Ann Clancy i   n
who has always been fascinated by family stories
of the early days of the colony. She has camped out
in the Serengeti, hiked through the jungles of Asia
and ridden a motor bike through the Himalayas,
but writing a novel has been her greatest achievement.

   She lives in Adelaide with her partner and their
young daughter.

The
Wild
Colonial
Girl

ANN CLANCY

PAN
Pan Macmillan Australia

First published 1996 in Pan by Pan Macmillan Australia Pty Limited
St Martins Tower, 31 Market Street, Sydney

National Library of Australia
cataloguing-in-publication data:

Clancy, Ann.
The wild colonial girl.

ISBN 0 330 35784 0

I. Title.

A823.3

Typeset in 10.5/12.5 pt Sabon by Post Typesetters, Brisbane
Printed in Australia by McPherson's Printing Group

For Peter, who had faith

Acknowledgements

I consulted many people and hundreds of sources during the research of *The Wild Colonial Girl*. I would like to thank all the people who gladly gave their time and those who made their resources available to me.

I particularly wish to thank Pearl McKenzie and family, and Cliff and Vince Coulthard, for their willingness to share their knowledge of the culture and history of the Adnyamathanha people of the Flinders Ranges. I used the *Adna-mat-na English Dictionary* by Pearl McKenzie and John McIntee as a reference for Adnyama-thanha language.

Ian Auhl's histories of Burra have been used extensively and I thank Ian for his great enthusiasm and encouragement.

The diary of Johnson Frederick Hayward, one of the early pioneers of the Flinders Ranges, has also been used extensively as a reference on the first sheep stations in the Far North.

In the interests of authenticity, I have used a number of original expressions, phrases and yarns which were written or told during the period in which the novel has been set. I am indebted both to the original writers of those letters, reports and stories, and also to those who have since collected them for later generations to enjoy. These sources include: E. Lloyd, *A Visit to the Antipodes*, 1846; Arthur Cannon, *Bullocks, Bullockies and Other Blokes*, 1983; Bill Wannan, *Bullockies, Beauts and Bandicoots*, 1983; L. Braden, *Bullockies*, 1968; A. G. Serle, *The Golden Age*, 1963; and Ellen Clacy, *A Lady's Visit to the Gold Diggings of Australia*, 1853.

Last of all, thanks must go to my late grandmother Miriam McDonnell and her sister, the late Emma Noble, who provided the inspiration for *The Wild Colonial Girl*. They were strong women who were inspiring in their own right. They told me many entertaining stories not only of their own lives, but also of the experiences of my great-grandmother and great-great-grandmother, two of the hard-working pioneer women of the mid-north and far north of South Australia. Those stories provided the seeds from which *The Wild Colonial Girl* grew.

Part
One

Chapter
One

'*J*aysus and Mary! Will you stop that cryin', Brigid? You'd think it was the end of the world!'

''Tis the end of the world, look at it!'

Kate looked across the wharves to the landscape beyond. It was like no place she had seen before. Low sandhills and wide pools of stagnant salt water stretched as far as the eye could see. The trees were grey and sadly stunted and the cries of the birds were mournful. She pulled the hood of her thick cloak over her head and wrapped the rest of it about her to keep out the bite of the south-westerly wind. She had expected sunshine, at the very least, for their arrival in the colony of South Australia, but it was heavily overcast, with dark ominous clouds scudding across the sky, driven by the wind.

The golden land of opportunity did look grey and forlorn but she was not going to admit that to Brigid.

''Tis just the port. Adelaide itself may be the prettiest spot you've ever seèn. You've got to look on the positive side of things, Brigid. 'Tis a new start.'

'They told us there'd be husbands waitin' ready for us with arms open wide!' Brigid sniffed.

'Oh, Brigid! You didn't believe all o' that, did you?' Kate laughed. 'Any husband worth his salt would not be waitin' on a wharf for an orphan from Ireland. They just told us that to keep us happy. They didn't want two hundred girls all worryin' and feeling miserable for the whole four months of the voyage.'

'Well, I'm miserable now that I see what 'tis like here. And scared. We have no idea what lies in store for us. Aren't you scared too?'

'Of course I am. Who wouldn't be? But we can't let it get us down.' She hugged her friend to her. 'Don't worry, we'll stick together, just like we have for the past two years. We survived that workhouse by looking after each other. This cannot be worse than that.'

'No, I suppose not.'

'And nothing, not even the colony of South Australia, could be worse than Ireland in the famine.'

'Well, I'm glad you're so confident.'

'We have to be confident. We have to put the past behind us and make the best of the future. I've decided what I'm going to do. I'm going to make my fortune, find a rich husband and eat as much as I can of the best food that money can buy!'

Brigid wiped her eyes and laughed. 'I bet you will too. You'd never let an opportunity pass you by. If it hadn't been for you we wouldn't have been included in the Orphan Scheme in the first place. It was only when you told them that we were fourteen that they said we could come. We'd not be here now if they knew that both of us were sixteen already.'

'Well, I've learnt the hard way. You've got to push like hell if you want to get anywhere in this world.'

''Tis all right for you, Kate, my dear friend. I've seen how men look at you. With your face and figure you probably will get yourself a rich man, and a good one too. I might still be waitin' on this wharf in ten years' time!'

'Nonsense!' Kate replied. 'You've a lovely face and you're a lovely person. Everyone loves you.'

Her eyes roamed over her friend's features. Brigid's hair was a warm velvety brown—almost auburn—and her eyes were large and soft. With her round and homely face, Brigid was the kind of girl who was liked by both men and women. But she had to be honest, to herself if not to Brigid. Her friend did not attract the intense interest of men as she did.

Kate was conscious from the reactions of others that her own looks were arresting. She wasn't sure why. Maybe it was her eyes. They certainly were a strange shade—something between violet and blue—with a startling brightness. Her brows were well arched and her lashes long and black. But as far as she was concerned her eyes were probably her only redeeming feature. Her smile was too wide to be pretty, even though her teeth were good. Her hair was that glossy black that hinted of the Spanish ancestry not uncommon in Ireland, but it had none of the warm highlights of Brigid's brown curls.

She looked down at herself. She had been described as petite, but scrawny would have been the better word for most of them, herself included. They had all suffered malnutrition, if not outright starvation, for so many years. Admittedly she had started to fill out a little since receiving hearty meals aboard the *Elgin*, but she was still as slender as a young boy, with narrow shoulders and hips and slim legs. She was better endowed now that she had started to fill out, but no one would ever be able to describe her as buxom. And that was what men liked, was it not?

She ran her hand over her heart-shaped face. In her view it was gaunt and her cheekbones stood out too much. Plump cheeks would look much better, she thought. And some rosy colour, like Brigid had, would improve her looks too. But her skin was very fair, almost white, and so fine in texture that it appeared translucent, as it often did in the black-haired Irish.

Her hand continued down over her determined chin to her slender throat as she took in the buzz of activity around her. Her looks were of much less interest to her than the unfolding spectacle of this new land.

The port was a forest of masts and spars.

Workers teemed over the wharf loading and hauling goods between carts and the waiting boats. There were other immigrants coming ashore and the sounds of greetings and excitement filled the air. No one had spared so much as a glance for the *Elgin* and its load of Irish girls. Irish waifs were no longer a novelty in Adelaide.

Their contemplation of the scene before them was interrupted by the booming voice of the Matron. 'Come on, girls, get ready to disembark. The port carts are here for your baggage, no nonsense now!'

The girls gathered up their meagre belongings from the deck and swarmed towards the Matron.

'Dirty brutes,' the Matron said in a lowered voice to the Depot Superintendent, as she eyed her charges distastefully. Her dislike of them had been obvious since the beginning of the voyage.

She then called more loudly to the girls, 'Come on, hurry up. You'll be walking the eight miles into town. There's only one road to follow. Ask for the Orphans Board Depot when you get to Adelaide. Get going or you'll miss your dinner at the other end.'

Ignoring the Matron's threats and abuse, the girls jostled their way down the gangplank, excited at finally going ashore.

'Come on!' Kate stepped off, dragging her faint-hearted friend by the hand, and set out across the wharf.

They picked their way through the trunks,

baskets and barrels piled up on the dockside, past the mounds of fishing nets and through the flocks of gulls waiting for morsels of fresh fish from the fishermen. Great bales of wool and grain sacks in huge mounds stood waiting to be loaded aboard the ships at anchor.

They were unsteady on their feet after the long months at sea.

'Hey! Watch out there, you eejit!' shouted an Irish voice.

Kate stopped in her tracks. The man who had yelled at her was pushing a handcart laden with sacks so full they were almost bursting. He cut across her path, nearly slicing across the toes of her boots.

'Watch out yourself!' she called back as he passed her. 'Don't you know it's ladies first?'

She laughed, tossing her head so that the wind would blow the dark hair away from her face, knowing her violet-blue eyes would be sparkling with mischief.

'Ha! They could go first if there were any!'

Then the tall, broad-shouldered Irishman grinned back at her, his wide mouth showing the perfect white of his teeth against the swarthy tan of his face. He disappeared into the crowd.

The track towards town was deeply rutted by laden vehicles. Kate, Brigid and the others made their way through the streets of Port Adelaide past the warehouses, the bondstores, the merchants' offices and the chandlers. An assortment of carts, drays and wagons passed them as they walked. Those coming towards them were laden with sacks of grain or piled high with loads of copper ore. Those that overtook them creaked under mounds of furniture and stores brought into the colony by the hundreds of new settlers arriving every week.

The road crossed a wide bush-covered plain that stretched almost as far as the eye could see. Rising in the distance to the east was a long line of thickly-wooded blue hills. The buildings they passed were crudely built of the most easily procured materials. Many were made of wattle and daub, others were made of rough-hewn stone. Small farms were dotted across the flat expanse over which they travelled. Chickens, goats, cows, pigs and sheep all wandered through the vacant tracts of land.

They were a couple of miles down the track when a loaded wagon drew abreast of them.

'Well, if it isn't the fair ladies of Ireland!'

Kate spun around to see the man with whom she had nearly collided on the wharf.

'And if it isn't the fellow who squashes young women under handcarts!'

'I'm surprised to see ladies of your class walkin' the track into town. Have you lost your carriage, then?'

Kate joked in reply: 'Have you no respect? Any real gentleman would offer a lady a ride, rather than drawing attention to her misfortune.'

'No fine lady would wish to be seen dead on an old wagon like this one.'

'Actually, we wouldn't mind at all,' called out Brigid.

The wagon drew to a halt. 'Hop up, then.'

'Should we?' Brigid asked, looking around to see if the Matron was within sight.

'I don't know about you, but my land-legs aren't holdin' up that well,' Kate replied.

'We would love a lift, thank you,' Brigid told him in her soft, almost breathless voice.

He held out a firm hand and helped Kate up onto the narrow seat beside him.

'Up on this chest behind me,' he said to Brigid as he gave her his hand and directed her to a place to sit.

'Rory O'Connor at your service, ladies,' he said, lifting his felt hat. Deep blue eyes twinkled with friendliness and his mouth curved into a broad grin. He flicked the reins and the horses continued their slow haul.

Kate studied his profile as they took off. He appeared to be on the young side of thirty. A strong jaw and a firm mouth were offset by the spark in his eyes and the smile lines creeping out from their corners. He was a big man but there was not a spare inch of flesh on him, his body was firm and strong, his skin tanned and healthy where it had been touched by the sun.

'Well, I am Kate O'Mara and this is Brigid Mulcahey.' Kate gave him her friendliest smile, pleased to be in the company of a compatriot. 'We've just arrived today, all the way from Cork.'

'From Cork are you, then? We're almost old neighbours. I'm from Castlemaine, County Kerry.'

'Ah, an O'Connor from Kerry! I knew an O'Connor from Kerry. Father of our parish he was,' Brigid told him.

'Father Daniel O'Connor?'

'Yes, 'twas him!'

'My father's cousin. How's that, eh? It's been two years since I've seen him. How is he keeping?'

''Tis more than two since I've seen him myself. 'Twas before . . . before I left there. Before my family died.'

'You lost all your family, then?'

Brigid looked at Kate. 'We both did.'

'I'm sorry.'

''Tis all in the past now,' Kate said, squaring her shoulders unconsciously. 'What about your family, Mr O'Connor? Did you come out here on your own too?'

'Yes, I came out on my own. But it was by choice. Poor old Ireland was in a sorry state. My family is still there. We were among the lucky ones. We survived the hunger. I'm still trying to talk them into coming out here to live. 'Tis a grand country.'

Kate was glad to put the subject of families behind them. 'Grand, is it? Tell us more.'

''Tis a beautiful country, there's no doubt about that, though you've not arrived on a good day. Usually the sun shines brightly and the birds sing out their hearts in praise o' the day.' He paused. ''Tis shaping up to be a good place to live but if you've come looking for work you've come at the wrong time, I must be telling you. A year or two back and you'd have had the pick of any job you'd like. 'Tisn't like that now, though.'

'We were told there'd be people lined up on the wharves waiting to hire us,' Brigid told him. 'And husbands too.'

Rory laughed, 'Yes, things have changed since the first boatload of orphans. There was plenty of sympathy for the victims of the famine then. Strangely enough, now that there are enough domestics, the sympathy seems to have dried up.'

Kate sat up. 'What? Is there not work for domestics, then?'

'No. Not now. They don't seem to be able to get the balance right. They founded the colony on the idea of free settlement—'

'We heard that there were no convicts here,' Kate broke in.

'That's right. They wanted to establish a different kind of colony. The idea was that the wealthier people would buy land, and the money that was raised from the sale of land would be used to bring out the workers needed for the farms.'

'So what went wrong?' Brigid asked.

'Well, at first they couldn't get enough domestics and farm hands. Everyone who came wanted to buy up their own piece of land, no matter how small. Then, just when they got enough people to come as domestics and farm hands, the whole colony went downhill and no one had the money to employ them.'

'So, 'tis not the golden land of opportunity we were told about,' Brigid said.

'No. It has been a tough start. Before they discovered the copper at Burra Burra and Kapunda it looked as if the lot of us may as well pack up and head east. The copper mines have put the place back on its feet, but we've now had a couple of dry seasons, the harvests are down and there's no money to employ people on farms.'

'How are we goin' to get work, then?'

'Good question. I think you'll be the last lot of orphans we'll see. If you were Cornish miners you'd have been right. There's plenty of work for them at the Burra Burra mines. The only other jobs you'll find on offer will be out in the bush.'

'But there's thousands more like us just waiting to get out of Ireland. There's nothin' more for anybody there; no hope at all. All the girls in the workhouse wanted to come here, we were just the lucky ones who got the chance,' Brigid told him.

'And don't I know it,' replied Rory. 'I don't imagine things have changed all that much since I left the old country. No one who lived through the famine would want to stay there to see the next one. But that's not the point. It isn't that there's no one wantin' to come. I might as well tell you honestly, 'cause you'll find out anyway, you're not wanted here and you'll not be welcomed.'

The two girls looked at each other in dismay.

'They don't like the Irish here, is that it?' Kate asked.

'That's part of it. They'll tell you it's a fresh start for all but many of the settlers just want their own sort here, the English, the Scots and the Germans.'

'Everyone's the same, I'm thinkin',' Kate reasoned.

'Mm . . .' Rory seemed reluctant to say more but he went on. 'Well, the Irish girls who arrived before you have earned for you all a bad reputation. There's been no work for those who came on the *Inconstant* in May. Not all of them were fit for working in the homes of the nobs and snobs anyway. So they've not had much choice of work, if you know what I mean.'

Brigid looked quite blank. Understanding was dawning slowly for Kate.

'Go on,' she said.

'I wouldn't want to offend you.'

'You couldn't. We lived in a workhouse, don't forget. There's nothing in this world that we haven't seen.'

He shrugged. 'Well, 'tis like this, most of the last lot who arrived are now prostitutes and most of the prostitutes in Adelaide are Irish. You'll all be lumped in the same basket together.' Rory flicked the reins and stared steadily towards the town in the distance.

Another look of dismay was exchanged between Kate and Brigid.

'Holy Mother of God! I wish that I'd never come,' whispered Brigid, crossing herself.

Kate was not one to give up so easily. 'Why don't they go out to the country then, you said there was work there. There is a choice, is there not?'

Rory looked into her eyes and laughed, 'You're what they'll call a "new chum" . . . and a green one at that. What do you think the bush will be like, then?'

Kate shrugged her slender shoulders and looked at the dull landscape around her. ''Tis like this, I imagine, without so many houses. Am I right?'

Rory laughed good-naturedly. 'This is a green paradise in comparison. Go up north and you'd find something altogether different. 'Tis hot, dry and downright dangerous.'

He nodded towards a group of people on the other side of the track. 'Take a look at the Aborigines.'

Kate and Brigid followed his gaze. Brigid paled a little but said nothing. Kate eyed them with frank curiosity. Their skins were dark and dusty. Thin arms and legs poked from bodies scarcely covered by a combination of fur and threadbare clothes. Children and native dogs scampered around them as they walked.

'They don't look too dangerous,' Kate remarked.

'Not here in town,' Rory replied. 'They've given up their fight for the land and they aren't allowed in the town unless they are wearing clothes. But out bush you'll hear a different story. They're thieving and murderous beggars and all dressed up in their paint they look pretty wild. They've been known to kill off whole families of settlers on remote farms.' His eyes returned to the road ahead. 'But the dangers of the bush are many: deadly snakes, ravaging floods, desperate droughts, uncertain supplies of water at the best of times, unbearable heat, bushfires, never mind the flies and the dust,' he said, shrugging his shoulders.

''Tis not much like Ireland, then?' said Kate, her tone innocent and her eyes full of mischief.

'No,' Rory smiled back at her, 'and there's one other thing that would get any good Irishman down and that's the isolation. There's no one else for miles. It's several days' journey between some of the farms, or stations, as they call them here. The Irish girls just won't venture into the bush to take on work, so they're stuck with the only work there is in the town.'

'Well, I'll go if I have to,' Kate declared.

Brigid nodded in agreement, her face more than a little doubtful. They both looked into the distance ahead, the wind on their faces, sobered by the seeming dearth of opportunities awaiting them. Kate pulled her cloak tightly around her once more.

'What's this?' Rory asked, slowing the wagon.

People were jostling for position outside a stone building with a sign proclaiming the 'Land of Promise Hotel'. The crowd was spilling out onto the roadway. A cart blocked the front of the building. On the back of the cart stood a roughly dressed man holding a woman by the hair.

The crowd was laughing.

'Drunk by the look o' them,' murmured Brigid.

'What am I bid, then?' roared the man, pulling the woman's head closer to his own. 'Not bad for a wife, if I say so meself!' He gave the crowd a leery grin. 'Come on, what will you bid for her, name the price and she's yours!'

'Mother of Mercy!' Kate exclaimed. 'He's selling off his own wife!'

Rory flicked the reins to move on.

'Mr O'Connor, wait!' Kate cried, grasping his forearm.

'You don't want to watch this, Miss O'Mara. We'd best be on our way.'

'No! The poor woman, we must do something!'

Seeing some poor downtrodden soul being mistreated was the kind of thing that could be guaranteed to upset Kate.

'Mr O'Connor knows best,' Brigid told her. 'We should go. There might be trouble.'

'Ten shillings!' called a skinny man with no teeth from the back of the crowd.

'Twelve!' called another, close by them.

'Ah, she's worth more than that! I can vouch for her. Cooks and sews, an' not bad in the sack, neither,' the husband leered at the crowd again.

'I'd keep her meself but I need the money bad. Come on, what am I bid?'

'Fifteen,' was called, and then 'One pound!'

The woman in question looked frightened, a bruise swelling over one eye, her dress torn at the hem and the neck. She writhed in the man's harsh grasp.

Rory flicked the reins and the horses started to move off.

'Stop the wagon!' Kate lunged across the Irishman, grasping for the reins to stop the horses herself.

'Kate!' Brigid dived off the chest and grabbed hold of Kate from behind. 'You'll cause an accident, you fool.'

Rory took the reins from her hands and halted the wagon again.

'We can't just let it happen,' she said, trying to stand up to see what was happening, tears forming in her eyes. 'I can't watch her being brutalised like that and do nothin'.'

Brigid did not release her hold. 'Kate, you've got to learn not to rush in like this. You can't help every single unfortunate man or beast that you come across. I've told you before. You'll land yourself in trouble.'

'She's right, Miss O'Mara. There's nothing we can do.'

Kate shrugged off her friend's hold. 'You might not want to do anything, but I will not stand idly by and do nothing. I'll tell that husband of hers a thing or two!'

She leapt down from the wagon in one swift and unexpected movement.

'Mr O'Connor! Stop her!' Brigid cried out.

'Hold the horses!' he tossed the reins to Brigid and leapt down, catching up to Kate within a couple of strides. 'Miss O'Mara, you'll get hurt,' he said, grasping her arm and pulling her backwards.

'Will you do something then, Mr O'Connor? Please!'

'All right, but let's not jump in boots and all before we've thought it through,' he said, dragging her as gently as she would allow him to back to the wagon.

Brigid was rolling her eyes in Rory's direction.

He raised both his shoulders and his thick black brows in response, as if to say 'what will I do with her now?'.

'Leave it to Mr O'Connor, Kate.'

They could hear the bids rising.

Rory turned Kate towards him and held her eyes with his. 'Listen,' he said, 'what are you trying to save the poor soul from? You want her to stay with a husband like that? She'd be better off without him!'

Kate searched his eyes and then looked back to the woman.

'He's right, Kate!' Brigid chipped in again.

Kate's eyes returned to Rory's face. Maybe he was right.

'Going, going, gone! To the feller in the grey hat, for one pound, seven shillings and sixpence.'

The man turned to his unfortunate wife, saying, 'And good riddance to you, you old crow.'

The woman was pushed roughly from the cart. The crowd cheered. It was too late to do anything.

'So much for the Land of Promise Hotel and this land of promise itself!' Kate said bitterly.

They were silent as they continued on their way across the plain. She could not rid her mind of the scene. How could people treat each other like that?

'Well that has cast a shadow over your day, hasn't it, Miss O'Mara?'

'Yes, it has. The poor woman. 'Twas criminal!'

'Not illegal though.'

'You've got to be more careful, Kate,' said Brigid. 'It wouldn't be much of a start if you got yourself into a punch-up on your first day here, would it now? And look, you landed in the mud when you jumped down. 'Tis all over your skirt, and on Mr O'Connor's seat as well.'

'I'm sorry, Mr O'Connor. I didn't mean to cause a scene.'

'No harm done, and call me Rory, both of you.' He had slowed the horses to go through a glue-pot of drying mud on the road.

When they were through, but still travelling slowly, he scraped his finger on the seat, lifting a lump of red clay. 'Now you two should have a good look at this. You'll be seeing plenty more of it.'

He placed his finger in front of Kate's face for her inspection.

Kate looked down. As quick as a flash, Rory wiped it onto the tip of her nose.

'Eh!' Kate cried, abruptly bending backwards.

She opened her mouth, about to tell him off, then she burst into laughter. Brigid and Rory laughed too. They had needed something like that to lighten the serious mood.

'You wretch! Don't you worry, I'll get my revenge sooner or later!' she said, wiping the mud off her nose and onto the back of her hand.

'Consider it part of your initiation into the colony. We all have to contend with it. The Road Board has done nothing to improve the situation and the colony has been here for thirteen years.'

'Thank you, then, for the thoughtful initiation ceremony!'

'Seriously, in the winter the streets are well-nigh impassable. A bullock actually drowned in a mud puddle on one corner of the main street last year.'

'No!'

''Tis true, I swear it.'

Then he gave a devilish kind of a grin, and said, 'I've experienced it first hand. During the winter the bogs in the main street are particularly bad. A few months ago I was walking down King William Street when an amazing thing happened.'

Kate leant forward to listen, her violet-blue eyes wide open as if trusting every word that would fall from his mouth. But there was a twinkle in her eye, too.

'Yes, there I was, walking down the street when I saw a hat lyin' on the road in the mud. It was one of those really expensive ones, so I figured I may as well pick it up, as no one else had claimed it.' He shook his head. 'I picked my way over through the mud and lifted the hat off the ground. Imagine my amazement when I saw a man's head underneath it!'

'Oh!' exclaimed Brigid.

'Well, worse was yet to come. I said to the feller, "Give me your hand, I'll help you out" and he said, "Thanks, mate, I would, but my horse is here beneath me!"'

Kate and Brigid both whooped with laughter.

'That's a tall story!' cried Kate. 'We might be "new chums", as you call us, but we're not so green as all that!'

Rory grinned in response and then drew their attention to the surrounding landscape. They had been slowly ascending a small hilly area and the land around them was green and lush. It was mostly taken up with small farms and gardens surrounded by picket fences.

'This is North Adelaide,' he said. 'Below us is the town of Adelaide.'

Kate looked ahead of them and down the hill that they were about to descend. Finally! There was Adelaide spread out before them. It was already a big town. Conflicting feelings vied for supremacy within her: sadness at having left

Ireland, excitement at the sight of her new home and relief at having arrived safely after a long and difficult voyage. A lump rose in her throat.

'Well, we're here at last, Brigid!' she cried out, her voice catching, and she turned to grab her friend's arm and to pull her forward for a hug.

Kate then turned to Rory, her eyes liquid and a jubilant smile upon her face. 'Thank God Almighty, we are here at last.'

Rory returned her gaze and in the few seconds in which their eyes were locked she read something there. He, too, had dreams. He, too, had come to the colony to put Ireland behind him. He, too, was here to seek out new opportunities. He said nothing, but his eyes mirrored her hopes and dreams. Her heart lurched in response.

Rory pulled up outside the Orphans Depot. Kate and Brigid were clearly the first to arrive as there were no signs of baggage or of others from the ship. Kate jumped down without waiting for help. Rory alighted and turned to help Brigid down as well.

The large double wooden doors of the depot were thrown open. A stocky young girl advanced towards them. 'Are you from the *Elgin*, then?'

Kate and Brigid both nodded.

'We've been waitin' for you all the mornin', come in!'

Kate and Brigid moved towards the doorway.

Kate spun around and said, 'Oh Brigid! We nearly forgot to thank Mr O'Connor, so excited we are to get here!'

'Thank you, Mr O'Connor,' Brigid called over her shoulder, continuing on her way into the depot.

'Indeed. Thank you,' Kate said, returning to him, shaking his hand. 'You saved our poor sea legs a lot of work!' She turned to follow Brigid.

'One moment,' Rory said, grasping Kate's arm to whirl her back to face him. He then took her hand again. 'Let me know if you're ever in need of anything. The colony is not an easy place to get on in when you're without friends and family.' His eyes were steady on hers. 'Ask for me at the Newmarket Inn, opposite the stockyards.'

'Newmarket Inn,' she murmured in response.

He then released her hand, raised his hat to them and said, 'All the best!'

He stood and watched as Kate and Brigid entered the Orphans Depot.

Kate glanced back once more.

He stood there still, watching her go, his face serious.

Chapter

Two

'I'll only tell you once,' said Mr Moorfield, the Depot Superintendent, with heavy emphasis. 'Once you have turned fourteen and you have left, you will not be readmitted. You are on your own and we will no longer be responsible for you, regardless of your circumstances.'

The girls from the *Elgin* were assembled in the courtyard inside the depot. They shifted on their feet and looked at each other glumly. They had heard much of today's news from those who were still at the depot since the arrival of the *Inconstant*, four months before.

'Any of you who can read might like to look at the newspaper today to see the poor regard in which your predecessors are held. The colony of South Australia is none too impressed with your value. There is a call to end the Orphan Scheme.'

Rory O'Connor had been right, Kate thought. The Superintendent looked at them sternly over his spectacles. 'Those few of you who can demonstrate that you possess skills as domestics have some chance of finding work. The rest of you must face reality; the only work for you is that of untrained labourers on the farms.'

The Matron from the *Elgin* added her piece. 'You will need to buckle down and work hard. Only those who are diligent, obedient and thrifty will be able to better themselves. Pray to our dear Lord that you will be one of those who will succeed in the new colony.'

The Superintendent nodded. 'While you are here you will be expected to cheerfully take on any work that is provided to the depot for your training. In addition, there will be a continuation of the reading and writing lessons that were provided to you aboard the *Elgin*.'

There were stifled yawns as Mr Moorfield continued his lecture. 'Infringements of the rules will be dealt with promptly . . .'

He read from a list before him, but Kate was not listening. She had little intention of staying long enough to infringe any of the rules.

'Heavens, Brigid! We've been here for three weeks and we've not had one job offer. We'll have to find another way to get work,' said Kate.

She was sweeping the courtyard of the depot, pondering her future yet again. Patience was not one of her virtues and she had no wish to idle away her time at the depot.

Brigid sat on a bench seat trying to darn linen neatly. 'Well I for one am in no hurry. For sure, it would be nice to get out of here, but with all the tales I've been hearing, it sounds like there are worse things that could happen. Did you hear of that poor girl Mary O'Leary?'

'No.'

'She took the first post she was offered, as a domestic on a farm near Adelaide. Her master turned out to be the very devil, drinking and abusive to her.' Brigid lowered her voice, 'And now she's having a baby, and he's accused her of playing around, though all the world knows 'tis his. She's been turned out without a reference and has nowhere to go. She came here yesterday but they won't have her back. It would be better, surely, not to go, rather than to go to someone like that.'

'The poor girl. I do feel for her, but there's nothing any of us can do for her while we are stuck here with no way of earning money. We must—'

'You there!' An imperious voice cut across their conversation.

Kate spun around to see who was addressing them. The great wooden doors of the depot were open and the gatekeeper was nowhere to be seen. A tall man with spurs and a wide-brimmed felt hat was tethering his horse to the hitching rail at the front of the depot building.

'Show me the way to the Superintendent's office!'

'Yes, sir!' responded Kate, making a great show of jumping to attention and saluting in military style.

Brigid rolled her eyes at Kate, dropped her mending on the bench seat, jumped to her feet and bobbed. ''Tis this way, sir, if you'll follow me.'

Kate laughed mischievously and watched the tall, lean stranger as he followed Brigid across the courtyard.

'Who's he?' Kate asked when Brigid returned.

'He introduced himself to the Superintendent as Mr James Carmichael, from some station or other,' replied Brigid. 'Good looking, was he not?'

Kate shrugged. That was the last thing on her mind. 'Is he here to offer work, do you think?'

'He certainly wouldn't have told us if he was.'

'That courtyard outside the Superintendent's office needs to be swept again.' Kate winked at Brigid and strolled off, her broom in hand.

'. . . I heard you were prepared to consider all offers of work,' the stranger was saying.

'I have considered your offer, Mr Carmichael, and it is a kind offer indeed. But I must be quite frank with you. I doubt that I can supply you with the workers you are wanting.'

'What is the problem?'

'Well, these girls—and they are just girls, Mr Carmichael, for there are few of them above fifteen years of age—will not want the post. Few of them had ever travelled outside their own small Irish villages before they came to South Australia.'

'They would be looked after, I assure you.'

'That may be so, but they are frightened by the stories they hear of the bush and its dangers. None of them would venture more than ten or twenty miles from Adelaide. The post you are offering is a very remote one indeed. Your station is two hundred and fifty miles from here. It is a wonderful thing that gentlemen like you are pushing out the frontiers of civilisation, but you won't find any of these orphans will be prepared to help you to do it.'

'I heard that they were desperate for work. I am certainly desperate for workers, preferably female. Shepherds make poor cooks and it is hard to keep the men at the station when there are no women there. I had hoped to get a number of girls to return with me.'

Kate's heart beat faster. It was just the opportunity she had been looking for. She was almost sorry she had responded in such a cheeky manner to his imperious tone.

'That may be so, Mr Carmichael, but they are unlikely to see it that way and I must warn you that they may not have the skills that you are looking for. Most of them are peasants. Many of those who hire domestics from here later complain to me that the girls are no good.'

The voices lowered and Kate could hear little more of the conversation.

A few minutes later the door opened and the

station owner reappeared, his hat in hand. 'Well let me know if you do find anyone. You can contact me at the Southern Cross Hotel.'

'I don't hold much hope but I will try. Good day to you, sir, and all the best.' The Superintendent went inside and closed his office door.

Kate watched as the station owner sauntered back to his horse. Could this be the chance she had been waiting for?

The next day Kate had heard nothing of the offer of work. Puzzled, she asked the others if they had heard anything.

'The Superintendent has his own ways,' advised one of the girls from the *Inconstant*. 'If he doesn't think it is a suitable post we won't hear any more of it at all.'

'Should I be asking?'

'I wouldn't if I were you. He doesn't like those who question him. Just wait your turn, something will come.'

'I'm not so sure.' Kate looked doubtful. 'What do you think, Brigid? Would you want to come to work on the station with me?'

Brigid looked torn. 'I would be happy to go work with you, Kate, but not so far away, surely. You have no idea what it may be like up there. 'Tis best to trust the judgement of those who know.'

'Well I don't believe there can be too much harm in just inquiring about it.' Kate smoothed her dress with her hands. 'I might go to see him now.'

Kate knocked on the door.

'What is it?' the Superintendent asked without looking up from his papers.

Kate cleared her throat. ''Tis about getting some work, sir.'

The Superintendent looked up at her over his spectacles. 'In good time, girl. You will be offered work when it is your turn. You're an *Elgin* girl, are you not?'

Kate nodded.

'Well then you will have to wait. There are others who have been here longer,' he said, returning to his papers.

'I'm anxious to get going and get settled into the colony, sir,' Kate continued, 'I'd be happy to take any job.'

'Well there are no jobs on offer.' He dismissed her with a wave of his hand.

Kate turned to go and then thought better of it. 'Beggin' your pardon, sir, but has the job on Mr Carmichael's station already been taken, sir?'

At this the Superintendent looked up at her again. 'And what would you know of Mr Carmichael?'

Kate felt the blush rise to her cheeks. 'I was here sweeping yesterday, sir, and could not help but overhear his offer.' She cast her eyes downwards.

'Hmmp,' snorted the Superintendent, 'eavesdropping no doubt. Yes, he did offer work, but the posting is not suitable for young girls and is too remote by far.'

'I wouldn't mind it at all, sir, I'll give anythin' a go.' Kate looked at him with a plea in her eyes.

'Don't question my judgement! Get out of my office, you'll be offered a position in turn, and when it's suitable.'

'Yes sir,' Kate said, swallowing her annoyance. There was no point blackening her name. She curtsied and left, closing the door gently behind her.

The gatekeeper looked closely at the Superintendent's brief note and then motioned Kate and Brigid through. They made their way down the main street. The October weather was warm and they had dispensed with the dark and heavy cloaks that they had worn into Adelaide on their first day. They were both attired in the clothes issued by the workhouse in Cork—thick dresses of dark grey wool with no ornamentation, and good solid leather boots.

''Tis the first real chance we've had of takin' a good look around the town,' Brigid said, taking in the scene around her. 'We were too busy talking to Mr O'Connor on the way in to take a lot o' notice. I wonder if we will be seeing him again? He was so nice.'

Kate did not respond, she was too busy looking around her.

The unpaved street was bustling with activity. Drays loaded with produce were drawn by four, six or eight bullocks. The drivers added to the din by shouting and cracking their long whips. Wagons and carts jostled for space with gigs and carriages. Most fascinating to Kate and Brigid, though, were the wild-looking figures of the bushmen. Belted, bearded, booted and spurred, sometimes with long leather leggings and broad-brimmed hats, they held enormous whips with thongs of fourteen feet coiled in their hands. Some sauntered along boldly. Others spurred their impressive horses through the streets, heedless of pedestrians and conscious of the dashing figure they cut.

There had been no rain since they had arrived and already the streets were dry and dusty in the patches between the thickening mud holes. The red dust soon settled over their boots and on the hems of their dresses. The same dust seemed to have stained the houses, the vehicles and indeed all the inhabitants of the small town.

Brigid and Kate wove around the clusters of half-naked and dusky natives, eyeing warily the spears and waddies in their hands. Dozens of dogs, some vagrant, some following along behind the Aborigines and their children, added to the general scene of liveliness.

Kate placed the order given to her by the Superintendent at one of the main stores. The goods were to be delivered, so she and Brigid were free to explore the town further.

'Should we not be getting back soon? We were not given permission to wander around the town,' said Brigid, wiping dust and perspiration from her face with her handkerchief.

'Soon,' replied Kate, looking up at another hotel sign.

''Tis it,' she said. 'The Southern Cross!' The look on her face was intent.

'What would we be wanting here, then?'

''Twould be where that Mr Carmichael is stayin'. I'm going to find out if he's still looking for workers,' she responded, looking up at the facade of the imposing hotel. It was three storeys high and was decorated beautifully with intricate ironwork.

'I don't think we should go in, Kate.'

'And why not?'

''Tis not the place for the likes of us. We will be asked to leave,' she said, eyeing the doorman uneasily.

'Rubbish,' Kate asserted, sounding braver than she felt, and she walked through to the reception, Brigid trailing along behind her.

'I'm looking for Mr James Carmichael,' Kate told the man behind the broad wooden desk.

'And what are you wanting with him?' he asked, looking down his nose at her.

'I understand he is engaging workers for his station and I've come to apply for a position,' Kate replied with as much confidence as she could muster.

Brigid shuffled her feet and looked uncomfortable.

'I will inquire as to whether he will receive

you,' the man offered, although he looked unwilling. 'Wait here, please.'

Kate and Brigid were kept waiting in the hall-way while the man disappeared upstairs in search of Mr Carmichael. Kate made the most of the time by trying to remove the marks of their walk through the town. Looking at her reflection in the glass of the windows, she smoothed her hair and tucked in the stray strands and dark tendrils which had fallen around her face. She wiped her dust-streaked hands on her handker-chief and tried, somewhat in vain, to shake the dust from the hem of her skirt. Brigid followed her lead.

'Will I do as I am?' Brigid asked.

Kate nodded.

Eventually the man descended the stairs. 'Mr Carmichael will see you. Come with me.'

He led them to a small coffee room which was quiet at this time of the day. 'Wait here,' he said and disappeared again.

Several minutes later Mr Carmichael appeared. Kate had barely looked at him when he had visited the depot, and besides, his broad-brimmed hat had hidden much of his face at the time.

He was a striking man, good looking, the bone structure of his face refined. Unlike the bushmen in the streets, he was clean-shaven, which gave him a smooth, urbane appearance. His hair was fair and several locks fell down in a sophisticated sweep over his brow. His eyes were grey, like the colour of the ocean on a cloudy day. His mouth was wide and his long, lean body was dressed today in clothes which marked the gentleman. A double-breasted dark blue frock coat fitted his slim waist and hips neatly. His thighs were encased in tight-fitting trousers which reached the instep and his waistcoat of embroidered silk in contrasting colours of red and grey set off the whole outfit to advantage. He was, every inch, the rich and successful station owner.

'What can I do for you?' he asked, coming straight to the point.

Brigid looked down at her dusty boots.

Kate looked up at his face. 'We've come about the jobs you have for women to work on your station. Have you found anyone yet?'

His eyes narrowed, almost imperceptibly. 'How did you know I was looking for workers, Miss, er . . .?'

'Miss O'Mara and this is Miss Mulcahey,' she replied and then ploughed on relentlessly. 'We heard at the Orphans Depot that you were lookin' for workers and we're keen to get work, so we've come to inquire for ourselves. We're willing to consider almost anythin'.'

'Er . . . take a seat, then,' he said, drawing up chairs for them and then one for himself. He was somehow both affable and condescending at the same time.

'My station is two hundred and fifty miles from Adelaide to the north, in the region we are calling the Flinders Ranges,' he began in his rather cultured voice and English accent. 'There are few stations up there but more are opening up all the time. There is plenty of land to be had for those with the courage to take on the challenge.'

Evidently he considered himself a man of courage.

He stretched out his long legs towards them. 'I established the station, called Wildowie, two years ago and have been stocking it with sheep since then. I was looking for some good strong lasses,' his eyes raked over their small frames before he continued, 'to return with me to the station to assist with general domestic and farm duties. But I doubt somehow that you'll do,' he said, looking them up and down again. 'The work is quite heavy. I didn't realise the girls from the depot would be so young or so . . . er . . . petite, shall we say.'

He began to rise from his chair.

'Oh, but we are strong,' Brigid broke in hurriedly, 'and gettin' stronger by the day. Why, we're twice as big now as we were when we left Ireland, are we not, Kate?'

James Carmichael gave a small, wry smile.

'And I'll be seventeen next week,' Kate said, crossing her fingers as she said it, hoping that the information would not get back to the Orphans Depot. They believed that she was younger.

James Carmichael sat down again with an

easy grace. 'Well I'd not take you on under any illusions about the work or the conditions. It is a hard life in the remote north. You've no doubt heard of the heat, the dust and the flies. The dangers of the bush are many. The station itself is quite isolated, you would no doubt be the only women for many miles.'

'What about the black women?' Brigid asked, eyes wide.

'They are of no account,' he said, waving his hand dismissively.

'What are the duties, Mr Carmichael?' Kate asked.

'You would need to be flexible. I want girls who will look after the homestead and do some outside duties. As well as that there would be some help for the men during shearing and lambing.'

Brigid looked at Kate with raised brows.

James Carmichael intercepted her look, and interpreted it correctly. 'Yes, I am asking a lot of anyone to take it all on, but in these hard times I'm sure someone will be prepared to do it. I will pay good wages for the right girls—eight shillings a week, which is roughly twenty pounds per year. You won't get better than that anywhere, and of course all your food and board would be included.'

Brigid nodded but Kate made no response.

James Carmichael picked a piece of lint from his sleeve and said, 'But I am not at all sure that either of you would be right for the job.'

Once again his eyes travelled down Kate's slender figure.

Kate didn't like the way he looked at her. She waited for his eyes to come back to her face and then looked him squarely in the eye. 'There's nothing I couldn't take on, Mr Carmichael,' she said. 'That's not to say that I have done all of those things that you mentioned—I doubt that you would find too many who have all the experience and are prepared to go to the ends of the earth,' she continued, hoping to sound more knowledgeable than she really was.

He looked at her, saying nothing.

'Would you be takin' us on, then?' Kate persisted.

He gave a small superior smile. 'If you're prepared to come, to work hard, and not to complain about the conditions then I am prepared to hire you.'

He stood as if preparing to bring the deal to its conclusion.

'One more thing,' Kate broke in. She bit her bottom lip before continuing, 'The wages are too low for what you are askin'. I'll take the job for twelve shillings a week.'

James Carmichael burst into laughter, 'Well that is rich, if ever I've heard it! Beggars cannot be choosers, Miss O'Mara.'

'If I am to come up to the Far North then I will need to buy some clothes for the heat. That will eat into my wages considerably,' she countered, thinking quickly on her feet.

'Nine shillings, then.'

'I'd not go up for less than ten.'

James Carmichael looked at her with grudging admiration and then he laughed, 'Ten it is, then.'

'And two months pay in advance, to make the necessary purchases for the trip.'

He laughed again, 'It is a deal, Miss O'Mara.' He shook her hand, and Kate felt the cool confidence of his presence course through her veins.

'And you, Miss Mulcahey, will you be joining us too?'

Brigid hesitated.

Kate knew that the thought of going north would be scaring Brigid witless, but they were loath to be parted. They had faced so much together.

'Miss Mulcahey will need time to think about your offer,' she said.

'Well think fast, Miss Mulcahey, for we leave the day after tomorrow. If you are coming, make your mind up by the morning.'

He turned to Kate once again. 'My overseer, Angus Campbell, will be here then. Present yourselves and he will provide you with your advance wages and make arrangements for your transport. Count yourselves lucky that he wasn't here this morning. He's been none too keen on my idea of hiring women so you'd have been out of luck.'

He stood.

Kate and Brigid made their way to the door he had opened for them.

'See you on the road,' he said.

'Yes, Mr Carmichael, and God bless you, sir,' Kate replied.

The two girls made their way back to the depot.

Brigid looked at her friend with increasing reverence. 'Well I'm not sure what to think! Good heavens, Kate, you get more bold as each day passes.'

'We have to grab at any chances we get.'

'Yes, but it might well be a case of out of the frying pan and into the fire! We know nothing of this Mr Carmichael or his station. I wonder whether we should have left it to the judgement of the Superintendent who knows more about these things than we do, surely.'

'I'm not going to sit about and let someone else decide my future, I know that! I am workin' my way to better things. I left the famine and Ireland behind me and I'm determined to go ever upwards from here. You don't have to come with me if you don't want to,' she said, referring not only to the station but to her place in the colony more generally.

Brigid looked at her anxiously.

'Oh, I'm sorry,' Kate said ruefully at the look on her friend's face. 'I shouldn't be saying that to me dearest friend. I know I'm more pushy than an Irish orphan should be, but isn't it the same for you, Brigid? Aren't you also scared of facing such hardship again?'

'I am that,' Brigid declared, 'But I'm not like

you. I don't have the same courage. I'd love to come, just to be with you, but the thought of the bush . . . well I don't know, I don't think it's the place for me.'

''Twould be fine, for we'd be together. We could protect each other like we have until now. We're a great team and there'd be no problem that we couldn't overcome. Don't stay here, there's nothing for you here, Brigid. The Far North would have to be easier than the workhouse and we survived that.'

Both Brigid and Kate looked grim as they remembered what they had been through.

The workhouse had been established in an old barn, built from stone and turf. The walls were damp, turning green with slime during the winter when the water seeped down them ceaselessly. The damp had combined with the constant draughts of bitterly cold wind, chilling Kate and Brigid to the bone, day in, day out.

The never-ending cold had been only one discomfort. Hunger had gnawed at them constantly. Their sleep was made uneasy by empty stomachs and they woke to face hunger again each morning. There was food, but little of it, and what there was would have been unappetising to anyone but the destitute. Kate's lip curled at the thought of the grey, half-cold porridge, the donated bread, dry and moulded long before it reached the workhouse, and watery soup with scarcely a vegetable or a piece of meat to be seen in it.

They had been covered in lice, their skin reddened and blotchy from the constant scratching. Sickness had been rife, the fevers killing with ease those already weakened by the long years of malnutrition and outright starvation. The workhouse, pitiful as it was, had at least saved them from the fate of their families. More than a million people had died in the famine. Those in the workhouse had counted themselves lucky to have received food and shelter.

Survival, for Kate and Brigid, had come from sticking together and sharing what little they had. They had nursed each other through illness and protected each other from the advances of the men. Many of the women had been prepared to give their bodies in exchange for an extra ration of bread or a moth-eaten blanket. Girls as young as Brigid and Kate had been fair game. But miraculously they had survived the workhouse with their virginity, if not their innocence, intact.

'Would you still go if I don't come with you?' Brigid asked.

'I'll not kick me heels in that blasted orphan home any longer!'

'Then would you take it against me if I said no?'

Kate looked disappointed but she gave her friend a warm hug. 'Of course not, maybe it would be best for you to find a position in Adelaide and wait for me here. You never know, I might not like the place and I could be scuttlin' back in no time!'

'It won't be the end of our friendship?'

'Nothing could spell the end of our friendship! You're the only one I have in the whole world. You're my family. We'll still be a good team. 'Tis just that I'll be up there and you'll be down here. We can share what I earn until you get a job and if 'tis good up there I will send for you.'

Her meeting with Angus Campbell came as a surprise. He did not share her enthusiasm for her trip to the Far North.

He stood in front of her, his face and neck almost as red as his hair and his eyes shining bright with anger. 'Yes, Miss O'Mara, I have been informed that Mr Carmichael has gone ahead with his damned fool idea of taking some females up to Wildowie,' he said in a strong Scots accent. 'I canna believe the naivety of the man. Women will be nothing but trouble! It will be no guid at all. He should hae left it up to me to hire the workers furr the station as he's supposed to do.'

He paced up and down the room on his rather stocky legs, so angry that when he spoke the spit sprayed forth from his mouth. 'I've seen just about everything in my time but never a gurrlie so unsuited to be working in the bush as you are. You'rre not strong enough furr the work. Any fool could see that. Damn him! As if my life is not difficult enough already . . .'

He ranted on, not giving Kate even a moment in which to respond. She decided it would be wiser to let him just wear himself out before she tried to get down to the business of organising the practical details for the next day. She simply stood there with a cool look on her face waiting for him to finish.

'I have given my commitment to Mr Carmichael,' she said quietly in her soft Irish brogue when he paused for breath, 'and since I am leaving tomorrow with the rest of the party we had best get on with the arrangements, had we not, Mr Campbell?'

Angus Campbell glared at her. 'Well I canna be making any special arrangements furr yourr comfort,' he said as if begrudging any kindness to her at all. 'You'll be riding on the wagon, except when the going gets rough and then you'll go on shanks's pony.'

'Pardon?'

Angus snorted, 'Shanks's pony means yourr own two legs, gurrlie.'

'Is there anything else that I will be needing to bring with me?' Kate asked, changing the subject.

'You'll need good strong boots and a wide hat, and furr God's sake try to get some clothes more suitable furr the heat. Don't bring too much, though, furr we've not got a lot of room. We are taking the stores up with us furr the next few months.'

Kate nodded. 'Mr Carmichael agreed to advance me the first two months' wages. I want to buy some suitable clothing. Did he mention that to you, Mr Campbell?'

'He did indeed, and if there is no talking you out of this foolishness then I'll hand it over to you, Miss O'Mara.'

Kate carefully counted all the money and placed it inside the pocket of her dress.

'Now then,' said Angus, 'we'll be on our way furrst thing tomorrow, so be ready from furrst light. We will pick you up from the front door of the depot. Be ready there or we'll come looking furr you to retrieve our two months' wages in advance.'

'I'll be ready,' said Kate. 'Have a good day, sir. I'll be seeing you tomorrow.'

Angus Campbell did not bother to reply and Kate saw herself out.

She could not think of a time in her life when she had ever held four pounds in her hand. She wandered through all the main stores in the town. She was determined to make the money stretch a long way. M. & S. Marks offered goods of reasonable quality at a fair price and Kate spent some time there poring over everything from shawls and ribbons through to stays. While the temptation was great to indulge her fantasies of silk chemises, cashmere shawls and décolleté evening dresses, she confined herself to the least expensive and most practical women's attire.

The shop assistants, though surprised at her destination, were eager to be helpful and they made some practical suggestions. She would need to take everything that she would require.

There would be no stores in the Far North and it could well be many months before she visited a store in the nearest town or returned to Adelaide to shop.

She purchased a pair of good stout leather boots, just in case her others wore through, two extra pairs of worsted stockings, six handkerchiefs, two towels, two plain aprons, a simple gown of printed cotton and one of plain dark nainsook, two calico petticoats, the same number of cotton drawers and a shift. That would have to do.

As she went along, Kate had been keeping a tally in her head. 'Could you total these items for me, then?' she asked the assistant, so that she could check her own figures.

Kate watched while he tallied them on paper in front of her. Her arithmetic was not quick, for she had only recently learnt it, but she was determined not to lose one penny through carelessness on her part or his.

'I make it two pounds and eight pence,' he said.

It was more than half of what she had, she thought. She would prefer to keep some money for the future. Some of it she would give to Brigid, so her remaining purchases would need to be carefully chosen.

'Now, I will be needing one or two other items,' she said, going through her mental list.

'Well, ma'am, of an absolute necessity is a sun bonnet. These are very popular with the ladies of Adelaide,' he said, showing her a straw bonnet with just a little ornamentation.

Kate looked at it critically. 'How much?' she asked.

'Not expensive at two shillings, ma'am.'

Kate thought it unlikely to last the rigours of the bush and looked around the shop for something more suitable. 'I have seen men in the town wearing very wide-brimmed and low-crowned hats which appear to do an excellent job of shielding them from the sun. Do you have any of those to show me?'

'Ah, the wide-awake hat; they are really for farmers and the like,' he replied dismissively.

'How much are they?' Kate pursued.

'One shilling, ma'am.'

'I will try one on.'

The hat, though a little strange-looking on her, fitted well.

'This will do the job,' she said.

'What about a coat and some warmer wear? It can get cold at night up north,' the assistant reminded her.

'No, the clothes I brought with me from Ireland will do well. Now, some trousers,' she said, watching for his reaction.

She had heard of other women who had worn trousers and while it was a shocking thought to most people, she could see that they may have some advantage, especially if she had to learn to ride a horse.

'Not for you, I hope! A wide-awake hat at a

pinch, but certainly not trousers. Not the done thing, if you'll excuse me saying so, ma'am.' He did look shocked indeed. 'The colony may be far from home,' he was evidently referring to England, 'but we have not dropped our standards that far.'

Kate smothered a laugh. 'Indeed no,' she said, 'I was instructed to buy trousers for one of the young shepherds, apparently he is a slight lad, not much bigger than me. He needs something strong for the rough life in the bush.'

She amazed even herself with how quickly the lie rose to her tongue.

The assistant looked somewhat suspicious. 'Moleskin would be the thing, ma'am, at ten shillings.'

'I'll get him just one pair,' Kate said, 'in case they are not quite what he wanted.'

'Is that all, now?'

'Surely,' Kate replied.

As the assistant wrapped the goods in brown paper and string, she looked idly around the shop again. She thought how much the other girls from the ship would have loved to have done what she had just done. It would be some time before they would see that much money, unless they met with extraordinary good luck.

On impulse, she turned to the ribbons. 'Just a couple of these as well,' she said, thinking of her friends.

Kate left M. & S. Marks, almost giddy with the fun of spending money but also satisfied that she had kept a little. She felt the remainder in her pocket. 'The beginning of the future! Some day I will be rich!'

Kate and Brigid lay on one bed in the darkness, whispering far into the night. After more than two years together they were reticent to let their last night together slip away too quickly.

'I wish you weren't goin',' Brigid sighed for the umpteenth time.

'You know I have to go. I can't wait here forever. I can't be waiting for the future to come to me. I've got to make the future for myself. Never, ever again do I want to be poor. Never do I want to lie in a roadside ditch praying that someone will take pity on me. If you don't want me to go on my own, then come with me. I want you with me. I will miss you so much if you don't come too.'

'I would if I could, but 'tis not for me. The slow and steady path is the one that I will tread. I'll get there, not as quickly, but I believe in being careful. I'd rather be here where I know that I'll get three solid meals a day. I would go almost to the ends of the earth with you Kate—'

'But not into the Australian wilderness!'

'No!'

'They won't let you stay here forever. You'll have to go some time. Eventually they'll find a job for you and you'll have to go.'

'Well then, I'll be prayin' that 'tis not two

hundred and fifty miles away. You don't know what might happen up there, Kate. You might be like the explorers, you might die of thirst and starvation—'

'Don't say it!' Kate interrupted, crossing herself. 'Pray for me, Brigid. Pray for us both that we never starve again.'

The discussion went in circles for hours. Kate could not stay and Brigid would not go. There was no way that they could stay together. Eventually sleep put an end to the discussion, but for Kate, the sleep was troubled. She dreamt of Ireland again . . .

. . . The wind blew bitterly cold across her body as they lay sheltering in the ditch. She clutched the body of her little brother closer to hers and pulled her threadbare cloak over the top of them both. He whimpered pathetically as she disturbed his unquiet sleep. It was the only way to keep him warm . . . If only they had not been evicted from their cottage. That had been the beginning of the end. How would they survive now? . . . Everything was gone. No land to plant another crop. No roof over their heads. Their last pennies gone on a pitiful handful of dried bread. Their father had died first. Then their mother.

Without land they had nothing: no hope, no security, no future.

It was so cold, so damp, the hunger gnawed at her insides and she could not sleep. The wind howled over her and the snow piled up in drifts around them. How long the night seemed. How hopeless and utterly miserable. She began to drift . . .

The thin light of the misty dawn wakened her. If they lay there any longer they would surely freeze to death. It would be better to walk and that way to get some warmth into their bones. She would wake up her brother and they would trudge to the next village. She had heard that there was a soup kitchen there. A bowl of hot soup would keep them going.

If she didn't get up soon they would simply die where they lay. Another day of staggering wearily, their legs weak from hunger. She had to get up.

'Wake up, Patrick, we've got to move on,' she said, shaking him.

His body was limp in her arms. Not Patrick too! Not her darling, her favourite brother. He was the one she had loved the most. The others had all gone—Ellen, Eamon, Kelly, the wee baby Michael. But not Patrick. Her favourite had been spared so far. She had given her own meagre portions of food to him to keep him going. She had carried him on her back most of the way from the last village.

She shook him again, panic rising in her voice, 'Patrick, wake up!'

But his body was cold already. His head rolled on his shoulders, his face grey and lifeless.

She looked up at the sound of wheels crunching

over the icy ground. She struggled to her knees,
Patrick clutched to her chest.

'Stop! Help me!'

The carriage drew level with her, the curtains
were parted and a supercilious face looked her
up and down.

The man inside tapped the roof of the carriage
with his cane. She heard his call to the driver:
'Don't stop. Drive on!' The accent was English.

The carriage disappeared into the mist. She
was alone.

Pain seared through her and she let out a cry,
a cry of terrible hurt and despair . . . She
couldn't help herself, her mouth opened again
and again, the screams of anguish piercing and
awful . . .

'Wake up, Kate, wake up, for God's sake! You'll
have the whole place awake!' It was Brigid,
shaking her, urgency in her voice.

Kate struggled up from the mist and the pain
and clung to her friend's arms, stifling the sobs
that rose in her throat.

'You were dreamin',' Brigid told her. ''Twas
that dream again, was it not?'

'Mm,' Kate sobbed, ''twas the dream again.'
She searched under her pillow for a handkerchief.

The dream that had haunted her nights ever
since the famine. The dream that returned to her
each time she was reminded of the horror of
watching her loved ones starve to death, one by

one, while she stood by, helpless to save them. Why had she been the only one spared?

'Are you all right now, then?'

'Aye,' Kate nodded in the darkness. 'I am, thank you, Brigid. Though sometimes I think I'll never get over it. I suppose I'm not as brave as I pretend to be.'

'We're both fragile, under the surface. But you're brave despite it. Far braver than I. You'll get what you want from life, I have not a doubt about that. You have spirit. It has kept you alive until now and it will keep you goin' still.'

'I pray that it will.'

'I'll be all right and so will you,' Kate said, reassuring herself as well as her friend, as they bade each other farewell in the morning.

Tears started down Brigid's face. 'Don't lose touch,' she said. 'If I get a posting I'll write. I'll also leave a message here with the post office, in case you don't get my letter. That way, when you come back you'll know where to find me.'

Kate gave her another hug.

A horseman and a bullock-drawn wagon piled high with stores came into view.

'This must be it,' Kate said.

James Carmichael's horse was tall and glossy. He spurred it on a little to reach them before the wagon did.

'Ready to go, then?' he called to Kate.

The horse was snorting the cool morning air,

frisky and ready for the long day's ride. To Kate, Mr Carmichael was a king perched high above them on the magnificent horse. His saddle and his top-boots were shiny black and embossed with intricate designs. His clothes, although of a practical nature for the journey, bespoke unlimited wealth. They were crisp, fresh, new and of very fine quality.

'I am indeed,' Kate called back with enthusiasm.

'And you decided not to come, then?' he said to Brigid.

''Twould take a braver woman than I,' she replied. 'I'm not so fearless as Kate.' She winked at Kate as she spoke.

The teamster pulled up the bullocks that hauled the wagon. 'Whoa, Blackie! Whoa, Lofty! Whoa, Pete, whoa!'

He tipped his hat to the orphans. He was an older man with a face that was wrinkled and tanned like an autumn oak leaf.

James Carmichael did not alight from his horse but introduced them from where he sat. 'Harold, this is Miss Kate O'Mara. Kate, Harold Simpson.'

'Good mornin' to you,' Kate said, unable to suppress the excitement in her voice. Harold responded in kind.

'I'm putting her in your care for the journey, Harold,' James said. 'She'll either ride on the wagon, or walk with you, that way I'll know where everyone is.'

He turned back to Kate. 'This wagon is

carrying all the supplies for the trip. You should acquaint yourself with its contents as you'll be in charge of all meals on the track. There's a quart-pot to make the tea at lunchtime and fresh bread and cheese for today. We'll be staying at an inn tonight, but when we're camping out this will be the roof over your head as well. If you spread the tarpaulin out over the top of the wagon at night you will have a dry place to sleep underneath.'

'It sounds grand.'

Brigid was rolling her eyes again.

Harold picked up Kate's bag and went to stow it aboard the wagon.

'You can trust old Harold,' James said to her. 'He'll look after you.'

Kate nodded.

'Our first stop will be Dry Creek tonight. Otherwise I will see you where we stop for lunch,' James told her. 'I'm off to catch up with the drays. Enjoy the beautiful morning.'

He spurred his horse impulsively and galloped back down the road from which he had come.

Kate hugged Brigid once more and climbed up onto the wagon.

'God speed you,' Brigid called.

'And God bless you, my dearest friend,' Kate returned, her eyes misting over.

As they took off, the sun slowly climbed above the trees and the buildings. The first rays bathed Kate and the wagon in golden light.

The journey to Wildowie promised to be one that Kate would never forget.

Chapter
Three

Myriads of birds sang their welcome to the day, some darting through the trees in flashes of bright green and vivid red, others swooping across the road, screeching as they went. The dappled shadows of the trees stretched their arms down the road in invitation to the travellers.

To Kate, the glorious spring day was an indication of good things to come. She looked ahead, up the long road, and felt her senses tingling with the excitement of anticipation. She was on her way! A new land, a new start, a new job, money . . . a new life. She was even wearing one of the new gowns she had purchased. She had chosen it because it was plain and dark and would not show the dirt and dust of the day's travel, but it suited her well. The darkness made her skin look even more translucent and her eyes larger and more deeply blue-violet.

She wondered if this new land looked as good

through the eyes of other travellers. The morning sun shone golden on the ripening fields of grain. Fat cattle and sheep grazed on bright green pastures. Chubby-cheeked children played in abundant gardens at the sides of the road. There were no cold, hungry waifs begging on the roadsides here.

Maybe God was finally going to smile on Kate O'Mara!

She started at the sudden sound of wild laughter echoing through the valley.

'What was that?' she cried out.

Harold was walking along the side of the wagon and he shouted with laughter at her alarm.

'You've just heard your first kookaburra! Don't worry, though, he's a friendly chap, and loves to laugh at the foolish ways of us humans.'

'I'm hoping he's not laughing at us, then,' she shouted, her pleasant reverie interrupted, 'for it's not every day I set off on a journey of two hundred and fifty miles in a strange country.'

'I'd be hoping not, either, Miss, for I've not done the journey before meself.'

Tired of trying to converse at a distance, she jumped gracefully from the back of the wagon to walk beside Harold.

'So, Harold, tell me all you know about where we're going,' she began.

'Well, it's a long way to go, and I'd just as soon be staying on with my family,' he said, grumbling a little as old men are wont to do, 'but times have been hard and Mr Carmichael will pay us all well for our trouble in carting his stores so far north. We'll follow the Great North Road as far as it goes. That will be to Clare Village, which is at least a week away. Then we leave the main road behind us and follow a rough track north, as best we can, for another few weeks. The track will take us past the stations which have just been established. I believe that Mr Carmichael's station is the most northerly settlement there is. It will be rough going and we're not likely to make more than six or seven miles in a day. But at least it will be safer with us all together.'

'Safer?'

'It is better that us teamsters travel in groups, not only for company on the long hauls, but to help each other out along the way. There's always the chance of breakdowns and lost bullocks. And there's the blacks to contend with as well. A lone teamster is easy prey.'

'They are rogues, are they not?'

'They can be that, Miss, but they are no fools. They know that they can have little chance of success against men with horses and guns, but a lone bullocky without the speed of a horse can easily be ambushed and killed.'

'Who makes up the rest of the party, then?'

'We're a reasonable sized party all up, there are several hired teamsters, including meself, two new shepherds and the overseer, Mr Campbell, as well as Mr Carmichael himself.'

'Mr Carmichael lives up there as well, or does he only go up to visit?'

'Ah, he's no King William Street squatter, that one.'

'King William Street squatter?'

'It's what we call the nobs who own the big stations but live in comfort down in town and have an overseer to manage the place entirely,' he explained. 'That lot only visit when the season is good and the weather cool and they have no understanding of how tough it can be day in, day out.'

'So Mr Carmichael is a reasonable sort, then, is he?'

'I've not heard ill of him,' he replied but offered no more information.

'He's married?'

'I've not heard that he is.' He seemed unwilling to discuss his boss any further with her.

'And what about you, then, Harold, d'you have a wife and family?'

Harold had no reticence in talking about them. She learnt that he had no fewer than six children. The oldest boy would soon take on the role of his father's offsider.

Her eyes roamed over the countryside. They journeyed through small patches of uncleared land that Harold called 'scrub' and which interspersed the small farms and tiny villages along the road. The trees were unlike any she had seen before. Most of them were a grey-green, unlike the emerald green of home, and they shed their bark rather than their leaves. The vegetation emitted a powerful aroma, both sharp and sweet. It was a bracing, clean smell which had been evident to Kate since their ship had first neared the coast of Australia. She knew now that it was the smell of the trees that they called the gums.

The road was busy with drays carting copper from Kapunda.

'I hear that copper saved the colony.' Rory O'Connor had said that.

'Yes, the place has gone mineral-mad now. Prospectors are combing the countryside. They are hoping for gold, of course,' Harold replied.

Blood surged through her veins at the very thought of finding gold. If a lowly shepherd had found the copper at the Burra, then there was no reason why a person such as herself could not discover gold in the colony!

Gold would fit in very neatly with her plans indeed.

German farmers came down the road towards them. Men and women alike were carting their produce to market by foot. Butter, eggs, vegetables, wheat—there was nothing that did not flourish on the German farms. Some carried the goods on their backs, others on top of their heads. The women made a fine picture, their bodies broad and strong in their national dress. Their golden hair was braided or tied firmly under their German-style bonnets and their blue eyes crinkled in smiles as they greeted Kate and

Harold with 'Guten Tag!' According to Harold, they were religious refugees who had come here with their Pastor. Within no time at all they had established bountiful farms and they now supplied most of Adelaide with fresh produce.

The young girls were much sought after as farmhands for they could pull a plough and thresh and winnow the grain by hand. Harold pointed out their villages with their neat gabled houses with large lofts and small windows, just as they would have lived in at home.

At midday the party stopped for lunch. Kate and Harold were at the tail end of the vehicles that were travelling to Wildowie. For the first time she saw the others who made up the party. The teamsters unyoked the bullocks so that they could rest under the shade of the tall gum trees. While they were tending to the animals Kate climbed back onto the wagon and delved through the stores to find the things to make the lunch. Keen to be contributing her share, she collected dry sticks, made the fire and took water from the barrel at the back of the wagon to boil the quartpot for the tea. The blue smoke that rose from the fire had that same fresh clean smell of gum trees.

As the teamsters and the shepherds finished their work they came to sit, one by one, around the fire that she had built. Harold introduced Dan and Sid. They dragged an old log and placed it well away from the heat of the fire and then sat down, telling Kate a little about themselves as they waited for her to serve their food. They were both younger than Harold and had been teamsters for a short time. Kate was pleased to find that Dan was an Irishman from Donegal. He seemed a pleasant sort of fellow, softly spoken, and it was good to hear his accent when so far from home.

Sid was a dark-haired Englishman with a bristly beard. His greeting to her had been brusque and his rather crooked features suggested a surly character.

The two shepherds were brothers by the name of Craig and Robert McInerney. They had fair complexions and sandy hair. Judging by the soft fuzz of new beards on their faces, Kate thought them little more than sixteen or seventeen years of age and on their way to their first job. Like her, they were full of enthusiasm and they shook her hand warmly.

James Carmichael and Angus Campbell had tethered their horses by the drays and had gone to a nearby public house for a more substantial lunch and a pint of ale.

The talk over lunch centred on the journey ahead of them. Even for the most experienced teamsters it would be a long, hard journey. Dan and Harold yarned about the journeys they had done before. Sid did not seem too keen on coming forward with much information about anything to do with his past. The McInerney brothers for the most part listened to the others talk. Like her, they were eager to hear all the information that they could about the journey and their destination. No one had been so far north before and they shared a sense of anticipation.

Lunch finished, the rest of the party sat with their backs against the logs, pulled their hats down over their eyes, lay back a little and took the opportunity to rest. The warm breeze drifted the last whispers of smoke from the dying fire. The bush hummed and clicked with the sound of insects. Kate sat, her head resting on her hand, and contemplated her first day out of Adelaide. It was all as it should be. Mr Carmichael seemed to be a good boss and a charming man, her fellow travellers were decent enough, the countryside was beautiful and the weather as fine as could be. If Brigid had come with her, her happiness would have been complete.

Then Kate felt the wind change. The warm northerly breeze swung around to a cooler south-westerly and brought with it soft grey clouds that hung down close over the land.

'Get with it, boys,' Harold said, 'we're in for a change and it looks like rain for later.'

The men pushed their hats back, stood up, and groaned as they stretched.

Just as they were finishing the yoking of the bullocks, James Carmichael and Angus Campbell returned from the inn. Little attention was paid to Kate as the party speeded up their preparations for the afternoon's journey.

They proceeded much as before, the two drays and the wagon, all piled high with stores and God knows what else, lurching along the deeply rutted dirt road. There was no conversation, just the ceaseless creaking and rumbling of the wheels over the rough track.

That night, Kate, James and Angus stayed at the inn, while the bullockies and the other men camped out with their teams. It rained overnight and on the following morning the road was heavy. The bullocks hauled the drays fairly well through the soft mud. The owners of the horse teams using the road were finding the going more difficult. The horses, by nature, did not pull as steadily. The horse teams plunged and reared, stopping, starting and lurching about all over the road.

By the end of the morning Kate had noticed that they had encountered fewer vehicles coming from the opposite direction, although plenty had passed them along the way. The mail wagons and passenger coaches had passed them at a spanking pace. Their drivers, or whips as they preferred to be called, were dressed smartly in their red liveries. They drove recklessly and the passengers held on for dear life.

It was at lunchtime that day that she had her next experience of the jibing tongue of Angus Campbell.

She had difficulty finding dry wood for the campfire. She was engaged in puffing on a small flame in the smouldering pile of sticks when Angus sauntered over on his stocky legs to give her the benefit of his wisdom.

'I've never known any lassie who was any guid at lighting a fire,' he said, standing well back and offering no assistance.

'This lassie,' she retorted, mocking his accent ever so slightly, 'has lit plenty of fires before.' She kept puffing and didn't look up.

'Plenty in the loins of young men but few in the bush,' sniggered Sid, the teamster with the crooked face and the permanent sneer.

'I've heard it's all these Irish lassies are any guid furr at all,' Angus added.

Kate kept her head low and continued to puff on the flame which had been growing little by little. She felt a slow blush rise up her face. Angus Campbell was getting under her skin but she bit her tongue, determined not to rise to his bait.

James changed the topic and the heated moment passed.

'Don't you know how to make an Australian cup of tea?' Angus jeered at her later when she had served the food and the pannikins of hot steaming tea.

'And what is wrong with the tay, might I ask?' Kate said in her Irish accent, little realising she was giving him more grist for the mill.

'Ah,' replied Angus, 'no wonder you can't make a proper cup of tea, you can't even say it. Let's hope you'rre better in bed than you are at the campfire.'

Sid laughed and the two young brothers joined in, albeit a little uncertainly. They wanted to be accepted as men even if it had to be at Kate's expense. Neither Dan nor Harold joined in. James Carmichael appeared not to be listening.

Kate ignored the latter part of his comment. 'So tell me, how would you be doing it better?'

'A guid cup of bush tea is made with a gum leaf in the quartpot,' he said in a scornful tone.

She gave him her sweetest smile, saying, 'Well I'd best be fixing it for you then.'

She strolled over to where Angus was leaning against the tree and took his pannikin from him.

'I'll make you another.'

She threw out the tea it contained and placed it beside the empty quartpot near the dying fire.

She then made a great show of picking a good gum leaf. Everyone was watching her now.

'Ah, this is the best I can find,' she said, returning to the centre of the group. She then proceeded to place the leaf carefully in the bottom of the empty pot. Picking up the pannikin and the pot, she returned to Angus.

Smiling, she said 'Now, I may be a poor Irish girlie but I'm thinking you did say to make the tay with a gum leaf in the pot. But how you'll be drinking it I don't know!'

The others all laughed outright. She gave him a grin as if to say that she was happy to join in some fun but would not be teased without teasing in return.

Angus's face was cold.

'Well, lassie, you'll have to rebuild the fire noo to get some more hot water.'

Kate's blue eyes sparkled with the challenge. 'Sure, and I would if I could, but you said you'd never known a lassie who was capable of building a fire so I'll be leaving it up to you!'

The rest of the group roared with laughter again.

An ugly flush of red suffused the face of the Scotsman, outdoing the red of his hair.

She purposely lowered her eyes, realising she had pushed too far. 'Oh, c'mon then, I'm just having a joke, I'll make it for you.'

She reached out to take the pannikin from him.

He threw both the pannikin and the pot onto the ground. 'Nae. Clean up the lunch things, we're off.' He stalked away.

She watched him go, the sparkle still in her eyes but somewhat less bright now that a sense of dismay replaced the thrill of the battle. She looked at Harold who shook his head at her slowly, and then at James Carmichael. His face, strangely enough, held a look of appreciation.

She returned to her work with a sinking feeling that as far as Angus Campbell was concerned, things could only get worse.

It was when they reached Gawler that evening that the party discovered why so few travellers had been coming towards them during the day. The rivers past Gawler were in flood and the River Light, the next river to cross, was impassable. It had seemed to Kate that there had not been enough rain to flood a river, but then the bush was famous for just that.

They decided to stay in Gawler town for the night and to continue their journey the next day, hoping that by then the river would be down in time for them to cross. Kate, by virtue of being the only female, was allowed to stay at an inn again. She was used to a rather more sedentary life aboard ship and the effects of long days of walking were sending her early to bed for the deep, relaxed sleeps which come only to the exhausted.

When they got to the River Light, they found, contrary to the advice they had been given, that it was still impassable. A number of vehicles had drawn up on both sides. Horses had been unharnessed, the bullocks unyoked, tents erected and campfires lit.

'Looks like we're stopping here for the night,' Harold called out to her. He then called 'Whoa, Blackie, whoa, Lofty! . . .' to halt the bullocks.

Kate scrambled down and walked over to the edge of the river. It was a torrent of swirling brown water. Logs whirled madly downstream pushing leafy debris before them. The punt had been tied securely on the other side where another group of travellers was waiting for the river to fall. James Carmichael joined her, his strong jawline taut as he surveyed the grim scene before him.

'A fine beginning to a long journey,' he said dryly. 'It may be days before the river is low enough for the punt to operate safely.'

'We'll have to wait it out, then?' Kate asked.

'There's no other way,' he said. 'But it's about time a few bridges were constructed on this road. God knows, the colony has been here for thirteen years.'

He walked off, without waiting for her reply, to issue instructions to the waiting teamsters.

'I'll help unyoke the bullocks,' Kate said, a wooden box in one hand.

'Ah, you don't have to, lassie,' Harold said, shaking his head.

'Why not? I like to do my bit. I'm learning new things all the time. I reckon the more I know, the better bushwoman I'll be.'

'True enough! But you're not doing a bad job so far.'

Kate used the box to get enough height to lean over the off-siders while Harold released the near-siders. He was a good teacher, explaining to her as they worked not only the yokes and tackle, but also the nature of the bullocks and how to work them, the commands to give and the pitfalls for beginners.

In return for her help Harold offered kindly to show her a bushman's trick or two for preparing the supper. She was engaged in kneading the damper when she heard a shout.

'Whoa there, Mick! Whoa there, Stump! Out o' the way, Spike, you eejit mongrel!'

That was a familiar voice! Jumping up from the ground, she saw Rory O'Connor directing a team of bullocks to stop at the side of the road. His dog was capering about in the way of the bullocks.

He was dressed in a bright red flannel shirt which stretched tightly across his broad shoulders and chest, corduroy trousers, leather gaiters and his familiar felt hat. His long whip was carried over his shoulder. She could hardly believe that one of the few people she knew should turn up at this spot.

She felt her heart fluttering at the sight of him. She waited until he had stopped his dray and had laid his whip on the ground. It was the sign that the bullocks could lie down too.

Then she called out, 'Well, if it isn't Mr O'Connor!'

Rory spun around to see who was addressing him. 'Bonny Kathleen, Lady of Cork, is it not?'

She was pleased that he had remembered her name. He strode over to say hello.

She quickly slipped her hands into her apron pockets.

''Tis grand to see you again,' he said, holding out his hands to her and looking into her eyes.

''Tis grand indeed.' She extended her hands, all covered in flour and dough, to meet his.

Even before he had noticed her mischief a bubble of laughter escaped her. She held his hands, covered in flour now too, up in front of his face for him to see.

Then she quickly stepped back. 'I warned you that I would have my revenge,' she said, laughing at him, her eyes sparkling with devilry.

'Oh ho!' was the only warning she got before Rory lunged forward, grabbed the hem of her skirt, and began to wipe his hands clean. Kate was too busy trying to get away to take notice of the fallen branch behind her. Stepping backwards with the hem of her skirt held tight in his hands she tripped over the branch and landed heavily on her bottom with a gasp.

'Mother of Mary!' Rory exclaimed, quickly stepping forward to help her up. He held both of her hands firmly in his own to bring her to her feet, 'I am sorry, Kathleen.'

She pulled the back of her skirt around to look at it. It was thick with wet clay. She just laughed again and shook her head. 'I think that this means that I still owe you one, Rory O'Connor!'

Kate turned to see James watching her, and Harold and Dan joining in the laughter. She duly introduced Rory to her party and James invited him to join them at their campfire and to share supper.

After supper was finished Rory produced a fiddle and some rum from a keg on his dray. All of the men took a measure of rum into their pannikins. Dan had an accordion and Harold had a tin whistle, so the group was entertained with some fine Australian bush ballads and heart-warming Irish melodies.

Kate felt her eyes straying to Rory time and time again. He had a lovely strong voice and was a fine figure of a man. Charming too. She could not help but be conscious of him. And he was evidently conscious of her, too.

All was quiet and the fire had almost burnt

away when she got up from her swag. She could not sleep and was not sure why. Whether it was the experience of camping under Australian skies for the first time, or whether it was the disturbing memories brought back to her by the old Irish songs, she did not know.

She sat on a log, quietly contemplating the dying embers of the fire and the alien night noises. A feeling of melancholy had settled on her. Home was so far away. She shook her head. Australia was her home now, she reminded herself, not Ireland! Besides, there had been no future for her there. The farm, the cottage, her village, her family . . . they were all gone.

Here there was hope. Her whole life, like the long rough road, stretched before her. At least she was going somewhere and there was somewhere to go! A year ago she had been stuck in a grim workhouse, cold, dirty, struggling to stay alive, and no opportunities in sight. Who would have guessed that just one year later she would be in another country, sitting by a warm campfire on a balmy night, pondering her fate? And where would she be this time next year? She would not be starving, that was one thing she would make certain!

There was the sound of a footfall on crunchy bark. 'Can you not sleep?' It was Rory.

'No.'

'Me neither,' he said. 'The night is too beautiful. Just look at those stars, have you ever seen anything like it?'

She looked up. 'Arrah, there are more stars here than in the whole of Ireland, it seems,' she said.

He smiled and said, ''Tis the southern hemisphere, there's a better view of the sky. There's no moon tonight. Come away from the campfire and you'll see them even better.'

They stood up and moved away from the fire. Kate stumbled over some uneven ground in the darkness and Rory took her arm. His hand was firm and warm.

Away from the light of the fire, and with her eyes accustomed to the darkness, she looked up.

The night sky was like nothing she had ever seen before. There was not a corner of the sky that did not hold a thousand stars. And they shone with such high intensity. A thick cloud, almost solid with stars, stretched overhead from one horizon to the other.

Kate took a deep breath and released it through pursed lips.

'The Milky Way,' Rory murmured, his eyes on her face as she looked at the skies.

'Glory be to God! I've never seen anything so beautiful.'

'Indeed, I have never seen anything so beautiful either,' Rory replied softly, still looking at her.

Kate looked at him, conscious of the undertone of admiration.

He was one of those men who engendered total trust. She put her hand on his arm. ''Tis wonderful to see you here on the road. I get the feeling that you and I are going to be good friends.'

Rory opened his mouth to speak, then closed it again, and instead took her hand to walk back to the fire. He then placed a few light sticks on the embers to give them warmth and light.

'What are you doing up this way?' he asked her.

She told him how she was headed up to Wildowie.

He whistled through his teeth, 'You're a brave one, then.'

'Not brave, just desperate to get a job. It was as you said, the only jobs are in the bush.'

'Wish I hadn't said it, in that case. The remote bush is no place for a young girl on her own.'

'Well, I have no choice. There's no family to look after me.'

'What of your family, then, Kathleen? What happened to them?'

'Gone in the famine,' Kate replied, a shiver running through her as she spoke.

'Was there no one left at all?'

'No . . . But let's not talk about all that, 'tis over now, 'tis in the past. That's where I want it to stay.' She sat down on a log. 'The one thing that I decided then was that I would never, ever, look back. I'll only look forward, and now that I am in the land of golden opportunity I have everything to look forward to.'

'I think there's some things you can never put behind you, my Kathleen,' he said softly as he sat next to her on the log.

It was strange how he had chosen to call her Kathleen. It was what her family had called her. Since losing them she had called herself Kate.

'Maybe you can't, but I can and I will! I'm determined to forget Ireland!' The sudden flaring of the fire lit the look of fierce determination on her face.

There was a moment of silence.

Kate looked up at him and grinned. 'So what of you, Rory, have you gone down in the world, then, for last time I saw you, you had a fine team of horses and now you have but a team of old bullocks? I do believe the gentleman has fallen on hard times.'

Rory laughed, accepting her change of subject, and he followed in a lighter vein. 'We gentlemen get sick of the high life from time to time, so we take to the roads for a bit of adventure and there's no better beast for adventure than the bullock. So I have left the team of fine horses at home.'

'There be no point letting the truth get in the way of a good story now, would there?'

'Indeed no, but the truth is that the bullock team is mine and the horses were not. I was resting my team before this trip and driving the horses for a friend when I first met you. But I've got fair cause to be pleased with myself.'

'Why is that?'

'I arrived less than two years ago with not a penny in my pocket. Through hard work I saved enough for the team, and it's a good living I am making with them, and money in the bank besides. So I'm better off already than digging the praeties back in Ireland.'

'What are you aiming to do now?'

'I'm on my way to Bungaree Station, just north of Clare Village.'

'No, I meant, what are you going to do now, with your life. Settle down?'

'No, the settled life is not for me,' he said. 'I'd like to see more of this great land. If I can make good money doing that, 'twill be good. My feet are restless. The thing that I learnt in the famine was that the only thing you really need in this world is food in the belly, and if you have that then there's nothing else worth striving for.'

'Do you really think so?'

'There's nothing you can take with you when you go. I survived the famine by living on my wits, travelling around, taking whatever work I could get and selling off the things I owned to buy food when I needed it. There was always work of some kind if you were prepared to move on. The less you took with you the better. It has been my philosophy ever since. I won't settle down while I've got life in me still.'

Kate smiled and stared into the fire for a moment.

'But 'tis the ones with the fine houses and the beautiful horses, like the landlords in Ireland, they're the ones who will never starve, no matter what. The more you can build up, the better.'

'Maybe.'

'Well, I want that, Rory, for 'tis the only way to be sure of the future. If there ever be another famine I'll be sitting pretty in a grand house and wearing a silk gown. The table will be piled high with more food than I could ever want.' She smiled, and the thought of all those riches lit her face with happiness.

'Good on you then, Kathleen, if it will make you happy, then 'tis what you must do.'

She smiled at him. 'I'll tell you what, when you get tired of your roaming then you can park your beasts in my grand garden and come in for the dinner of your life.'

'And won't you be green when I tell you my tales of adventure! 'Tis a bargain.'

Kate stretched out her hand to shake on it. 'Yes, 'tis a bargain,' she said.

His grip was strong and she felt the beat of her heart lift a little as he touched her. She felt at home with him, at peace with him, warm towards him. There were other, stronger, feelings there too, feelings she did not want to analyse too deeply.

If only he wasn't Irish, and a part of everything she had left behind her. She wanted to get ahead. A roving Irishman could hardly lead her to the grand house of her dreams.

Chapter
Four

*T*he next morning James Carmichael stood, his long legs wide and his hands hooked on his belt, looking at the river still swollen and muddy.

'Dangerous still,' he said, frowning a little.

'We'll not be crossing today, then?' Kate asked.

'No, there have been people drowned here trying to cross when it is flooded. We will not take the chance. You may as well settle in for the day. Angus, take one of the boys with you and see if you can purchase some fresh meat from one of the farmers.'

Kate wandered back to their camp to organise the breakfast. It was when she had cleared up later in the morning that Rory approached her and invited her to go out with him while he shot some bush fare to add to the supper.

After he had shot two ducks and a cockatoo he offered to show her how to use the gun.

She was surprised that he would think she would need to know how to use a firearm, but accepted the offer anyway. She might need to find something for the stewpot one day herself.

He showed her the shotgun, explaining the various parts and how they worked. He stood so close to her that it made her heart thump against her ribs, but she put the feelings aside as she tried to concentrate on what he was saying. He watched her as she followed his instructions for loading it. First she tipped the powder funnel into the muzzle and shook it a little so that the required amount of powder fell to the end. She put in a small wad of old rag and pushed it down with the rod, the given weight of shot went in on top of that, then another wad to hold the shot in place. Finally she placed a new percussion cap on the back.

She felt the weight of the shotgun and Rory showed her how to place it up against her shoulder to take aim. She was conscious of the light touch of his hands upon her body as he adjusted the position of the gun against her shoulder. She aligned the foresight and the rearsight notch and then focused on the foresight.

'Watch out, for it will give you one hell of a kick!'

Kate aimed for a pink and grey galah in a tree nearby and pulled the trigger.

The explosion sent her reeling.

The bird took off with an indignant shriek.

'Jaysus! You're not wrong.' She rubbed her

shoulder where it had taken the impact. A puff of black smoke hung in the air around her.

Rory smiled. 'Wide of the mark but pretty good. Try again, this time just aim for the tree.'

She reloaded carefully and tried again, this time missing the tree completely. Then once more. This time she hit the tree.

'Well done!' Rory patted her on the back. 'That's enough for today or you'll be so stiff you won't be able to knead the damper for dinner!'

He looked at her, his eyes shining with admiration, and leaned over close to her to wipe the smudge of black powder from her cheek with his thumb. Kate looked down, conscious of her reaction to his hand's feathery movement on her cheek. She stepped away from him and wiped the black from her hands onto her handkerchief. They headed back to the camp.

Other groups of travellers had arrived throughout the day. Those gathered by the river spent their afternoon variously engaged in washing their clothes, mending, writing letters and reading. Those who could read swapped books. Some just sat about telling yarns or discussing the different breeds of bullocks.

James was reading and Rory was, of course, a main player in the yarn-telling. Kate sat back a little from the rest of the group while her muddy dress soaked in a tub of soapy water and listened to the men talking.

'Well 'twas the worst trip I ever had,' said Dan, 'the year before last. I was taking a load to a farm south of Adelaide. My bullock team and the wagon went over the edge of a cliff and down into a gorge. Both the leaders were killed. It was impossible to get the rest of the team and the wagon back up again. I was really in a pickle . . . Well, I skinned the two dead ones and cut their hides into strips. I made a long rope out of the strips, tied one end to the wagon and the other to a stout tree. As the sun dried it, the hide shrank and gradually pulled the wagon to the top o' the gorge!'

The others all laughed. Kate smiled over at Rory.

'Well, I've seen worse than that,' he said. 'A mate and m'self were working down at Langhorne's Creek when my mate got his wagon badly bogged. We tried everything to get that wagon out. In the end my mate told me to keep going, for if I didn't make our destination by nightfall I'd not be paid. I was just about to go when he put his head under the wheel of his wagon and called out to his team, *"Put me out o' me misery, you rotten bastards!"* . . .'

He turned to her and said, 'Excusing the language, ma'am, but those were his very words,' and he turned back to the group.

'At that moment one of the polers lurched and slightly moved the wheel. My mate sprang to his feet, calling them all the murderin' so-and-so's he could lay his tongue to, and with the swearing and the whip they lifted the load out o' the bog. We made it by nightfall and earned a bonus into the bargain!'

The group all laughed again. Rory looked over to her and winked.

A number of other travellers arrived as the afternoon wore on. One of the parties opened a keg of rum and by supper time many of the men were rolling drunk.

Rory sought Kate out after she'd cleared up. 'You'd best be making yourself scarce, Kathleen. Some of these men have had way too much and things could get ugly 'fore the night is out. The air is blue already with the language being used. Go to bed early and shut your ears to everything you hear.'

James Carmichael had been watching her and when he heard this advice he added his support. 'Yes, disappear now while no one is looking. That way they won't notice that you've gone.'

The singing and the swearing got louder as the night wore on but Kate lay quietly in her swag, forgotten by the men. Eventually sleep got the better of her. It was later in the night, after it had been quiet for some time, that she heard some of the men returning to the camp.

They were very drunk and noisy. A woman's scream rang out.

Kate sat up in her swag. Another scream, definitely female again, but Kate could not pick up her words.

She crawled out of the swag and towards the front of the wagon. In the flickering firelight she could just make out a number of figures. It was

Sid, Angus and a couple of the men who had arrived in the afternoon.

'Tie 'em up, Sid, we'll teach these black bastards!' Angus called out.

She saw Sid pummel his fists into a writhing figure who was held fast by another man. It was a black woman! Kate realised that there was another one on the ground, struggling as her assailant lashed her with a whip.

Kate watched in horror. 'Mother of God!' she whispered. These women were being beaten to within an inch of their lives, right here in front of her! She could watch no more but, heedful of Rory's warnings, she stayed put, curled over with her head on the ground so that she could no longer see the cruelty. Her heart hammered in her chest as she tried to shut out the noise with her hands.

Another scream, this time more bloodcurdling than before. Kate looked up to see one of the men advancing on the woman with a burning stick from the fire.

She could not sit by any longer! She crept out towards the back of the wagon to where the pots and pans lay on the ground. She picked up the heaviest pan with a long handle and moved stealthily to place herself behind the men. No one had seen her.

Without warning she launched herself towards the group and hit one man as hard as she could over the head. He dropped down as if dead. Sid and Angus swung around to see what had caused their mate to fall.

'Leave them alone,' she screamed, her pan poised for more action.

Sid dropped the arm of the black woman and advanced on Kate instead.

Two shots rang out, close by and almost simultaneously.

Sid dived for cover. No one else moved.

Rory's voice was rough as he yanked her arm. 'Get out of the way, Kathleen, you're in my aim.'

She looked, but she could not see the owner of the other gun.

'All of you, let go of those lubras,' came the stern voice of James Carmichael.

The men let go sullenly and the women struggled to their feet.

Rory stepped forward into the light of the fire. 'Keep me covered, Mr Carmichael, I'll check for weapons.' He took Sid's knife.

James entered the circle of light as well. 'Get going!' he shouted and motioned the women to go.

They fled silently into the darkness.

'Disgusting behaviour,' James said coldly, eyeing Sid and Angus. 'They might be savages but that is no excuse. Any repeat of that type of behaviour and you'll find yourselves, at the very best, without a job and without your pay.'

He looked at the one that Kate had knocked out. 'Kate, tend to him, we don't want any deaths here,' he said. He walked off again in the direction of his own swag.

Kate went to fetch a cold wet cloth to place on the man's head.

'High and mighty squatters,' muttered Sid, and he and Angus skulked off.

Rory remained with the wounded man. 'You're a bloody fool, Kathleen, for they'd have done you as well!' he reprimanded her when she returned, his voice barely above a whisper. 'I told you to stay put, and that's what I meant.'

He undid the collar of the unconscious man while Kate held the cold compress to his head. There was a huge lump swelling up where Kate had hit him and he groaned loudly as he regained consciousness.

'I couldn't have stood by, Rory,' she said. 'I couldn't let something like that go on! Did you not see what was happening to those poor women?'

'I did, and you've got a heart of gold, lass. But you shouldn't have interfered.'

'Surely we're all God's creatures?' her voice caught a little.

'Of course we're all God's creatures! But hell and damnation, you'd be on your way to meet your God if I hadn't been there ready to help you!'

Kate dropped the cloth and stood up. Why was it that she always landed in trouble whenever she tried to do anything for anyone else? And for Rory, of all people, to be telling her off!

She turned her head and began to walk away, embarrassed that she was upset by his reprimand.

Rory caught up with her in two strides. He

seized her arm and whirled her round to face him.

'Whisht, I'm sorry, Kathleen,' he said, taking in her teary eyes. 'But you should leave these things to the likes of James and me. You could have been hurt.'

He pulled her into his arms and rested his chin on top of her head. She buried her face in his broad chest, smelling the warm male smell of him. A couple of sniffs escaped her before she got herself under control. But she was in no hurry to remove herself from Rory's strong arms and warm chest. A liquid warmth flowed through her veins. She closed her eyes, revelling in the sensation.

Behind them the injured man stumbled to his feet, grumbled loudly and lurched away, back to his camp.

'We were there, Kate,' he whispered to the top of her head, 'just waiting for the right moment to intervene. You should have been trusting someone else to come to the rescue o' the blacks. There's only one thing you need to be learning about life in the bush, and that's to keep yourself out o' trouble. Now, go to bed.'

'I don't think I could sleep,' she replied as Rory released her.

He looked at her for a moment. 'Wait here,' he said.

She sat down on an upturned stump near the fire. Rory returned a few moments later with a pannikin that had a little rum in the bottom.

'Have a drap o' this, 'twill settle you down.'

She turned up her nose as she took the first mouthful but as it slid down her throat she felt its heat spread through her. She finished what was in the pannikin and stared into the darkness of the bush. The night's sounds were hushed, lost against the ever-present murmur of the river. The camp was quiet. Heavy drunken snores were the only sign that there were other people present.

'I can't believe that they could treat them like that!' she said, thinking of the black women.

''Tis not the first time and it won't be the last. They're treated like animals.'

She thought about the poor woman who had been sold by her husband back in Adelaide and that Mary O'Leary who Brigid had told her about. Just what kind of place was this colony? Beneath the thin veneer of English morality lay a society which mistreated its weakest members. The men in the colony were a rough lot. No wonder her friend Brigid had been reticent to come with her.

'Are the men here always so violent towards women?'

'Men all over the world, like the women, are pretty much the same,' Rory shrugged, 'but don't be lumping us all together, now, will you, Kathleen?'

'Of course not, I'm sorry, Rory. A few of you are decent enough, men like you, and Mr Carmichael.'

He raised his eyebrows. 'You're sure of his motives, are you?'

She nodded, dismissing his question. 'Maybe I've just run into some of the wrong ones so far.'

'You may have done. Or you could be right. Maybe the colony does have more than its fair share of bad characters. Some of the men here were lags who've come over from the eastern colonies—'

She interrupted him, 'Do you think that Sid was a convict, then?'

He shrugged his shoulders again. ''Tis not the kind of thing you ever ask out here in the colonies. People here prefer to leave the past behind them, and they have many different reasons for doing that. But there's no reason that they should be any worse than free settlers. Think of some o' those you knew in Ireland who were convicted of stealing to save their families from starvation. You wouldn't call them criminals, now, would you?'

'Indeed no.'

He shook his head slowly. 'Maybe 'tis the bush. Only those who are prepared to live a rough life want to come out here and to take their chances. You've got to be strong and prepared to live on your wits.' He stretched out his legs before him. 'Then again, maybe 'tis the bush itself. There's so few women out here. It lacks their civilising influence. We need more women like you, Kathleen, women who're prepared to set the standards of what is right and what is wrong.'

'But you said that I shouldn't have interfered, to leave it to the likes of you and Mr Carmichael!'

He laughed, acknowledging her argument. 'You're right, I did,' he said, 'I mean you should set the standards, but with less danger to yourself!'

'Ha!' she exclaimed, raising her shoulders and rolling her eyes. 'And how might I be doing that?'

He smiled. ''Tis too late at night to be pondering the ways of the world, Kathleen. Go to bed, for we'll all be back on the road in a few hours from now.'

She rose slowly, her body now relaxed from the rum. 'G'night to you then, Rory,' she said, 'and thanks.'

She would have liked him to ask her to stay longer. She was drawn to him, more than to any man she had met before.

''Night, sweet dreams,' Rory replied.

Her dreams were sweet, despite the events of the night. She lay wrapped snug in her warm swag, cosy and secure as if still cradled in Rory's arms.

The river was down by the next morning. The drays and wagons were punted across without much more ado. The Gilbert River further on, however, was still flooded. Not having a punt, it was harder to cross than the Light. Rory stayed with the Wildowie party so that the teamsters could help each other as they hauled the loads through the muddied, swollen waters. An experienced teamster and an entertaining character, he was a welcome addition to the party. James invited Rory to travel with them as far as Bungaree Station, where Rory would be finishing his journey.

The countryside on the way to the village of Clare was the most beautiful that Kate had yet seen. They passed through the charming villages of Auburn, Watervale and Penwortham. The gentle rolling valleys were green with lush spring growth. The gum trees rose majestically and towered over the road. The orchards, vineyards and market gardens, now a few years old, overflowed with produce to sell to the Burra. There were plenty of well-watered green glens to suit the bullocks along the way.

Clare was the centre of the agricultural district supplying the mining towns of the Burra. Blessed with high rainfall, it seemed almost as green as Ireland after the dusty drying plains they had travelled across after leaving Adelaide. Officially it was the last place on the Great North Road. From here on there would be very little traffic. The only people further north were the bravest of the settlers. The next day's journey would take them to Bungaree Station, home of the Hawker family and the station to which Rory's team was hauling his load.

Kate was already feeling that she would miss him and almost wished that it was Rory who was carting for James Carmichael, rather than Harold, or Dan, or especially Sid.

'Where to from Bungaree?' she asked Rory as she walked beside him on the way out of Clare.

'I'll come back here to Clare,' he said. 'It should be easy to find a load to take south again, though Mr Hawker at Bungaree may have something for me anyway.'

'And then?'

'Wherever the next job takes me.'

Kate was silent for a moment.

'I would hope that we cross paths again, Kathleen.'

'Surely we will, I'm thinking it must be fated, for I've met you twice already,' she smiled.

She liked Rory, a lot. He was charming, funny, a tower of strength. But he could never be part of her plans. He wanted to roam. She wanted wealth and security.

'So where to for Kathleen O'Mara after Wildowie?'

'I'll be staying there for some time, God willing,' she said. 'I want to save up some money, maybe to buy for myself a business, like you've done, and a home.'

'And a room full of silk gowns and a gigantic table piled high with food,' Rory said, his grin wide and his eyes sparkling.

'To be sure, 'tis what I'm after,' Kate agreed, laughing even though she was deadly serious about it all.

'I thought the Irish orphans all come here looking for husbands,' Rory said, glancing at her sideways.

'Not Kate O'Mara! I know the law, I've been told that once you marry all your money is your husband's, and knowing my luck I'd find m'self with a devil who drinks and gambles!'

'And he'd trade all your silk gowns for grog!'

'Exactly!'

Then she became more serious. 'No, I will only get married if a rich man comes my way. Love won't keep the wolf from the door. My mother and father married for love and they were still in love, for all the good it did them, when they starved to death.'

'You won't be lonely?' he asked, with another sideways glance.

'Certainly not, with fine friends like Brigid and your good self, why should I be?'

She looked ahead, down the track. A flicker of dismay passed across Rory's face.

'What about you, Rory, are you looking to be married?'

'No, indeed, I'm not the type to be settling down, Kathleen. 'Tis the roaming that makes me happy, so the life of a bullocky suits me fine. The less you have, the less you have to take with you and the more free you can be. If you start to tie yourself to something or to someone, then you're stuck.'

'You might find a good woman who likes the roaming too, and you could still be footloose and fancy free.'

'Arrah, they're a rare breed. I've only met one woman who might love the bush life,' Rory replied, looking up the track ahead.

'And have you asked her?'

Rory shrugged his wide shoulders. 'She wants to settle down. Gee off, Mick! Up there, Stump!' he called to his leaders, and the conversation was lost as he manoeuvred the team across another small creek.

Kate was left thinking that he'd be a great catch for anyone with lesser ambitions than herself.

Bungaree Station was like a small village. For years it had been the most northerly settlement in the colony. The homestead itself was a large whitewashed cottage with wide verandahs. There were other buildings including a large woolshed and a variety of outbuildings. These were surrounded by an expanse of orchards containing grape vines, peaches, nectarines and other fruits. Watermelons grew abundantly in the vegetable garden fenced with palings. The whole scene was dominated by a gigantic haystack.

Kate looked over the settlement with a sense of satisfaction. Bungaree demonstrated just how quickly wealth could be made from wool. Wildowie would be similar and she would have a hand in making that money.

While James Carmichael had dinner with George and Bessie Hawker, Kate and the teamsters ate supper with the workers of Bungaree Station. Bungaree hospitality was good indeed. After a hearty meal the station hands took out their musical instruments and put on some entertainment in the woolshed. It was an enormous building with a high pitched roof thatched with reeds. Great bales of wool were stacked at one end of the woolshed and the smell of lanolin was strong in the air.

Rory joined in with his fiddle and Dan with his accordion. After warming up on some pretty Irish airs they moved on to jigs and then to reels. Kate found herself being asked for every dance. Even the two brothers McInerney asked her to dance. Kate had noticed that the younger one, Craig, had scarcely taken his eyes off her for the last two or three days. Even surly faced Sid had asked her for a dance. She felt pretty in her new gown of printed cotton. It was very simple, with just a narrow piece of lace that trimmed the neckline. The fabric was covered in tiny sprigs of blue and purple flowers that reflected the unusual colours in her eyes. The cut of the gown, with its bodice that narrowed to a 'V' shape at the front, below her waist, accentuated her tiny waistline and slender hips.

There was only one thing that worried Kate. Throughout the evening Angus had stood leaning against one of the thick poles of the barn watching her with a cold look in his eye. Kate wondered if he was too shy to ask for a dance, or whether he didn't wish to lower himself to dance with the servants. She shrugged her shoulders. Maybe he couldn't dance at all and that was why he looked peeved. Rory eventually handed the fiddle to another musician and asked Kate to dance.

Kate talked and laughed with great vivacity as they whirled around on the floor of the wool-shed. She really enjoyed Rory's company and was determined to make the best of her last evening with him. She loved the feel of his firm hands and strong arms around her and she looked up into his eyes with absolute trust.

A week on the track and Kate's face was no longer pale. Her cheeks were pink where they had been touched by the sun, her face was alive with the excitement of the dance, her eyes sparkling and her mouth inviting. Rory looked as though it was all he could do not to kiss her right there and then in the middle of the barn.

The musicians took a break and Rory led Kate outside for a breath of the fresh night air. Angus's eyes followed them as they went. They strolled through the orchard and the garden, the cool evening air flowing over their damp skin.

'Stay here, Kathleen, I've got something to give you,' Rory said as he disappeared towards the bunkhouse.

He was back in a moment and he took her hand in his.

'I want you to take this,' he said, pressing a tiny derringer pistol into her hand.

She looked at it with consternation. 'And what would I be wanting with this?' she asked.

'You'll never know when you'll be needing it,' he replied, 'and I'll feel more confident with you going tomorrow if I know you can protect yourself.'

'Surely I don't need it!'

'There's the blacks, Kathleen . . . and don't be fooled into thinking that you can trust the whites either!'

She sensed that he was serious, despite the humour. She placed the derringer in her pocket.

'I'll be missing you, Rory—' she said.

He reached out to take her in his arms. Her words were cut off as his lips touched hers and her heart skipped a beat.

The woolshed door opened, flooding pale yellow light around them.

She stepped back, dragging her lips from his. 'No, Rory.'

Her heart raced, whether only in response to Rory, or at being surprised by an intruder, she did not stop to consider. The silhouette against the door was short and stocky. Kate knew immediately that it was Angus standing there.

Rory grabbed her hand firmly and pulled her further into the orchard.

'Rory—'

'Sh, don't say a word, not yet. I must talk to you, but not where we'll be overheard.'

The door closed and with it went the light. She looked back at him.

'You must know how I feel about you—'

'Rory, don't—'

'No interrupting me now. Admit it, Kathleen, you feel it too.' He tilted her chin up so that he could look down into her eyes.

Her answer was there for him to read. She had never been good at dissembling.

'We haven't got much time and there's much to discuss.'

Her eyes were growing used to the darkness again and she could see his eyes glittering strangely, reflecting the starlight.

'The remote north is dangerous, too dangerous, 'tis why there are no women up there now. Anything could go wrong and no one would ever ask what happened to the young Irish girl who had headed for the bush. Life will be too tough up there for you, you must not go.'

'I must go, 'tis a job and I'll be paid good money—'

'What does money count for?'

'It counts for a lot! I for one never want to starve again.'

'Jaysus, you can't starve out here, 'tis the land of plenty!'

'You don't know that, anything might happen.'

'Kathleen, listen to me. You're going to one of the most remote places in the whole world. Starvation will be the least of your troubles. You could die of thirst, or the blacks might get you. Give up on this crazy scheme!'

'I want to go, I must go. 'Tis my only chance. 'Tis like you said, there are no other choices except prostitution—' She held up her hand. 'No! Don't interrupt me, 'tis my turn to speak now. I won't be alone. Mr Carmichael, Angus Campbell—'

'Those two! Angus is a snake, you've seen the way he watches you, and given what he did to the black women; and as for Carmichael, my God, I'm positive he'll be wanting more than a maid.'

'Mr Carmichael is a gentleman!'

'He might have been born in the upper classes but that doesn't make him a gentleman. Being born with a silver spoon in his mouth doesn't guarantee you that he'll behave with respect to you. He is a man, a normal red-blooded man.'

'And you're no different, Rory O'Connor!' He was red-blooded, hadn't he just proved it?

'Of course I am! I'm too red-blooded not to be attracted to you! But I'm not luring you north with false promises of a grand sheep station and the lifestyle of an English lady!'

'And neither is he!'

Rory shook his head and looked into the distance. 'You're a frustrating woman.'

She reached up to place her hands on either side of his handsome face, turning him back to look at her. 'Rory, listen, you're seeing things that don't exist. Sure, Angus and I will never be the best of friends, but he's all bluster where I am concerned, and Mr Carmichael is a gentleman. He'll act like a gentleman. I want to go with him.'

'For a smart girl you're one hell of a fool, Kathleen O'Mara.' His eyes were now piercing, 'What d'you think you'll get from the likes of Carmichael?'

'I'm not a fool, but I see where the future lies. This colony will be built on wool.' She could picture herself on the wide cool verandah of Wildowie in a flowing gown, surveying the green pastures, mistress of all she could see. 'I want that life. I want to own a sheep station and be mistress of a grand house. Maybe this is my chance.'

'Jaysus, Kathleen! You don't think that he'd marry a brat from Ireland, d'you?'

'I'm not a brat!'

'No, you're a beautiful young woman, desirable, spirited and utterly irresistible to any man. But it doesn't mean he'll want to marry you. The upper-class English just don't marry Irish orphans. They have other uses for them!'

If only he would not put those thoughts so crudely into words!

She wasn't mercenary, she didn't want wealth for its own sake. She just wanted to be secure!

'We'll see!' She turned away from him to look at the low hills in the distance. Anywhere but his eyes. She didn't want to acknowledge what he had said. And she didn't want to see the hurt in his eyes and know that she had caused it. She almost wished that she had never met him!

He turned her back to face him this time, his hands on her slender shoulders.

'For the love of God, take some advice from someone who's seen more of the world than you have. There are other ways to get ahead.'

He was close to her. She looked up at his mouth, soft and wide above hers, then at his eyes. They beseeched her to trust him, to believe him. She felt herself drawn to him, more powerfully than to any other man. More powerfully than to James Carmichael. More powerfully than to Wildowie and all its potential riches. She placed her hands against his chest, ready to push away from him.

'Stay with me,' his voice was barely above a whisper.

'I . . . I can't.'

'Why not?'

How could she explain why not? She could not deny that her attraction to him was strong. Very strong. Her fingers uncurled against his chest. He felt so solid, so dependable. Part of her wanted to stay with him. But could she consider abandoning her plans, her hopes, her dreams?

He was strong, he was virile, he was utterly, utterly charming. He was adorable. But she shouldn't be here with him, doing this. There would be no financial security with Rory O'Connor.

His eyes pleaded with her.

She hadn't forced her way onto the Orphan Scheme or endured four months aboard a stinking ship to stand here in his arms. She hadn't left Ireland behind her just to join up with a teamster, a rover, a footloose Irishman.

He pulled her closer still, his hands running up and down her back, making her gasp at the intimacy between them.

Her arms tightened against his chest, forcing him away from her. 'No, stop!'

'Don't deny it!'

'I must deny it,' she cried out, breaking away from him completely. 'It cannot be, Rory. There is no future in it!'

'You've not given it a chance!'

'There's no time to give it a chance. I'm leaving in the morning!'

Rory spun away from her, agitated, and ran his fingers through his crisp dark curls. He was disgusted with her. She could see it.

'Don't be mad with me. You're one of the only two people that I count as friends in the colony!'

'A friend is it? I'd like to wring your neck. Is that all you can say about me? What kind of friend would I be letting you walk into certain trouble?'

He was hurt. She could tell. But she couldn't help that. There was no way that she could give in to the attraction she felt for him. No way at all. Not when she had come this far. Those years of starvation were not that easily forgotten.

'Rory, I do care for you, I do. But I came out here to do something and I must do it. If I fail then I fail, but I have to give it a try!'

He was watching her, the muscles in his jaw flicking in the pale starlight.

He shook his head. 'If all it needed was spirit then I'd lay my bets on your success . . .' he took a deep breath and ran his fingers through his hair again as if despairing of her, 'but your spirit will not change the way an Englishman thinks.'

'Well, my plans do not depend only on James Carmichael. I'm going anyway and there's nothing you can do to stop me.' Her voice fell away, lacking conviction. She started towards the woolshed.

'Just one moment, don't go yet. I'd better show you how to work that bloody thing.'

'What bloody thing?' she asked, mimicking his words, trying to break the thread of tension that stretched tautly between them.

'The derringer.'

She had forgotten all about it.

She took the pistol out of her pocket and he showed her its working parts. Her heart beat an erratic rhythm as she listened to him, hearing his words, reading the deeper messages that flowed beneath the surface.

The loading procedure was much like the shotgun, except that it held six shots. He showed her how to leave one cylinder unloaded so that there was less chance of the firearm discharging accidentally.

His businesslike tone soothed the discomfort between them. 'Remember, hold it straight out in front of you with both hands to keep it steady,' he said, and paused, adding in a dry tone, 'I hope you never have need to use it.'

'Thank you, Rory,' Kate said. 'And God bless you for thinking of me. I'm just sorry—'

He cut her off with a shake of his head, 'We've said all we can say.'

Miles and Bungaree had been left behind. Ahead of them lay a further journey of one hundred and fifty miles. There was little in the way of a track, no towns, no inns, and precious few travellers in either direction. The days took on a familiar routine. Up at first light to find the bullocks, two or three hours on the track before lunch, another two or three hours following the dusty trail after their repast before they stopped to rest for the night under tall gum trees by the side of shallow creeks. Kate grew more accustomed to the days on the track and the nights under the stars. Progress was slow and steady and the party was relaxed.

There were ever-increasing numbers of kangaroos, dingos and emus. Kate watched with pure pleasure the graceful rhythmic bounding of the 'roos across the plains. The animals seemed almost without fear and for the most part allowed the party to come quite close to them before they bounded away. Both the emus and the kangaroos had featured on the menu at dinnertime when Harold had shown Kate how to prepare quite tasty dishes. The men voted Kate's kangaroo stew to be the best that they had tried. Not only was the wildlife more frequently seen but so too were the blacks. The party had stopped at a waterhole. Kate saw the native children diving into the water and splashing about.

The bullocks soon put an end to the crystal clear water and the blacks moved off. Kate, hot and dusty from a day on the track, envied the freedom they had to play naked in the fresh cool water. Strands of her hair, thick with the dust stirred up by the bullocks, stuck to her neck and the swish of her skirts had sent that same dust up her legs and through her petticoats. A wash in a bucket every evening was refreshing but a long soak would have been the only way to remove the ingrained dirt.

The next afternoon they reached the River Broughton. Although it was early in the afternoon, there was plenty of good water and green feed for the bullocks, so they decided not to press on but to take the opportunity for a well-earned rest. Everyone sat under the shade of the tall gums, thankful for an early break from the warm day. The river was flowing well and the sound of the water bubbling and gurgling as it cascaded over the rocks in the river bed was soothing to the foot-weary travellers. Several of the men nodded off.

Kate sat pondering her decision to part from Rory. He was certainly a charming man. In fact he probably had too much charm and not enough of what it would take to make a good husband. If she was going to marry, it would be to someone with more prospects than he had. It was a shame that she had left him behind; Brigid too. She could do with some friends on the track with her.

She listened to the water flowing and thought back to the black children and their joyful splashing in the waterhole on the day before. She had been told that some of the new colonists had gone native themselves and had been known to bathe naked on the isolated beaches near Adelaide! The more Kate listened to the water the more she became convinced that a dip, if only up to the ankles, was the only way to soothe her hot feet and cool the blood that flowed through her veins.

All was quiet, most of the men were resting and those that weren't were deeply engrossed in a quiet game of cards. Kate got up and wandered casually away from the camp and up-river where the animals had not stirred up the water. She sat down on a large boulder that jutted out into the river, took off her stockings and boots and, holding up her skirt, dangled her feet into the crisp cold water. A sense of relief swept through her body as her blood began to cool. She shifted her weight forward on the rock, lifted her skirt a little higher and immersed her slender legs as far as the knee. She kicked and swirled her legs in the water, rejoicing in the feel of its flow over her skin.

There was still no sound from the camp downstream. She looked around her. Fat sleek magpies, bold in their black and white, warbled their liquid, crystal-clear song in the tree above. White galahs screeched and whirled against the blue cloudless sky. She was entirely on her own. Unable to resist temptation a moment longer she pulled her legs out of the water, stood up and began to undress. With each garment she removed, she looked around her warily, fearing that one of the men might venture nearby.

Finally, completely naked, she stepped quickly into the water where it flowed over a sandy bed. She splashed out quickly to where the water came up to her thighs and bobbed down, still anxious lest someone should come.

The coolness of the water sucked her breath away and she gasped as her warm body adjusted to the temperature. She swirled her arms about her, revelling in the satin feel of the water over her breasts and belly. Looking down, she realised how she had begun to fill out now that she had a decent meal three times a day. Where before she was slender, almost boyish, she now had curves and soft flesh.

She regretted that this bathe had been a spontaneous thing, for if she had planned it, she could have brought soap to wash her hair. She undid the pins that held her hair, ducked her head under the water and washed it as best she could with her hands. Coming up again, she rubbed her skin vigorously all over with her hands, removing the ingrained dirt and dust. She had never bathed naked in the open air and she revelled in the sensation, entirely forgetting her earlier fears of prying eyes.

She rolled in the water, from her back to her front and over again. Gaining confidence she dived and came up, throwing her wet hair back through the air in an arc and down her back to her buttocks. The droplets of water spun through the air, the sun catching them in a circle of diamonds. It was glorious.

Gradually the cold began to seep into her bones. Rubbing her skin over once more she stood up and walked from the water. A light breeze had sprung up and it chilled Kate's already cool skin. She sat in the sun on a warm rock to wait for her body to dry before she pulled her clothes back on. Her skin, as white as marble, had never seen the sun before. She sat there, basking in its soft warmth, her wet black hair flowing down softly over her back to her buttocks.

James Carmichael could scarcely believe his eyes. He had never seen a white woman bathing naked in a stream. And he had never seen any woman bathe with such total lack of self-consciousness, glorying in the sensations of the wild. He knelt on one knee and watched her, admiring the lithe way that she moved and the young innocence of her maturing body. He had appreciated the beauty of her eyes and the glowing freshness of her face but he had certainly never been particularly conscious of her as a woman. Now, as he looked, he couldn't understand how it could have escaped his attention that she was so desirable, her innocence so beautifully highlighted by her passionate, wilful nature. He realised that Kate was no longer the half-starved Irish waif of his first impression, but a girl ripening into a ravishing woman.

A great red kangaroo came springing through the bush at that moment and bounded down towards the river with great, slow leaps. She followed him with her eyes as he came ever closer, oblivious of her presence. He jerked and skidded to a halt not twenty yards from her, as though danger was in his path. She knew that he had not seen her for she had sat absolutely still on the rock. He vaulted sideways, turned and sprang away.

Kate's eyes darted back to the place at which the kangaroo had startled. There, fifteen yards from her, stood James Carmichael.

Chapter
Five

Kate's heart jumped to her mouth. He was looking straight at her, not moving a single muscle, his whole bearing relaxed. His gun, forgotten, was lying over his shoulder.

For a moment their eyes held.

Kate hesitated. What should she do? Leap back into the water? Dash behind the nearest tree? Make a run for it to pick up her clothes? Maybe cover her nakedness with her hands?

She decided to brazen it out.

'Avert your eyes, Mr Carmichael, so that I can finish my bathing and get dressed!'

After a slight pause, he turned away and walked back towards the camp.

Rory was wrong, she thought. James was a gentleman.

One intruder was enough. As soon as he turned, Kate bolted for her clothes and hastily pulled them on. Everything in place, she took a long, deep breath. She combed out her hair with her fingers and twisted it into a thick, damp rope which hung over her shoulder. Much refreshed, she made her way back to the camp along the side of the river. In places the brush was thick and Kate pushed it out of her way with determination.

James stepped out onto the path in front of her. 'Not so fast!' he said, grabbing her arm. 'What do you think you were doing, Kate?'

She avoided his eyes and ignored his question. 'Let go of me!' she said, pulling her arm away.

James looked her over slowly, his gaze travelling from the top of her head, over the fresh-washed skin of her face and throat, past the damp patch on her gown where her hair hung wet against her breast, and down over her hips and her legs, outlined by the gown clinging damp against her body. She had seen that look before—hot and intent. The men at the work-house had looked at her like that. She was not so naive that she did not know what it meant.

She felt her pulse quicken. This was not the way she had things planned. She had thought of making herself indispensable to him, so that he could not run the station without her. She did not want it to begin like this. He would be the one in command. He would dictate the action. And the pace was already too fast to suit her plans. If she was not careful she would find that Rory had been right. She would be used for James's ends, not her own.

She had seen that look on Rory's face, too, but

it was different. Rory admired her, respected her, found companionship with her—as well as wanting her physically.

But James?

She took a step backwards. James's arm came up to grasp hers and Kate looked up at him with defiance in her eyes. The sound of a shotgun from the direction of the camp took them both by surprise. James's head went up, his whole body jerking suddenly to attention.

'Stay where you are until I give the all clear!' He turned and ran towards the camp.

Kate followed him. If there was trouble then she would help too. She wasn't going to wait there for this scene to be continued later!

Back at the camp the men had their firearms poised and pointed towards the thick bush down-river.

'Blacks!' called Angus with loathing.

'What happened?' James asked.

Angus lowered his gun but the others kept theirs poised and ready to fire. 'They came here scavenging furr food, when I told them to clear off they raised their spears and threatened us—'

'I grabbed my gun,' interrupted Dan, 'that seemed to scare them a bit, for they started shouting and moving away.'

'One of them then ran back towards us, his spear ready to throw, and Dan shot at him. Must've hit him in the leg, furr he shouted out again and limped away.' Angus's face was filled with abhorrence.

'They all disappeared quick-smart after that,' Dan added.

James Carmichael nodded. 'They might be back, keep your guns ready!' he told the men.

He turned to Kate: 'Don't leave the campsite again unless you take someone with you for protection!' A double meaning was contained in his eyes.

'I won't. You never know who you might meet out there.'

James looked at her for a moment before Angus spoke.

'Should we move on from here?'

'I think not,' he replied. 'They would be more than able to keep pace with us, even if we did. I would be very surprised if they came back now that they've seen the guns.'

The men dropped their shoulders, beginning to relax.

'I thought we'd not meet dangerous natives until we were further north,' Kate commented.

'It is unusual,' James agreed.

'They were hungry, no doubt,' said Harold. 'It would be the only reason they would have come to our camp in these parts. It is unlikely they were here for the grog since they've probably not had it before.'

As usual, it seemed to be Harold who showed the greatest understanding of the blacks. He had covered more bush tracks than anyone else in the group. It showed.

'Well if they were hungry, why weren't they fed, surely we have plenty?' Kate said.

'They'll only want more, they become dependent,' growled Angus. 'It's no guid to feed them, it's better in the long run to send them on their way.'

Kate was aghast. Vivid recollections of the famine in Ireland flooded her mind; images of her family, of starving people clad in rags, of young babies giving up the fight for life, of the decimation of disease on frail bodies. It all flashed in front of her eyes in a matter of seconds.

''Tis what they said about Ireland too!'

'These people are savages, Kate,' James said gently, as if it excused whites from all responsibility.

'They are still people! If they're hungry they must be fed!'

Kate looked from one face to the next. Angus looked belligerent. She was obviously overstepping the mark with him. James looked concerned but she knew already that he would do nothing for the blacks. Dan looked pensive, for he too remembered hard times back in Ireland. But he would not dare to contradict the boss or the overseer. Young Craig looked at her sympathetically, but he had stars in his eyes and would have agreed to feed all the blacks in Australia if it would have made her happy.

Sid's crooked face was an ugly sneer. 'Let the bastards starve, I say, the faster they go the less trouble for all of us.'

Angus nodded his head in agreement.

Kate thought back to Rory's warning. It was no doubt one of those times when he would say that she should keep her mouth shut and stay out of scrapes.

'Time to prepare for the meal,' she said, shrugging her shoulders as if the topic was closed. She left the group to continue the discussion without her. There were more ways than one to skin a cat! A few rations left behind would not be missed.

That night they retired early, a sense of tension in the air. Kate noticed that the men took more than the usual precautions before retiring. Each of them carefully laid his gun by the side of his swag. The horses were left saddled and tethered to trees close by, ready to mount in a hurry if needed during the night. The bullocks were hobbled so that they would stay close to the camp. Being sensitive animals, they would stir if they heard or smelt anything unusual in the night. Kate took out the pistol that Rory had given her and placed it within easy reach, under the edge of the blanket where no one else would see it. From now on she would keep it ready.

For the first time since the afternoon Kate had time to think about the incident with James Carmichael. Her very first impressions of him had been of a charming and typically reserved Englishman, someone who was way above her reach. Then she had caught him watching her and she had begun to wonder just how far above her reach he really was. His actions today suggested that he found her very attractive. Thank God for the sound of the gunshot.

Brigid was not here to protect her now. Neither was Rory.

She knew that to give in to James would be the sheer height of folly. The last thing she needed or wanted was to become involved with him here and now, on the track, where their relationship was only one of master and servant. It could have no future, could it?

She thought back to Bungaree and to Mrs Hawker, confidently in charge as the station owner's wife. She had reigned over the station community like a queen: gracious, competent, worldly, well dressed, wealth at her fingertips, owner of a beautiful and desirable homestead. She could see herself in that role. Nothing was beyond her, was it? South Australia was supposed to be a society where all people were equal.

Marriage to a wealthy man would give her all the financial security she could ever hope for. There would be no need to fear famine ever again. Or was she being a fool? Was Rory right? She would have to be careful. James was used to getting what he wanted, on his own terms. His terms might not include marriage. There was no point deluding herself. She would have to keep him at arm's length until she understood what motivated him.

First light slipped across the plains while the

camp was still sleeping. The pure lilting call of a magpie pierced the stillness and Kate stirred. One of the men tossed some sticks and dry leaves onto the hot ashes of the fire. She stretched, listening to the crackle as the leaves started to burn.

The night had brought no return of the blacks and the tensions of the evening before evaporated with the morning dew. As they took off Kate realised just how much more she was becoming attuned to the bush. She could recognise the calls of the various birds. She noticed for the first time the red tips of the new growth on the gums and the infinite variety of wattle flowers. Some of them hung in lemon yellow showers, some made golden balls of fluff, others were just tiny puffs of amber on sparse dry branches.

She thought about James. He had not approached her since the incident near the river yesterday. In some ways she was relieved, for she knew that she should repel his advances. But in other ways she almost hoped that he would pursue her, for it increased her confidence in herself. She wasn't just a troublesome Irish servant, she was an attractive woman, a woman who was going somewhere. Maybe she did have some hope of bettering herself through marriage. She shrugged her shoulders. It could have been nothing more than a passing desire on his part.

As the day wore on, Kate was no closer to knowing her own mind about James. It looked like rain was on the way. Dark clouds moved down towards them from the north and the air was heavy and oppressive. Once again some of the tarpaulins were tied tightly over the loads while others were draped over the drays to form shelters for the teamsters.

Black crows cawed, their sound despairing and desolate.

Kate began to get the evening meal ready, aware that later the weather might not be conducive to cooking over the fire. James Carmichael unloaded a tent from the wagon and set it up close to the campfire. It had a flap which opened out at the front and he sat under this, consulting his map and compass and sending Kate long, speculative looks.

'God, I almost wish it would rain,' she commented, looking up at the sky for the umpteenth time.

'Yes, it may be the last rain we'll see for some time,' James replied. 'From here on be thankful for any that we get.'

She could feel a tension building between herself and James, even though their outward conversation would have sounded unremarkable to anybody else. He wanted her, she knew that. She looked over at him as he studied his maps. Her eyes roamed down over his long lean body, from the soft blond hair over his clean-shaven face with its strong jaw and cheekbones, over his flat muscled belly, his narrow hips and those long strong thighs. Her heartbeat lifted.

He was an attractive man and very much the gentleman. Everything about him appealed to her: his manner, both authoritative and gentle at the same time, the way he dressed, moved and rode his horse. His gestures were those of the aristocrat. Even his possessions spoke of the man. They were expensive, tasteful, quiet, masculine. To Kate, he epitomised the life she wanted herself.

He looked up and caught her eye on him.

The rain began with large infrequent drops that fizzled on the fire. The men donned their oilskins, and Kate her cloak, to shield them from rain as they ate their supper. It was not yet cold but there was no point letting those heavy drops dampen them through to the skin as the cool night began to fall. The birds came alive with the rain. Hundreds of small green and red parakeets darted in and out of the foliage, setting up a chorus of screeching and squealing. The smell of the rain on the eucalypt trees cleansed the cooling air.

Thunder rumbled in the distance. There was more rain to come. The men left the fire, leaving Kate to clear up as they made their preparations for the night. James watched her as he sat in the dry under the tent flap. The thunder came inexorably closer. The darkening sky was now rent with frequent flashes of lightning to the north.

The tension in the air was almost unbearable. Suddenly the storm crashed overhead. She stowed the last of the dinner things, stood up and turned, to find James confronting her. His eyes devoured her. Without warning he reached forward with both his arms and pulled her towards him in one deft movement. His lips met hers as if he could wait not a moment longer. They were firm and cool, covering hers in a way that left no room for protest. Kate stiffened for a moment and his hands tangled in her hair, holding her to him, while his lips closed over hers again, demanding, conquering her instinct to cry out.

She pulled away from him, her heart hammering within her breast, and looked up into his eyes. At that moment the skies opened up and the rain crashed down upon them. Large droplets splashed onto their faces. It seemed as though minutes passed as they looked at each other, although it could only have been seconds, the rain running in rivulets down their faces. Kate was searching his eyes, wondering just what she might mean to him. Time stood still.

He kissed her again, their lips fresh, their faces cooled by the splash of the soft clean rain, their bodies steaming under their damp clothes. She did not resist him, but nor did she respond. She was lost in indecision. What should she do? Repel his advances? Hold him off, hoping for time to become more sure of just what he wanted?

And how could she get out of this without offending the man who was her master?

Thunder crashed overhead again and the

lightning arced down to earth not far from the camp.

James grabbed her hand. 'Come on, it's dangerous out here,' he said and pulled her with him towards the tent.

If she went to his tent now, all would be lost. She shook her head and droplets of water were let loose from her hair as she did so. 'No!' she said firmly.

She pulled her hand from his grasp and scooted underneath the dray, like a rabbit into its burrow, to the dry patch of ground where her own swag was waiting for her. She did not look behind.

She wanted him—lock, stock and barrel. She had no doubts about that. She wanted his lifestyle, his confidence and his place in society. He was powerful, sophisticated, polished, urbane. He would never be amongst those who would starve. He would be wealthy, successful and secure.

She wanted him, but only if she could get the whole deal.

That day they stayed put, the rain making it impossible to go on. Although the rain was light, it would cause the yokes to rub against the bullocks' skins, rubbing off the hair and eventually the skin itself. They would not move until the skies had cleared. It was a good opportunity for the bullocks to rest up and to take their fill of the soft green grass by the creek.

James wrote in his journal and Kate was left to watch him and contemplate the events of the last few days. For some reason her mind returned to Rory again and again. She couldn't help but wonder just what he would have thought if she had let James Carmichael get his way.

They were such different men. With Rory, she knew what he was thinking and what he was feeling. There was no pretence. With Rory, what you saw was what you got. He was raw, powerful, exciting and, not least of all, fun.

In contrast, the squatter was refined, polished, reserved. And he had what she wanted.

Rory, Rory, Rory. Thoughts of him spun around in her head no matter how much she tried to push them away. Handsome, devil-may-care Rory. If only he and James would swap places. If only Rory was the squatter. No sooner had the thought crossed her mind than she realised that Rory and James could never swap places. Rory was too footloose and fancy free to ever tie himself to a long-term scheme like a station. James was not carefree enough to be a rover and too refined to work with bullocks. She wanted both of them in their own ways. She could have Rory tomorrow, if she had not sworn on the graves of her family that she would never, ever, starve again.

James and Angus went hunting in the afternoon. The others sat about enjoying the day's rest. Kate examined her derringer in private, reminded by Angus's constant animosity and now by James's interest, that she would need to be ready and able to protect herself at all times. There had to be a way to keep it on her without the others knowing it was there. She got her needle and thread, a spare stocking and a handkerchief, and she fashioned a holster that she could wear under her gown against her thigh. This would be better than in her pocket where it bumped against her leg and where anyone who might brush past her would feel it. And better still than in a holster on her hip where everyone would see it and know that it was there. Here, alone with a group of men, she began to understand just what Rory's real fear was and how astute he had been.

She shook her head. If only thoughts of Rory could be banished from her mind!

The next day they reached Jacob's Station and the need for protection was brought home to Kate in another way. She heard that there had been more trouble with the blacks in the area. One of the hut-keepers on Jacob's property had been speared and the local settlers had joined together to carry out reprisal raids. No one talked about just what had happened as a result but evidently the remaining blacks were now pretty fierce. Kate's party would need to be on guard against attack.

She sat on a wooden railed fence watching the station hands herd the sheep for the night.

'Why do they do it?' she asked Harold.

'Why do they do what?'

'Attack the settlers when they have no guns and no real chance of winning?'

'Desperation.'

Harold had been about the bush for a long time and considered himself to have a good understanding of the blacks. He had learnt from previous experience, however, that his views were not well received by many of the colonists. They did not want to know about the plight of their fellow humans. They did not consider them to be above the status of wild animals.

'Tell me more about them, Harold. Why are they so desperate?'

Harold shrugged his shoulders and then looked around. It would do him no good for the others to hear his views.

'Well, there's a number of things that happen when settlers take up the land. The sheep eat the food that the black fellers used to eat themselves. The native animals start to move away because their food has gone too—'

Kate interrupted him, 'But we have seen so many kangaroos!'

'Even they are no longer as fearless as they used to be. They've been shot at by guns and they are afraid of humans now. Before the white man came, the people could just approach a 'roo and club him over the head. They can't do that now. As well as all that, the waterholes get fouled by the stock.'

'So they come to the stations for food?'

'Or worse, they knock off the sheep, and

that's what makes the squatters so angry. The black feller is punished harshly and before you know it the hatred has sprung up between them and the whites.'

'I can understand it,' Kate said. 'They are the victims of cruelty, like those poor women who were attacked back at the Light River.'

Harold shook his head. 'There's always wrong on both sides, Kate. The blacks have attacked white women and children too, you know. Anyway, it all goes to explain why they get so desperate. Once they know what white settlement means they are scared for their lives. They simply decide that they won't take any more of the white man's treatment and that they'll put a stop to further settlement. They attack. But they'll never win in the end.'

'There must be another way to solve all these problems!'

'No one has thought of anything yet,' Harold replied sadly.

Kate thought of the English landlords in Ireland, the evictions and the hardships. Was this any different?

'How much further now, Mr Carmichael?'

'We are about two-thirds of the way there.'

'Sure and I'll be glad when we are three-thirds of the way!' replied Kate emphatically.

'Good heavens, you are as Irish as they come!' James laughed at her.

The miles took a long time to cover now that the track was rough. In fact there was almost no track to follow. Had she known how far she was to travel, or how long it would take, would she have decided to come?

They often stopped to clear roots and fallen trees from the track. The wheels of the drays, and more particularly the wagon, caught on boulders jutting out on the narrow path. When Kate rode on the wagon she was jolted about until her teeth rattled in her head.

On the crest of one wave of the undulating hills, James rode back to where Kate was walking.

'Look up ahead!' he called.

She looked north into the distance, and there, arising above the horizon, stood a majestic blue and hazy mountain, higher than any she had seen so far on the journey.

She turned to James, a question in her eyes.

'Mount Remarkable, the first of the mountains in the Flinders Ranges!'

Kate grinned. It was a sign that their eventual destination was within sight. 'How long till we reach it?'

'Another few days,' he called back, 'that's where Gillies' Station is, the same distance again to Beautiful Valley and then again to the Flinders Ranges proper. Wildowie is a stone's throw from there!'

This tangible reminder of their increasing proximity to the Flinders Ranges seemed to both cheer and relax the whole party. The mood that night around the campfire was a happy one. Once again they joined together in music and song. So close to their destination, their guard was down.

The next morning began clear and still. They could not hear any of the bells at breakfast, which signalled that the bullocks had roamed far in the night. The party spread out, searching for the cattle. Kate was helping too. She and Dan headed out eastwards along a shallow gully to look for the bullocks, talking about Ireland and their happier days there. They were chatting quite merrily when she heard a dull thud. Dan stopped speaking. A single hoarse cry issued from his mouth and filled the air. He fell, a spear protruding from his back.

Her heart stopped still, then began to beat furiously. Her instinct was to run but she threw herself face forward to lie in the shelter of his body. She grabbed his gun with one hand and felt for his chest with the other.

He was dead!

She looked around frantically. There was no one in sight, but brown eyes must be watching her from the cover of the bush. She placed the gun firmly into her shoulder, no mean feat from a crouching position. She fired the gun once in the direction from which the spear had come. At least they would know she was armed and it would alert the rest of her party.

The sound seemed to ricochet against the hills

and then the bush was still, the frogs and crickets silent. Kate's mouth was dry. Her body felt like jelly. Every inch of her pounded with fear. She tried to slow her breathing. Panic would be her downfall otherwise. A gunshot sounded in the distance. She waited a short while. Still no movement. She reloaded, using Dan's ammunition pouch, her hands shaking and sweating.

'Mary, Mother of God!' Kate prayed softly. 'Save me from death.'

Her hands were wet with a slick film of perspiration. She took them from the gun, one at a time, and wiped them down the skirt of her gown.

All the time she was scanning the bush, her heart still hammering, her mouth dry. She felt for her pistol. It might be needed. It would be difficult for her to reload Dan's gun if under attack.

There were more gunshots, and shouting in the distance. Kate lay still where she was.

Three black men shot out from the cover of the low scrub. She would not have known they were there if she hadn't seen them, for they made no sound at all. They ran, fleet-footed, straight past her. Her heart in her mouth, she raised her gun to take aim. They took no heed of her and she could not bring herself to shoot. James, Craig and Angus burst through the bush noisily behind them.

'James!' came Kate's strangled cry as she staggered up and into his arms.

'Which way did they go?' James asked.

Kate pointed, 'There!'

Craig and Angus followed the direction they had taken. James let go of her and dropped to the ground where Dan was lying.

'Dead!' he said, after examining Dan quickly.

Kate nodded, still shaking.

'Keep that gun ready!' he said, putting his own to his shoulder. They knelt back to back, keeping watch on the circle of scrub around them. The minutes ticked by, she knew not for how long. It seemed like hours. They watched, waiting, scanning the bush. Her heart pummelled in her chest. Perspiration ran down her face, between her breasts. Her gown clung to her.

A sound from the bush! They whirled round, guns raised, ready to fire. There was a heart-stopping moment as she saw the bushes part not ten feet from where they knelt.

'Don't shoot, it's us!' cried Angus as he sprang into view.

Her finger eased off the trigger as he emerged.

'We lost them,' Craig called as he, too, leapt through the bushes.

Both James and Kate lowered their guns.

Craig looked in horror to where Dan was lying by their feet. Blood had been trickling from where the spear protruded from Dan's back and was now congealing in a dark puddle on the bright red earth. Ants gathered at the perimeter.

Kate felt her body dissolve into jelly as the sense of danger gave way to shock. Just ten minutes ago she and Dan had been chatting as if they had not a care in the world. Now he was dead. She had been walking right next to Dan and she, too, could have been killed.

They all stared at the body, panting as the adrenalin pulsed through their veins.

'What about the others?' asked James.

'There were other gunshots,' Kate told them.

'We'd better find out,' Angus said, stalking off towards the camp.

'Come on,' James said, taking Kate's arm and motioning Craig to come too, 'we had best stay together in case the blacks come back.'

Craig's eyes were riveted on Dan and his face was a sickly colour against his sandy hair. Freckles stood out green on his skin.

'There's nothing more we can do for him right now, lad. We'll get the others and come back to bury him later. Come on, hurry!'

Craig followed the other three as they raced back towards the camp. They called as they went, both hoping that the others were alive to answer and afraid of running into gun barrels themselves.

The camp was empty and undisturbed, just as they had left it a short while ago. Sid and Harold were nowhere in sight. Kate prayed that they had not been killed too. They moved through the bush, desperately seeking the remaining members of the party.

'Cooee!' Sid's voice came faintly from further down the gorge.

'Cooee!' James called in reply as they stumbled through the boulder-strewn creek towards the source of Sid's voice.

Sid was sitting on the ground. Harold was lying sprawled on the ground in front of him, his head cradled in Sid's lap. Both he and Sid seemed to be covered in blood.

'Oh my God!' Kate ran towards them and fell down onto her knees by Harold's side, feeling for his heartbeat and assessing the wound.

The stump of a spear was still protruding from his shoulder, below the collarbone. Sid had evidently broken it off while trying to pull it out. Blood seemed to pump up in bursts from deep inside the wound.

James was with her, feeling for Harold's breath on his hand.

'Still alive,' he said tersely.

Kate nodded. But what a mess!

Craig looked down on the scene, his face still green. He began to sway on his feet.

'Come with me, Craig,' Angus said, pulling him away. 'We'll have a quick look around to make sure the blacks have all gone.'

Robert moved to go with them.

'No, you stay,' James ordered Robert. 'We are going to need your help here!'

'He's done for!' Sid spat out.

Not Harold! her mind screamed. He couldn't die! Of all the party, he was the most endearing. He had looked after her like a father. His family would be waiting for him to come home. She couldn't let him die! She would do everything in her power while there was still breath in his body.

'Not yet! He's still alive. There's a chance of saving him!' There was no sign of blood bubbling from his mouth, so with luck, the spear had not touched the lung.

'We're going to have to get the tip of this spear out!' James said. He turned to Kate. 'What are you like as a nurse?'

'I'll give anything a try,' she replied, her eyes blinking away a tear. 'Where do we start?'

'Let's get him back to the camp.'

Kate's arm shot out to protect Harold from being lifted. 'No, we should not move him, I'm thinking, the spear is too close to his heart and lungs, we'll have to get it out here.'

James nodded, looking as if she must know more about these things than he. He looked at her, ready to take her instruction.

'We've got to stop this bleeding first, or he'll be gone before we get near the spear tip. Bandages, we need bandages!' She lifted her dress to reveal her petticoat underneath. Taking the fabric in her teeth, she tore through the hem and then ripped it right around with her hands, making a broad bandage.

James pulled a large handkerchief from his pocket and said, 'Sid! Your scarf too.'

They were all looking at Kate, waiting to be told what to do. Kate began to issue the orders. While they stood paralysed, Harold's life was being pumped from his veins.

'Robert, run back to the camp. We need a sharp knife, a pot to boil water, anything to make bandages, some blankets. Sid, build a fire, hurry!'

Kate grasped the handkerchief and the scarf and folded them briskly into wads. 'Hold these hard against the wound, Mr Carmichael,' she told him, as she began to rip another bandage from her petticoat.

They watched as the wads quickly soaked with blood.

'Push harder against the wad!' Kate cried.

Harold moaned and stirred. Fearful of causing more pain, James pulled his hand away from the wound.

'Jaysus!' Kate hissed at him, 'more pressure or he'll bleed to death!'

She placed her hands on top of his, adding her pressure to the wound. Blood seeped out through their fingers and over their hands. 'Hold it still until we're ready to get the spear out.'

'What happened, Sid?' James asked while they waited for Robert's return.

'They must've been following us,' Sid replied. 'I should have guessed something was up, my dog kept whining this morning over breakfast, remember?'

Kate and James nodded.

'They were probably watching us then, waiting for us to split up and become easy prey. We had no idea they were following us, though. The first I knew of it the spears were raining down upon us. I turned around. There would have been four or five of them, all painted up. Fearful-looking they were. By the time I had my gun aimed they had disappeared. I looked around and Harold was on the ground with the spear sticking out of him.'

'The same happened to Dan and me,' Kate told him. 'Dan is dead.'

Harold moaned again. Every now and again it seemed as if he drifted into semi-consciousness. She took Harold's hand in her own and murmured words of comfort, not sure if he would hear her. She could not sit and watch his life ebb away without doing something.

'You'll be all right, Harold, we'll stop this bleeding and then we'll get the spear out. You'll be back with your family in no time. You'll be fine, Harold, just fine.'

It didn't matter what she said, she figured, as long as she kept talking to him, willing him to hang on to his life, to keep going. Words were small comfort against the pain and he stirred again.

'You'll be fine, Harold, we'll fix you up in no time,' she murmured, 'we're looking after you. Only a few minutes more.' She squeezed his hand and felt the faint answering pressure from his.

He was partly conscious, Kate realised, and the pain would be ghastly when they tried to remove the spear.

'Sid, leave the fire. We need some alcohol for him! And more saucepans to boil water!' she said. Sid took off in the direction of the camp just as Robert emerged from the bush carrying all the other things she had requested.

Robert filled the pot from the creek and placed it on the fire.

By the time Sid returned they had torn more bandages and taken the first pot of boiled water off the fire to cool. The knives had been sterilised with the boiling water. More pots were placed onto the thin bed of coals.

'Who is going to do this?' James asked her, his eyes full of fear.

She looked back at him. 'You do it.'

James shook his head. 'Your fingers are much more nimble. You seem to know what to do.'

Kate was dismayed. Other than helping out in the workhouse infirmary she had very little experience as a nurse. And the infirmary had hardly been the place to learn anything at all. The poor wretches there had been left to suffer and die. There was nothing much that could be done for people so weakened by starvation. It had certainly not prepared her for this!

She took a deep breath. 'I'll do my best but you'll have to help me.'

James nodded.

She turned to Sid and Robert. 'You'll have to help too. Bring the rum and pour as much as you can into his mouth. Everyone will have to help to hold him still.'

Sid poured the rum into Harold's mouth, waiting for him to splutter and cough before giving him more. He did this several times. James and Kate worked to cut Harold's shirt away from his chest and shoulder. Without the steady pressure on it, the wound began to seep blood again. They would have to work quickly. Kate washed her hands thoroughly with the cooled boiled water and poured some of it over the wound to clean it. She took another deep breath and looked up at James. He nodded for her to go on.

Kate began to prod gently, feeling the angle of the spear. Blood welled up over her fingers and she gritted her teeth. She would have to probe deeper. She took the knife and inserted it along the shaft of the spear, trying to find the barbs. Harold moaned and writhed as the knife tip slid in.

'Hold him still!' she ordered. James and Robert placed their weight down on his arms and legs and averted their eyes. Only Sid had the stomach to watch. Maybe he had seen worse in his time.

Kate wished that she, too, could avert her eyes. Her stomach turned over as she probed again.

She probed once more, then recoiled as Harold roared in pain.

'Keep going, Kate!' said Sid, who was watching and helping her.

She worked at it again and could feel what was probably a barb. Fortunately it was not wide. She slid the knife down the opposite side, freeing the other barb from the flesh as well.

Swallowing hard she moved the knife down to what she thought was the tip of the spear and prised it up a little. The stump moved. She slipped the knife in a fraction further. She picked up the second knife and slid it into position on the other side. Harold squirmed again.

'I'm going to lift it up,' she said to James. 'When I say so, pull on this end of the stump.'

He looked hesitant.

'Sid, you do it!'

'Ready,' he said.

Beads of perspiration had formed on her face. Her gown clung to her body and dark tendrils of hair shone wet and black with perspiration against the white of her neck.

'Now,' she croaked, her voice evidence of the strain she was under.

The remainder of the spear seemed to float upwards on a spurt of blood. Harold jerked and then lay still, no longer drifting close to consciousness, but still breathing. Kate dropped the knives and grabbed the boiled water. She washed the gaping wound liberally, the water turning into red rivulets as it touched Harold's body. Sid clamped a dry wad of clean cloth back over the top and placed pressure on it.

'D'you think that's it?' Kate asked, after a few minutes.

'Best check it to see nothing is left inside,' Sid said, removing the wad again.

The knives were lying in the dirt. Kate rinsed her hand again and felt the wound for debris. She splashed water over it again.

'Pressure, quickly.'

Sid slammed the wad back down. Robert followed up with another. Sid held it firm for almost a minute, the blood flow slowing as the moments ticked by.

Kate took a long shaky breath. 'A large wad, then we'll try to bind him up.'

Sid and Robert helped to hold him in a sitting position while Kate and James wrapped bandages round his chest and shoulder, working faster and faster as they could see the blood seeping through. Finally they were finished and there was no more blood seeping to the surface. Harold started to shiver and they covered him with blankets.

Kate sat back on the bare earth, heaved a great sigh and sank her head into her hands. She had done all that she could for the moment. The enormity of what she had just done began to dawn on her. She looked down at her hands, sticky with blood, and she shuddered. She staggered up and washed her hands in the remaining warm water and sat down again heavily.

'Thank you, Kate,' James said, his voice a little detached.

Kate looked up.

Sid was squatting by the dying fire, watching her. 'Good on you, love,' he said, the surly look on his face for once replaced by admiration.

'You're a braver man than I,' said Robert, smiling at her, easing the tension a little.

'Robert, you keep an eye on Harold while Sid and I try to fashion a stretcher,' James instructed.

As they talked about the best way to do it, Angus and Craig reappeared.

'There's nae a sign o' those black bastards,' Angus told them. 'We've been back to bury Dan, though, the poor mon.'

'What about Harold?' Craig asked with concern.

Sid told them of Kate's courage and skill in extricating the spear. Kate looked up.

Craig looked at her, his face full of compassion.

Kate wished that at this moment someone close was here with her. How she wished she could sink into Brigid's warm embrace or Rory's bear-like hug. She took some long, slow breaths, willing herself back to a state of control. The drama was over. But Harold hovered near death still. She couldn't afford to fall in a heap just now. The task of nursing him had only just begun. She took a few minutes to pull herself together while the others took Harold back to the camp on the stretcher.

Slowly she walked back to the camp. When she got there she checked Harold. His face was white and pinched, the lines on his face deeper than they had ever appeared before. His body still shook with shivers. She kicked a rock from the campfire and wrapped it in a blanket to place at his feet. She then took both his hands in hers and kept them warm, talking to him as she had done before.

The others left her to this job while they fetched the strayed bullocks. Only Craig stayed with her, his gun poised ready in case the blacks returned. Kate prepared meat and vegetables to make a broth for Harold, ready for when he floated closer to consciousness.

When the others returned a long discussion ensued on what to do.

'We're like sitting ducks here just waiting furr the blacks to attack again,' Angus complained.

Kate's main concern was for Harold. 'A wagon ride over a rough track like this will surely start him bleeding again. Move him now and we may as well be kissing him goodbye,' she said. 'He needs a few days' rest before we move on.'

James considered both their opinions before adding his own thoughts. 'We're not all that far from Mount Remarkable now. There is a police outpost there and they need to know what has happened. We should warn other station owners that these blacks are up to no good. It might also be better to place Harold in their care until he's well enough to go on.'

'You'd not get better care than Miss Kate's,' Craig interrupted, 'and that's a fact. Look what she's done already.'

It was the first time she had been called 'Miss'. 'Kate' had been sufficient before.

Sid, Robert and James himself all nodded in agreement. There was a new respect for her. She had passed the unwritten test of the bush. She could hold her own in a crisis. Her handling of the gun had not gone unnoticed and her courage in dealing with Harold's wound had been nothing short of remarkable. It was only Angus who showed none of that new-found respect. He had not seen her in action.

James decided that they would stay put. Once again they tightened the camp, hobbling the bullocks and tethering the horses close by. Kate tended to Harold while each of the others took turns as guard. There was no further sign of the blacks.

Over the following days they talked about the attack over and over again, each telling it from a different perspective. Kate continued as nurse, Sid took over as cook and James wrote the letter to Dan's family in Adelaide. He would offer to keep the team and the dray at Wildowie and he would send them the money they would have made by selling them. It was the least he could do, thought Kate.

She could now see why her compatriots had been so wary of heading into the remote wilderness. It was dangerous. And she was not as invincible as she once had believed. There were plenty of perils in life other than famine. Rory had tried to tell her that.

Rory.

She shoved the thought of him from her mind

and looked around. It was not all bleak. The beauty of the Australian bush was growing on her every day. At this moment the landscape was bathed in golden light and the sky stretched wide and blue from one horizon to the other. Vivid lorikeets flashed red, green and purple through the trees. Galahs with breasts as pink as the sunsets sat chattering on the old branches of the gums and the magpies warbled their songs to celebrate the day.

Days had passed since Harold had been speared. The few times he had surfaced since then, Kate had carefully spoon-fed him broth while one of the others held him a little upright. His condition was deteriorating. No longer pale and racked by shivers, he was developing a fever. His skin was mottled red and covered with a thin film of sweat. He began to call out in his sleep for his wife, Jo, and for his children.

Kate heated water till it was lukewarm and gently washed him. For a while the fever abated, then it returned more fiery than ever. As the day and then the evening wore on, Kate bathed him more frequently. Through the night he began to call out loudly in distress, for his mother, for Jo, and for others whom Kate had never heard of. He was keeping the whole camp awake. Sid was keeping watch during the wee hours and it was he who helped Kate by holding him still while she bathed him.

An unlikely companionship was growing between her and the rough and surly Sid. His new-found respect for her had changed their relationship entirely. Kate had discovered, beneath his sour manner, a man undaunted by fear, not dismayed at the sight of blood, and loyal to his companions.

The next day dawned hot and still. At least the chill night air had helped to cool Harold's flushed skin. His face, in the morning heat, was now a deep red. More ominous still was that he no longer called out. Kate found it hard to raise him to pass a little water between his lips. She realised with dismay that infection had taken over the wound and there was nothing left to do but to hope.

Kate remembered, a little guiltily, that since leaving the depot she had not been near a church or a priest. She found the simple rosary, previously forgotten, buried deep inside her baggage and she sat with Harold, his hand in hers, hoping that God would hear her prayers despite her lapse.

'Our Father . . .' she began, murmuring quietly.

The others, seeing her rosary and hearing her prayers, fell silent too. It seemed that even the crickets and the birds became still. The frogs in the nearby creek stopped their croaking.

'Hail Mary, full of grace . . .' she continued.

It mattered not that Harold was not a Catholic, for surely it was the same God to whom they all prayed, Kate reasoned.

The bush was quiet, tense, waiting.

'Pray for us sinners now and at the hour of our death . . .'

Others silently joined her; Angus, Craig and Robert saying their prayers for him too.

Harold's eyes fluttered open and for a moment he looked up at Kate. They fluttered closed again. She felt a fleeting pressure on her hand and he heaved a long, shuddering sigh. The blood ebbed away from his skin, leaving it paler than it had appeared for some time.

Kate stared down at him intently. She could no longer see the laboured rise and fall of his chest.

She had lost him.

Kate dropped the rosary beads on the ground and with a strangled cry began to loosen his clothes to feel for the beat of his heart. James strode quickly to where Kate sat and felt for the heartbeat too.

'He's gone!' she cried. She had tried so hard to save him. Dear Harold!

'No, Kate,' James said, and he took her hand and placed it over Harold's heart, 'he's still alive, feel here.'

Tears sprang to her eyes as she, too, felt the faint pulse beneath her fingers.

'Thank God!' she said, her voice catching on her tears.

'I think he's going to make it,' James told her, his hand on the old man's forehead. 'He's passed the worst of it. His fever has almost gone.'

Harold's eyes fluttered open, focused on her

and closed again. Kate bowed her head on his chest and wept tears of relief.

She heard footsteps close by.

'You've saved him, love!' It was Sid's voice. 'Three cheers for Miss Kate!'

Another two days of rest were allowed for Harold before it was time to get going. Although a lot better, he was only just able to get up and move about. Any exertion cost him dearly.

Kate spent the day thinking back over the whole experience. She wished that James Carmichael was not so detached, so distant.

She longed for words of comfort and an understanding ear. It had all been traumatic; the attack, Dan's death, having to extricate the spear tip from Harold's chest . . . She longed for strong arms encircling her, holding her, making her feel secure. She was not an invincible woman. The famine had not toughened her completely. Beneath the bravery and the determination was a vulnerable girl. A girl who needed more sustenance than food alone could provide.

But the arms she longed for, the ones she saw in her mind's eye, were not the arms smooth with fine golden hair, the hands slender and graceful. They were muscular and strong, the forearms sprinkled with dark, thick hairs, the hands square and capable. They were the arms she wanted, no matter how much she tried to deny the thought.

Sid had been the only one to offer her any real words of sympathy, even if his manner was laconic. 'I used to think you were just a money-grubber, love, but there's more to you than that. There must be a heart buried in there, if you're prepared to dig through the ambition to get to it. Harold wouldn't be here if it weren't for you.'

Kate realised it was meant as a compliment, but it revealed the way she presented to others and she was surprised. She wasn't that ambitious, was she? She did care about others— Brigid, Rory, the blacks, the poor beasts that drew their drays and wagons . . . Surely a life experience like hers would make anyone appear a little hardened?

With Dan gone and Harold still weak they were two teamsters short, but they had to move on. James assigned Kate and Craig to look after Harold, his team and his wagon. Robert and Angus were assigned to Dan's team, leaving the spare horse hitched to the back of the wagon and James as outrider.

Kate would have a slight advantage over Craig as far as the bullocks went. Having attached herself to the dependable Harold for most of the journey, she knew each of the team by name and was familiar with the commands as Harold had called them. Harold lay on the wagon with his head propped up where he could see the team and instruct the two beginners. This alone would be tiring enough without walking all day and wielding the heavy whip. The yoking up had gone smoothly and Kate was eager to get started and to try her hand. She was the first to pick up the whip.

'Have a practice with that whip before you try to do anything else,' advised Harold.

The bullocky's whip was fourteen feet long and was so heavy that she had to hold it with both hands. Kate could remember watching Rory. He was a skilled teamster and a strong man and he had used both hands to wield the whip.

'Now stand along the left-hand side of the team, just in front of the wagon and behind the bullocks!'

Kate moved into place, her face turned across her shoulder to take Harold's instructions.

'Hold the whip aloft to your right side with your right hand uppermost . . . that's it! Now, swing the whip forward, parallel to the team, as if you were going to lay the whip on the bullocks' backs. Go on!'

Kate swung the great heavy whip forward as hard as she could. Far from cracking in the air to the side of the bullocks, it landed with a heavy thud on the ground just in front of her. She could hear Craig laughing at her and she turned around and said to him with a grin, 'Don't be forgetting that it's your turn next!'

'Give it another go,' Harold called. 'This time put your whole body into the swing!'

Kate practised making the movement without actually swinging the whip. When she had the feel of it she swung the whip backwards in an exaggerated arc and then lashed it forward.

She heard a shout from behind her and turned around just in time to see Harold's hat falling to the ground. She had caught it with the whip!

'First you want to save me life, then you want to knock me block off!'

Kate and Craig burst into laughter, with Kate laughing so hard that she bent in two.

'Have another go. Craig! You better duck for cover!'

When Kate had the whip under control it was time to try the commands.

'Gee up, Blackie! Gee up, Lofty!' she called to them but her voice came out weak and thin, even to her own ears.

The bullocks just stood and stared ahead. They did not move a single inch.

'Speak as though you mean it!'

'Gee up, Blackie! Gee up, Lofty!' she yelled as confidently and powerfully as she could, snaking the lash forwards. The team started to move. They took off, pair by pair, like the segments of a serpent.

Kate grinned as she looked back at Harold.

'That's the go!' he called to her.

At the first turn in the track Kate took a deep breath and called to the bullocks again. 'Whoa back, Blackie! Come here, Lofty!' and the leaders slowly turned the team around the bend.

'You're up to the knocker, there's no doubt about it!' Harold declared as Kate pulled the team up to stop for lunch that morning.

As each day passed she learnt more about handling a bullock team and even became proficient at wielding the monstrously long whip. She got to know the bullocks better and to understand their individual characters. She loved to see the sunshine glistening on the dark coat of Blackie and to watch the ripple of Lofty's fawn coat as he walked. The leaders were worth their weight in gold. Harold had chosen them by the width of their foreheads, since the leaders need to be the most intelligent beasts in the team. Cocky and Ping were the second pair in the team, or the body bullocks. Cocky was long and lanky and lurched as he walked along. Ping tended to be a little lazy and was always the last to get up. Stump and Bluey were the polers. Stump had short legs, as suggested by his name, and needed to move them quickly to keep up with the rest of the team. He was a good, hard worker. Bluey was a quiet fellow who stared at her silently, as if to gauge whether she really was in control.

By the time they reached the Gillies' property at Mount Remarkable, both she and Craig were claiming that they could turn the team on a threepenny bit.

The news of the black attack caused a great stir. The overseer and station hands talked of collecting a group of men together to clear the blacks out once and for all. They had no faith in the local police. Not only were they too few to track the blacks and really teach them a lesson but also they refused to take action unless the culprits could be positively identified. Kate and Sid had been in no position to get a good look at them and thought that they would be hard to identify.

The whites on the station talked about retaliation. The station blacks began to look nervous and there was tension in the air. They claimed that the attackers were not part of their own tribe, the Nukunu, but were Jadliaura people from further north. Kate hoped fervently that the blacks who had attacked them were not Jadliaura people. Wildowie was situated smack bang in the centre of Jadliaura territory.

James claimed that the tribes above Mount Remarkable were linked anyway. They all knew each other, held corroborees together and planned and carried out joint attacks on settlers. They were known collectively as Adnyamathanha, the people of the hills.

There was little support for a reprisal from the party bound for Wildowie. They were conscious that increased hostilities between themselves and the blacks would not serve their purpose. They feared a repeat of the attacks either on the way or when they reached Wildowie. They were keen to move on. Mount Remarkable towered overhead, reminding them that compared to the distance they had already travelled, there was not far to go. James would have no part in a reprisal raid. Kate had no doubt that when they left for

Wildowie the people at Gillies would take things into their own hands.

Kate herself was the object of much attention. She was the only white woman who had been seen so far north. The eyes of the station hands followed her hungrily wherever she went. The station blacks were very curious about her, too. They had already given her the name Udnyuartu, which meant 'white woman'.

The Gillies' property was large but Kate noticed how primitive the buildings were in comparison to Bungaree. They must have only settled here recently, she decided. The main house was a wattle and daub cottage and the outhouses were little more than bark lean-tos. The laundry where Kate spent her day washing her own and James's clothes was simply a stone chimney and hearth to heat the water.

After a spell of two days the party moved on. What surprised Kate was that although they had reached the Flinders Ranges, there was still a long way to go. It seemed that everything in this country took on enormous proportions. The razor-backed mountain range, rugged and blue, seemed to stretch forever northwards. Huge eagles hovered high in the vast blue sky and lizards several feet long leapt across their paths. Had the kangaroos and emus stood next to Kate they, too, would have towered over her.

Although they had come one hundred and seventy miles they still had about eighty to go. As far as Kate could remember it was about three weeks since they had left Adelaide. The last eighty miles could well take them another ten days if nothing else went wrong. It was now well into December and each day grew hotter as they travelled.

Their day's journey was dictated by the location of water. The creeks were sluggish and little better than a series of stagnant pools. Kate strained the water through a piece of muslin to remove the tadpoles, the wrigglers and sometimes the slime. There was often no fresh water to drink through the day, so she made up bottles of cold tea to wet their dry throats along the dusty track. The flavour of tea covered the brackish taste of the water.

Harold explained to Kate that if they didn't reach water in time for the camping down, they would have to unyoke the bullocks and take them back to the campsite of the previous day. Then they would bring the bullocks forward, past the drays and the wagon to the next waterhole. The following day they would take the bullocks back to the loads and bring the loads forward to the waterhole. To get from one waterhole to the next would end up taking them three days. They might have to repeat these steps several times if water remained scarce. They could cart enough for the people but not enough for the bullocks.

A few days from Gillies' they met two teamsters heading south. They were the first travellers they had met on the track since they had left Bungaree. They all camped down together, happy to meet others, swap yarns and give advice on the track and its condition in both directions. Kate loved these starry evenings on the track, swapping yarns and singing the old songs.

The teamsters were carting wool south to be sold in Adelaide and much of the yarning was about working the bullocks in such dry conditions.

'There was one old bullocky up 'ere a while back,' one of the teamsters avowed, 'it was dry for so long 'e hadn't worked 'is team for months. It was so long since this bloke 'ad seen rain that one day, when a drop of rain fell on 'im, 'e fainted dead away.'

'Good heavens!' Kate said, playing along as if she was believing every bit of it.

'Yes indeed! We had to throw three buckets of dust in 'is face to bring 'im to!'

Kate laughed, 'I'm thinking it must have been that feller's team I saw further back along the track. They were so poor that they had to stand in one spot for half an hour before they could cast a shadow!'

Everyone laughed. She was learning as much about the telling of yarns as she was about the bullocks themselves. The teamsters assured them, on a more serious note, that there was reliable water further ahead. The next morning they broke camp, bade the other travellers a reluctant farewell and continued on their way.

Harold was well enough to look after the team for most of the day now. Craig took over late in the afternoon when Harold began to tire. Free of the worry about finding water and no longer working the bullocks, Kate was able to appreciate the fine country through which they travelled.

The river red gums stood sentinel along the watercourses like great sleeping giants. As well as the gums there were casuarinas and, as they progressed north, more of the small native pines with their deep green foliage and fresh smell. On their western side the majestic ranges towered over them, blue and purple in the changing light of the day. The limitless plains to the east, covered in wild flowers of every colour, were broken occasionally by rugged red gorges. At dusk the animals gathered to feed by still waterholes.

At times they saw blacks moving in the distance. They were family groups with women and children tagging along. It appeared that they wished to avoid the settlers and there seemed little danger of attack. The remainder of the journey passed uneventfully.

'One more day and we'll be at Wildowie,' James told them all as they camped down for the night by a large waterhole.

'I'm dying to get there,' Kate replied and everyone else nodded in agreement.

'It will be good to get off the track for a while, that is for sure,' Sid said.

'Wildowie,' said Kate, 'does it have a meaning?'

'Wildu is the Adnyamathanha word for eagle, and cowie, or owie, is the name for water. Wildowie is the place of eagles and water,' James shrugged. 'That is as much as I know.'

'So that is why all the place names here end with "owie",' said Kate. 'How fitting that they be called water places in a land that is so dry. Tell me, what is it like, Mr Carmichael?'

James smiled. 'Wildowie? You will see it tomorrow with your own eyes. Don't expect anything too much, though.'

Angus snorted, 'You can say that again.'

'I grew up in a cottage with mud walls and a thatched roof, so nothing would be too rough for me,' she told them.

'Then you'll noo doubt feel at home,' Angus said smugly in reply.

Kate took special note of their surroundings the next day. She was aware that what she was looking at was the country that was to be her home for the next few years. They were travelling across a wide plain of shimmering golden grasses. The mountains on their left appeared like mammoth prehistoric animals crouching on the plain. The golden grasses gave way to steep iron-red cliffs, then to misty blue foothills and eventually to the hazy purple of high, rugged ridge tops. The colours were soft and muted in the early morning light. As the day progressed the sun rose to rob the colours of their vigour, just as it sapped the strength of the travellers. The gold became parchment, the gums lost their rich green and turned to grey and the blues and purples became dusty, pale lavender. It was as if the entire landscape was bleached by the strength of the light.

The more she tried to peer into the distance to take stock of their destination, the more the shimmering heat threw up a mirage to prevent her seeing too far. She was impatient to see Wildowie. It was as if she had used up all her patience over the long weeks of the seemingly endless journey and now she could wait no longer.

Chapter

Six

'Mother of Mercy! You must be kidding me, surely?'

Kate stared at the rough shelter nestled in a glade of small native pines. It was nothing more than a hut made of pine and pug with neither chimney nor door. There were two small windows, unglazed and completely open to the elements. It was thatched with rushes, the type that she had seen growing in the creeks. Attached was a yard made of mallee, to hold the sheep, and a smaller one with a shelter for the chickens.

She picked her way through the mutton bones and other rubbish that lay strewn about on the ankle-deep grass. Peering inside the doorway, she saw the floor was made of the vibrant red earth of the Far North. The hut had been divided into two small rooms. The one that she could see contained little but a rough table and chairs made of pine slabs, bunk beds fashioned from poles and chaff bags, and an open hearth made of rocks and clay.

She whirled around to face Angus and James. 'This is just one of the shepherds' huts, not the homestead, isn't it now?' An uncertain smile hovered on her lips.

Sid, Harold and the McInerney brothers looked at James and Angus hopefully.

'This is it, the only homestead there is,' James drawled.

Kate's face was a picture of dismay. 'It hardly deserves the title of homestead!'

Angus's face twitched in silent enjoyment of the moment.

'God spare us!' whispered Kate to herself.

Where was the charming stone house with wide cool verandahs, the lush productive vegetable gardens and orchards, like those she had seen at Bungaree? Was this all there was to show for two years of settlement? Where were the cheerful workers she had looked forward to meeting, the hot clean bath to soak her tired legs and wash the dust out of her hair? What about the hearty meal awaiting them?

'We knew it would be rough but not this damned rough. You should have warned us! Fancy coming all that way for this,' Robert spat.

'I did warn you, all of you. You had a choice then and you decided to come. If it is rougher than you imagined it would be, then it is hardly my fault,' James said, shrugging his shoulders. Without waiting for an answer he continued, 'It will look more civilised in the morning when you've slept, I've got no doubt. And don't forget that you'll get a bonus for every year you stay on.'

He looked around the group at the glum faces. 'Let's get everything organised before nightfall,' he said.

Kate, Craig and Robert stared at their new home.

'Get going,' James said. 'Kate, you concentrate on dinner. The rest of you, get the bullocks unyoked!'

'Let's make the best of it,' Kate said, squaring her shoulders.

They each went their own way to prepare for the night.

'Is there no one living here, then?' Kate asked Angus a moment later as she pulled pots and pans from the back of the wagon.

'One of our shepherds, old Ned, is minding the home flock and looking after the homestead. He has a hut-keeper, a half-witted boy named Gerald. They'll soon be back wi' the sheep noo doubt, but Ned will move out to one of the outstation huts with one of the new boys noo that we are back.'

She wondered just where exactly she was going to fit into the arrangements. Would she sleep here in the cottage? What about Ned and Gerald, would they continue to sleep here too? And where did Angus stay? She did not want to be forced into his company any more than was absolutely necessary.

'Fancied yourself as the lady of the castle with James as your laird, did you?' he taunted.

She ignored him. She was tired and disappointed. It was not the time to rise to his bait. She made her way into the hut to prepare dinner. She was conscious that Angus's eyes followed her as she went. He was going to make the most of her discomfort.

Everything was covered in dust and cobwebs. The room was thick with the stench of wood smoke. Chop bones and dirty blackened pans sat in a heap in the corner. Kate went back to the wagon and pulled an apron from her bag. Ned might be a reasonable shepherd, she thought, but neither he nor Gerald rated well as housekeepers.

Before she prepared dinner she was going to make the place more habitable. She peered into the adjoining room. There were more bunk beds and two cupboards. Sacks of flour and sugar and boxes of tea leant haphazardly against one wall. The insects and the ants had found their way into them. The room was musty. Flies circled lazily in the centre of the room. She would clean that room tomorrow.

Only a new chum would have taken a post like this, Kate seethed, as she dusted the main room, swept out the fireplace and then the floor. No wonder none of the old hands had wanted to come. Spiders scrambled to get out of the way as she turned the place upside down. Damn James Carmichael! He had warned her that it would be a rough life up here but he didn't say that the place wasn't fit to live in! Her family home in Ireland had been poor but it had never been dirty!

She lit a fire in the hearth and immediately the room filled with choking smoke.

'Jaysus!' Kate cursed as the smoke stung her eyes.

At that moment James walked in.

'What's up?'

'Don't you be asking me what's up, Mr James Carmichael. This blasted fireplace is a devil of a thing.' She kicked the rocks which made up the fireplace. 'Look at the smoke!'

'Don't go wrecking the place, Kate,' he said calmly, a sardonic smile on his lips.

''Tis a wreck already and you damn well know it!' she retorted, her eyes flashing and her hair tumbling down, loosened by her exertions.

James leant against the doorway, one eyebrow raised. 'I like to think of it as a rustic retreat.'

'Rustic be hanged! A clean bed is not too much to expect, or a clean kitchen in which to cook.'

He shrugged his shoulders. 'It's serviceable.'

'Well if you think 'tis serviceable and if you like living in smoke so much then you can cook your own meal! I'm staying outside!' She tossed her hair over her shoulder and strode towards the door.

James grasped her arm as she passed him.

'Kate!'

'Let me go!' she tried to wriggle out of his grasp.

James held her in an iron grip. She would never have guessed that those long, slender gentleman's hands could have been so powerful.

'Kate,' he said softly, 'you're even more adorable when you're all stirred up.'

Kate tried unsuccessfully to pull away from him again.

'Let me go!'

But he held her fast. His grey eyes turned as cold as steel as he looked into hers. 'Don't forget who is boss here.'

Without thinking, Kate raised her other hand and slapped him across the face. 'And don't you be forgetting that I can leave here any time I please.'

He let go of her and stepped back immediately, rubbing his face. She walked through the doorway.

'Make a campfire outside and we'll eat out there!' he called after her.

Kate was fuming. How dare he treat her like that! She collected up some dry sticks and broke them over her knee, enjoying the sharp crack they made and wishing that it was James's neck she had in her hands. As much as she would rather that he went without dinner tonight, she had a responsibility to the others to get the meal on. They were all tired and hungry.

Craig came past with a sack of flour from the back of the wagon.

'Craig,' Kate called as he headed for the door,

'don't put that in the dirt in there, leave it on the wagon for now.'

'Mr Carmichael told me to.'

'Well tell Mr Carmichael that I'll be cleaning the place up before anything goes in. It can wait for tomorrow since it has been weeks on the wagon already. One more day won't make any difference.'

James overheard her and came to where she and Craig were talking.

'Do as Kate says,' he said, and shot Kate a look which was meant to mollify her.

Ned was back with the sheep by nightfall and was glad to see that the party had arrived. He was an old fellow with a long beard that once would have been white but was now stained dark brown with tobacco juice and God knows what else. His clothes were filthy and Kate could smell him and his dog from the other side of the campfire. Both of them looked as if they hadn't been washed for years.

James introduced him to everyone.

'Didn't think they could lure a woman up 'ere,' he said when he shook Kate's hand, 'and not such a pretty one either.'

Kate smiled at Ned, 'I don't know that I'll be staying all that long.' Her eyes flicked to James and back again.

'We'll treat you so good you won't want to leave,' the old fellow chuckled and then he winked at her. He was clearly quite eccentric.

Gerald appeared midway through dinner,

although he should have been there long before by rights, ready with dinner waiting for Ned. He was a quiet boy and looked quite vacant. He said little to the group. As it was already getting dark he took his dinner out with him and went to watch the sheep for the night.

After dinner James talked to the group about his plans for them.

'The first priority is to get the homestead in a reasonable condition,' he said, shooting Kate a sideways glance. 'We'll start tomorrow by building on some more rooms. It was good enough in the short term for Angus and me but it needs to be bigger now. One day it will be a station that is as fine as Bungaree. Tomorrow we will start to build it into a place we can be proud of.'

'You need a proper storeroom where the food can be kept free of ants,' Kate said, not looking at him.

'That's a good idea. We'll eventually need it to keep the blacks from thieving, too. They are getting to be more of a problem. We'll also build a chimney so that Kate can cook inside when the weather turns bad and a place to do the washing down near the creek.'

'Don't you be going to too much trouble on my behalf,' she said dryly.

The others looked a little puzzled at her tone, as if they could sense the tension between her and James.

'We do need a woman's touch here,' he said smoothly, 'that's why you were hired. I'm sorry everything wasn't ready for you. We'll soon put it all to rights.'

She looked up at him, unsure of how to take his comments.

He noticed her intent stare. 'What are you thinking now?'

She stood up and leant over next to him. 'Open your mouth for me a moment,' she said.

'I beg your pardon?'

'I just wanted to see if that tongue of yours is planted firmly in your cheek or not!' Kate said, her eyes dancing with mischief.

James smiled and the others relaxed visibly, pleased that the tension had been broken. A hearty meal and a yarn around the campfire had done a lot to restore her usual good humour.

'Once we've got this place fixed up we'll be building another shepherd's hut so that we can split the flocks. The flocks have been too big since the last lambing season. As it is we've got two shepherds out there without hut-keepers and that makes it pretty tough. We'll place Craig out with Ned.'

He turned to Craig. 'You can start with hut-keeping and then learn your way from there.'

Craig nodded.

'What about me?' asked Robert.

'You can stay here with Gerald and the home flock until you find your feet, then you can go to one of the outstations as well.'

Kate could see that the two brothers were just a little apprehensive at the thought of being taken out into the wilderness and being left to their own devices.

'You'll be top shepherds in no time,' Ned told them, reading their faces accurately.

'What about the blacks?' asked Robert.

James began to answer, 'We've not had too much trouble with them—'

'Yet,' Harold broke in. 'They're always quiet at first. Then they realise just what white settlement means. Just wait until someone mistreats 'em and you'll hear more.'

Kate looked at the boys.

'You'll need to provide us with firearms,' Robert told James.

'Of course,' James replied.

'Shoot as many of the black bastards as you can,' Angus broke in.

'That won't be necessary. I would prefer it if everyone stayed as well clear of the blacks as they could. Harold's right. They'll give us merry hell if they get upset.'

'I'd be shooting first before they had time to raise their spears if I were you!' Sid asserted.

'The lads at the outstations have been complaining bitterly about the sheep the blacks are stealing. Between them and the wild dogs it ain't no easy job looking after the sheep. The blacks have been about 'ere lately, too,' Ned said, 'asking for tucker and baccy, but I've sent 'em on their way.'

'That's the way,' James said. 'Treat them firmly but don't stir up any trouble.'

James brought the conversation back to the plans for the coming few days. 'Now, Harold and Sid, we've got wool ready to be carted south again if you are willing to take it.'

Harold and Sid nodded. James had made the offer of the return loads before they had left Adelaide.

'If you want to rest your teams for a week or two I can also offer you some work here. We're going to need help building onto the homestead and with the new huts and yards, splitting posts, weaving the scrub fences and the like.'

Harold nodded. 'I can turn my hand to anything,' he said.

'Likewise,' Sid told James.

'We'll stay until you've got most of it knocked off and then we'll head south together,' Harold said.

A little later James came over to speak quietly to Kate. 'I am sorry it wasn't all ready for you,' he said.

''Tis me that should be saying sorry, Mr Carmichael, for flying off the handle. You did warn me but I had built up a different picture in my mind. 'Twas not your fault at all.'

'Think about how you would like it to be, Kate. We'll build a station as good as Bungaree.'

'Better. We'll have the best station in the Far North!'

The night was clear and mild so Kate decided to avoid the fleas and dirt in the hut and sleep under the stars. The rest of the party did likewise.

Only old Ned slept inside with his dog and his pile of dirty old blankets.

Kate stared up at the sky and thought about what James had said before they had retired. *Think about how you would like it to be . . . We'll build a station as good as Bungaree.* What did he mean? That the future here was better than a servant might reasonably expect? Did she dare hope? Was he looking for a woman with whom he could share his life in the bush? A woman who could put up with the hardships, the isolation, the heat and the dust, the insects, the blacks . . . Could she fill that role?

The next morning they were up early. Kate took charge of the homestead while the others went on with the preparations for the building.

She took everything that she could carry outside, scrubbed it down then left it in the sun to dry. She cleaned the insects out of the flour and the sugar and stacked the sacks on the dry table and seats. Then she dusted and swept the hut thoroughly. James found a roll of calico that he had brought up on the drays and she cut it up to fix under the thatched roof, as a ceiling, to keep the insects from dropping down upon them. She cut out extra pieces to cover the windows and after lunch Harold came in to help her nail it all into place. He also promised to make her a door. When she had finished everything inside she boiled gallons of water to pour on the floors to kill off the fleas and the ants.

She would have to stay outside now until the

water had soaked away. She wandered outside the cottage, her hands on her back, and stretched her spine. Noticing the charcoal left by the fire the night before, she took a piece in her hand. A smile of mischief lit up her face. She went back to the doorway with one of the chairs to stand on. Above the doorway, on the lintel, she wrote: 'The Grand Hotel, Wildowie'.

She finally had a moment to relax and to take stock of her surroundings. Her mind had been so taken up with the shortcomings of the homestead that she had hardly spared a glance for their surroundings. She ambled up the hill behind the house and sat down on a large rock in the warm sunshine to look over the valley in which the homestead nestled. It really was a pretty spot.

To the north ran a range of low hills knuckled with granite. To the west lay a high razor-back mountain range, clear, blue and majestic in the early morning light. Opposite was the tall red rock wall that formed the gorge through which the creek ran. She had noticed yesterday that the afternoon sun lit up the red rock, making it glow like hot coals in the campfire.

Fine native grasses covered the floor of the valley like a carpet and when she looked closely she saw tiny flowers of pale blue, and miniature yellow and white flowers like stars dotted through the green.

The pines were unlike any pine trees she had seen before. They were small with emerald green foliage and tiny black cones. The bark looked ancient and deeply lined. It was patterned with fungus and lichens of soft green and vibrant orange. The creek itself was pretty with its rocks sprouting great splotches of pale green lichen echoing those on the pines.

A flock of white corellas screeched as they flew overhead. They settled in a ghostly white gum that stood out stark and dead against the green of the hills. The eagles for which the area was named whirled high, suspended in the air currents, searching for their prey.

The view really was wonderful, now that she looked at it properly. She could picture a grand stone homestead with wide verandahs nestled on the hillside above the spot where the hut stood now. She pictured the garden with roses rambling up over the verandahs, flower beds, stone paths and a pretty garden seat from which to appreciate the view. To the right she would plant an orchard with every kind of fruit tree that she could imagine—lemons, apples, pears, grape vines . . .

A small movement caught her eye on the other side of the valley. She looked but she could see nothing. She shrugged her shoulders. It must have been her imagination, or maybe a bird moving silently through the bush. She stretched her back again and yawned, looking up at the wide powder-blue sky. A movement again.

Kate sat up. She could have sworn she had seen a tree move! She stared at it intently. Was she going mad or what? She rubbed her eyes. The tree in question was a half-dead she-oak some distance away. It had a bare branch sticking out halfway up the trunk. She sat back again, half closing her eyes.

It moved again! It was all she could do not to jump up with a shout. She took some long, slow, deep breaths. She was not going mad. There was someone behind that tree and she was going to find out who it was.

She yawned loudly as if there was nothing amiss and felt for her derringer. It was still there, nestled safely against her leg. She slipped her hand through the pocket of her gown and carefully withdrew the pistol through the opening. When she stood up she brought it to nestle in the folds of her gown. She walked nonchalantly past the homestead and towards the creek as if stretching her legs.

She gave the doubtful tree a wide berth until she had passed it. She then turned and looked behind her. That tree was a black man! She could not believe her eyes. The branch poking out halfway up the trunk was his arm. There was no doubt it was a man for all he had on was a loincloth, and a brief one at that. He was standing absolutely still. She pulled out her gun so that he would see it but she didn't aim it at him.

She called out in a gruff voice, 'Hey! I can see you. Come out of there. What are you up to!'

The black man took one look at her firearm, dropped the tree he had been holding and dashed past her towards the scrub line not far away. As he reached it, Kate realised that there were other figures standing there quietly. She saw two women and some children disappear into the bush.

She ran after them, calling, 'Hey come back, come back!' but they took no heed. She followed the way she thought they had taken. She came to a dead end.

'Damn!' she said, her chest heaving. They were fleet-footed. She had no hope of catching up with them, not that she knew what she would do if she had.

She stood still for a moment, panting and holding the stitch in her side. She didn't even know why she had chased them. She had been fascinated by the blacks ever since she had seen them on that first day on the Port Road. She made her way back to the homestead and went to find James to tell him of the blacks.

'Mr Carmichael, you'll never guess what I've seen with my very own eyes!' she began. James turned from the work he was doing, and so did Angus.

'I . . .' she began.

Then she had second thoughts. Angus hated the blacks. They had done her no harm this afternoon. It might be better that Angus didn't know the blacks had been nearby. He might go after them.

Angus and James were looking at her expectantly.

She thought fast. '. . . 'Twas . . . 'twas a snake, a big one, down by the creek!'

'What colour?' asked James.

''Er . . . Black, 'twas a black one! It stayed ever so still for a moment and then it took off into the bush with hardly a sound!'

'Red belly?' Angus asked.

'Yes,' she said.

'Red-bellied black snake it was, then. Don't worry, they're not too dangerous. They're scared of humans and aren't terribly poisonous, even if they do bite. It is the brown snakes you need to watch out for,' James said and they resumed their work.

Kate went down to the creek later to have another look for the blacks. There was no one in sight except for Harold, further upstream. He was collecting reeds to thatch the roof of the new building. Harold didn't loathe the blacks. She thought it would be all right to tell him the amazing thing she had seen this afternoon.

'To be sure, Harold,' she told him, 'I was sitting there for ages and just thought it was a tree. If I hadn't seen the movement in the corner of my eye I would never have realised it was a man. Do you believe me?'

'I do, Miss Kate, I've heard of them camouflaging themselves with boughs to appear like trees down in the Clare village district. What I wonder is why they were so curious. And why didn't they just walk right up to the homestead rather than watch unobserved?'

She shrugged her shoulders. 'I don't know. Don't tell the others though, will you?'

'You can trust me.' He continued his work of cutting the rushes.

The next morning, on Harold's advice, she collected dry fresh gum leaves in a couple of sacks. With these she could make herself a reasonable mattress that would insulate her from the cold floor of the homestead. While she was collecting the leaves she saw two black women watching her from the edge of the bush. When they had gone out of sight she returned to the homestead, dumped the leaves and collected some cold damper and mutton left over from dinner the night before. She wrapped them in a sugar bag and placed them at the spot where she had last seen the blacks.

After lunch she stole a moment to wander down by the creek to where she had seen the black women. As she got close to the spot her heart jumped into her mouth. The sugar bag had been moved! She had left it under a small gum. It was now in the fork of the same tree. She peered around her cautiously. There was no one in sight.

She pulled the bag from the tree and looked inside. The damper and the mutton were gone. They had been replaced by a cake made of grass seeds and a blackened piece of flesh which looked like snake. They were obviously meant to be eaten. She looked around again. An eerie feeling travelled down her spine. She could see no one but she was absolutely certain, she knew not why, that brown eyes were watching her from the bush.

The food was a symbolic gesture to her, just as hers had been to them. It was important that she eat some of it, here and now, while they were watching her. The snake, if that was what it was, did not look appetising. The seed cake, though, looked reasonably inviting.

She sat down and took a large bite. She nodded, smiling, as if she was enjoying it. It wasn't too bad, either, fairly bland and tasteless, but quite edible nonetheless. She heard a hushed giggle from the bushes not ten feet away from her. She wondered what she should do. Before she had a chance to make up her mind, a small figure came hurtling through the bushes, giggling and pointing at her.

It was a small boy, no more than two or three years old by the look of him, chubby and naked. He stopped a short distance from her, looking at her with great lustrous eyes, unsure of whether to approach her further. She held the remainder of the seed cake towards him and he toddled closer.

'Pst!' came a sound from the bushes behind him. He ignored it, clearly fascinated by the sight of Kate.

He came up close to her, took the remaining seed cake from her hand and placed it into his mouth.

'Hello, little fellow.' She held out her hand to

him and he advanced just a little further and held his own hand out to meet hers. She touched him and he giggled again. Kate looked up to see that a woman had appeared behind him. His mother, perhaps.

'Hello!' Kate said again, knowing that if they did not understand her words they would know her intent.

'Nunga!' the woman said softly.

Kate nodded. 'Nunga,' she repeated and the woman smiled.

She was a young girl, much the same age as Kate herself, with dusky skin and high, pointed, bare breasts. All she wore was a woven loincloth and she carried nothing in her hands.

Kate knew only one Aboriginal word. It was the name they had called her at Mount Remarkable. This was a different tribe and it may not work but it was worth a try.

'Udnyuartu,' she said, pointing to herself.

A momentary look of surprise flickered across the girl's face and she broke into a string of words. Kate gave her a puzzled look.

She then pointed to Kate and repeated 'Udnyuartu!' and nodded vigorously. She had understood!

She called out. Suddenly and noiselessly two more women appeared. One was old, her eyes set deeply in a face more wrinkled than Kate had ever seen. Her breasts hung down, thin and saggy, to her waist, and she carried a stick. Her dark eyes twinkled black and friendly from their deep sockets. The other was older than the first woman, with a broad face, a flat nose and a mass of curly hair that stood out from her head.

'Udnyuartu!' Kate said again and they all nodded vigorously. It was the first time they had ever seen a white woman!

'Udnyuartu,' the young woman said. She walked over to Kate and touched her hair, a look of wonder on her face. Her fingers travelled over the skin on Kate's forearm.

'Yuraartu,' she said, pointing to herself.

'Yuraartu,' Kate repeated, pointing to the woman. If udnyuartu meant white woman then yuraartu must mean black woman. They grinned with delight. Kate tested it out further.

'Yuraartu!' she said, pointing to the old woman, 'Yuraartu!' she said, pointing to the third one, and finally 'Udnyuartu!' pointing to herself again. The three woman clapped their hands and grinned, nodding all the while.

They were communicating!

'Yakarti!' the old woman said, pointing to the child.

'Yukardee,' Kate repeated.

'Yakarti!' they corrected her until she got the pronunciation right.

The black women cocked their heads abruptly and listened. Kate heard the repeat of a loud bird whistle. The young woman snatched up the child and they vanished from sight.

Kate was left staring at the spot where they had stood not a moment before. It was as if they had never been there and their meeting had never happened. She would come back tomorrow and see if they returned.

'Very tasty indeed!' James said, as he finished the rich, thick gravy of the stew that Kate had made for them that night. He smiled at Kate warmly.

'Beats the mutton chops we had week in week out before Kate came, don't it?' Ned commented.

James nodded.

Angus, of course, said nothing. It didn't matter how well she could cook. He would have preferred that she hadn't come at all.

'You've made a difference to the place already, Kate,' James told her. 'A clean place to come home to, clean clothes, neatly mended. A hearty meal ready after a long day's work. You've made the place more bearable.'

'Sure have,' Ned said, winking at her again. The others agreed.

Ned continued, 'You'd make a fine wife for a station man. That's saying a lot, for there's not too many who would.'

Kate's eyes slid over to James and she looked at him through her eyelashes. She wondered if things could lead in that direction. She doubted that she should aim that high but then ladies of James's class were highly unlikely to come to a rough and remote place like this.

Later that night as she and James were

preparing to retire, James again broached the subject of her staying.

'I meant what I said over dinner, Kate,' he said softly, looking at her body as she moved around the kitchen. 'You really have made a difference already. I'd miss you now if you left.'

'Would you?' She sounded a little harsh, even to her own ears.

James looked at her silently.

'Is there any real future for me here?' she continued on a softer note.

'Oh, Kate,' he said. 'You're a perfect woman for Wildowie. I want you here. I need you here.'

'But you've not answered me. What future is there for me? I've got to know or I may as well head back with Harold and Sid. Harold has offered to take me if I decide not to stay.'

A slight look of alarm flitted across James's face. 'What more future could you want?'

'I don't want to be a lowly servant for the rest of my life, Mr Carmichael,' she said quietly.

'Leave the future to look after itself. There will be opportunities for you, believe me.'

Kate just looked at him.

James knew that she wasn't satisfied. 'Kate, listen to me. This is all a big gamble. Wildowie may never pay off or it may be a huge success. I took a big risk settling so far north. Stay with me here, work side by side with me, let's build this place together. Within a few years I will have enough money to pay back my father's investment in this. We'll see what comes of it and we can make our decisions from there. To all intents and purposes you are the mistress of Wildowie and you will continue to be in the future—if you stay.'

Kate looked at him, afraid of pushing her luck too far too fast. If she pushed him she may well lose him, and what else was there for her? A long lonely journey back to Adelaide where job prospects were few and far between.

'Stay, Kate, there's nothing for you to go back to,' he said, reading her mind. 'Your only hope is here with me. At the least you have a job, money of your own, a place, albeit rough, to call home. You aren't just a lowly servant. You are the housekeeper. Sure, it must be lonely for you at times but I'll look after you, I promise. Together we could build this station into a place to be proud of. I'd say it was worth a try!'

He argued persuasively, not actually making any promises, but inferring there were better times to come. Anyway, he was right. There was nothing for her elsewhere in the colony.

'I thought you were the type never to look back, never to retreat, Kate O'Mara.'

God, he was so smooth, so damned sure of himself!

'I am! I'll not look back. 'Tis what I promised myself when I left Ireland.' She squared her shoulders. He had found her Achilles heel. 'I'll stay on, Mr Carmichael, but just remember, I'm not just an ignorant Irish lass who can be used. I'm in this for what I can get, too!'

'And you will get your rightful share.'

Of Wildowie? Of the profits, should there be any? Of James too?

'Go to bed, Kate, the world won't get better for worrying about it.'

The words rang a bell in her mind. Rory had said that too.

Rory.

Chapter
Seven

The wagon and the dray were piled high with wool. The bullocks were yoked and ready to move off. The sun was already scorching hot, even though the morning was still young.

'Take care o' yourself, now, Harold,' Kate murmured as she hugged him and wished him farewell.

'I will, young Kate,' he said, 'and you too. Just remember, if you want anything bad in this world, you've got to fight for it.'

'Ye know me, Harold. I will,' she replied.

'I have every faith in you, girl.'

'Thank you.'

'Remember, now, when you come down to Adelaide, you must come to stay with us. I mean it. I've given you my directions. I owe my life to you and there's not too much you could ever ask of me. I'll be offended if you don't. I want to find some way to thank you for what you did. If you hadn't been so brave and so caring I'd be pushing up gum trees right now.'

'But at least your ears would be in one piece!' she replied, referring to her prowess with the whip.

Harold laughed. 'Come and stay and meet my family. Don't forget, now.'

'I won't,' she said. 'You have been a good friend to me, Harold. You looked after me as well as I looked after you.'

She looked at the old man fondly. His hair seemed to be more grey than when she had first met him. The wrinkles in his dear face were deeper. There was no doubt that he'd had a close brush with death.

'I won't argue that now,' he said. 'Just remember that nothing would ever be too much to ask of me.'

She hugged him again and then turned to Sid. 'Goodbye, Sid, all the best,' she said, shaking his hand.

''Bye, Miss Kate. Look after yourself. You're a top lass and they're lucky to have you here,' he said, a grin stretching from one side of his crooked face to the other.

'Thanks, Sid.' That was one hell of a compliment coming from him!

She would miss both of them, even surly Sid. She could never countenance his attitude towards the black women but he had never, since the black attack, been anything but kind to her. She sensed that he had lived a hard life. He probably had been a convict just as she had surmised when she first met him. She had seen lash scars on his back when he washed by the creek.

Kate had won his respect and that was no small achievement. And she had learnt a lot from him too—she had learnt not to judge a man too quickly, for behind that surly face and sometimes cruel behaviour there was a heart of gold. He was the one who had helped her get the spear out of Harold and he was the one who stuck up for her when the going was rough.

The homestead would be quiet without them, that was for sure.

Ned and Craig had already moved on to the outstations. Only she, James, Angus, Robert and Gerald were left at the headstation. She hardly ever saw anything of Gerald and when he was there he almost never spoke. James and Angus were often out working and she was usually on her own during the day. Unlike his brother, Robert took little notice of her. It was a lonely life for a woman out here on her own. She would miss them both.

Kate waved goodbye until both teams had snaked their way down the track and out of sight. This was it. She was now stuck here until God knows when. It was too late to change her mind. If she had wanted to get back to Adelaide her only chance had just left. She prayed that she had made the right decision. Would it all work out from here?

She turned back to the homestead. It was

certainly more substantial now that three extra rooms had been added on. It still looked rough, as the additional rooms were also made of pine and pug. But James had unearthed a number of things from the back of the drays that would make life just a little more comfortable. These had included some comfortable chairs, a hip bath, a large brass bed for himself and some rugs for the floor. When he next went south he would bring back the tools and workers needed to build a proper house made of stone. Slowly it would take shape as the elegant homestead that Kate had pictured it would be. Next time anyone left for stores she would get some fabric for curtains and sew them up herself. Little touches like that would make it so much more comfortable.

Kate's day was busy every day. It was hard work from sun-up to bedtime. It seemed sometimes that there was no end to the work that awaited her. She swept the fireplace out each morning, cooked three meals a day and cleaned up after everyone. Managing the food was a job in itself. Ants found their way into just about everything and the flies and heat combined caused the food to go off almost before it could reach their mouths. Meat that had been killed for too long had to be soaked in the flowing creek and rubbed with vinegar to make it more edible. And there was a limit to what could be done with mutton and damper.

The washing alone could have filled her days.

The wood had to be chopped, the fire built, the water heated. She had to cart the water by hand from the creek, careful not to spill one precious drop. She would then stand in the blazing sun over the steaming tub, turning and stirring with a big stick, her long gown clinging to her perspiring body. Then she would wring it by hand and hang it on bushes to dry. After that came the mending and darning. Fortunately there was little ironing, as the men's work clothes could do without it.

She looked after the chooks, milked the cow and churned butter. She helped the men whenever they needed an extra hand to hold up posts, slabs and beams as the huts and fences were built. Then there was the making of soap and candles and the other hundred and one tasks that happened not daily but nevertheless regularly.

It was in this way that the weeks and months went by.

James was teaching her to ride a horse. When she was able she would ride out to wherever the men were working with a basket of food and the tea. Eventually she, too, would take her turn in riding the five or six miles in each direction to the outstations to take the rations to the shepherds and the hut-keepers. She helped to weigh it all out. The rations were twelve pounds of mutton, ten pounds of flour, a quarter of a pound of tea and two pounds of sugar per week for each man. The hut-keepers had to find their own firewood.

Often alone, she spent her days fantasising about a better life. She pictured herself in the years to come, riding a spirited horse, fitted out in a riding habit of the latest cut. Mistress of the station, she would take baskets of food to the sick and needy workers and their families.

The hard work was to be expected, it was what she was being paid for and she did not begrudge it in any way. It was all a part of building her future. It was the isolation that was hard to tolerate. She had no one that she could call a real friend. No one with whom to share confidences or talk with about her hopes and dreams. She wished that Brigid had come with her or that Rory or Harold were here. They were all people with whom she felt something in common. There were no other white women for miles. James was nice enough—smooth and charming—pleasant company, someone whom she admired greatly, but he was not the type to share confidences with. As for the shepherds, they were not unpleasant, but she had no special relationship with them. Of course, there was Angus, but who wanted to be friends with a red-haired brown snake?

She had to admit that she did feel attracted to James. There was so much about him that was alluring. The way he did things—she supposed it was his upbringing. He was always the gentleman, always polished, a little aloof, but that enticed her all the more. She thought of him a lot. A lot more than she should. She yearned to be closer to him, more in touch with his feelings and for him to be more in touch with hers. She needed someone to be close to. But he was hidden from her, behind a wall of English reserve.

It was obvious that he still wanted her, but she was not sure of exactly what he was prepared to give in return. His eyes followed her when he thought she wasn't taking notice. If he brushed past her his hand would linger for a moment on her shoulder or her arm. She didn't mind. She liked it, she wanted to be touched.

She yearned for his friendship. Wildowie was a lonely place for a woman on her own. Rory, once again, had been right. He had said that any Irishman would feel isolated in the bush. She did feel isolated, she did feel alone.

Whenever she could spare a moment, and no one was watching, she would wander away from the homestead and further down the creek to a secluded spot the black women had shown her. It was a safe place to meet them, where they would not be seen. She never knew who to expect or when they would come. The young woman and her son were often there. Sometimes she brought others whom Kate thought were her sisters but the old woman came only rarely. Kate continued to raid the stores to give them food.

Today she lay under a tree on the soft grass waiting to see if her black friends would appear. She did not mind waiting, at least she could have half an hour to relax. The longer she waited for them, the more sorry for herself she began to feel. Self-pity was not something she indulged in often, but it would be so nice to have someone to talk to out here.

Eventually, tired of waiting, Kate made her way back to the homestead. Even the brisk walk did nothing to restore her usual good spirits. What was she doing up here on her own? She should have stayed in Adelaide where she had Brigid and the companionship of her other friends from the *Elgin*. Had she found a position in Adelaide she would have been working with other women, or have been close enough to others to go visiting.

The feeling of despondency stuck with her through the remainder of the afternoon while she prepared the dinner.

'You are unusually quiet tonight, Kate,' James said as they ate.

Kate shrugged her shoulders in response.

'What is up? Is something wrong?'

'No, not really. I'm just not feeling my usual self. I must be tired, I suppose.'

She couldn't say more than that, not while Angus was there, although she would have liked to talk to James since the invitation had been open. She missed having someone to share her feelings with. Maybe tomorrow she would sit down and write a letter to Brigid.

After dinner she sat at the table and pulled a candlestick close to mend a shirt for James. Angus had disappeared as he often did in the evening. She and James were left alone.

'Still feeling low?' James said, putting down his book.

'Mm, I can't seem to shake it off. I don't know what has got into me,' she gave a hollow kind of a laugh.

'I've got the very thing to help.' He disappeared into the store room and returned with an unopened bottle and two small glasses in his hand.

'This will cheer you up a bit, help you sleep.'

'No, thank you, Mr Carmichael. I don't drink.'

'Call me James. There's no need for formalities up here.' He showed her the bottle. 'It is muscat, very sweet, you'll like it.'

She shook her head.

'Oh, come on, have a drink with me. You're not the only one who feels low from time to time. We are so isolated here. We've got to look after each other a bit. I'd like to have a drink with you.'

When he put it that way it was hard to refuse. He had read her thoughts quite accurately. He, too, was looking for company.

'Oh, all right then, if you insist.' She placed her sewing down on the table.

James pulled the cork and poured her a small glass. 'There, you just have a taste first and see if you like it.'

He was not forcing it on her if she didn't want it.

She picked up the glass and took a tentative sip. It was delicious, very sweet, almost viscous, with the flavour of ripe, dried raisins.

'Mm, lovely,' she said and took another sip. James reached over the table to fill her glass.

They started to talk, first about things in general, then about Wildowie. All the time she was sipping at the muscat as they talked.

She pushed her glass forward to be refilled when James filled his own. He filled hers too.

'Don't drink it too quickly now, will you? If you're not used to it, it will go to your head.'

At least he was not trying to get her drunk. He was looking after her and that gave her a nice feeling. Sometimes she felt that she was almost totally ignored by the men on the station, but not tonight. The wine was warming her, softening her, making her feel more relaxed.

'It must be hard up here, being the only woman.'

'It is that.'

'I wondered when you would start to feel it.'

'I don't know why it came over me today. Maybe because I have been hoping for a letter from Brigid and I haven't had one yet. It would be nice to hear from her. I do miss her. I wish she had come.'

'Write to her, see if she has changed her mind, she could come up with the men I bring up for the lambing in June.'

'Could she still have a job up here?'

'Certainly! If it would keep you happy you can have anyone you like up here.'

'Thank you, Mr Carmichael—'

'James,' he corrected her.

'Thank you, James. You are very kind to me.' The muscat was working on her now and she was beginning to feel languid, liquid, relaxed. She knew that Brigid would not come up but that was beside the point.

James reached for her hand across the table. 'No, I should thank you, Kate, not many women would come up here and put up with the hardships as well as you have. I appreciate you and what you have done for Wildowie.'

Kate looked into those grey eyes of his, now glowing with warmth. She should pull her hand away. It felt good, it felt so comforting for her hand to be held in his. It was what she had needed, someone to be close to her, to show some care for her.

He held her eyes with his. She was not conscious of the way her eyes had become dreamy. Her lips parted softly on a sigh and curved into a tender smile. It was an intimate scene, just the two of them here in the middle of the wilderness, the candle glowing softly, the night air balmy, talking about the things that were close to their hearts.

In one smooth motion he rose from the table and walked around to stand next to her. He drew her up to face him and took the glass from her hand.

'I think that is enough, you're getting tiddly.'

She was getting tiddly and her legs felt as if they would no longer support her. But it was all right, James was looking after her.

He placed one hand under her chin and tilted her face up to his. 'Stay up here with me, Kate, don't ever think of going. You've made this place bearable. You've given it that woman's touch, turned it into a real home.'

His face moved slowly down towards hers and she knew with absolute certainty that he was about to kiss her. She wanted him to and she swayed towards him slightly, lifting her face to his.

His lips touched hers, at first softly, tentatively, waiting for her response. They were sweet with the taste of muscat. Her hands moved without conscious thought to his chest and up around his neck. She had given him the sign that he had been looking for and he kissed her again. Their kiss became deeper, stronger.

His arms slid around her to encircle her body and to pull her close up against him. His arms around her felt wonderful, secure, loving. It was what she wanted, this feeling of being close, of being loved and wanted. The kiss seemed to go on forever, she was drowning in it, revelling in it, opening all her senses to its power.

'Oh, Kate, I've wanted this for so long. I'm so very fond of you,' he was searching her eyes with his own.

It looked very much like her dream was coming one step closer.

She pulled him towards her again, relishing his closeness, wanting him closer still, but he pulled away from her a little.

'Are you sure that this is what you want?'

She nodded and moved closer to him again.

But he held himself away. 'I don't want you saying that I got you drunk to seduce you.'

'No . . .'

There was a gleam in his eye as he looked at her. What was it, triumph? Pleasure? She didn't care. She wanted him as much as he wanted her, and if she had to give up her body for some love, then that was the way it would have to be.

He took the candle in one hand and led her to his bedroom.

Inside his room he stopped to kiss her again, his hands working at the fastenings of her gown. She felt a hot dampness surging through her. He peeled off her gown, tossing it onto the floor, then her cotton chemise and underclothes. He loosened her hair. It tumbled in heavy curtains down over her body. Everything happened so smoothly. She stood before him, swaying ever so slightly, naked, unashamed, her heart beating like a drum, her breath rising and falling, waiting.

He stood before her, his hands on her shoulders, looking at her nakedness, the luminescent white of her skin and the ebony of her hair shining in the candlelight. 'By God, Kate, you're beautiful,' he whispered, and he pushed her gently backwards to lie on his bed. He began to slip out of his own clothes.

She watched, not caring if he thought her bold, as his naked body emerged, his skin smooth and golden in the candlelight, his masculinity rigid and upright.

He stopped and looked at her again as if to savour every morsel before he partook of her. He picked up the candle from the table and brought it to her, drinking his fill of the sight of her beautiful body. She felt like a flower in first bud, ready to be plucked.

Then he placed the candle by the side of the bed and moved over her gently, restraining his passion, taking the shell-pink skin of her nipples into his warm mouth. Her body trembled in response and she cried out, pulling his head closer to her breasts. His gentle hands, the skin not harsh or calloused, stroked her belly and between her legs, sending a liquid warmth through her. He was a skilful lover, sophisticated, refined, holding himself back for her pleasure, conscious of her innocence, savouring her purity and claiming it reverently as his own.

'James,' she gasped as he brought her to the peak of excitement, the tension within her unbearable agony. He was poised above her, his manhood pressed against the centre of her femininity.

He took a few deep breaths, bringing himself under control. 'Thank God I got to claim you first, Kate,' he whispered, and he entered her. She gasped as he did so, the tension at its peak, the hot sharp pain giving way to a feeling that left her breathless. She placed her hands on the smooth skin of his buttocks, pulling him deeply inside her, wanting more and more of him. His control gave way and they moved together, Kate's instincts coming to the fore, in an ever upward spiral of motion and feeling. She felt the storm reach its height inside her and she gasped again, her body quivering with release. His release followed hers and his body fell gently onto hers, spent.

James lay down beside her, his hand resting along the line of her jaw, the light of the candle shining full on her face.

'You are a beautiful and desirable woman, Kate,' he said, his tone urbane.

Kate did not know how to reply. Thoughts tumbled through her mind. She rolled over and his hand came round from behind her to cup her breast.

The candle flickered as an enormous soft brown moth flew about, attracted by the light. She watched as it blundered towards the flame, hopelessly attracted, caught in its spell and doomed to be burnt. Already its soft brown wings fluttered wisps of smoke. It dived for the flame once again. She could watch no more. She turned into James's chest, wondering if she was like the moth and if so, whether she would get burnt too. What would tomorrow bring?

The deed was now done. She could say that circumstances had forced her into it but if she was entirely truthful she would admit that there was more to it than that. She had not been drunk, at most maybe more relaxed and carefree than she would have been otherwise. But she had wanted him, she had wanted to be held and stroked. Her body had responded to his, willingly. The first kiss by the river had wakened desire within her, a desire that was somehow inextricably linked with all that she wanted from life. She was not only falling in love with James, she was falling in love with everything that he represented. He was the only one here who could possibly fulfil her needs; her need for companionship, for love and, above all, for a secure future.

Are you sure that this is what you want? he had asked her. She had said yes. She did want him—lock, stock and barrel.

In the following days she spent a lot of time thinking about James and wondering if she had done the right thing at the right time. She probably hadn't, but how much longer could she have tolerated that desperate loneliness?

He was a good lover, polished, sophisticated, smooth. He was always the gentleman, but it seemed sometimes as if it was all technique and little real passion. And in a strange way, she sensed that he only wanted to meet her needs so that she would meet his. It was not an entirely mutual kind of thing. There was something missing.

Sometimes, when she made love with him, unwanted thoughts slipped through her mind. She wondered what it would have been like if she had been with Rory instead. When Rory had kissed her at Bungaree, sparks had flown, the earth had tilted on its axis. His presence was raw, virile, powerful. If his kiss could make her feel the way it did, if it could effectively blot out the rest of the world for her, then what would it be like to make love to him? She imagined it, even when she was in James's arms.

She wished she hadn't met Rory. She wished that she could forget him now that she had. There had been no future for her there.

Her life at Wildowie began to change in subtle ways. James, although distant and reserved during the day, was attentive to her needs at night. If she could get through the days on her own, seeing no one, talking to no one except the blacks, then she could have him at night. He would hold her and talk to her, making her feel loved, important.

Maybe that was right and maybe it wasn't.

When guests arrived from nearby stations, for a duck hunt or a kangaroo shoot, James ignored her, not wanting others to know the nature of their relationship. At these times he was distant and she felt that she was relegated to the role of servant again. It was hard to fathom just why he did this. No doubt he had his reasons.

Kate found her mind returning to Rory yet again. What would he say to all of this? If he was James, would he have treated her with the same casual indifference throughout the day then lavished attention upon her body at night? She doubted it.

Over time, Kate was reaping the benefit of James's experience and was no longer the passive recipient of his attentions. Gaining in confidence, she was learning ways to further heighten his pleasure and to get him wanting more. Slowly she began to feel more in control of where her relationship with James was going. He did consult her about things, about the lay-out of the garden, about his future plans for the homestead. She felt as though there really might be some kind of a future for her there. He never mentioned love, but then he was a typical Englishman, reserved about matters of the heart. He never mentioned marriage, either. But she was patient. She could wait.

The men began to treat her with more defer-ence. They were obviously aware of the chang-ing nature of the relationship. Only Angus continued to be rude, but that was Angus. He was number two at the station and he wanted it to stay that way.

The days and weeks began to slip past more quickly.

Eventually Kate received the much awaited letter from Brigid. The envelope, addressed in a careful script to Miss Kate O'Mara, care of Mr Carmichael, Wildowie Station, the Far North, was very grubby. It had been passed from hand to hand, teamster to teamster, station owner to shepherd, until it had reached her.

> *Third day of January 1850*
> *To My Dearest Kate*
> *I do be hoping that this Letter reaches you*

well and happy. I am stopt here in the Orphans Depot for there is no work here still. We are all in health and am thankful to God in his kindness for that at least.

I think of you often and wonder how this Letter has found you. I seen Mr O'Connor and he told me how he had seen you on the Grate North Road. Singing your praises, he was. You have won a heart there, I'm thinking. He said to tell you that he is going up to the Far North to cart some goods for another Squatter who is opening up a Run near you. Later in the year I think. He will call to see how you are going when he is there.

Should I be coming up to join you at Wildowie? There is not much work to be had in Adelaide. Write and let me know what you are thinking and how you get your health.

God Bless You Kate.
With all my love,
Brigid.

Kate smiled again. It was all just so typical of Brigid. Fancy her staying so long at the Orphans Depot! She had patience, not like Kate herself. That stifling environment would have provoked her to do outrageous things just for a bit of excitement.

The next day she wrote back, telling Brigid about Wildowie and her life there. She wanted to be honest with Brigid about her relationship with James, but it was still way too early for her to have anything to crow about, so it was better left unsaid.

Just thinking about writing it down in a letter to Brigid made Kate think it over again. Yes, it was going well with James, in some ways. They got on well—very well in the bedroom—but she still felt that she knew so little about him, about what he was thinking and feeling, about his past and his personal plans for the future. It did her no good to ask him either. When pushed, invisible shutters would simply be drawn down and he would divulge nothing more about himself.

It would be good if Brigid were here and she could have a heart-to-heart with her. It was the kind of thing that could not be written down in a letter.

The other thing that went unspoken was Kate's fear about becoming pregnant. She would have liked to discuss it with another woman, but there was no one here for that. She knew that it was possible, for it had all been explained to them quite clearly on the orphan ship. Most of the girls had their first monthlies on the voyage. It had been the first time that they had received three square meals a day and their bodies had come rapidly to maturity. At least on that voyage the authorities had planned for the contingency, unlike on the first Irish orphan ship where one hundred and fifty girls had all begun menstruating at the same time. Not one spare piece of linen could be found on board and no provision had been made for the girls to wash their personal things and to dry them away from the prying eyes and vulgar comments of the sailors. Kate had hardly believed it when she was told the story back at the depot.

Her monthlies had never been regular. Since she had been sleeping with James she became anxious if they were late. But eventually they would come again, she would heave a sigh of relief and promptly put it all to the back of her mind until the next time. It was certainly not the kind of thing that she could ask him about.

She really should do something about it, but she knew not what to do. She had started feeling tired lately, too tired to think about it, too tired to worry about much at all. Maybe it was the never-ending heat and her long, hard days of work that made her feel like this.

The days began to drag for her and she was simply glad to get to the end of each day.

Desperate for some female company, Kate wondered if the black women would appear. She decided to leave the candle-making for the next day and to go down to their secret meeting place by the creek.

They did appear and this time the old woman was with them. Kate liked her. She sensed a certain wisdom in those ancient eyes. Like the other women, Kate now called her Adnyini, which, Kate thought, probably meant grandmother. Over the months that Kate had been here she had learnt more of their language and they had in turn learnt some of hers. They now had a few words in common and for the rest they used mime and drew pictures in the dirt.

Her relationship with them had developed very quickly, given the few months since she had met them. She was obviously the only Udnyu who had ever shown an interest in them or their culture. Sharing, whether it be food or information, seemed to be integral to the way that they lived and they were evidently very keen to share their culture with her. She in turn was appreciative of their company and sought them out as often as her duties would allow. There was no one else, other than James, with whom she had any real relationship at all. And James was her lover, not really her friend, as Brigid and Rory, God bless them, had been.

She was fascinated by the black women, the food they ate, the way they walked, talked and played together. They began to show her the ways of the bush. Each time they met they would show her some plant or animal and how to use it for food or for medicine. The changing of the seasons was more important to them and they showed her the signs that would tell them when a fruit was about to ripen or an animal return to the area, ready for them to hunt . . .

'Udnyuartu sick fella?' they asked her.

'Tired,' Kate said, drooping her body and yawning to explain the word.

Adnyini nodded sagely and repeated Kate's gestures to show that she understood. She took one of Kate's hands in her own and examined it, first the palm and then the back. Then she looked into her eyes and pulled down the lower lid.

She nodded her head and spoke slowly in her own language in the hope that Kate would understand what she said.

Kate shook her head and looked bewildered. The old woman was trying to tell her something about her tiredness but she knew not what.

Adnyini pointed to her belly and repeated her message but still Kate failed to understand. Maybe she meant that Kate didn't eat enough and that was why she was tired.

'I eat a lot,' she said. She knew their word for stomach was warlla. 'Warlla full,' she said, 'eat plenty.' In fact her appetite was enormous and she was putting weight on her tummy and breasts. She gestured with her hand over her stomach to signify her belly was full and that she was eating a lot.

Adnyini nodded to her, signalling that she understood. Then Adnyini spoke to the other women, quickly and softly, and Kate had no hope of following her words. Two of the women left and appeared again ten minutes later with some leaves of a plant.

'Ngarlkuka!' Eat! Adnyini told her, giving her the dark green leaves.

Kate ate them slowly, for the flavour was none too good, but she trusted that the old woman knew what she was doing.

Finally she swallowed the last mouthful and Adnyini looked pleased.

'Warndu,' she said. Kate knew that warndu meant good. She nodded to show that she understood.

'Warndu, yakarti,' Adnyini motioned to Kate's belly again.

Kate shook her head, puzzled by this reference to children. She couldn't understand why Adnyini was on about it again.

'No yakarti,' Kate said.

Adnyini looked frustrated and she spoke to the other women again. They all looked at Kate and then at her belly. They shook their heads. Discussion went on for some time. Every now and again they would glance at Kate. She knew that something was bothering them but she couldn't understand what it was.

They couldn't make themselves understood and as the shadows were lengthening Kate knew she had to get back to the homestead.

'I'll come tomorrow,' she told them as she left.

On the following day they were waiting for her. This time there were a couple of women whom she had not seen before. Altogether there were five or six of them, all sitting in the dust underneath a spreading gum tree. Adnyini and her granddaughter were there. Kate sat down cross-legged on the ground with them and the little fellow who had come to her on that first day rolled around in her lap. Adnyini had with her a little bag made of hand-woven string.

'Malaka,' Adnyini said, showing her the bag. Inside were more of the leaves they had gathered for her the day before.

'Warndu,' good, Kate said to Adnyini. She had felt better yesterday evening and wondered if it was the effect of the herbs she had eaten.

Adnyini nodded and gave her the rest of the bagful. She then motioned with her hands to show Kate that they could be found under trees near creeks.

'Thank you,' Kate said, chewing on the leaves.

Adnyini then took Kate's hand and placed it on Kate's belly, all the time talking to her in words that Kate had not yet learnt.

Kate spread her hands and shook her head. She did not know what Adnyini wanted. Adnyini motioned for one of the women to stand up and to come closer.

She was a young woman with high cheek-bones and wide eyes. When she stood up her rotund belly became more obvious. She was pregnant. The skin that stretched over her tummy was shining and tight like a drum, even though there must still be months before the baby would be born.

Adnyini placed her hands on the young woman's belly. 'Muldurru,' she said. It must have been the word for pregnant.

Then she placed her hands on Kate's belly and repeated the word: 'Muldurru.'

'What . . .?' Kate began, and then 'My God!' she exclaimed. She sat up straight. The connection Adnyini was trying to make hit home suddenly and with a terrible force. 'No, I'm not pregnant!' Her eyes were wide with shock as she looked into Adnyini's eyes and then down at her own body. Her heart began to beat at a furious pace. Her mind rebelled against the thought entirely. She looked up at Adnyini again. A baby wasn't part of her plans. Not now, at any rate.

'Muldurru,' the old woman nodded.

Kate's hand went to her brow and her jaw dropped. Could the old woman be right? Is that why she had been so tired? Is that what Adnyini had been trying to tell her? The thought had not entered her mind before. How could she have been so stupid? But maybe Adnyini was wrong. How could she be so sure anyway when Kate herself had no idea of it?

Adnyini began to draw in the dust by her feet. She pointed to the moon still present in the day-time sky and made gestures that indicated menstruation. When did Kate last have her period?

It was six weeks ago—maybe more. She had not been counting. It was so easy to lose track of time up here. The last time her monthlies had been due she had been worried for nothing and she had put dates and times to the back of her mind.

Adnyini pointed to the pregnant girl, then to the moon and held up six fingers. The other girl was six months pregnant.

Adnyini pointed to Kate and then to the moon. How long had Kate been pregnant?

Kate held up her hands and shrugged her shoulders. She did not know.

She bowed her head in her hands. It seemed too awful to be true. She didn't want to believe that it was so but she knew somehow that it was. It all made sense now. The tiredness, her appetite, her breasts becoming larger and more tender, that strange melancholy feeling that had come over her.

'Damn! Damn! Damn!' Kate swore loudly. She could have kicked herself for such stupidity. She had known that she was taking a risk but she had continued on blithely, ignoring the reality. She could ignore it no longer.

She was no better than the other foolish and ignorant Irish girls she had heard of. That woman, Mary O'Leary, whom Brigid had told her about, for instance. Although she had felt sorry for her, Kate had thought the O'Leary woman was naive. Now she herself had made the same mistake!

Adnyini leant over and took her hand. Kate looked down at her own hand, slender and pale inside Adnyini's brown, broad and wrinkled one. Kate knew nothing about having babies, nothing really about her own body. This was no place for a woman to have a baby. Who could she go to for help? There was no one, not a single white woman anywhere on the remote stations. These black women were the only women for miles. She would have to rely on them for help.

'Virdni?' Adnyini asked.

'Yes,' Kate nodded sadly. Yes, it is bad. It was so stupid to have fallen pregnant. Here in the most remote corner of the colony. There was so much work she had to do to get the homestead how she wanted it. And James, what would he think, surely it was not part of his plans either?

Adnyini clucked sympathetically and held her hand more tightly. When Kate got up to go, Adnyini's hand restrained her momentarily. She pointed to the afternoon sky glowing red as the sunset approached. She then signalled the setting of the sun and the rising again tomorrow.

'No come.' She gestured to the group of black women around them and then pointed to Kate herself, 'No come!'

Kate kneaded the dough for the damper and wondered just what to do. There were no firm promises. No plans for marriage, no certainties. They still had not talked of marriage or of the future in any practical terms. What would he think of them having a baby, here and now? He might not be too keen. There was so much work for them all to do.

She had heard of women who tied their babes in a sling and hung them from a tree while they worked in the fields. She pictured a baby sleeping, hung from the river red gums down by the creek. Her fears began to evaporate. There was no need for her to worry. As James would say, the future would look after itself. He would look after her, she had no doubt about that. She would be able to stay here no matter what happened. She would not be like Mary O'Leary who was cast out onto the streets to look after herself. Kate would not be destitute. James loved her enough to look after her.

Kate smiled to herself. The more she thought about it, the more she realised just how much she would love this little baby. James would love him, or her, too. It might be just the thing they needed to put the seal on their relationship. This might be all that was needed to bring him to tie the knot. Yes, it could all work out for the best.

There was no point in delaying the inevitable any further. She had waited until dinner was over and the other men had retired to bed. She and James were sitting on the floor in front of the hearth. The fire was warm on their faces and James had put his arms around her.

'James, I have something to tell you,' she began nervously as he undid the buttons down the front of her nightgown.

'Later,' he said, nuzzling her neck gently.

'No, now,' she said and she pulled his hands away from her gown and did up the buttons again.

'James, I don't know how to tell you this,' there was a nervous flutter in her tummy, even though she knew there was nothing she should be nervous about.

James suddenly became very still, as if a premonition of what she was about to say had flashed through his mind.

'I'm going to have a baby!' The words tumbled out in a rush.

'What?'

'I said,' she cleared her throat, 'I'm—'

'I heard what you said.' His eyes turned as hard as the shale that littered the slopes of the ranges. It was as if a shutter had rolled down over them and Kate could not read his response.

'You're sure?' he asked, his tone terse.

She nodded, the uncertain smile leaving her face.

His aristocratic mouth hardened to a thin line. 'Whose is it?'

'Why are you asking me that? Of course it is yours, whose else would it be?'

He shrugged his shoulders.

He had said that he knew she was a virgin when he had taken her. That had been half the pleasure for him. He had said so.

'You were the first, James, you know that is so, surely?'

He did not answer.

'And the only one, James, you know it! James! Don't you?' Kate could hear the hysteria rising in her own voice.

'I know no such thing.' His eyes were cold and calculating.

She was confounded by his response.

'I've not been with anyone else and you know it!'

'How can I be sure? What about that O'Connor chap, you were pretty friendly with him, weren't you?'

He was sitting back, his arms folded across his chest. The flicker of firelight reflected on his eyes and it was if she could no longer see into them. She could not tell what his thoughts might be.

'God Almighty, how can you say such a thing?'

She was not a woman who had been free with her favours. A hot pink flush rose to her cheeks at the very thought of having been with Rory.

'You knew I was a virgin when you took me and that was well after Rory had left us. You know it!'

'Do I?'

He was completely calm, totally controlled and horridly remote. He had withdrawn behind the mask of the ever so proper English gentleman. To Kate, it was like dealing with a stranger. She stared at him open-mouthed. She felt as if she were in the grip of a nightmare where everything familiar and comfortable had dropped out of her world, where certainties slipped through her frantic grasp. One where she would try to scream but no sound would come and struggle to crawl but make no progress. She was enclosed in a fog of incomprehension.

She looked at James, her eyes wide with shock. What was he saying? What was he doing to her? If he was any closer she would have shaken him in the hope that the James she knew and cared for would reappear.

'James, don't do this to me.'

'What are you going to do about it?' he asked her guardedly.

'What can I do?'

'Is it too late to get rid of it?'

'Get rid of it! I don't want to get rid of it!'

'You might have to.'

'And how would I be doing that, can you tell me?'

'I thought all women knew these things.'

'Well I don't. I've not needed to know before!' Her mind was still reeling from the shock that he did not want the baby at all.

He must know that she would have no idea. He had told her that it was her innocence that had attracted him so much in the first place. Unlike the women with whom he had had affairs before, she was not calculating, she was not careful, she was not selfish.

'What about ladies' pills?'

'I've never heard of 'em,' she said. 'D'you think I grew up in a chemist shop, for God's sake?' She had heard of pennyroyal and castor oil being used to stop a baby but where would she get such things up here?

He was thinking of his reputation, she could see that. Some people would say that what he had been doing with an Irish servant was only one step better than the men with their black velvet. He had said once that he had never stooped so low as to take a black woman, no matter how lonely and desperate he had felt up here in the wilderness.

'James?' she said and his name came out as a plaintive cry. Tears welled on her lower lids and began to slide slowly down her face. Her face beseeched him to show compassion.

The calico ceiling flapped in the evening wind. The fire crackled and pockets of air that were trapped in the greener wood popped and snapped as the flames caught them. But he gave no immediate reply.

'There, there, dear girl,' he said finally. 'We'll think of something.'

But he made no move to comfort her.

'You won't get rid of me, will you?' she asked, a frightening thought creeping into her mind. She felt so terribly alone, and wondered what on earth she would do if he did.

'No need to cross any bridges before you come to them,' he replied. 'Let's sleep on it and make our decisions in the morning.'

Kate made her way to bed in a state of total shock. She could never have pictured, even in her worst dreams, that he would respond like that. The tears rolled noiselessly down her cheeks and into the pillow as she tried to fathom his response.

James stayed by the fire.

From time to time she let go a stifled sob, but he did nothing to comfort her.

Kate awoke in the morning to find the other side of the bed cold and empty. She knew not whether James had come in at all during the night. When Angus came into the homestead for breakfast he told her that James had ridden to the outstations and would not be back until later. Angus looked piercingly at her heavy eyelids but said nothing.

James arrived back at the homestead at dusk. Angus and Gerald were nowhere to be seen.

'It's all fixed,' he said to Kate as he laid his hat on the table.

Her eyes flew to his.

'You will marry Craig McInerney and act as his hut-keeper.' His tone was final, as if he would not enter into negotiation.

'I beg your pardon?' She was unable to believe her ears.

James repeated word for word what he had just said.

'I don't believe it!'

'Well you had better believe it.'

'But I don't want to marry him!'

'I don't think you have a choice in the matter. He is prepared to marry you and to treat the child as his own.'

Kate felt her spirit return to her in a rush. She was no longer sad, she was angry. Damned angry! 'How dare you speak to him about my business without so much as a by-your-leave? How dare ye?'

'You put the matter in my hands. I am the boss here so it is my business. You are an employee of mine.'

'An employee, is it?' she gasped. 'Is that all I am to you now? Last time we talked I was to be a partner and work by your side!'

'Don't be ridiculous, Kate.'

''Tis what you said yourself! I'm your lover, James, remember?'

'That is all in the past now.'

Kate was struck dumb.

'What else did you expect, for pity's sake?'

The words froze in her throat. She could not utter them now without looking like a total idiot.

'Don't tell me you expected marriage, Kate!'

She didn't even look up at him. She had not precisely expected it but she had, in the back of her mind, hoped for it.

'You know how my family would view that, don't you? They don't know you, they don't know what you are like. They would believe that you are a conniving fortune hunter from the gutters of Ireland! The English gentry do not marry peasants from Ireland.'

No, she thought, they prefer to let them starve. 'Does it matter what they think? You know different, don't you?'

'Yes, I do, but it does matter. If I was to marry without their approval I would very likely be cut out of the inheritance.'

'They would not, surely?'

'They would, my dear. It is the way of the English gentry. How else could they have amassed and maintained their wealth? I would not wish to cut myself off from all that. I would be a fool. No, I'm afraid that you will have to go, as much as I regret it.'

Kate looked at him, still shocked.

'Go where?'

'To Craig.'

She had forgotten that outrageous idea already. He would marry her off to another man, just like that. Was that an indication of how deeply he felt about her?

Kate felt her pulse rate quicken. Did he think that he could do something like that and get away with it? Did he think that he was free of all responsibility? Did he think that she would take all this lying down? How little did he know Kate O'Mara!

'Oh no you don't, James! You don't get off this one so lightly. The child is yours. He will be your son, your responsibility. You will not foist me or him onto another man.'

'No?'

'No! For I'll not be putting up with it! I'll not let you walk all over me that easily. This baby is your problem.'

'No, it is not, my dear. You slept with me willingly. I asked you, I remember it well. You agreed that I wasn't seducing you, that you wanted it as much as I did. You were lonely, I was only looking after you.'

Is that why he had asked her? What a fool she had been. She thought he was being a true gentleman!

Kate was speechless with anger. Absolutely speechless. The two-faced bastard wouldn't outsmart her that easily!

'James, I don't like making threats, and I never make one unless I intend to carry it out, but I promise you, on the graves of my family, that unless you let me stay, unless you recognise this child as your own that I will make it clear to all the world that it is yours and that you have used me for your own ends and then cast me off.'

'Your threats don't concern me, Kate. There is no one up here for you to tell.'

He was trying to bluff her.

'You would hardly want me to tell your Adelaide circle, or your family. I know their addresses, for I've seen it on their letters. I can write, James, and I'm bold enough to do it.'

There was a faint look of alarm on his face.

He put his hand on her arm, but she shook it off.

'I'm sorry, Kate, I should have handled this more delicately, I can see that now. You are distraught. No wonder. I know women get that way at these times.'

'Ha! Women get distraught when they find out they are being used, you mean!'

'Don't say it, Kate. If anything we have used each other. You wanted love, I gave it to you. You were lonely, I gave you friendship. You wanted to get ahead, I gave you that chance. You cannot deny it. But you have to live with the consequences of your own actions.'

Kate felt so angry she could burst. 'It's your actions, it's your consequences, it's your baby and I won't be letting you forget it!'

'Look,' he said, trying to mollify her, 'we may not have to worry. You may miscarry. We can hope.'

A surge of protectiveness shot through her, surprising her with its power. No, not her baby, she would protect him, she would pray that no harm became him. She would fight tooth and nail for him, for his life, for his welfare, for what was rightfully his. She would never, ever let James forget him.

Never.

'Let us discuss this when you are calmer, my dear.'

'Don't keep calling me your dear! Just don't! You don't mean it, that's clear!'

'See what I mean? You are not rational. You have never minded before. We will wait for a better time.'

He had never treated her like this before!

If Kate had a knife in her hand she would surely have stabbed him.

She sat down with a thud on a chair, totally flabbergasted. It was beyond her comprehension. She thought that gentlemen always took their responsibilities seriously. He was an out-and-out rogue!

There was a cough outside the door and Angus appeared. He did not meet Kate's eyes. He had probably been listening outside, she thought. 'We've just finished counting the sheep. There are forty missing. The blacks have got them, noo doubt,' he said.

'Do another count, to make sure. I'll be there in a minute!' James said, dismissing him.

Kate was seething with anger, her skin whiter

than usual. Her eyes were huge and glittering in her heart-shaped face.

'Kate, you've got two choices. One, you can marry Craig, or two, we'll take you as far as Clare Village, pay you out for the year and you can look after yourself from there. It's up to you.'

Kate was aghast. This was like a nightmare that continued on even though she tried to wake herself out of it. She stared at James in dismay while her mind raced through her options. Marry Craig and live on Wildowie with James so close but out of her reach? Her dreams of being the squatter's lady were in shreds. Not a gracious homestead but a lowly shepherd's hut. Not the charming and sophisticated squatter but a shepherd who was no more than a boy. Neither she nor Craig would have any real chance of bettering themselves, no matter how hard they worked.

Escape from Wildowie would have to be better than that! Could she go to Clare? What chances would there be for her then? Would it be the most attractive option? She had only a short while left before her condition would become obvious. No one would hire her then. Clare would be no good to her at all. No friends, no opportunities. The child would never see his father. They would be destitute and reliant on charity! Marrying Craig would have to be better than that! But what kind of marriage would it be?

'I can't be marrying Craig, there's no priest up here!'

'That didn't stop you living with me,' he shot back at her. 'It is the done thing to live as man and wife until a priest is found who will come so far north, or until you travel down to Clare.'

'What have you done to convince Craig to marry me?'

'You are not blind, Kate, he's been totally infatuated with you ever since we came up here.'

'I'm sure he doesn't want your leftovers, though. He does have his pride.'

'His pride was easily overturned. I offered to pay him not only his own wage as a shepherd, but also yours as a hut-keeper and a little more besides. There is nothing to spend it on up here. He should be able to save a tidy sum.'

He had offered Craig the money. He hadn't offered it to her or to the child. She was a woman! Unwanted baggage, that's what she felt like.

'James, don't do this to me! Have you no feeling? We've had a good relationship, haven't we?'

James looked at her. His eyes grew warm, like hot ash in the fire. He pulled her into his arms. His mouth crushed down upon hers, choking the protest that formed on her lips. She felt him harden against her and she twisted her head away.

'My God, Kate, you are so desirable, I could never stop wanting you,' he muttered into her hair as he pulled her up against him again.

She felt her body melt towards him treacherously.

Then she saw his face above hers, superior, worldly, possessive, sure. It was as though a volcano erupted inside her. She raised her hand and slapped him hard across his arrogant face.

'Don't touch me again,' she hissed at him.

Who did he think he was that he could treat her as if she didn't matter to him at all and then take her in his arms? His arrogance was insufferable.

'The decision is yours,' he said and picked his hat up from the table. 'Make up your mind by tomorrow.'

He spun on the heel of his expensive leather boots and left the homestead.

She sat heavily and rested her head down on her forearms at the table. 'Merciful God! What will I do now?'

Surely there was some other option. Craig and Clare were equally distasteful. There had to be something else she could do. Was there some way of getting rid of the baby? She didn't want to do that but what sort of life would the poor little mite have?

Harold! Harold would have helped her. What dreadful timing. If she had woken up to this before he had left, he would have taken her back to Adelaide. He owed his life to her and he said that nothing would be too much to ask. He did have a big family to support though, and she would be an added strain on his already meagre earnings. No, she couldn't do that to him, it would not be fair.

Brigid. Could Brigid help her? She would want to, Kate had no doubt about that. But how could she when she did not even have a job?

Kate laughed to herself but it was not a happy laugh, it was bitter. If only she had Brigid's patience she would not be here. She would not be pregnant. She would not be broken-hearted. No, it was highly unlikely that Brigid would be in any position to help her.

Maybe, just maybe, she could ask help from Rory. Her heart knocked against her ribs as she thought of him. Would he support them? He probably would and he probably could. He was making a success of his life. He had enough to get by on. She shook her head. She could not ask him. He had helped her out already and their friendship was not of such long standing that she could encroach that much upon his goodwill. On top of that, she didn't think she could face Rory. She would feel so ashamed. Not only had he warned her, he had asked her to stay with him and she had turned him down. She had kicked him in the face and she couldn't go crawling back to him now.

What on earth was she going to do?

If only she had listened to Rory's warnings. He had been right about the gun, he had been right about James's motives and he had been right about James's priorities.

Angus was smirking when he came in to dinner. James had obviously told him of her condition. Kate was sure that when she was alone

Angus would find a suitable moment in which to say, 'I told you so'. She was not going to discuss the matter with James while he was there, that was for sure.

James himself was as cold and as distant as the English winter.

The loss of forty sheep from the home flock was the main topic of discussion over dinner. It seemed that the blacks had stolen them, yet again. There was no sign of where they had gone.

'They will hae tekken them to a hiding place and will be having a fine feast at our expense,' Angus was complaining.

'It seems that we are to be plagued by them forever, doesn't it?' James commented. 'It is because we are the furthest north. There are no stations past us to take the brunt of the thievery. In a way, we protect everyone else from the worst of it.'

'Between the blacks and the wild dogs we'll be lucky to get ahead at all,' Angus said.

'You're right there.'

'I've heard of other stations baiting them with poison,' Angus continued.

It sounded as though he considered them both pests to be eradicated.

'Are you talking about the blacks or the dogs?' Kate interrupted.

Angus did not even deign to answer her question.

James ignored her too. He continued his discussion with Angus. 'The fact that we are so isolated means we are more at risk of attack. I'm convinced that we should do nothing that would stir them up. If you could be sure of getting the ringleaders, though, we could make an example of them.'

'I'll keep an eye out tomorrow when I'm out,' Angus told him.

'I will too,' said James, 'though I think you are more likely to come across them than I am.'

The next morning James left for the station of their nearest neighbour some twenty-five miles to the south. He hoped to negotiate for the two stations to jointly move a large flock of sheep up from Adelaide. Angus left early to scout out the bush north of the homestead. He was looking for another area to establish an outstation and the end of summer was a good time to do that. If there was water there then, there would be water there all year.

Kate was glad to be alone for the day. Her decision weighed heavily on her mind. Try as she might, she could think of no other options and it looked like marriage to Craig was the best that she could do.

'Better the devil I know than the one I don't,' she said as she fed the chickens.

There was only one other possibility she hadn't considered seriously and it was something that Kate was hesitant to even think about. Maybe the black women knew how to get rid of a baby in the early stages of pregnancy. It was not something that Kate wanted to do. But would it be any sort of a life for a child in these dangerous and remote conditions? She would see the women this afternoon. The least she could do was to ask.

Kate was sweeping out the ever present dust from the homestead when she heard what she thought was gunfire. She dashed outside, her ear straining to determine the direction. She felt for her own pistol. More gunfire!

What should she do? Maybe Angus was shooting at 'roos. Or maybe he really was in trouble. There was no one else who could go to his aid. James had ridden down to their neighbour's station. Gerald and Robert were tending the home flock. It was better to be safe, she thought, as she ran to get a saddle, a spare gun and some ammunition. She had never ridden out on her own before. Catching a horse and saddling up were more difficult than she thought.

More gunshots. Whatever was going on? With great difficulty she leapt up onto the horse and swung her leg over the saddle. Modesty could go to hell.

She had only walked a horse before, or trotted gingerly, but spurred on by fear, she rode fast in the direction of the gunshots. She was tossed up and down roughly in the saddle, her bottom and thighs slapping against the hard leather each time she and the horse came together. From time to time another gunshot rang out. She was getting closer all the time. She stopped for a moment, determining which way to go. Taking out her pistol, she fired into the air to warn of her presence. A gunshot came in answer and she veered off to the right.

A little further on she heard a horse galloping towards her. Seconds later Angus came into view. Kate swerved wildly and her horse came to a sliding, slithering stop. Angus, too, pulled up in a cloud of dust.

'What's up? Are you all right?'

'I am,' he said. His horse was lathered and Angus himself was breathless from exertion, his skin red and smeared with dust and sweat. He took off his hat and wiped his brow with his forearm.

'I caught the blacks red-handed,' he gasped. 'Feasting on the sheep. Half of them slaughtered, the rest with their legs broken, herded into a dead-end gully.'

'The blacks attacked?'

'Nae, I surprised them and shot doon at them from the hilltop. Got some o' the bastards, too!'

Kate felt her heart sink. 'How many?'

'A guid few in the gully. The rest got awae. I managed to chase some o' them, got a couple more on the run.'

The look on his face could only be described as elation. Kate had a sinking feeling in the pit of her stomach. He had killed some of the blacks. He had been waiting a long time for an excuse like this. Now he had done it.

'What 're you going to do now?'

'I'm coming back to get Gerald. We'll bring

the rest o' the sheep back. What are you doing here anyway?'

'I heard gunshots, I thought you were in trouble. I came to help you.' She almost wished she hadn't. Thank God she hadn't been in time to watch as the Yuras were murdered!

Angus looked a little taken aback that she would have come to his rescue. He saw the ammunition and the gun she had brought with her.

'I nae needed yurr help.'

'Fine. But I was the only one around, I thought I had better come.'

'Ah well, you can get back noo,' he said, rather ungraciously.

Kate whirled her horse around and trotted back to the homestead. She could hear Angus's horse behind her. Lord! What did she have to do to win that man's respect?

Kate was glad when Angus and Gerald left to retrieve the remaining sheep. It gave her a chance to get down to the creek to see the women. She hoped they had not been involved in any way and she was thankful that Angus had never discovered that she had met with them there.

The tranquil glade was empty when she got there. That in itself was not unusual, for they travelled from one area to another and would not always come here during the day. But she felt a deep sense of foreboding. She suspected that Angus had not told her everything about his morning's activities.

She waited. It was imperative that she see Adnyini. Not only did she want to check that they were all right, but also she had to find out if there was a way to stop this baby. It was not something that she would want to do, it would break her heart, but she was getting desperate. She sensed once again that she was being watched. She stood up and looked around. Her eyes were sharper now, more used to picking out the silent black figures from the bush. There was Adnyini's daughter, Arranyinha, watching her from the other side of the creek. Her face was daubed with clay, the sign of mourning. She had seen it before.

Kate waved her arm. 'Nunga!' she called. Arranyinha remained motionless. Why was she hanging back? Kate advanced on her slowly. When she within ten yards Arranyinha began to retreat. She was terrified. She knows what has happened, Kate thought.

Kate held up her open palms to show that they were empty.

'Nunga?' How are you? She asked gently. Kate could now see that her eyes were red-rimmed and the clay on her dark cheeks was streaked with tears.

The black woman broke into a wail that sent a shiver down Kate's spine. It was a cry of terrible pain and anguish. Tears sprang to Kate's eyes in response and the blood ran cold in her veins. Something was terribly wrong.

At the sight of Kate's response, Arranyinha sat

down and wailed even louder. Kate could finally approach her. She hurried over and sank down next to the distraught woman, placing an arm round her shoulders.

'Arranyinha, what is it?'

'Crackaback! All fella gone crackaback!' she cried out. It was the word they used for gunshots.

'Who? How many?' She held up her fingers.

Arranyinha held up five fingers.

'Five!'

'Yuraartu,' said Arranyinha and she held up two fingers. Kate was horrified. Angus had killed two of the women as well!

'Who? Who?' Kate asked urgently, a horrible thought crossing her mind. He would probably have shot the slowest of the group.

'Adnyini?' Kate asked her, her voice urgent.

Arranyinha wailed again. Oh no!

'Tell me!' Kate implored her.

'Adnyini gone crackaback!' she cried and sobbed into her hands.

That bastard had shot Adnyini, an old woman! Kate could scarcely believe her ears! He had shot a defenceless old woman. Her Adnyini, the woman who had adopted her as a granddaughter. Harmless, loving, wise Adnyini.

Tears sprang again to her own eyes and she clung to Arranyinha as they cried together.

Arranyinha pulled away from her, 'Warrikanha gone crackaback!' she said.

Her younger sister had been shot. Kate was

not sure who she meant. Their family relationships were so complicated. Kate looked puzzled. Arranyinha motioned with her hands—a pregnant belly.

'Oh God, no!' Kate groaned.

Angus had shot the girl who was in an advanced stage of pregnancy. He was barbaric! Did he have no human feeling at all?

Kate hugged Arranyinha to her again, the smell of her smoky skin strong in her nostrils. It was too terrible to be true but, knowing Angus, she had no doubt Arranyinha was telling the truth. The news could not have been worse. At least, that was what she thought . . .

'Yakarti gone crackaback!' said Arranyinha and held up three fingers.

Three children dead as well! Why on earth would he have shot three children?

Arranyinha motioned again to show Kate what happened.

As far as Kate could work out, they had heard a gunshot and the men picked up the children, not only to get them away from danger but because they thought that the white man would not shoot a man with a child. In this way they could protect themselves as well as the children. But Angus had no compunction. He had shot at them anyway and that was how the children had been killed.

Five men, two women, one of them old, one of them pregnant, and three children. It was a nightmare. Kate was surprised that Arranyinha had even come to tell her. She was amazed that they would trust her at all now. How could he have done this dreadful thing?

She asked if there was some way that she could help. Arranyinha shook her head. If she came near the blacks' camp now she would probably be speared. Arranyinha had only come to bring her the news and now she must go. It was hardly the time to ask about stopping the baby.

They hugged once more and went their separate ways.

Angus was already back at the homestead when Kate arrived.

'What have you been up to?' he asked her suspiciously when she came in.

'Minding my own business!' She was in no mood to be kind to Angus Campbell. He was a thorough scoundrel. But she couldn't mention where she had been or what she knew or she might place herself and the Yuras in greater danger.

'Don't speak to me like that!' he thundered back at her.

'You be hanged!' she said dismissively, turning her back on him to continue with her domestic tasks.

She felt him rather than heard him immediately behind her. The hairs on her neck rose and the next moment his arm was around her throat, holding her in a lock.

'You bitch,' he snarled. 'You're not so high

and mighty now. Don't look down yurr nose at me.'

Kate struggled to remove his arm but he held her in a vice-like grip. 'Let go of me, you animal!' she shouted.

'I get the last laugh,' he said and thumped her on the side of her head with his free hand.

Kate squirmed to get out of his grasp.

'You're a bastard, you'd stop at nothing, would you? If you were more of a man you'd not be hurting and killing women and children!' Her wretched temper! The words were out of her mouth before she realised it.

'What?' he thundered in her ear. 'What are you saying?' Both hands came to her throat.

'Nothing,' gasped Kate as she struggled ineffectually to prise his fingers from her throat.

'Tell me what you mean or I'll choke the living daylights out of you!' he roared.

Kate struggled, his hands tightening the grip around her neck. She didn't think he would kill her, he was just trying to frighten her. She could feel her face suffusing with blood and her own heartbeat began to pound in her ears.

'What did you mean?' he snarled.

Spots appeared before her eyes. She could not speak, his hands were crushing the air from her throat. She kicked back at his shins and clawed his hands but he would not let go. Another moment or two and she would surely lose consciousness. He must be serious. He was really going to kill her.

The derringer! She had the derringer on her! She slipped her hand through her pocket.

'I'll say the blacks did it! Good riddance to you. James won't mind now, I'm sure!' he grated.

Kate's fingers struggled to get a grip on the end of the butt. She could not reach it. She pretended to slump and her fingers reached the pistol. She grasped hold of it but it caught as she tried to pull it through the pocket. If she didn't fire soon it would be too late! Blood pounded in her head and blackness threatened to engulf her. She spun the chamber with her thumb, pointed the derringer away from her leg and pulled the trigger.

The explosion was deafening.

Angus let go of her, surprised by the gunshot, and she fell to the floor. He whirled around, looking to see who had fired the gun and Kate pulled the derringer through her charred and smoking pocket. Angus turned back to her to find he was looking down the barrel of her pistol. His eyes widened and it appeared to Kate that his red hair stood on end.

She held the pistol up in front of her, her hands shaking. 'That was just a warning,' she rasped, her throat sore. 'One step closer and I'll shoot you dead!'

'You wouldn't dare!' he said, but he advanced no further.

'I would dare. You had no compunction shooting down defenceless women and children and I'll have none with you! Yes, I know you did it and I'm not telling you how I know. One more time, Angus, one more attack on them, or me, and I will tell the police to lay charges against ye!'

'And I'll tell them about the stolen pistol!'

'It's not stolen. Rory gave it to me. He could see you for what you are. Now get out of here! Don't come back in until James returns or I will shoot you dead as soon as look at you.'

He strode out through the door and into the yard. She heard the hoofbeats as he rode his horse down the track away from the homestead.

What was she to do? The baby, the Yuras, and now this. Her own life was under threat. Her position at Wildowie had become more untenable every day. James did not want her here. She was not likely to see the Yuraartu again and she could not go on living at close quarters with Angus. He was dangerous and it seemed that he would stop at nothing to wreak his revenge on women and blacks.

If only she had not fallen pregnant!

If she left, James would dismiss both her and the child from his mind immediately. There would only be some hope for them if she stayed within arm's reach. She would not leave Wildowie. She would go to Craig and maybe, just maybe, James might change his mind when he missed her. Even if there was no chance for her, there might be a chance for the child. A chance of being recognised and acknowledged and the chance of a little help to get on in the world. The kind of help that Kate herself had prayed for and never received. It would be different for this child than it had ever been for her, she would make sure of that.

That evening she listened while Angus told James his version of what had happened that morning. Angus told James that he had been forced to defend himself because the blacks had attacked when he confronted them. It was terribly unfortunate that he had killed three of them in self-defence, he said. Angus's glance flicked to her every now and again, daring her to tell James what she knew.

Kate thought it would be better to keep Angus guessing about what she knew and how much. That way she had some small degree of power over him. If she told James it might all blow over.

'And Kate here came hurtling across the plain to see what hae befallen me,' Angus told him, looking at her as he said it.

James looked at Kate thoughtfully.

'Well, Angus, I do wish that you had consulted me before you took matters in your own hands. You know that I had no wish to stir up the blacks—'

'They needed to be taught a lesson!' Angus interrupted.

'That may be so,' James went on smoothly. 'Let us hope that you've done no more harm than good. You also took an unjustifiable risk. If you had been killed there would have been even more trouble, for then we would have had to punish them more. And, quite frankly, I cannot do without a good overseer!'

Angus said nothing. He shot a look of self-satisfaction in Kate's direction.

'Please do not take these matters into your hands again,' James continued. 'If the police were to find out, there would be hell to pay. Whatever your opinion of the blacks, the law would cry murder.'

'There is no evidence. Don't worry, I'm no fool. The bodies, their digging sticks, the spears, waddies—everything has been burnt.'

Kate was sickened by the conversation. The blacks were not considered as fellow humans at all. She wanted no further part in the discussion. She bid the men good night and walked a little awkwardly across the room towards the bedroom. The ride had left her stiff and sore, her inner thighs chafed. Sleep came slowly and dreams returned to haunt her again.

'Well, Kate,' James asked coldly, the next morning, 'what is it to be?'

Kate looked up at him, her face a little pinched from a restless night, but her resolve stronger than ever. As much as she feared that awful dream, it had served a purpose. It had reminded her of the harsh lessons of her past; of what it was like to try to survive with no family, to be without protection, to be utterly destitute and to have a child die the slow agonising death of starvation in her helpless arms.

This was not going to happen to her child. Never.

'I will not go to Craig,' her voice was soft but the tone was one of iron resolve. Nor would she consider for a moment longer that she might abort the child. Never again would a dead child be on her conscience.

'Then you may as well pack. I'll take you down to Clare. We'll leave tomorrow.'

'It's not that easy, James.'

'What do you mean?'

'I'll not go to Clare. I'll not go anywhere that will give you a chance to forget your own child. You have a duty. I will remain here long enough to see that your duty is done.'

'Don't be ridiculous. The child is your problem, you bedded with me willingly, knowing the risks. Anyway, you can't stay here if I have told you to go.'

'It will be hard for you to remove me forcibly. And if I'm to hang around here then you may as well be paying me and I may as well be your servant. I can live with that. But I'll not go anywhere else without a guarantee that you'll claim the baby as your own.'

James stood with his wide mouth slightly ajar. It was clear that no one had defied him in this way before. He had been the boss for so long.

'Ye see, James, you were born with a silver spoon in your mouth. Everything has been handed to you on a plate. Ye've grown up thinking that you owe nothing to nobody, that in this life you only have to suit yourself. But that has changed now. I am changing it. I'll not let you forget that this child is yours. You have no sense of loyalty, you have no sense of duty. Not now you don't, but you will have and I'll be the one to make sure that you learn it.'

James just looked at her, a puzzled frown on his face as if she was speaking a different language.

'So I'm not going to Clare. I'm not marrying that poor boy Craig. Your clever plan will come to naught. I'm stopping right here.'

James shook his head. He had never been one for confronting things head on. 'We shall see about that.'

'Indeed we shall.'

That night she sat sewing by the light of the candle at the table. James hovered around her as if unsure of what he should be doing next.

Finally she felt his hand on her shoulder and she turned her head to look at it—that smooth, slightly tanned hand with the sprinkling of golden hairs looked strange against the dark fabric of her gown.

'Kate?'

She tilted her head to look at him.

'Do you still think that I've done the wrong thing by you?' He drew her up from her seat.

'You could make it right, James, it would not take much on your part to do that.'

His hands slipped up to cup her face and he looked at her, silent for one moment. Then his face moved towards hers and he kissed her, as softly as the brush of a butterfly's wing.

She turned her face away. He could not treat her like he had and then expect that she would willingly give herself to him all over again. She was no longer as naive as she had been when he had first kissed her down by the River Broughton.

'Forget all of that for a moment. I do love you, you must know that. There has been this hiccup in our relationship, but that is all it has to be. Let us forget our differences and let things go on like they were before. I do care for you, Kate, and you care for me.'

He turned her face back to his and his lips came down over hers again, not softly this time, but passionately. He did not let go his hold on her face until he felt her soften and weaken. Until she returned with equal fervour the passion of his kiss.

As she responded to him, his hands loosened their hold and moved down her throat, over her collarbone, one fondling her breast, the other slipping around her hips to pull her up hard against him. She could feel his arousal against her. He still wanted her and she, in return, wanted him. She wanted his love, she ached for that blissful release of the tension simmering between them. She wanted it to be all right again. Her nipples tingled at his touch, the pathways of sensation which ran from her breasts, down her body and between her legs, came alive, a sensation of heat flooding through her.

She arched herself against him. Yes, this would be the easy way out. To let him love her, to love him in response, to let their desire wash away the differences between them, to submerge for a short time the reality of the conflict.

But it wouldn't work like that. He was deluding himself and deluding her in the process. Their child was there, between them, living and growing. She must never let him forget it.

She placed her hand on his chest and pushed her throbbing body away from his.

'James, I cannot go on like this.'

'Kate, it will be all right, we'll find some way out of this tangle. There must be some way of getting rid of the baby.'

'No, I'll not get rid of the baby. I've lost too much family already. No more, James. There'll be no more children dying if I can help it.'

'Well, I still think we might be crossing bridges before we get to them. Let us deal with the baby if and when it is born. In the meantime, why not continue on as we were?' He reached for her again.

'No, we can no longer do that. It is not the same as it was before. It can never be the same as that. You talked about us building the best station in the Far North, another Bungaree. We were in it together, you said. And now I know that we're not in it together. We never will be, unless you change your mind. If you want to change that

241

fact, if you want to claim me and the child as your own, then we can talk about continuing on as we were. Promises aren't good enough. It's deeds that count. They are my conditions.'

'You act as if you are the one who makes the rules here!'

'On this matter, I am. You might be the boss of Wildowie Station, you are the boss of the shepherds, you are the boss of me as a servant. But that is where your authority ends. You do not own my body and until you claim this child as your own then you have no authority over him either.'

'We'll see about that.'

'You can see all you like, but I will look after myself. I've learnt that you don't have my interests at heart and you cannot deny it.'

James looked at her, utterly at a loss. Kate could see the thoughts written plainly on his face. How had she claimed so much power for herself? A lowly servant, an Irish one at that! How dare she set the conditions by which he could make love to her? Who was she to give the orders? But he couldn't convince her that he had her interests at heart. There was no way he could do that when what he wanted was to get rid of her child.

Kate left her sewing on the table and went into their bedroom. She pulled her clothes from the wardrobe, laid them over one arm and marched down the short hallway towards the guest room.

'What are you doing?'

'Moving my things into the guest room,' she replied, without turning her head.

Kate looked forward to the following January when the baby would be born. Surely, when James saw the child, things would be different. His feelings as a father would undoubtedly be stirred and he would not be able to withhold his love and support.

Kate had to hold these hopes, for nothing in James's approach indicated that he cared at all about what would happen to the child. He had no interest in the health of Kate and the child growing within her.

He still had interest in her body, though—she could feel his eyes upon her as she moved about the house. His eyes often drifted to her breasts, no doubt noticing their size as they swelled in preparation for feeding the baby. He had approached her to move back into his bedroom many times and she had been steadfast in her refusal.

She would not let him use her like that again, as much as she craved for loving arms around her, for someone close enough to hold at bay her loneliness at Wildowie. No, she would not give in to James. She had her child to think of now. If she lost the upper hand there would be no hope. Her son—for she had always imagined the child to be a boy—would never claim his rightful heritage.

She had to stay close enough to James to maintain the pressure of the child's claim for paternity, but not so close that James would take her presence as his mistress for granted. It was a fine line that she had to walk and she often felt dangerously close to falling to one side or the other.

As much as James and Angus would now allow, she kept a close eye on the workings of the station. One day, she vowed to herself, one day she would be mistress of a station. One day, if all went well, her child would inherit Wildowie from James and at that time she, too, would need to know just what it took to run a station.

If it wasn't for Angus she could have kept a much closer eye on things, but it was Angus who deliberately excluded her from his conversations with James about the management of Wildowie. For Angus, the pregnancy had relegated Kate to her rightful place. The place of a lowly female servant who had no hold on the boss at all. He took great pleasure in emphasising Kate's lack of status.

Kate herself took great pleasure in planning her revenge on Angus, fantasising about her role as mistress of Wildowie, imagining that her first step would be to sack him, or better still, to demote him to shepherd! That would teach that woman-hating devil a thing or two!

Kate found that as the months rolled on, it was harder to get through the day. The hard physical work of washing and cooking some-times sapped all her energy. The shearing, in September, was a particularly busy time and everyone worked from dawn to dusk and, when needed, throughout the night.

It was the Yuraartu who were Kate's main support throughout her pregnancy, for there were no white women from whom she could get advice. They seemed to accept that she had played no part in the massacre and slowly her relationship with them was re-established. They collected herbs and berries for her when, at different times, she felt the ill-effects of pregnancy. They gave her advice on what she should and shouldn't do. Some of the advice seemed sensible, and she took it seriously. She must never eat the meat of the mandya, or the euro as it was known to the settlers, for it was too strong for a baby. Mandya were the kangaroo-like creatures that roamed the rocky ledges high above the valley where the hut stood. Nor should she eat the tail of the urdlu, which the Udnyu called kangaroo. The urdlu tail would cause the baby to be bound up inside her and the birth would become difficult.

For Kate it was no trouble to avoid the euro or the kangaroo tail as their diet consisted of mutton and damper, day in, day out. And for someone who had survived the potato famine, this was no hardship. The guarantee of three square meals a day was a source of great security, even if it was monotonous.

That kind of advice she was prepared to follow, but other bits of advice were harder to believe. They warned her particularly that she must never go out in a thunderstorm as the soul of the baby would then be out in the storm too. The lightning and thunder would harm the baby as well as the pregnant mother. Nor were women to make a noise during the storm, as that would cause the storm to become worse. Only the men had the power to deal with storms. They could make them or break them. Women, however, were powerless in that regard.

Now that she no longer had the intimate company of James she sought the Yuraartu more often. The more time she spent with them, the more she was able to understand how they felt about the settlement of whites. In fact, settlement was not the term that they used. Invasion was the way they described it. It was a shock to Kate that the Yuras regarded the whites as having invaded, for she had never considered it that way before.

She began to understand the reason for the petty pilfering that went on. As Harold had once explained to her, the game that the Yuras had once hunted was now more scarce and harder to hunt. The sheep were not part of the Dreaming, the system of religious beliefs that tied together the Yuras, the land and all the animals and plants that it contained. With no significance in the Dreaming, sheep were not considered sacred and there were no sanctions involved in who could kill them or how they could be killed, cooked or eaten. They did not run away from the hunters, but stood still, waiting to be killed. It was Yura land, and anything that had lived there, from time immemorial, had been there for the Yuras to use. They had no concept of property, no idea that the sheep belonged exclusively to the white men. The whole thing was beyond their comprehension. What they had, they shared, it was as simple as that. They shared the land and all it contained with the white man. Why did the white men not share too?

It reminded Kate of Ireland in so many ways. The English had invaded Ireland, seizing the land and renting it back to the Irish. When the tenants could not pay, they were evicted. The land that had been theirs was no longer theirs. Anything taken from the land by the peasants was considered poached or stolen. Anyone caught poaching, no matter what the reason, was convicted. Many had been transported to Australia for the crime of feeding their families! There were many parallels. She had always been one for championing the underdog. Slowly and surely she was beginning to see things through the eyes of the Yuras.

What she saw was not pretty.

She was glad that she had kept her meetings with the Yuras a secret from James and Angus. They both hated the blacks in their own ways. James was simply arrogant about them. He bore them no personal ill will, as long as they did not have an impact on the profitability of Wildowie. To him, they were of no value and encouraging them onto the property was simply asking for trouble of one kind or another. The less that he had to do with them the better. For the most part they were simply beneath his notice.

Angus, however, was malicious in his attitude towards them. If he had been allowed to hunt them down and kill them one by one and to rid Wildowie of them forever, he would have. To Angus, blacks were the only things lower than women in the social order.

Kate knew that many of the men in the bush resorted to black velvet in the absence of white women. There was proof of it here at Wildowie, even though James had ordered them to stay well clear of the blacks. The women had sought Kate's help in treating diseases that they had never seen before. Diseases that Kate had seen before, amongst the women in the workhouse— the ones who had sold their bodies for favours in the desperate struggle to keep one step ahead of starvation.

But she did not know how to treat these diseases either. She could only warn the women to stay well away from the white men. She watched as these diseases, like so many others, spread quickly through the Yuras.

Kate also saw another side to the Yuras. They were not simply the innocent victims at the hands of the whites. They, too, contributed to the silent war that raged throughout the Far

North. Their own culture was harsh and unjust in so many ways. She saw young girls, many years younger than herself, married against their will to old men. She saw women who had been punished brutally and beaten senseless by thick waddies for minor transgressions and men who had erred and had been speared through the leg as a consequence. These were almost everyday occurrences. The whites had no monopoly on violence or on rough justice.

The initiation scars they bore demonstrated the level of blood-letting that was integral to their culture. As far as Kate was concerned, the circumcision of ten-year-old boys was torture.

They were neither gentle nor innocent, but they were certainly hard done by. They were slowly but surely being driven off the land that they loved and it broke Kate's heart to see the effect it had on the women whom she had come to consider as friends. Adnyini, Warrikanha and others were gone. The remainder were saddened and defeated, as if they now knew that nothing would turn back the terrible tide of white settlers.

Life at Wildowie did not change very much as Kate's pregnancy developed. She was still expected to do the work that she had always done. Gerald and Ned both gave her a hand with the heavy tasks if they saw that she was struggling. James, for the most part, shut his eyes to her condition. Angus gloated on her downfall and did nothing to help.

'What are you going to do when your time comes?' James asked her as she stood stretching her back, once again.

Kate was clearing up after dinner. 'That I don't know, for there's not a white woman for miles, is there?'

'Maybe as your time comes closer we should send you down to Clare. There is a lying-in home there.'

Kate looked up at him sharply. Was he trying to get rid of her again? Was it yet another ploy to help him evade any responsibility he had? Would he take her down to Clare and leave her there? It was not worth the risk.

'I'd rather not go down there.'

'Well I think you should. There is no one here who could help you. You could get into difficulty.'

'It's no more complicated than the lambing. I'll be fine.'

James looked at her cynically. 'Then if you won't go, I'll have to get someone to come up here to help you. I'll see Mrs Hughes when I'm on my way south, she might know of someone.'

'That would be better,' she replied, and she continued washing the dinner dishes.

'You do know that I'll never claim the child as mine, don't you?'

They were words that Kate just did not want to hear. She did not reply.

'Kate, are you listening to me?'

She did not reply, she did not want to

acknowledge what he said in any way. She heard him rise from his seat and come to stand behind her. His hands came down gently on her shoulders and he turned her around to look at him. She kept her eyes lowered and he placed his hand under her chin, to tilt her face up so that she would look at him.

James stared at her. At this stage of her pregnancy she was positively blooming and she knew it. Her cheeks had a soft rosy tint, her hair shone black like the wing of a crow and her eyes sparkled bright and dark. Her breasts were straining against the fabric of her gown.

She could see that he wanted to kiss her. It was in his eyes. They had lost that cool hard look they had taken on of late. The grey became the warm grey of ash and his lips softened.

But she wouldn't let him kiss her. That would be foolish. She looked down again.

'Kate, you must understand something,' he began softly. 'You walked into this with your eyes open. You were willing. You knew what the risks were and you took them. I can never claim the child as mine. I would be the laughing stock of South Australia, never mind the shame I would bring upon my own family. You've got to understand that. I have no choice. If the child stays here, he will be disadvantaged. Everyone will know that he is a bastard. You would be better off going somewhere else and saying that your husband has died.'

'He is your child, I'll not let you be forgetting

him. He has a right, at the very least, to your support, and so do I. This will be his station one day. He should grow up here, learn how to run the place.'

'Don't be ridiculous!'

She shrugged her shoulders and his hands left them and fell to his sides. He looked into her eyes.

'Kate, all of this has turned your brain. You're no longer rational.'

'It is no surprise. You're not treating me with the respect that I deserve, are you now?'

James sighed and shook his head as if he would no longer try to reason with her. He stalked outside.

He had only his own interests at heart, there was no doubt about that. But he was not confrontative and he was not cruel. He would not force her to go against her will. He was too gentle to do that.

The next day Kate received a letter from Brigid.

> *18th day of September 1850*
>
> *My Dear Kate*
>
> *I hope you are well and happy. I am sorry, it has taken me so long to write but you know how it is that time slips away so quickly. I was waiting for some good news before I set pen to paper. Finally I do have some good news for you.*
>
> *Two weeks ago I left the Orphans Depot*

*to take up a position as nanny to a dear lit-
tle baby. My master and mistress, Mr and
Mrs Jensen, are most kind, although they
are not able to pay me very much. I get five
shillings a week as well as my board and
food. It is not as much as you get, but I
guess I did not have to travel out to the
bush. I am close to town, here in North
Adelaide. Five shillings a week is better
than the nothing I got at the Depot.*

*So I will save steadily and surely get
ahead.*

*How are you going up there with your
rich and handsome squatter? Well, I hope.
Have you saved enough to buy your first
station? . . .*

Kate smiled at Brigid's light-hearted comments.
Little did she realise how far from the truth they
were.

*. . . I have met the gardener here who is
very nice and also a bit sweet on me, I'm
thinking. His name is Jonas. If all goes well
we can put our savings together and one
day buy our home. But more on that in the
next letter since it is early days yet. He
might not be a squatter but he is very
sweet.*

*You no doubt will be making your way
in the world very fast but I will get there
slowly and surely like the tortoise.*

> *Please write back soon. God bless you.*
> *Your loving friend,*
> *Brigid.*

What could Kate write in reply?

Two days later James left Wildowie to go south. He was going to Adelaide to bring up another mob of sheep before the weather became too hot and the water dried up. If he had left it any later there may not have been enough surface water to water the sheep along the way.

Kate stared along the valley, watching the puffs of dust arise from his horse's hooves as he left. In one way she was relieved that he had gone, for if she had capitulated she would have been dumped at Clare on the way. But in another way, she was sad. She had been left there all alone again, with only Angus and the shepherds for company.

It was early November 1850. If Kate had worked it out correctly then the baby was due some time in January. Eight weeks away. James would bring a midwife of some description back with him. That was the plan. She hoped that he could get back in time.

Chapter

Eight

Angus's animosity towards her became more obvious as each day passed. It seemed as if he wanted to make life uncomfortable for her—so uncomfortable that she would leave. She almost wondered if it was part of a plan hatched by the two men. These days her tolerance was low and it was all she could do to put up with him. Until James returned she was at his mercy and he wasn't going to forget it.

'Wash my clothes today,' he ordered her one morning before he left to take rations out to Craig and Robert.

'I did the washing yesterday,' she objected. 'They will have to wait for the next washday now.'

Carting and boiling the water was heavy work, especially in the heat. It was now December, she was big with child and water was already scarce. The landscape was dry, dusty and colourless. Near the homestead the creek was now little more than a series of waterholes. If she wanted clear clean water for washing she would have to walk a good way to get it. And if the clothes were not clean enough Angus would tell her to wash them again. That was what he had done last week.

'Do as yurr told, lassie!' he snapped back at her, 'and while yurr at it, there are fleas in here again, tek out everything and treat the floor like you did the last time.'

That meant another load of boiling water and she had not noticed any fleas at all.

'I've got the soap and candles to do today,' Kate replied, 'I'll do the floors and the washing tomorrow.'

'Don't talk back to me! I'm the overseer, and don't you forget it!' He cuffed her on the ear as he passed her to go outside.

Kate bit her tongue and pressed her lips together. Her ear was smarting. But it was not the time to stand her ground. She could never afford to anger Angus when she was alone with him.

She went to the door and watched him saddle up.

He saw her watching him and turned back to her. 'If you hae the time to stop and watch then you obviously don't hae enough work to do.'

She turned back inside wordlessly and went on with the unending work. Later she left Angus's clean, dry trousers and shirt on the table while she prepared dinner for the three men. The soap and candles would have to be done tomorrow.

At sunset they came in for their dinner. Kate was already preparing food for Ned to take with him for the following day's lunch and had not yet returned the trousers and shirt to Angus's room.

'Och!' she heard Angus say.

She turned around to see that the clothes had been knocked off the table and onto the floor. It immediately entered her mind that it might not have been an accident.

'Arrah,' she exclaimed, her blue eyes rolling, 'they're the clean ones I did for you! Watch out or they'll be dirty again.' Since he was making no moves to retrieve them, she walked over from the hearth to pick them up herself.

Angus moved to get out of her way and as he did so he trod carelessly on the shirt.

'Oh! Now there's mud on them,' she scolded. The floor was still a little soft from the boiling water poured on it to get rid of the fleas. She passed them to Angus, saying 'Put them away before they get any dirtier.'

'Nae, I canna wear the shirt, it's too dirty. You'll have to wash it again tomorrow. Sorry,' he said but his tone inferred that he was not the least bit sorry at all. He handed it back to her.

She just stood and looked at him, measuring his mood and deciding whether to make a stand. They were not on their own now.

'If you cart up some water for me I'd be happy to,' she said. 'Otherwise I'm only carting water for the washing of the clothes once each week.'

'You were hired to do the job, do it yourself!' he said, his tone derisive.

Ned clicked his tongue. 'That's no way to talk to Miss Kate!'

'It is about time she remembered she is the servant, not the mistress here,' Angus scowled at all of them, daring them to challenge him.

Ned shrugged his shoulders and then turned to Kate and said, 'You are only a wee lass and you shouldn't be carrying heavy things in your condition. I'll bring up the water for you in the morning.'

He went back to filling his pipe as if there was no more to be said.

'If Kate canna do the work then she shouldn't be here,' Angus insisted. 'James should hae realised that a bog-Irish whore canna look after a homestead. If she canna do the work then she'll be turned off.'

Kate fetched the stewpot from the fire and began to serve dinner. Ned winked at her and Gerald patted her silently on the arm, but no one said a word to Angus. They had his measure and were on Kate's side, but it was not worth an argument.

The next day, tired of the company of Angus and the shepherds, Kate was longing to see the black women again. She hadn't seen Arranyinha or any of the black women since James had left a month ago. It seemed that they moved around with the changing seasons. Arranyinha had described journeys that took them many days. They would walk from one cowie, or waterhole, to another. Many of those cowies were kept secret from the whites. Not even Kate had been entrusted with knowledge of their whereabouts. They had told Kate that they were moving to the 'big-one-cowie', or the big waterhole, or the 'big-one-cowie walk', by which they meant flowing water. They never once told her the direction they would take. They were no fools. Once the white men knew of their water they would take the sheep there and that would be the end of it for the Yuras.

Kate's reverie was interrupted as Angus came crashing through the door.

'Get the gun loaded, Kate!' he called.

Kate dashed to get the rifle and some ammunition from under the bed where it was hidden. She was not going to bring out her own pistol. She always kept that hidden under her skirt.

'What's happening?' she called out as she began to load it.

He was already loading his own gun.

'Blacks! By the creek!' was all he said but his tone spoke the rest for him. He hated the blacks even more than he hated women.

'What have they done this time?'

'Who knows what the thieving beggars have been up to,' he said, fumbling as he loaded his own gun.

'You're not going to shoot them?'

This time there had been no provocation, not even one sheep stolen! She held the gun that she had loaded firmly against her with both hands. She did not want Angus to take it. With two guns loaded he would be able to shoot twice as many Yuras.

He grabbed the gun and in no time had wrestled it from her hands. He raced outside with Kate following him.

'Angus, don't shoot them. James will be furious.'

He ignored her as he mounted the horse.

'I'll tell him myself, not just about this time but the last time as well!' She was desperate to stop him.

'Go right ahead. He won't believe you,' he tried to bluff her. 'Yurr days are numbered here anywae. There's plenty more of yurr sort but he canna afford to lose his overseer!' He flicked the reins to go but Kate caught hold of the bridle.

'Angus, don't do it! They've done no harm, have they?' She was almost pulled along as the horse reared and plunged, unsure of whether to obey her restraining hand or the pressure of the spurs.

'Get out of my way!' he roared, flicking the whip lightly across her shoulders and digging his spurs into the horse at the same time. She let go as the horse plunged forward.

She jumped backwards, out of the way of the frightened horse. Angus galloped off in the direction he had seen the Yuras. It was the direction she usually took to get to the secret meeting place. Had he come across them there by accident? Had they been waiting there for her? If he killed them it would be her fault!

What was she to do now? She had to warn the Yuras. The last time Angus had gone on a reprisal raid, men, women and children had been killed. Adnyini and Warrikanha had been shot in cold blood. Who would he murder this time?

She started to run after him. Panic had set in and she was not thinking clearly. Her gait was ungainly since she carried so much extra weight. God! She would never get there fast enough! She decided against it and slid to a halt, the extra weight of the baby on her body threatening to overbalance her. She would have to go on horseback.

She raced as fast as she could back to the yard that held the horses. She climbed up onto the top rail and whistled the horse she had learnt to ride. He trotted over obediently and with her heart in her mouth, she leapt across onto his bare back. There were no horses saddled and there was not a moment to lose. She hung on hard, her fingers knitted tightly into his mane and her knees close in. She leant forward and slipped the gate undone.

She didn't stop to close it behind her. Too bad if the rest of the horses escaped! She dug her heels into his belly and took off towards the meeting place further downstream.

She felt her bottom slip and slide over the horse's back as he moved.

'God keep the babe safe!' she whispered, conscious that this was a risky ride. She had never ridden bareback and this was not the best time to try it. She leant low, her belly hard up against the shoulders of the horse, avoiding the branches which might otherwise knock her to the ground. Her heart was hammering. Was there any chance she could catch up with Angus before he shot them?

What irony! The last time she had done this, it had been to help Angus. This time it was to hinder him and to help the Yuras!

She was almost there. The place where they met. The sound of a gun discharging rent the air.

'Oh no!' The sound hit her like a physical pain as she imagined Angus's target.

Another discharge!

Through a belt of dense bush and she would be there.

She pulled up the horse in a cloud of dust and slipped to the ground. She pulled her derringer from her pocket and dashed through the narrow path that led through the bushes. She could hear the sounds of terror as she approached.

A gun discharged once more as she emerged onto the other side.

The once-peaceful glade was a scene of mayhem.

It was a perfect place for a planned ambush, though Angus had surely come upon it by accident. The glade was surrounded, on this side by the patch of thick bush, to the left by a steep hillside and to the right by tall outcrops of rock. Straight ahead, forming the backdrop, was the wall of a shallow gorge.

It was like a small enclosure. Inside, black men, women and children ran in panic, trying to escape the aim of Angus Campbell's gun. Some were scrabbling up the side of the hill, children screaming in their arms. Some were climbing over the rocks, trying to get over the top and into the shelter the rocks would provide. Others were at the gorge wall, cowering in terror or lying over the bodies of their children in a pitiful attempt to protect them.

This side provided the escape route but they would have to run straight into Angus's gun to get out. Angus was there, his back to her, aiming his gun at the people against the gorge wall.

She rolled the chamber of the pistol past the blank and brought the pistol up, aiming it at his back.

'Angus! Drop that rifle or I'll shoot!'

He whirled around to face her, his gun still ready to fire.

She realised her mistake. In her panic to protect the Yuras she had failed to get cover before alerting him.

She held her gun steady. 'Drop it, I said!'

'My perfect chance,' he snarled, taking aim as if there were no gun in her hand. 'You and the blacks in the one day.'

He took a step towards her and she watched in horror as his finger tightened on the trigger. This was it. Her, the baby, the blacks. It was the end for all of them. She must fire now!

At that moment a spear sliced through the air by the side of his head and he ducked in defence, reacting without thinking.

It gave Kate the moment she needed. The moment it took to decide to shoot.

She pulled the trigger. The charge exploded. There was the acrid smell of gunpowder, a puff of smoke and Angus crumpled in front of her eyes.

A spear thudded into his back, then another. The Yuras were not taking chances.

She lowered the gun slowly, shock taking over where panic had left off. She had killed Angus Campbell!

She swallowed and looked again. He was not moving. She spun the chamber again and walked towards him, the gun poised ready to fire. She would not be taking second chances either.

She kicked him tentatively, then with more strength. There was no response. He was face down with the spears protruding from his back. She squatted down, pushing him onto his side to feel for his heart.

But there was no need.

Where his heart had once been there was now a gaping hole in his shirt, a hole with blood still pumping from it.

She had shot him in the heart. He could not have survived a shot like that.

Kate started to feel sick, the world began to spin, strange pricks of light appeared before her eyes.

She fainted.

She woke to the sound of groaning. The groaning, she realised, was her own. She opened her eyes to the harsh daylight, the sun overhead. She was hot beneath her gown and she was soaked in perspiration. What the hell was she doing lying out in the sun? Why was she here? What was going on?

She drew a total blank.

She placed her hands against the coarse sand and pushed herself to sit upright. The sight of Angus, lying on his side in the sand, flies crawling over the drying blood brought it all back with a hideous impact. She had killed Angus.

She remembered now. He had been shooting the Yuras in cold blood. She tried to stop him and he had turned on her. She had to shoot him. She had to. It was her and the Yuras, or it was him.

She must have fainted, for the blood on Angus was no longer free-flowing. The number of flies attested to the passing of time. The Yuras had fled, taking their wounded with them. They had not stopped to help her, but who could blame them?

She suddenly felt very sick. She fell forward onto her knees and vomited into the sand. Eight months pregnant and she had committed murder.

'Jaysus and Mary!' What was she going to do now?

Slowly, testing the strength of her legs, she stood up. She staggered over to a pool where water still trickled through rocks and she washed her face, neck and hands.

She must try to think clearly, to overcome the panic rising within her.

What was she going to do?

With that gaping gunshot wound it would be obvious that he had not been killed by the blacks. The blacks did not have guns. They would not even know how to use one. No one, no one at all, would sympathise with her motive for killing him. It would be considered the most heinous of crimes—to kill a fellow white man to save the life of a handful of treacherous blacks. She'd be hung, drawn and quartered!

Jesus, what had she done?

No one who knew of the antagonism between her and Angus would believe it was an accident. She had no choice, she could not give herself up. There was no way that she would have this baby behind bars. She would have to run and hide, quickly. She would have to get out of the Far North as fast as she could. They would track her mercilessly.

Eight months pregnant and on the run from the law!

She had to think this through clearly. She

splashed her face again. Why wasn't her brain working properly? Normally she kept her head in a crisis. She would have to run, but not empty-handed. She would go back to the homestead. Now, while no one else was around. Pack a few things and flee into the cover of the bush. Make a good start before Angus was discovered.

She got up and started to run. There was not much time before Ned would return with the flock and Gerald came in for dinner. She crashed through the bush, back to the horse. How could she mount him without a fence to climb? She whistled the horse to follow her as she set off, looking for a fallen log or a stump. Eventually she found what she was looking for, scrambled onto his back and made for the homestead as fast as she could manage.

She looked around before coming up close to the homestead. All was quiet.

She slipped off the horse and ran inside.

God, she would have to be quick. What would she need? Not too much, it would weigh her down. She grabbed a flour bag. Two bottles of water, cold chops left over from the last meal, the damper that she had baked that morning. A tinderbox. A knife.

Clothes. Her hat, the sun was fierce. A spare gown. Her trousers, as yet never worn, an old shirt of James's to wear with them. That would have to be it.

Anything else? Ammunition for her pistol.

Her heart was beating fast. Any moment Gerald could walk in on her. Anything else?

A blanket. Cold nights.

She threw the blanket onto the floor and placed everything onto it. Then she rolled it up, tied the ends with a long piece of twine and slung the swag over her shoulder.

Now, to take a horse or not?

No, it was not hers. She would not add stealing to the list of her crimes, and horse-stealing was a serious crime. Besides, they would track her by the hoof prints. She could not afford that, despite the advantage that the horse would give.

She opened the door just a fraction and peered outside. No one in sight.

She dived for the cover of the bush and began to run as fast as her skirt and her condition would allow.

Deep into the bush she went. They would come after her, she knew that they would, so she could not take the track. She would have to move through the scrub, keeping close to the track so that she knew where she was going, but out of sight of her pursuers.

Then she remembered Brigid's letter. Rory was coming up to see her. Damn! How she wished that he had arrived before she had shot Angus! If Rory had been there he would have protected her from Angus. None of this would have happened. Maybe she could still intercept him on his way to Wildowie.

No, it was highly unlikely that she would see

him. It was better to keep out of sight of her pursuers. She didn't stop, she ran, then walked when she was too tired to keep running, putting as many miles as she could between herself and the homestead. Branches whipped across her face and tore at her clothes. She did not look behind, for they could not be that close behind her. They may not even find Angus until tomorrow.

Darkness slowly settled over the land. Kate did not light a fire. She could not afford to, in case they were already on the lookout for her. She stopped under a tree. Sitting on a fallen log, she ate one of the cold chops and a hunk of damper. This food was going to have to last her for some time.

It was then that she began to realise how ill thought-out her flight had been. It was the beginning of summer and she was in no state to run fast for a long period of time! She had walked almost the whole way to Wildowie and she had worked like a slave ever since, so she was fit. But she was so cumbersome!

She had only two small containers for water and that would hardly be enough now, when the rains were still a long way off. She should have brought more food. Even if she ate sparingly this food could last for only a day or two. She could shoot animals with her pistol but the sound would alert anyone within cooee. As she thought of what else she should have brought with her, the moon, nearly full, rose through the trees, bathing the landscape in strong silver light. She got up. The moonlight was a blessing. She could move in the cool of the night.

It was just before dawn when Kate dropped down onto the ground near a small, sluggish creek to rest. She found a little green moss, which she used to strain the putrid water. It was better than going thirsty. She would rest here for an hour or two, take another drink, refill her bottles and take off again.

It was in this way that she continued through the next day and the next night. Then her food and her water were gone.

She would have to survive on what the land could provide. Kate began to search for the sources of food and water that the Yuraartu had shown her. At breakfast time she pulled the long, narrow leaves from the spiny ata and nibbled on the soft ends that had been buried in the plant. Ata was the name that the Yuras used for yacca. Some settlers called it blackboy.

In the middle of the day she dug into the roots of a needlebush, using a sharp-edged stone, and sucked the moisture retained inside. As she walked her eyes combed the bush for other sources of food. The more she looked the more she began to notice. There was pigface, or arkala, as the Yuras called it. And there were the telltale signs on the river red gums that they contained the grubs that could be eaten raw or cooked on the fire. She was not desperate enough to eat those; not yet anyway.

It was when she was struggling to reach the upper branches of a small minga tree that she first got the uncanny feeling that someone was watching her. She looked around over both shoulders and then stayed absolutely still. There were no sounds or unusual movements. She shrugged her shoulders. She must be imagining things. She pulled the lump of gum that was called minga nguri from the tree. She sat down and ate it slowly. It was tasteless and not unpleasant but not the sort of thing that she could wolf down.

Wildowie had been a long and disastrous chapter in her life, she thought, as she chewed. The baby, James, Angus—all of it had been wrong, all of it had ended in disaster. She would never see Wildowie again. Even if they survived, her child would never know his father. He would never get to claim his heritage.

She had not stopped to think about Angus since the moment the gun had discharged. Even now she had to force herself to think about what she had done. Flashes of the scene flitted through her mind: his hand tightening on the trigger, the spear streaking past, the sound of her pistol firing, the smell of the smoke, the way he dropped like a stone.

The congealed blood, crawling with flies.

Would God ever forgive her for this? She would have prayed for her soul but her rosary, like everything else, was back at the homestead. When she had time she would pray but, right now, she must think about other things, she must fight to survive.

She couldn't have chosen a worse time to leave than at the beginning of the long, hot, dry summer. She hadn't found water since this morning. The moisture from the roots had wet her mouth but had not quenched her thirst. Walking through the heat of the day required a bottle full of water every hour. Her bottle had been empty since an hour or two after dawn. She hoped that by nightfall she would find a waterhole or a creek that hadn't yet dried up. She had not crossed the track since last night so she wasn't entirely sure where she was. As long as the sun was at her back, she was heading south. That was all that mattered. As long as she was heading south she was putting distance between herself and Wildowie.

She could see a line of tall river red gums ahead. They signalled the presence of a watercourse. She hoped that it would contain water, no matter how stagnant, no matter how muddy. By late afternoon she was there.

It was bone dry.

The rocks and boulders that covered the watercourse were baked hot in the sun. Far from being a cool haven, it was a long oven of radiating rocks. Her head had started to throb from dehydration. She peered through the shimmering heat waves in the hope that she would see a place that might hold water. It looked as though she was surrounded by cool wide lakes in every direction. The more she tried to focus on them the more they shifted. It was no use dashing off to dip her hot body into them, for they didn't really exist. She knew that they must be mirages. She would rest for a while and then search the creek bed in both directions.

In the cool of the late afternoon she walked along the creek. There was not one small pool of water anywhere. She would not even have to fight the wrigglers and tadpoles for her right to a stagnant pond this time. She sat down, dispirited and scared. She should go on, now the heat of the day was over, but she was too hot, too dry, too thirsty. She did not even look up in appreciation of the sunset as the clouds blushed pink and scarlet above their gilded rims.

A solitary dismal crow mocked her from the top branches of a dead gum, stark against the mauve sky. Kate began to feel desperate. She got up again, conscious that the longer she was immobilised, the less chance she would have of going on. Her tongue was starting to swell in her mouth.

She cursed herself for a fool. It might have been better to wait at Wildowie to be taken south by the police rather than to have tried to escape, only to perish in the bush. When she had walked up to Wildowie it had been late spring and a far cry from December and no rains. It was months since they had received a single drop. If only she could get water then she might make it to the next station.

Then Kate shook her head. No! A pregnant woman, on her own, stumbling through the bush to get help at a station would cause an uproar, even if they hadn't yet heard of the murder of Angus Campbell. It was a last resort, that was all. And it looked like she might not even manage that.

She thought hard, trying to remember the lessons that the Yuraartu had taught her about bush survival. There was always water, they said, you just have to know where to look. They had talked about digging in creek beds. She would try that.

She found an outside section of a bend that was not covered in rocks and boulders. With her hands, she began to dig through the coarse sand. The rocks were hiding underneath. She dug the sand from around them and then prised them up with her hands, her fingernails breaking and her fingers bleeding. The sand underneath was damp. She prayed that the hole would fill with water overnight. Meanwhile she lay with her head and hands in the hole, trying to soak the cool dampness in through her skin.

At first light Kate awoke to the noisy commotion of birds. But she did not greet the day with joy. Her mouth dry and her eyes gritty, her first thought was water. During the night she had pulled the top half of her body from the hole and curled up on the soft coarse sand, exhausted from her frantic flight from Wildowie. It was four days since she had left. Four days of panicked escape, of hardly stopping to sleep, eat or drink.

She peered anxiously into the hole. There was nothing there. The taste of disappointment was bitter in her mouth. She was in trouble. The baby too. It would be impossible to walk another day in the hot sun. She would have to stay where she was until nightfall and try to find water then. She dug the hole deeper still and, as she had heard that the early explorers had done, she sat right down in it to absorb any cool moisture that might be present.

She dozed. It was a strange kind of sleep that she had no control over, as if she were slipping in and out of consciousness. When she slept she had weird dreams of drinking, running creeks and deep waterholes. When she woke it was to see the mirages floating across the plain beyond the dry watercourse.

'When the sun goes down,' she told herself. 'When the sun goes down, I will get up and look for water.'

The sound of moaning woke her up. She realised the unnatural noise was coming from herself. God, her head ached so fiercely! Maybe she could find more of the trees that were suitable for root tapping, or some she-oaks with the young green cones that she could chew to allay the feeling of thirst. But not right now, it was too hard to get up. Her tongue was swollen in her mouth and her muscles twitched and flicked.

She was dreaming. There were voices, quiet at first, and then louder. They were shouting to her in a strange language. She struggled to understand their words but her head was too dizzy, too fuzzy, too slow.

Slowly she opened her eyes and started with surprise. There were two young Yuras, their spears poised over their shoulders, ready to throw. They were only a few feet from her.

'Nunga!' she croaked, her greeting automatic.

They both stepped backwards, puzzled by her use of their language.

'Nunga!' she greeted them again. It was only a croak that emitted from her mouth.

The boys made threatening gestures with their spears. Their eyes were round and full of fear, the whites showing starkly against their black skin.

Kate felt her head begin to spin once more and the light seemed to fade from before her eyes.

'Awi, awi,' she muttered as she lost consciousness. Water, water.

Her eyes opened again. It was late afternoon. The boys were gone. Her only hope of help had disappeared with them. They had not understood her. They probably thought that she was someone from the spirit world. She had heard that it was something that the blacks often thought when first seeing white people. Or maybe she was the one who had been seeing spirits. Maybe there had been no one there at all. Was she hallucinating? Her thoughts were so confused, she knew not which things were dreams and which were real.

She thought of James. If only James had returned, all this would have been unnecessary. She tried to picture James but it was Rory's swarthy, handsome face that rose up before her eyes.

Rory grinning, Rory telling yarns, Rory teaching her how to shoot that blasted pistol.

'I think there are some things you can never put behind you, Kathleen,' she heard him say softly. She was dancing with him, spinning and whirling on the floor of the woolshed at Bungaree, her face tilted up to look into his laughing eyes and his wide ever-so-kissable mouth. Whirling and swirling to an Irish reel . . .

And suddenly she was back in Ireland again, starving, the hunger gnawing at her, the cold deep in her bones. Everything grey and dark. Misery and despair eating at her insides. Her beloved Patrick in her arms.

She floated to consciousness. She was burning hot, not freezing cold. The hunger had gone but the terrible thirst remained. If she did not get water soon, she would die. The baby would die too, just like Patrick had. She put her hands on her belly, holding the baby. Another child would die. Once more, she was helpless.

She closed her eyes. The harsh light of the

Australian sun was too bright. A ghastly headache pounded away behind her eyes.

'*There's nothing that you can take with you when you go,*' Rory's voice whispered over the hot plains and waving golden grasses. '*You could disappear and never be seen again, there'd be no one who would ever ask what happened to the Irish orphan girl who was headed for the bush.*'

Then James seemed to take Rory's place, '*I want you here, I need you here, you are the mistress of Wildowie.*'

Then Rory's voice took over again, this time fading into the swish of the wind in the gums, '*Goodbye, my darlin' Kathleen. Goodbye, my darlin'.*'

She had not realised that she had lost consciousness again until she felt hands on her face and a squirt of water into her mouth. She opened her eyes to see the Yura boys close up to her, their spears on the ground and their young faces wrinkled in concern.

'Awi,' she croaked. She wanted more, a drop was not enough.

They spoke to her in Adnyamathanha, the only words she caught were 'water' and 'sick'. They knew how thirsty she was. They continued to squirt water into her mouth, a drop or two at a time, from an andupi, a wallaby-skin bag. And between each drink her head fell forward and she sank into the strange dream-filled world that she had existed in all day. Her dreams mixed everything up: Angus, James, Rory, the baby, the hunger, the thirst.

It seemed that the process of giving her a drink had taken them hours. Gradually her mind became sharper and she ceased to lapse into periods of unconsciousness. They pulled her out of the hole but she was still weakened from her ordeal and could do little but lie on the sand while they tended to her. They cooked a long lizard over a small fire and fed her morsels between the drinks which had become progressively more generous as the evening wore on. She realised, as they had obviously done, that if they had given her the whole lot at once she would never have kept it down.

Now she was tired. She rolled over onto her side and fell into a deep, dreamless sleep, oblivious of the clear crystal night. The boys slept too, their heads on their hands, their bodies nestled close together near the still-warm fire.

First light was slipping pink and orange across the golden plain. She awoke to the sound of young voices talking Adnyamathanha. She stretched her aching limbs. Magpies gurgled their morning song. She was alive!

They signalled to her that she must travel with them. Kate picked up the swag and they set off towards the south as the first rays of the golden morning sun lit up the plain ahead of them.

Part way across the plain they climbed some low rocky outcrops. They stopped and there was some discussion, almost an argument, between the boys. They kept looking in her direction as they spoke. Kate knew it was about her. Finally the taller, more slender boy shrugged his shoulders, seeming to acquiesce with the other boy's view.

They walked on about twenty yards over the face of the flat rock. Kate could hardly believe her eyes when they shifted a small rock that lay on top of the almost horizontal rock slabs they had been walking on. There where the rock had been was a waterhole. It would have only been a foot in diameter but it was deep. The boys each took a small drink from their hands and then they invited Kate to do the same. It was cool, clear and very fresh. She looked up after a few desperate gulps, conscious that this water was precious. They nodded. She could drink more.

That was why the discussion had taken place. The presence of this rock-hole was a well-guarded secret and they had not wanted to show her. She would have given anything to take a wash in the cool water, but she knew how precious it was. The accumulated dust and sand would have to stay on her skin until she reached a better supply.

'Thank you,' she said, wiping her mouth.

The boys refilled the andupi with water. The feet of the yellow-footed rock wallaby had been fashioned into a strap. The taller boy slung it around his neck. He shifted the andupi onto his back and then covered the rock-hole carefully so that animals could not get to it. They continued on their way. Kate was not concerned where they were taking her. It was towards the south. That was all that mattered.

As the sun rose higher in the sky she began to feel the heat. Each time they passed deep shade she would take a rest. The boys, however, did not appear to be hot, tired or even thirsty. She knew that they stopped only because she needed to. At one stage she was amazed to see the smaller boy suddenly leap through the bush. He grabbed hold of a lizard that she had not noticed, swung it so that its head hit the ground with a thud, and then hung it tail-down from the string around his hips. They stopped from time to time to dig roots and yams from the soil and to pick the fruits of several bushes and trees. Kate knew that it was usually women's work but they were hardly going to rely on her to find the food for them. The latter they gave to Kate to eat through the day but the lizards were kept for the evening meal.

As the sun began to sink towards the horizon, the mountains took on the deep purples and blues that Kate loved so much. They began to climb into the rocky foothills below the towering peaks. The boys then led her along a gorge. There, in the cool, sat the rest of the group. There must have been ten adults and the same number of children. Kate's entrance caused quite a stir.

The women, grinding seeds on flat rocks,

paused with their hands in mid-air. The children stopped their running and calling and shrank behind the adults. The men stopped their tool-making. They all looked up at her in total surprise. Some reached for their spears and waddies. Had she not been with the boys they would have either attacked or run, she was not sure which.

All at once there was talking from many voices. Then an old man came to his feet and addressed the boys. Kate watched as the boys explained how they had found her, buried in the sand and dying of thirst. They all looked shyly at her and then away. She waited for the boys to finish their explanation. Then she spoke to the old man in the little Adnyamathanha that she had been taught.

'Hello, how are you?' she asked him.

She heard the sharp intake of breath from the people. Few whites knew anything at all of their language. If they were ever spoken to, it was in pidgin, or broken English. Kate had never understood why they had used pidgin and not plain English or indeed the language of the Yuras. The Yuras were not stupid, after all.

'Well,' he said, his eyes opening a little wider in surprise.

'I am called Udnyuartu,' Kate said.

'Udnyuartu,' she heard the name on many lips at once.

It was not just that she was a white woman, she was Udynuartu, the white woman from

Wildowie. She saw the understanding dawn on their faces. They knew of her. The tension evaporated.

She explained, using gestures, English and Adnyamathanha, that she had shot the red-haired white man. She had left Wildowie and she had to go south, to where the white men came from. She must escape the land of the Yuras or she would be in trouble. Big trouble. The Udnyus would come after her, they would bring the police.

The blacks knew of her fear, for they had felt it many times themselves. They had seen their men dragged away, beaten, whipped, killed. There were those who had been taken away and never heard of again.

She had made herself understood. Although wary of her, they welcomed her into their camp. She sat with the women. They nodded at her shyly and she introduced herself to them. She spoke of Adnyini and Arranyinha. They knew the women who she named and Kate heard them saying 'sister of this one' or 'auntie of that one'. Kate could never keep track of their complex system of relationships but there was no doubt that they were of the same people. They nodded and said 'Udnyuartu'.

They knew who she was. The fact that Kate had tried to converse with them in their own language and gone bush with them to learn their ways had made her famous among them. They were used to the white men who only wanted their women, or the station owners who wanted them to tell the secrets of their waterholes. Someone who took an interest in their culture had stood out.

That night Kate shared a meal of kangaroo with them around the campfire. It had simply been tossed whole into the ashes. Kate had smelled the hair burning off. Then it was pulled out again some time later, still not fully cooked, and torn into pieces. The animal seemed to be divided in a particular way, with the best parts going to the men and the rest to the women and children. The kangaroo's legs had been discarded.

She relaxed with them, watching the slow dance of the stars across the night sky and listening as they told their ancient stories and sang their mystical songs. Sitting with the women at Wildowie had been fascinating but not nearly so intriguing as living in the middle of them: men, women and children all together. Before then she had seen only the women's business, for they seemed to keep women's and men's activities quite separate.

One by one they lay down to sleep for the night: dogs, babies, men, women and children all together. Kate pulled her blanket from the swag and covered herself. Sleep did not come immediately. She began to wonder just what she was going to do from here. It was tempting to stay with the Yuras for as long as she could. At least then she would neither starve nor die of thirst. The baby could be born here with them—

better that than on the track somewhere, alone and without help. If she stayed in the Far North for too long, though, she would eventually be spotted by someone from a station and they would hunt her down like a criminal.

Not only that, but also she must begin to make a new life for herself and her child. She had nearly died of thirst. Her baby had nearly died with her. It was not the first time in her life that she had survived by the skin of her teeth.

She would not let it happen to her child, she was sure of that. She had lost all the family she had ever had. Her resolve that never again would a child die in her arms grew stronger each day. This child must live. This child must never experience what she had been through.

She would fight, she would strive, she would sacrifice everything she had ever wanted in life to ensure that this child had the best. A new job, a better way of earning money, a secure place in society. Next time she would be the one who would call the shots. She didn't want to be at the beck and call of the Angus Campbells of this world.

And as for James? She was beginning to hate him for what he had done to her. If he had done his duty, she would have been mistress of Wildowie and Angus would have had to show her respect. The more she thought about it all, the more she realised that James was the one who was to blame for all this. James. He had seduced her so cleverly, she could see it now in retrospect. He had played, so skilfully, so smoothly, on her feelings of loneliness. He had used her. It had never been a two-way street at all. He had used her and when he had discovered her pregnancy he had done nothing to help her. His idea, that she should marry Craig, had only been to help himself, to get rid of her, to foist his responsibilities onto someone else. Then the idea of sending her to Clare to the lying-in home—that had not been to provide her with support for the birth. It had been to get rid of her.

That James! He was shrewd, she had to give him that. But she, too, was clever. She would find a way to make him pay. She would force him to give to her son what was rightfully his. She still wanted what James had, but not now for herself. It was for her child. How she could do that she was not sure. For she must never see him again. If she did, she would be taken up on a charge of murder.

At that thought her heart sank. She would never see Brigid again, or Rory, or old Harold, her bullocky friend. She would have to start again, somewhere else, another name . . .

It was on the third day of her sojourn with the Yuras that Kate broached the subject of continuing her journey south. They had been hospitable and she was safe from harm as long as she stayed with them. But she should go. Her child's future was not improving while she collected yams and seeds and ate kangaroo around the campfire each night.

The old man, named Mawaanha, told her to wait, for there were other Yuras coming to discuss what they should do about her. Kate was unsure exactly what there was to discuss but she knew better than to try to hurry any decisions. These people seemed to have quite a different concept of time. To them, there was never a hurry.

The next day three men whom Kate had not seen before arrived in the camp. With them was her old friend, Adnyini's daughter, the one who was called Arranyinha.

'Arranyinha!'

Kate and Arranyinha hugged like sisters. God, it was good to see her again!

'Nunga?' Arranyinha asked.

'Warndu,' Kate replied.

When they had finished exchanging warm greetings Arranyinha held Kate at arm's length and looked her up and down. She held up the net bag and the bark dish that Kate was carrying.

Arranyinha looked around at the people assembled around them. 'This is not Udnyuartu!' she said, shaking her head solemnly.

Kate's heart skipped a beat. What was Arranyinha saying that for? They had only accepted her into their group because she was Udnyuartu!

A slow grin spread across Arranyinha's face. 'She now lives with the Adnyamathanha, she is Yuraartu! Blackwoman!'

The whole group broke into shouts of laughter, not least of all Arranyinha herself. She and Kate hugged again.

While Kate and Arranyinha swapped their news, the men all collected together under the shade of an overhanging rock. Kate could tell by the frequent glances in her direction that she was the subject of the discussion. After hours of talk back and forth between them all, Mawaanha, the old man, approached her again.

He told her that they had decided they would help her get south again. But not now. It was too risky for her to travel so far at this stage of her pregnancy. Nor did they want to undertake a long journey outside their own territory at a time when the waterholes were drying up. The further south they went, the less knowledge they had of permanent sources of water and safe hideaways. She could not survive in the bush on her own with the little knowledge she had, that was obvious to them. So she could not go on her own. She must stay with them and they would look after her and her child as they would if she were one of them. They were right.

She would not cross paths with Rory, that was her only disappointment. And she had wanted to see him so badly. He was someone she could talk to, someone who could shoulder the burdens that weighed heavily upon her. She needed to tell someone the whole story of Wildowie and the tragedies that had overtaken her there. And Rory would have been the perfect person.

That night there was singing around the fire. The voices droned the old songs and the children clapped sticks and hands in rhythm with the singing. There was dancing around the fire. First the women danced. Then the men, daubed with different coloured ochres, did their dance, stamping their feet to stir up the dust. The dust and smoke were lit up in the warm light of the fire, making the whole scene appear mystical and wondrous. The constant droning of the voices seemed to send Kate into a trance. There was magic at work and she had the privilege, granted to so few white men or women, of being part of their ceremony.

If Brigid could only see her now, Kate laughed to herself, she would be horrified. She had gone native. Here she was, pregnant, dressed in a tattered gown, barefoot, dusty from head to toe, eating great hunks of blood-red kangaroo meat and dancing around the fire with the 'savages'.

James, she knew, would be revolted. Ladies of James's class never even ate with their fingers! But she didn't give a damn about James. It was well and truly time to stop chasing him and to start chasing a future for her child.

The next morning they made preparations to break camp. They would all travel together: the family group, the newcomers, Arranyinha and herself. They were headed for the 'big-one-cowie' the place of much water, the place Kate had heard mention of but had never seen. The place that had been kept a close secret by the

Yuras since the coming of the Udnyu. It was no small mark of respect that they were now taking her there. She felt both honoured and humbled by the trust they had placed in her.

It was the place where they would spend the remainder of the long, hot, dry summer. Not all of the Yuras would be there, though, since they were careful never to overload the land. If a large group stayed for too long then the resources of food and water could become too depleted for use in future years. Over-use of the area by humans could also cause contamination of the water. Kate began to glean the real reasons for the walkabout, as the Udnyu called it. It had nothing to do with shiftlessness. It was about spirituality, about ceremonies, finding food and water, meeting friends and family. It was survival.

The family sorted out their belongings. There would not be much to carry: spears, waddies, flint knives, bark dishes, the best of the digging sticks, skin bags for water, slings and pouches made from animal skins in which to carry the babies.

Everything else was simply left to fade back into the bush from which it had come. There was no mess to clean up, no houses to lock. By the time they came back next year there would be few signs of habitation other than the remains of long-dead campfires and the stories depicted in symbols on the walls of the gorge.

They didn't need wagons, they didn't need

drays. They simply picked up the few belongings they had and they started walking. The pace was slow enough for the children, the pregnant women and the elderly to keep up. It allowed them to gather or to kill any food that they needed along the way. They covered the distances in good time but there was no sense of urgency.

How different it was to the trip up to Wildowie! Kate did not walk in the choking dust stirred up by the bullocks. There was no need to feed and water the animals, no need to tether them at night. No one had to scout out a smooth path for the wagons.

The Yuras knew the way to go. They had been travelling these tracks for as long as they could remember and they could go by foot through places that vehicles could never negotiate. There was a feeling of freedom. The life of the Yuras may have lacked the comforts known to the Udnyu but there were fewer cares, less to work for, less to look after and almost nothing to clean. Life was more simple in many ways, more attuned to nature.

To live like this for a short while was refreshing. The culture of the Yuras was absorbing in every way. She knew, however, that it was not for her. Once the baby was born, they would leave. It would not be possible to live this life forever.

Eventually all of this land would be settled by the Udnyu. The Yuras would be driven away or would succumb to the Udnyu diseases. This idyllic lifestyle would come to an end.

Even if it didn't, Kate could not remain undiscovered by the Udnyu. She would eventually be identified and then it would only be a matter of time before she was hunted down and caught. She would be imprisoned, if not hanged. Her child would go into a workhouse, just as she had done. He would never claim his birthright. It would be a repetition of history.

The Yuras walked for days. Eventually they passed by the boundary of Wildowie. They were travelling across that wide plain of shimmering golden grass where the mountains crouched at the edge like mammoth prehistoric animals. It looked much the same as the last time she was here. The golden grasses gave way to the steep iron-red cliffs, then to misty blue foothills and eventually to the hazy purple of the high, rugged ridge tops.

But instead of continuing through the middle of the plain, to Wildowie, they veered to the left. They made their way towards those towering peaks and into a narrow, twisting gorge that at first sight appeared to come to a dead end. But there was a pass to one side. They climbed over the top and into a broad valley that nestled between two mighty mountain ranges. Had she climbed up over the hazy purple ridge tops to the east she could have looked down onto Wildowie.

Kate would never have guessed that this lush

green valley with its wide flat floor lay hidden in here. From Wildowie the lofty rugged mountains had seemed to form one great impenetrable range. No one from Wildowie had ever attempted to explore the country to the east.

They had explored the land to the north, for it was easy to travel up the flat plain. The land to the south was already well known and partly settled. The plains to the west drifted into desert, made blue and grey by saltbush, with waterways that trickled away into a great salt lake. Those plains had been judged unsuitable for thirsty sheep.

This was a hidden paradise. No one but the Yuras knew it was here. What a magical hideaway! There was no fear that she would be discovered, unless an intrepid or very lost explorer came to it from the east. God knows what lay that way or whether anyone could get through from that direction!

She felt like jumping for joy. Her legs, tired and aching from the long walk with the extra weight of the baby, were ready to walk on, ready to explore this green haven. The baby kicked and rolled inside her, as if he, too, was joyous about the sanctuary they had found for him.

The trees were red gums, tall and majestic like those she had seen near Clare Village. Their size indicated the presence of plenty of water. The grass on the valley floor was still green, unlike the gold and brown of Wildowie. Soon they came across the big-one-cowie—a wide, deep waterway that flowed strongly, even in these dry months. It was a sanctuary for animals and birds. Attracted by the availability of food they, too, had made this their home for the summer.

The Yuras called it Elatina.

The men made bird-like calls which were answered from beyond. A little later Yuras emerged from the bush ahead of them. First in twos or threes, then by the dozen. Soon they were surrounded by them and there was a mighty welcome for the latest group to arrive. It was a homecoming.

Kate was welcomed by the women who knew her and then by those who didn't. For the first time in many years, she too had a family. A great, big extended family. The long lonely months at Wildowie rolled away. She brushed the tears from her eyes as they made their way to one of the camps. She felt that she had finally come home.

Everyone wanted her to tell the story of how she had killed the red-haired one, even those who had been there. They clasped themselves and danced about in glee as she told her story. They patted her and grinned at her as if she had come in answer to their dreams.

That night there was a party. There was plenty of food of all kinds: wallaby, kangaroo, euro, emu, snake, seed cakes, roasted yams, witchetty grubs, the fruit of the iga. Kate, remembering their advice, avoided the euro and the kangaroo tail. There was dancing and singing well into the night. One by one the children fell asleep, then the adults began to nod off. Kate curled up in the sand and fell asleep to the sounds of a few Yuras still talking around the campfires, exchanging the news of the months they had been separated.

The time passed quickly. Each day she joined the other women as they collected and prepared food, played with the children and sat about in the sand telling yarns. It was a relaxed way to spend the day and she did nowhere near as much work as she had done in a day at Wildowie.

She learnt more about the Dreaming, their system of spiritual belief. She heard how the two great Akurras, or serpents, came down from the north. They were thirsty and they drank up all the water in the huge salt lake on the way. They slithered down through the mountains, carving out great valleys as they came. Finally they came to rest not far from here. They showed Kate the two highest mountains in the distance. Each of those was the head of the Akurras. They heard great rumblings sometimes, as if the mountains themselves were moving. But it was not thunder and it was not an earthquake, it was the Akurras, rolling over, deep beneath the mountains.

The Dreamtime story of the Akurras was just one of the many stories she heard as she sat around the campfires at night and in the creek beds where she sat in the daytime, talking with the women. There were some stories told by the men and some told by the women. The stories had meanings at many levels. They explained how the world came to be and they defined the relationships between the Yuras, the land and all that it contained. They taught the children the morals and the behaviour expected within Yura society. In a very simple and memorable way they taught the children how to find their way through the Adnyamathanha lands so that they could move, as the seasons and the ceremonies dictated, from one area to another without losing their way. The stories emphasised the use of landmarks as signposts. Each story linked the landmarks with events in the story and demonstrated the path to follow across the sometimes harsh and dangerous terrain.

It was in this way that Kate learnt about the Far North, the Flinders Ranges and the Gammon Ranges, as they were called by the Udnyu. It was the kind of knowledge as yet not shared with the Udnyu. She knew now where the permanent waterways could be found, where the game was plenty and at what times of the year. She learnt the areas where only women could go and the areas where only men went. She learnt about the sites that linked the people so powerfully with the land. To the Yuras, these places were as sacred as the Holy Communion wine, the holy shroud or the holy grail. They did not need great cathedrals in which to worship, for they had the spectacular and mystical places provided by nature.

To her surprise she discovered that the Yuras did not just walk upon the land, they cultivated it in subtle ways. They burnt off tracts of land early in the summer when the fires would burn cool and not destroy everything in their paths. The burning off caused the land to replenish itself and to provide fresh feed for the animals and birds. She noticed how the Yuras picked the seeds up from under the urti, or quandong trees, and carried them to other places where urti might also grow and flourish.

They were not just the hapless wanderers that the Udnyu thought they were. All their movements and stories were purposeful. Survival in this harsh land was the ultimate aim of everything they did.

If only she had her own station, she thought, then the knowledge that had been shared with her by the Yuras could be put to good effect. She would not treat the Yuras like the other squatters did. She would protect them and their sacred sites. She would work with them in looking after the land so that Udnyu and Yura could live peacefully together.

But there was no time to think about that now. The baby moved inside her, reminding her that the birth would come soon. The older women watched her carefully, asking her how she felt and telling her how to prepare.

She woke up one morning, a strange sensation coming in waves across her belly, and she knew that the time had come.

Chapter
Nine

Arranyinha and one of the most experienced women took her in hand. They helped her down to the creek where they washed her face and hands with water and sat her in the shade to wait and rest.

Gradually the pains increased in intensity.

'Come,' Arranyinha said, and they began to walk her along, stopping each time Kate felt the pains were coming on again.

Up and down by the side of the creek they walked in the shade. Kate had thought it strange that they would make her walk like this, for she thought the best place for her would have been on her swag. But they were right, the walking somehow eased the pain, or at least made it more bearable. Kate got the idea of walking between the pains and stopping, leaning against a tree, when the pains returned. Then they coached her in the breathing, taking a long slow breath and relaxing as the pain began and another long slow breath after the pain had subsided.

When Kate tired they encouraged her to squat down rather than to lie down.

An old woman, one whom Kate did not know well, came to join them. The old woman leant on a stout stick for support and carried a malaka and a bark dish called a yardlu. The bark dish was empty. She did not look as old as Kate's friend Adnyini had been. Her hair was grey and crinkled and her broad nose and full lips stood out from a face that looked like crumpled tissue paper. She had the large dark twinkling eyes, like Adnyini's, that seemed both ancient and wise. Arranyinha introduced her as Unakanha.

Unakanha was skilled in midwifery. She examined Kate and talked to Arranyinha. She laid both her hands on Kate's belly and left them there for some time, feeling the muscles as they contracted and relaxed. She felt Kate's hands and head. Then she took her hands and spoke to her earnestly, soothing her fears. Unakanha then spoke to Arranyinha. Arranyinha stood up and, motioning for the other woman to go with her, they left Kate and Unakanha under the trees.

The old woman nodded her head and sat down in the soft earth, her eyes on Kate as she continued walking back and forth under the short shadows of the midday sun. From time to time the old woman would feel Kate's belly or tell her to take a drink of water from the creek.

Arranyinha and her friend returned a short time later. Unakanha stood up and the three Yuraartu then guided Kate to another creek bed, this one dry and insect free. It was here, some time later, that she squatted, her back against the top of the ditch, to give birth. It was Unakanha who took hold of the baby as he emerged.

Unakanha laid the baby on the bark dish while she wiped the tiny face with her fingers. Arranyinha helped Kate to settle back and rest for a moment.

The baby started to cry softly and was handed to her. Tears sprang to her eyes as she examined the child. Everything, from the top of his head to his miniature fingers and toes, was perfect.

She looked at him in awe. The fine down that covered his head was a dark honey-gold. He opened his eyes and looked at her. They were grey, that unfathomable grey of the ocean on an overcast day. The eyes of James Carmichael. No one, looking at him, could doubt his paternity.

He continued to look into her eyes. There was someone else there in his look. She had seen that same trusting appeal in the eyes of a baby before. It was as if he knew he was relying on her for his life.

Memories returned to hit her with their force. Patrick. Something about him reminded her of Patrick! That same tender trust had been in her brother's eyes when she had first held him. It had been the beginning of the unusual closeness between them. A closeness that had continued until that cold misty morning when he had died in her arms.

She would call this baby Patrick, for her dearest brother, and James, so that his father would remember him. Patrick James O'Mara.

'His name is Patrick James.'

'Virdianha Patrick James,' Unakanha said to her.

'Pardon?'

'Virdianha,' Unakanha repeated. 'His name is Virdianha, Yura name for the first-born.'

Arranyinha built a small fire in the ditch and Unakanha threw some green branches that Arranyinha had collected onto the coals. They held Kate over the smoke, explaining that the smoke was to cleanse her body. The afterbirth was buried deep in another hole in the sand.

They erected a shelter for her. She would stay here for a while, until the bleeding was over and her body was cleansed. Then she would rejoin the group. Arranyinha and Unakanha would stay with her, teaching her how to feed and care for the baby and looking after her until she was strong again.

While she remained apart from the group the women visited her. There was nothing that she had to do for herself. They brought food for her, fed her, and washed her and the baby. In the days before her milk came in they even fed Patrick from their own breasts. She was not sure whether they did it to teach Patrick how to suckle, or whether it was simply their way of building family relationships.

She offered silent thanks to God. What would it have been like if she had given birth at Wildowie? She would have counted herself lucky if a midwife had arrived at all. And there would have been none of this tender care. They'd have put her back in the traces immediately—cooking and cleaning for the men.

When she returned from the shelter she was welcomed back like a long-lost daughter. The men, so fond of babies and children, made a great fuss of Patrick. They cuddled and kissed him, and cooed over him as if he was a child of their own.

Mawaanha, the elder, held Patrick as if he would never let him go.

'You look like Virdianha is your boy,' Kate teased him.

'He is. I have claimed him. He is Mathari,' he said.

'Pardon?'

'He is Mathari, same as me, same as you. He is part of our skin group.'

Kate looked puzzled.

'All Yuras belong to Mathari group or Ararru group. It follows the line of the mother. You are Mathari group, so your son is Mathari group too. He can only marry someone of the Ararru group, same as you, if you were to marry again.'

He went on to explain the custom of skin groups. It prevented intermarriage between close blood relatives so that the genetic stock remained strong. Initiation also helped in that process, since a mother would prevent her child from becoming initiated if she believed that the child had any genetic weakness. An uninitiated man was unable to take a wife or to have children. It was all recorded, he told her, and she had seen the records on the rock walls of the gorge. There had been circles, and circles crossed through with vertical lines, the patterns hammered indelibly into the rock walls. These told the genetic history of the Yuras.

But she was not of their race, or their group. 'But I have no skin group, I'm an Udnyu,' she said.

'Yes, you have a skin group. You have been claimed.'

Arranyinha broke into the conversation. 'I claimed you as my skin group, last summer, not long after we met you. I wanted to claim you first before anyone else did.'

Kate was amazed. They had claimed her without her even knowing. She had been part of this family for longer than she had realised.

'Thank you, then, I'm proud to be Mathari,' she said, recognising the respect that Arranyinha had shown.

An outcast in her own society, she had been accepted into theirs in ways that she had never imagined. To the colonists, she was on the lowest rung of the social ladder, for she was both Irish and female. As a murderer, she was outcast by her own actions. Here, she was accepted as an equal member.

The women were sitting together in the cool sand of a dry creek bed when the autumn rains began.

At the first splash on her bare arm Kate jumped up. 'Rain at last!'

She held up her arms as if to capture the rain as it fell. The feel of clean rain splattering onto her skin was divine and the smell of rain on the hot dry earth was even better. It was a smell that could never be forgotten by anyone who had waited through months of the dry for the beginning of the rains.

She tilted back her head, so that the drops would fall on her face.

'God, how wonderful!' It was a time to rejoice.

She wanted the feel of it all over her. She knew that the others would not mind if she took off her clothes, so she did. She peeled her dusty old gown down over her body, removed her underclothes and stood naked, the heavy drops of rain washing her skin, drop by drop, making it cool and washing away the dust. The rain came down more heavily and the water trickled down over her body, renewing and refreshing her, turning her skin to silk.

She had regained her shape quickly after Patrick's birth. Her skin was firm and her muscles toned. She supposed that it was the life she was leading. Many miles were walked in a day and the diet of meat, seeds, vegetables and fruits kept her lean and fit.

The other women laughed at her as she stood in the rain. They were not desperate for water on their skins. Their entire lives had been spent in the dust. As the rain became heavier they moved to the sheltered areas under rock overhangs.

The rain did not stop. It dripped on and on until the air was saturated with the smell of the gums. The dry gullies turned into instant rivers, the waters racing and tumbling, hurling aside the gum trees and rolling great boulders down towards the plains.

Kate washed her clothes and changed into her trousers and James's shirt. She still had those boyish hips and thighs and now her curves had disappeared under the loose thick shirt.

The landscape looked different. The rain had washed the dust from the trees and everything seemed to glow with a new vigour, including Kate herself. It was time to think about moving on. She knew now, as she had known from the beginning, that she could not stay with the Yuras forever. She had to secure a future for Patrick. She could not allow him to grow up in the same poverty that she had experienced. The longer she left it before she started, the longer it was going to take her to save enough for him to be educated and to buy a farm or a business that would provide for his future. Life here with the Yuras was good, but it could not last forever.

Patrick was growing stronger every day. He could now hold up his heavy head and clasp things with his tiny fingers. In a way it would be a shame to take him away from the Yuras. They adored him and Kate knew that he, too, loved them, even at this early age. As much as she didn't like to acknowledge it to herself, he was as happy in their arms as he was in hers. It was the way that they related to children. They handed them around from one person to the next. They were suckled by more than one mother. Kate's friends were her 'sisters' and were not only aunts to Patrick, they were mothers as well. All the adults around him were loving and caring. The men were all fathers to him too.

He would not have that when they went south. And what would she do with him when she worked? There would be no loving aunts and uncles. She would have to hire a girl to watch over him. Or worse, if she had to work long hours she would have to put him with a baby farmer—a woman who took on children and was paid for their care. Kate didn't much like the thought of that. Some baby farmers were wonderful, but most were drunkards, desperate for any extra money they could get their hands on.

The future was not going to be easy for either of them. But it had to be done. She couldn't postpone the move forever. Eventually they would be discovered living here with the Yuras and this idyllic existence would come to a nasty end.

And the sooner she left, the less he would weigh. Since she was going to be carrying him, at least as far as Clare, if not further, that was a serious consideration.

The other problem which she had been pondering was her identity. People in the Far North would be looking out for a young Irishwoman with a baby. How was she going to evade capture while she was looking for a job which would pay her enough to get away from South Australia?

She wished that she had been thinking more clearly when she had run away from Wildowie. She had lost sight of the things that were most important to her. She had even left all her precious savings behind. So much for her great goal of becoming rich one day! If she had thought to take the money then she could have simply caught a coach down to Adelaide, then paid the fare for a boat to take her to one of the other Australian colonies.

The Yuras were certainly in no position to give her money for her fare. Money was entirely unknown to them. How was she going to get out of South Australia with a young baby in her arms and not a penny to her name?

She talked with Arranyinha about her dilemmas. Arranyinha, in turn, spoke to Mawaanha, who discussed it, of course, with all the elders. Her business was now the business of the whole group. They were one.

Mawaanha approached her to tell her their decision. They would stick by their promise to take her south. Now that the rains had come, it would be easier and safer to travel. They would escort her to the boundaries of their own territory, then they would negotiate with the Nukunu, the people further south, for them to take her as far as Clare.

It would be better that way, since the Adnyamathanha would not be trespassing onto Nukunu territory. It would also be better for the Nukunu to take her on to Clare since they knew the hideaways and best paths to take. While in more settled districts, she would need to be more careful about being seen by Udnyu. Once she had reached a busy place like Clare Village she could hide behind the mask of anonymity.

'And we will look after Virdianha until your return,' the old man finished, as if it had already been agreed.

Kate's head jerked up. 'What?'

'He will stay with us and we will love him, for he is one of us now. When you are ready, when you are free of your fears of the Udnyu and you are able to look after him properly, then you can return for him.'

'Oh no! You don't understand. I love him. I cannot possibly leave here without him. He is everything to me!'

'We love him too. We can look after him and teach him well. What would happen to him if the Udnyu caught you and hanged you? What will happen to him if you leave him to seek work? We think it is better that he stays with us, where he is safe.'

'But I am his mother. He must go with me!'

'We are also his mothers, his fathers, his aunts and uncles. He is a grandson to me. It is the Yura way. It is our responsibility to watch him grow and to guide him. Think on it. Do not set your mind against it now. Think of him and his needs. You also have needs and you must meet them, but what is best for him? Tell me your answer on this when you have slept on it.'

Kate was horrified. Leave her son here? Her whole life now revolved around him. She must see to his future. She must make sure that his father one day claimed him as his heir.

She could see that the Yuras only had his interests at heart, but to leave him here? What sort of mother would do that?

That night the dream returned to haunt her.

The mists swirled around her, the snow drifted with the wind, settling in the ditch where she lay. Patrick, her baby Patrick, lay in her arms, death slowly claiming him as surely as it had claimed the others.

'Patrick, my darlin', wake up, 'tis time to go now.'

She shook him. His body flopped in her arms.

'Patrick!' her scream of anguish cut through the mists like a knife, 'Patrick!'

Dogs barked around her. The baby stirred and cried in her arms. Gum smoke drifting from a nearby fire filled her nostrils. Thank God! She was not in Ireland. She was here, in Australia, with her baby. He was alive. They were warm and well fed. She cuddled her own Patrick closer to her, murmuring to his soft downy head, 'My baby, thank God you're safe.'

The dream unnerved her, as it always did. It brought back the memories that her conscious mind sought to thrust behind her. It came at times of hard decisions to haunt her, to remind her that she must strive for a life where hunger would never stalk her again.

What did it mean this time?

Was she selfish in wanting Patrick with her? Was there a chance that she might one day lie destitute, with him in her arms, just as she had with her brother? The journey south would not be easy. Working and saving, and getting ahead, would not be easy for a woman with a baby.

Maybe the Yuras were right. Maybe she should leave Patrick in their care. It might be the only way of keeping him safe, at least over the next year or two. She cuddled Patrick to her. She did not want to leave him.

The next morning she told Mawaanha and Arranyinha of her decision.

Arranyinha took Kate in her arms, acknowledging that it was a hard decision to have made. 'It is the right thing,' she said.

Then an awful thought went through Kate's

mind. What if the Yuras were attacked? Angus was gone, but there would be others who would follow in his footsteps. There was no shortage of Udnyu who hated Yuras and without knowing it the Udnyu might kill one of their own.

'What if you're attacked by the Udnyu again?'

'We will protect him, I promise you that as your sister. We will keep him well away from Udnyu. We will make sure that no harm befalls him.'

'How will I find you when I return?'

'All the Yuras know of Udnyuartu and her child Virdianha. Just come, ask for him, ask for me, and the Yuras will lead you to him. If there is any fear, if there is any danger, then we can meet in the Secret Gully. The Udnyu do not know the Secret Gully. It is our hiding place. The place where all the Yuras will gather if ever there is great troubles with the Udnyu. We have heard stories. Stories of the terror of the other black groups when the time has come for them to be hunted down and killed like animals. When this time comes for the Yuras, we will be ready. No one but us knows that the gully is there. We have made many trips there, to hide spears and waddies, to hide our sacred objects. When the time comes, that is where we will go.'

'What Secret Gully is this? I do not know it.'

'I will show you. Come.'

Kate put Patrick into a sling made of animal skin. Arranyinha led her north of Elatina, up over the hills and through a wide pass which looked over a small valley beyond. It was not far, maybe two to three hours' walk.

'There it is.'

'What makes this so secret?'

'Can you see it?'

'This valley?'

'No, not this valley, the Secret Gully.'

Kate peered intently. There was a dry flat dusty area, sparsely vegetated, crisscrossed by dry eroded waterways. On either side were watercourses, marked by the odd tall gum. Their upper branches were bare, indicating that water was not abundant here. It would be no good for sheep.

Wildu soared in circles overhead, looking for prey. There was nothing anywhere to suggest a secret gully.

'Follow me!'

Arranyinha led her forward over the low foothills and down to the plain. They crossed some of the dry, shallow waterways.

Suddenly Arranyinha grasped her arm and cautioned, 'Look out!'

Kate stopped in her tracks. 'What?'

She had been looking well ahead and Arranyinha's warning had pulled her up short. She looked down in front of her feet and into a yawning chasm.

'Jaysus!' She stepped back two paces.

She looked to her right and then to her left. The chasm stretched almost all the way across the plain. Here it was maybe five feet across.

Towards the end, where it opened out to join the watercourse, it was thirty feet across. She would never have guessed that it was here.

Here where they stood, the sides of the chasm were steep. Too steep to climb down. It must have been about thirty feet deep and she could feel the cooler damp air flowing over her face as she stood over it. Pools of water dotted the bottom, reflecting the sunlight above.

'Come this way.'

Kate followed Arranyinha as she made her way along the edge of the chasm towards the perimeter of the plain. Where the chasm opened out the edges were not steep and they scrambled down to the bottom.

They then walked back along the cool, darkened chasm, alternately crossing dry sand and splashing through cool pools, until they came to the place where the walls were only a few feet apart and the light from above was a narrow shaft. Here the water had been forced to rush through a narrow tunnel and had eroded the earth out from under the rock, leaving open caverns on either side below the rock walls.

Patrick began to cry and Kate sat down at the edge of the cavern to feed him. It was so cool here. So quiet. No one on the plain above them would know that they were here. It was the perfect hideaway. There was shade from the sun, shelter from storms and plenty of water.

'This will be our meeting place if we need it. If there is any danger, to us, to you, or to Patrick, we will meet here. No one knows of this place but the Yuras. If there are any problems when you return to us, send a message through any of the Yuras and I will come to meet you here.'

Kate finished feeding Patrick and then leant over the edge of the cavern to look down into the water. Her image was sharply reflected and she was surprised by the sight of the tangled hair forming a halo around her head. She put her hand up to touch it. It was dirty, knotted and full of prickles and burrs. She wished that she had brought a brush with her. Yet another item that she regretted leaving behind when she fled from Wildowie.

She tried to comb the tangled tresses with her fingers but they caught in the knots. She tried to pull out the burrs with her fingers, but long tangled strands came with them. It would be easier if she just cut it off.

That was it!

She would cut off her hair. The thought struck her with its beautiful simplicity. She was wearing boys' trousers and the over-large shirt belonging to James. With her hair cut short she would look like a boy. Her hips and legs were slender, like a boy's. The police and the station people would be looking for a young woman. A young woman who might have a baby with her. A lad on his own, making his way south, would attract little attention. It might even be possible for her to keep the disguise and to get work on a farm. Why hadn't she thought of it before?

The more she thought about it, the more appealing the idea was. It would mean an end to the problems of unwanted attention that her presence as a female had caused ever since she had left Adelaide. Kate did not stop to contemplate the matter further. She and Arranyinha strode back to the camp. Arranyinha found a good sharp yurdla and began to remove her hair, a lock at a time. The other women gathered around, each of them taking a lock of hair as it was removed. It was silkier and smoother than their thick hair and the texture was fascinating to them.

Then it was finished. Kate put her hands up to feel her hair. It was short all over. For the first time since she was a child she felt her neck and ears bare to the air. The warm breeze sighed over her skin. There was no mirror to see the effect. She would look later on at her reflection in the water when she went to get a drink. It was time to help the other women collect their contribution of food for the day.

The next morning she talked to Mawaanha about the journey south. He was still adamant that they would take her only as far as Nukunu territory. From there, he said, the Nukunu must look after her. It was their land.

'Why should they look after an Udnyu who means nothing to them?' she asked.

'You are known to them, Udnyuartu. They know of your bravery in defending the Yuras from the Red-haired One. They know what risks

315

you have taken by protecting the Yuras.'

'I am worried. Maybe they will tell you that they will take me south and then they will not do it. They may leave me in the bush.'

'They will do it. Their reputation amongst the black people depends upon it. It will be a fair trade.'

'Trade for what?'

'I will show you. Do not follow me. Wait here.'

Mawaanha was gone for two hours. When he returned he held out his closed hand to her. She placed her hand below his and he dropped into it a ball of red earth.

'What is it? Ochre?'

'It is. We will trade it.'

'Trade it?' How could they trade something that was freely available from the earth for anyone to dig out?

She let the ochre fall to the ground and brushed off her hands.

'Tut!' Mawaanha said sharply and he picked it up again. 'This is precious, look at it!'

He rubbed the ochre between his fingers. It was smooth, fine-textured. Where he had rubbed it on his fingers the ochre was a bold colour, red and shiny.

'It is ochre of the very best kind. Other groups walk many, many days to get this ochre from us. Sometimes other groups raid our ochre mine and attack us to get it. Very valuable. The Nukunu want this. They will take you to where you want to go if we give them some.'

'If it is so precious you must not give it away for my sake!'

'You are important to us. You are a friend to the Yuras.'

'Thank you.'

'We want you to do something for us in return,' Mawaanha continued. 'You know the ways of the Udnyu. You speak the language of the Udnyu. We have seen the Udnyu, coming from the south like a horde of hungry animals. They are taking up the land, driving away the Yuras, killing those who resist. We want you to try to save our land. Speak to your elders down south and ask them to let us keep our land. Otherwise there is no hope for the Yuras. Will you do this for us?'

Would she do this for them? There was nothing that she would not do for them. They had befriended her, saved her life, welcomed her into their family, looked after her, adopted her child as their own . . .

But little did they know that she had no power to influence the Udnyu elders. How could these people comprehend that in Udnyu society there were those with power and those without? The Udnyu were not like the Yuras. They did not reach a decision by taking everybody's needs into account and then making the decision that would benefit them all.

Those with the power took whatever they could and be damned to those who had nothing.

She was a woman. She was Irish. She was a peasant, as poor today as she had been in Ireland. What power could she possibly muster on behalf of the Yuras? She was barely one step further up the social ladder than they were.

Besides, she was a criminal. A hunted criminal. She dare not show her face publicly!

She tried, as best she could, to explain these things to Mawaanha. But she knew that there was no way that he could understand the complexities of the white man's world unless he experienced it for himself. And God help him if he ever had to.

He put his hand on her arm. 'I understand, Udnyuartu. It will be hard. It will take many seasons. But we trust you. We know that you will do this for us. You will find a way.'

She would do all that she could.

The next morning a small group of men made preparations to leave. They mixed a quantity of ochre with water to form a thick paste. This was shaped into a large cake with an indentation underneath so that it could be carried easily on top of the head. It must have weighed quite a few pounds.

Kate began her goodbyes. First she bade her friend Arranyinha an affectionate farewell. Arranyinha, daughter of Adnyini, was the one that she would miss the most. They had been together through thick and thin. She had been one of that small group of women that she had first met, down by the creek. She had been the one who had come to tell her of the death of the men, women and children when Angus had carried out his reprisals for the stolen sheep. Arranyinha had been there for the birth of Patrick. Arranyinha had shown her the Secret Gully. Arranyinha was her sister.

She kissed Arranyinha's broad face and hugged her once more.

Then all the women and children crowded around her to say goodbye. She spoke to each of them in turn.

Kate wished that she had something to give them. All she had were her two old dresses, the water bottles, the blanket and the flour bag. She could never give her derringer away. The few things she could give were better than nothing and her simple gesture of gratitude would be understood.

One of the dresses she presented to Arranyinha, the other to Unakanha. The bottles she gave to the two boys who had found her. The blanket, probably the most useful of the items, she gave to Mawaanha as a mark of respect for an elder.

It was her old friend Arranyinha who gave her the urdlupi, the kangaroo-skin rug, in return. She would need it on the cold nights heading south, Arranyinha said.

The flour bag had been reserved for a special purpose. She had written on it, carefully, in a strong dye that Arranyinha had made for her, the following words:

This boy is Patrick James O'Mara. Son of Kate O'Mara and James Carmichael of Wildowie Station. Born January 1851. Entrusted to the care of the Adnyamathanha people April 1851.

It was signed Kate O'Mara.

She hoped that it would suffice. If she did not return by the time he was due to be initiated, Arranyinha was to take him and the bag to James Carmichael at Wildowie.

If ever the Yuras were attacked, or if blamed in any way for abducting a white child, then they could show the Udnyu this bag.

She took Mawaanha's hand and thanked him for his care of her.

Then she took Patrick from Arranyinha's arms and sat down in the dust with him. 'Patrick, my darling boy,' she said, looking into his grey eyes, 'I'm going away now, but I will come back as soon as I can. I love you and I wish I could take you with me, but I cannot. The Yuras will look after you until I return.'

She held him to her and he began to cry as if sensing her sadness. His tears acted like a trigger and she, too, began to cry. The more she cried, the louder he wailed.

She kissed him on the face. 'Hush now, 'twill be all right, I promise you.' She looked at him. There were the grey eyes like James had, the blond hair, the smooth charm already evident.

But he had her heart-shaped face and deter-mined chin. And her determination, too, even at three months old.

He had quietened down and she kissed him once more. 'Remember that I love you and I will get back as soon as I can to look after you. I promise.'

Arranyinha took him from her arms and she rose up from the dust. She wished them all well, turned on her heel and went. She did not look back. She did not want her heart to be wrenched apart. She would miss them all so much. It was yet another set of goodbyes in a lifetime of say-ing farewell to people she loved. Her family, her friends in the workhouse, Brigid, Harold, Rory . . .

Kate knew that she would be missed. She was the only Udnyu to have ever given these people one iota of respect.

With the few men who had been chosen to accompany her, Kate began her journey out of the Flinders Ranges and back to Adelaide.

They never hurried and yet they seemed to cover great distances. Each night they camped in a place that was a known shelter to the men. Sometimes it was a gully protected from the wind, at other times a wurley built on a previous occasion at the edge of an open creek bed.

One night they camped at a place the men called Yura Pila, 'the place of the two men'. They pointed out to Kate the surrounding rock slab hills that looked like the two men, and told her the story of how these ancestors had camped at this place on their journey north. The two men had eaten the last of their emu meat there.

Kate and the men camped under some overhanging rocks where Kate saw paintings marked on rock walls. The paintings were representations of kangaroo tracks, just like those they had shown her in the dust on their way south. There were other markings to do with their ceremonies which were not really explained and which Kate did not fully understand. This place was obviously very important to them. Nearby there was a spring with fresh, clear water. The setting sun sent the colours spreading like flames through the cloud banks and lit up the warm red tones of the rock paintings.

After another few days travel they made contact with the Nukunu. Kate kept well away while the complex negotiations went on between the men. It was particularly important that the Nukunu people guarded her well as she passed through their district, for it was where the police outpost was located. From now on the district was more settled and they would have to take back-ways that were unknown to the whites. They told her that they would take her to Burra Burra, rather than Clare, since the lands above Clare were already thick with settlers. The Udnyu would expect her to go that way.

They accepted that a friend of the Adnyamathanha was a friend of theirs. That she had killed a white overseer was of no concern to them. In fact, in their view, Kate had carried out the retribution that was due to Angus, and her actions had been entirely consistent with their system of law.

Kate found that the Nukunu had a similar language to the Adnyamathanha. While they used many words she did not know, they could understand most of the words she had learnt from the Yuras. Her days travelling were fascinating, more so than during her time on the track up to Wildowie, because now she was really learning about the world around her, the plants and animals and the way of life of the people who knew the land better than any settler ever could. The time passed quickly and before Kate realised it, she was on the outskirts of the northern areas of settlement and was saying farewell and thank you to her guardians.

And she could not thank them enough. If it wasn't for them she most probably would have perished. They had done it for her because she was Udnyuartu. But her gratitude to them and her pride in herself took equal place in her mind. She was elated. If she could survive a journey like that—a white woman travelling on her own with the Yuras—she could survive anything.

Nothing, nothing in this world was impossible, no hurdle was insurmountable. She was about to start again and there was nothing that would stop her this time. She would get what she wanted for her son and herself.

Kate knew that she was close to the Burra Burra township of Kooringa when the undulating hills turned into a dreary wasteland, stripped bare of trees, and the skyline was muddied by the smoke of the smelting furnaces. It seemed an awful contrast to the rugged beauty, statuesque gums and clear, clean air of the Far North.

It was ironic. When she had travelled north to Wildowie the wilderness itself had seemed strange; relentlessly bleak, almost an enemy of the settlers. The dangers had appeared almost insurmountable, from the attacking blacks whom she neither knew nor understood, to the teeming wildlife underfoot. Snakes, scorpions, ants, flies and spiders had all posed a threat of one kind or another. Wild dogs and eagles were enemies of the shepherd. Bushfire and flood had been ever present and very real threats.

It must now be June or thereabouts. For eighteen months she had lived in that harsh and threatening wilderness. The only civilisation had been the rough homestead and the shepherds' crude huts. Other than the Yuras, there had been no more than a handful of people with whom she could converse.

But the endless harsh beauty of the bush had become familiar and beloved. The knuckles and knobs of ancient granite, she knew now, always appeared softer in the violet and gold of the setting sun. Angry red rock-faced gorges had been hushed by the cool blue-greens of the native pines. What seemed like endless red bulldust had given way to hill after hill of delicate grey shale. The hard, rearing upthrust of the mountains was contrasted with the soft, almost transparent skin of the gecko. The grand expanse of landscape and wide open skies were simply a foil for the dainty shimmering silk of a dragonfly's wing and the fine design on the back of a slippery skink.

In time she had come to appreciate all of these things. Since she had shot Angus, the inhospitable land had welcomed her with open arms, in time becoming a safe haven and a welcome shelter. And because of the Yuras, the bush had become a place where survival was no longer a relentless struggle against the odds. It was a bountiful provider of all that she needed for survival.

She paused on top of the smoke-hugged hills that looked over the Burra Burra settlements. She was back to civilisation, as it was called.

It was ugly, it was dirty and it was bleak.

Now the roles were reversed. It was white settlement that was harsh and threatening. The mass of buildings and smoking chimneys seemed strange to eyes accustomed only to bushland. The threat came not from the wild, illiterate Yuras but from the powerful, cultured, literate whites—those who would have read about Kate O'Mara, the 'wanted' woman.

Chapter

Ten

Kooringa was the main settlement nestled in the valley below. The mine site was large, probably as much as one hundred acres. It was crowded with stone buildings, dozens of sheds of all shapes and sizes, machinery and engine works, engine houses, storehouses, tanks and dams of water. And of course there were piles of copper ore everywhere. Towering above it all was a gigantic white chimney spewing smoke across the undulating hills.

The mines looked singularly unattractive and she had no desire to work there. Her first task, nonetheless, was to find a job. She strode purposefully down the hill and towards the town.

Now well-used to trousers, she had picked up the stride of a boy. Her hair was still short. Black curls clustered around her head. All that she owned right now were the clothes upon her back, her wide-awake hat, a wallaby-skin bag full of water, a kangaroo-skin rug, a flint knife, a net bag that held a little food and her precious derringer. Once she had a job she would buy decent clothes, some more food and eventually enough for a ticket out of the Burra. She rubbed some dirt on her face to disguise her clear skin, pulled her hat down low, and strode down to the town.

'Mornin', Father,' she said in her soft Irish brogue as she came up alongside a young man dressed in the black flowing robes of the priest-hood.

'Good morning to you, young fellow,' he said, nodding his head with every intention of continuing along his way.

Kate skipped a couple of steps to keep up with him. 'I'm new into town and looking for a job. D'you know of anywhere I might find work, Father?' she asked.

'What kind of work are you after?' his accent was Irish but not as strong as Kate's.

'Anything will do, for I've no money at all. I've been a hut-keeper and a bullocky's offsider before now.'

'Well then I'd track down the bullockies, lad. There's plenty of them here in the Burra. Upwards of eight hundred are on the road cart-ing ore to the ports on any one day and then there's several hundred carting the wood from the Murray scrub for the furnaces. You'll find that most of them are Irishmen, so you'll be at home with them. They'll find you something to do, I've no doubt.'

Kate approached three bullockies and the third one took her on as a billy-boy. His name was Aidan Duffy and he was an Irishman from County Clare. Not much taller than Kate herself, he had a long beard, almost completely white, and the kind of face that engendered trust. She gave her name to Aidan Duffy as Declan O'Leary. True to the colony's protocol, she was not asked about her background nor from where she had come. The one set of dusty clothes that she owned and wore bespoke hard times, and the things given to her by the Yuras caused one white tufty eyebrow to be raised. But nothing was said.

He was a very old man and had not employed a helper before. As he explained to her, the work had become tiring for him. She began work that afternoon. Her duties consisted of finding the bullocks and helping Aidan to yoke up and load the dray with wood to take to the smelters. As well as that she was to boil the billy, make the tea and undertake any odd jobs that Aidan found for her to do. By the end of the day she was into the idea of things, swearing and joking like the rest of them.

'Arrah, Declan's too big and grand a name for such a slight young lad,' one of the other bullockies joked. 'We'll call you Dec.'

The other bullockies laughed. One of them added, 'It's a babe he is. There's not a single whisker on his cheek!'

Kate spat on the ground as a boy would and

hooked her thumbs into the belt loops on her moleskins. 'I might look like a babe, but I can do a man's work any day,' she said.

'That he can,' said Aidan, clapping her on the shoulder. 'And he can turn the team on a three-penny bit. He's no new chum, regardless of his tender years.'

Later that afternoon when they knocked off work Aidan offered to give Kate, or Dec as she was calling herself, a bed for the night at his place. Kate was amazed when he led her down to the Burra Creek.

'Welcome to Creek Street,' he said.

The entire creek was a scene of bustling domestic activity. Women were washing clothes. Others were scouring out pots or preparing the evening meal on open fires. Red shirts flapped on clothes-lines in the wind. Pigs sniffed through the refuse looking for food. Chickens scratched around in the dirt. Children raced helter-skelter among the adults, having fun along the edge of the water dyed saffron from the mine.

Kate and Aidan walked along the creek banks. Kate was so busy watching the children at play and thinking longingly of Patrick that she almost fell into a barrel cemented in mud atop the bank. She lurched over the top of it and was immediately overpowered by the combined smells of cooking onions and smoke that arose from inside the barrel.

'Watch out or you'll end up in someone's dinner, young lad!' Aidan warned her.

Kate looked around in astonishment. The banks were covered with chimneys of all descriptions; as well as those made of barrels there were some constructed only of mud and others made of wood. It was then that she realised she was actually walking across the top of people's homes!

'Mother of Mary!' she exclaimed, looking around her.

People had made their homes by burrowing into the side of the banks. Some had mere holes for windows and doors, others had substantial doors and glazed sashes. They made their way down the slope of the bank to the edge of the creek and walked on, passing little houses with shingled verandahs and even whitewashed walls. Kate had never seen the like of it before.

Eventually they came to a dugout that on the outside looked much like any other.

'This is it, the place I call home,' Aidan said as he opened the door and led her inside.

The last rays of the sun were enough for Kate to see that he had two rooms, both small. The walls were of untreated mud. One of them had a chimney that went up to the open air above. The furnishings consisted of a rough-hewn table and bench seats in the kitchen, and a low bed against the wall in the other room. Various bits of tackle for the bullocks lay scattered about.

'You probably wonder why anyone would live in a place like this,' he said, registering the look of incredulity on Kate's face.

'I do!'

'Cheapest accommodation there is,' he replied, 'for there's no rent and they cost nothing but a few days' labour to build. You can't buy land here as it is all owned by the South Australian Mining Company. "Sammy", as we call it, is too mean to build homes for its workers.'

She heard the heavy rain begin outside. 'God! You'd get washed out in a storm, though, would you not?'

Aidan's face broke into crinkles as he laughed, 'It has already happened once or twice, but there's no harm done, just sweep out the mud, dry everything out and it's ship-shape again.'

She shook her head. What a place to live in!

'There's been no one drowned, then?'

'More chance of dying of typhoid or smallpox, they say. With more than two thousand living in the creek all told, diseases are the real worry,' he said. 'But burrowing out a home, 'tis only natural, for most o' them are Cornish miners and digging underground is what they do best.'

Aidan lit the slush lamp on the table. The piece of rag set in a dish of fat emitted little light, but a lot of malodorous smoke. He told Kate some of the more interesting stories of the dugouts while they ate their simple supper. The tradesmen, such as bakers, butchers and grocers, simply called down the chimneys to let the women know that they had arrived on the banks above to sell their goods. Mischievous children would also call down the chimneys, or worse still, drop dead rats or pebbles down into the frying pans as dinner was being cooked. There was even one account of a young man who came to the dugout of his lover for a clandestine meeting. When the parents arrived home unexpectedly he tried to leave by the chimney and became stuck inside it. The girl's unsuspecting father lit a fire, causing the young man to come back down again in a great hurry.

Then Aidan fell silent and they listened to the rain trickling down the chimney and hissing on the embers of the fire. After living in the Far North the trickle of rain was still a welcome sound to Kate's ears. Aidan declared himself ready for bed. He fixed some blankets to make Kate a bed on the bare earthen floor. It didn't bother her, for she had slept on the bare earth ever since she had left Wildowie.

She settled down early for the night with a feeling of satisfaction. She had found a job and she had a safe place to sleep. Her disguise had obviously fooled Aidan Duffy. Not that she was too pleased about lying to the fellow, for he was such a dear. She could hear his snores as she lay contemplating her future. She had found out today that the date was the tenth day of June, 1851. It was the first time she had known the date for quite some time.

She had been in the colony for only twenty months but it had been a lifetime of adventures.

It made her wonder just where she would be when another twenty months had passed. At seven shillings a week her wages were not high. But they would be enough to save for her fare and food for the journey. The question was, where could she go from here?

She would love to go back to Adelaide. She wanted to see her friends Brigid, Rory and Harold. But it would be very risky. She knew not how seriously the police would be tracking her. Heaven knows, they might even be watching her friends' houses in case she turned up! And, of course, there was always the chance that she might get to Adelaide and not be able to find any of them.

Harold might be away carting goods. Rory might even be on his way to or from the Far North. Brigid may have taken a position elsewhere. Her journey might be for nothing. It might be that her best chances would come from staying in the Burra, for there was certainly a copper boom in this part of the colony and more work to be had here than in Adelaide. She would bide her time, save her pennies and watch for opportunities. She fell asleep with those thoughts on her mind.

'Turn out, turn out!' she heard the cry.

She sat up suddenly in her bed of blankets. Had she just dropped off to sleep and dreamt of a voice raised in alarm?

'The bridge is down, turn out, turn out!'

This time she had heard it for certain. This

was no dream. She could hear the heavy foot-steps of people running along the bank above her.

She jumped out of bed. 'Aidan, Aidan, get up quickly!' She heard no response so she stumbled through the darkness to his bed and shook him hard. 'Quickly, get up! The bridge is down! We are about to be washed out!' She helped the old fellow get to his feet.

He was very groggy and seemed unable to think about what should be done.

'Light, we need light!' Kate said and she heard him feel about him for the slush lamp and tinderbox.

As soon as it was lit Kate looked around. The water was already lapping under the door and across the floor.

'We've got to get out!' Kate cried.

'Take some of these blankets with you!' Aidan said, handing them to her. 'I've got to get the money out!'

Kate was amazed to see him attack the mud wall with a sharp knife, digging the clay away as fast as he could.

'What the devil?' she began.

'It's hidden in the wall, for there's no bank in the Burra,' he explained as he continued to scrape and dig.

Kate had worn her shirt to bed, so she had only to pull on her trousers and boots and jam her derringer into her pocket. She then picked up the blankets and her few belongings and made for the door handle. Her mistake was not thinking ahead to what lay beyond.

The door was pushed back with a whoosh and a wall of water two feet high flooded across the floor. Kate was pushed off balance and landed on her bottom. Fortunately the slush lamp was up on the table and they could at least see what was happening. She scrambled to her feet, collecting the wet blankets in her arms again.

'Get out!' Aidan called and they both struggled out of the door and waded through the fast-flowing water and up onto the bank.

The moonlit scene was pure chaos. Anything and everything floated past in the rapid water: horses, pigs, carts, fences, empty casks, tables, chairs, pots and pans. There were the sounds of panicked voices all around them, women screaming, men shouting in alarm, children crying.

'Stack them here!' Aidan called to Kate as he put the blankets down by the flour barrel chimney. 'You stay here and mind our gear, I'm going back for more!' He jammed the money further into his pocket as he ran.

Kate would have stopped him but he had gone before she could make a move.

A moment later he struggled up onto the bank with the pots, pans and other kitchen paraphernalia in one arm and the bullock tackle in the other. He dropped them at Kate's feet and disappeared again. The same scene was being played out above every dugout in the creek.

The next load was the bench seats.

'Now for the table!' he cried as he spun around to return to the dugout. The waters were rising fast now and Kate was getting worried.

'Hang on! The table is nothing compared to your life! It's getting too dangerous!' she said as she grasped at his sleeve.

'I'll be right!' he cried, and he was gone again.

A couple of minutes passed but there was no sign of Aidan.

Hang the valuables! Human life was the most precious thing there was. She abandoned her post and ran down the bank. She waded into the cold, muddy water flowing through the dugout door. The slush light was gone and she struggled to see in the darkness. She felt something big bump hard against her thighs. Her hands shot out to push it away before it knocked her feet from under her.

It was Aidan!

His body swirled past her in the water and out of the door. She lunged through the water after him, trying to get a hand-hold before he disappeared. She grasped a handful of his clothing. She was pulled off balance, lost her footing and was catapulted into the swirling, muddy maelstrom.

'Help! Help!' she called each time her head bobbed above the water. She had hold of Aidan now with both hands. She would not let him go. She could not grasp a secure hold on the bank without him being pulled away from her. Her cries were heard and people rushed along the bank calling to those ahead of them.

'Man in the water! Man in the water!'

Someone ahead threw in a heavy table. It splashed into the water ten feet ahead of Kate and she lunged for it, crashed into it painfully, and grasped it with one arm. The table began to move too, but only slowly. The next moment rough hands were holding her and pulling her out of the water. She was coughing and spluttering. Two big fellows had hold of both her and Aidan.

They were safe.

Someone draped a blanket over her shoulders and she quickly drew it around her to cover herself. She thanked God for the cover of darkness and the atmosphere of confusion. She hoped no-one had noticed the wet shirt clinging to her breasts. Aidan began to cough.

'You all right?' she asked him anxiously, wiping the mud from her face and eyes with the back of her hand.

'Yes,' he gasped. 'Lost me footing.'

'Thank heavens I came after you.'

Aidan laughed and gave a watery-sounding cough. 'He who's born to be hanged will not be drowned,' he said, winked at Kate and coughed again.

He looked older and more eccentric with his hair wet, his face muddy and his long white beard dripping muddy water.

She helped him to stand and they struggled up the bank together. Their rescuers had already disappeared. There was no one whom she could

337

thank. In the semi-darkness she was sure she had heard a familiar voice. Her ear strained for more but whoever it was had now gone.

They struggled back to their own chimney-place. Fortunately the things they had saved were still there. Aidan sat atop the pile and minded their gear while Kate helped their neighbours. Finally there was nothing more that could be done. News spread that they could spend the night in the great assembly room of the Burra Burra Hotel. Kate and Aidan joined the exodus of weary people trudging down the main street.

The scene in the hall was chaotic. Children were crying and grizzling, unaccustomed to being disturbed in the middle of the night, others lay sleeping on the floor or in their hapless parents' arms. Men and women were trudging mud through the place, trying to get their possessions under shelter for the night. Others were claiming that possessions should be left outside to leave more room for those who needed a place to sleep. Anxious-looking souls ran about asking if others had seen this person or that. The whole place smelt of wet, steaming, dirty clothes.

Kate was unable to change her clothes, for she had no others. She supposed they would eventually dry out from the warmth of her body. She pulled the fabric away from where it clung to her breasts and made sure she was well covered by her kangaroo-skin rug. She sat down on the floor next to Aidan, and watched the people around her. The reactions of humans in adversity, now that the danger was over, was fascinating.

Kate noticed, as she had at times like these before, that some people became heroic and almost noble, some became more caring and generous and there were inevitably those who took the opportunity to take what they could, whether it was someone else's blankets or a larger patch of floor than they needed. Natural leaders sprang up. Sometimes they were the ones that you would expect to take control and at other times they were the ones you had thought least likely to have the wherewithal. There were several men who had dumped their own things in a corner and, heedless of their own troubles, were helping the women and children, finding a place for them to lay their heads, offering to look for lost families or find blankets.

The incessant crying of a baby nearby caught Kate's attention. He sounded like Patrick and her heart went out to him. The mother looked tired and worn down. Kate knew instinctively that this was not the only trouble that had beset her. The woman had a number of very small children and no husband anywhere in sight. She was changing the baby's clothes and as she did so his infant wails were becoming more insistent. A toddler was standing nearby, shivering, and his older sister was grizzling, obviously cold and wet too.

'Here, I'll help you,' Kate said, getting up. 'Where are the clothes for these two?'

The women pointed to a large cloth bag and Kate delved through them to find some dry clothes. She started with the boy first. The mother nodded in silent thanks and put the baby to her breast. It was when Kate had almost finished getting the girl dressed that she heard once again that familiar voice, deep and strong.

'There's a bit of space over here for you, ma'am! Move over a little, would you, mate?'

Kate's heart skipped a beat, or it may have been two. Then it hammered away in a burst of excitement. That voice!

It was Rory!

She didn't think twice. She jumped to her feet, letting go of the child, and spun in the direction from which his voice had come.

'Rory!' her voice rang out joyously right across the hall, although he was only a few yards from her.

Chapter

Eleven

Rory looked at her, his face blank. That should have been enough to bring her to her senses.

It didn't.

The space between them closed in a split second as she launched herself towards him. She kissed him full on the mouth before he had a chance to fend her off.

'What the devil!'

Kate drew back, surprised at the almost hostile reaction she had received. 'Rory, it's me!'

Rory was totally bewildered, as if he had never met her before.

'It's me,' she urged.

Then she remembered that she was disguised as a boy. Her hair was cut short, her curves were covered and in all probability her face was covered with mud. She had been so excited to see him that she had even forgotten her disguise. She leant up towards him to whisper her secret in his ear but he held her off, wary of being kissed again by an unknown boy. She grabbed his arm and pulled him towards her.

'It's Kate, you fool!' she hissed.

His expression was ludicrous. It would have sent Kate into peals of laughter if she hadn't been so determined to keep her disguise. His face drained of all colour and he looked as though he had seen a ghost.

Kate put her finger to his mouth before an exclamation could escape him.

'Don't say a word!' she warned, her eyes dancing with mischief.

'Well if it isn't . . . um—'

'Declan.'

'Yes, Declan.' The look of shock was being replaced by one of unmitigated joy.

'O'Leary, Declan O'Leary, how could you forget?'

'Must have been the shock of seeing you again so unexpectedly. Declan O'Leary indeed! You've changed since I saw you last, young Declan!' Now he was playing the part. He grinned at her wickedly, which was fine, as long as he didn't give her away.

'Oh Rory, I'm so happy to see you, I could burst!'

'Well I'd best step back out of the way, then!'

'Indeed!' she laughed. She looked around her quickly, hoping she had not given herself away by kissing Rory. Almost everyone was attending to their own troubles. Only Aidan watched them, his eyes piercing beneath his muddied brows. She swallowed hard.

'Rory, come and meet Aidan. Aidan, an old friend of mine, Rory O'Connor. Rory, this is Aidan Duffy. I'm working for him as a billy-boy,' she said and shot Rory a look of warning.

The two men shook hands.

'You're a brave man if you've taken on this madcap as a helper!' Rory laughed as he shook hands with the older man.

'You should have warned me of that yesterday before I took him on,' Aidan laughed.

'Too late now!' Rory replied.

'And where did you two meet, then?' Aidan asked, his eyes alert as he watched their response.

'On the Great North Road. We travelled together for a while,' Rory replied smoothly.

Kate looked over at the children whom she had been dressing before she had heard Rory's voice. The mother was now finishing the job.

'Can you spare the lad for a while? I could do with some help outside,' Rory asked.

'Sure, we're all organised now, aren't we, Dec? I'm going to get forty winks before the sun comes up.'

Rory strode towards the back of the hall and through the door. Kate followed him as he made his way across the yard, through the drizzling rain, towards the stables.

He motioned with his finger against his lips,

took Kate's hand and led her inside. 'This looks like a quiet place where we can talk.'

There was a lantern, turned low, on a hook by the door. Rory picked it up and led her down past the assorted paraphernalia stored away from the rain, towards the back of the stables where the hay was stacked in bales.

The light of the lantern shone soft on the warm gold of the hay. There were the subdued sounds of horses snickering in their stalls.

He placed the lamp carefully on the floor and turned around.

'I thought you were going to give me away in there—'

She had no time to finish her sentence. Rory swept her into his arms, clasping her to his chest, crushing the air from her lungs.

'Oh, Kathleen!'

Her body was held up against his, breast to chest, thigh to thigh, hip to hip. His arms were tight around her, as if he would never let her go. His skin smelt of fresh rain and it blended with the sweet summery smell of the fresh hay. Being held by him was like coming home.

She arched back to look up into his eyes. 'Rory.' The word came out like a sigh and the hard, lonely months seemed to roll away.

'Oh, God,' he muttered, searching her face, 'I've missed you. I thought I'd never see you again.'

'I've missed you too.'

'Where the hell have you been?'

'You know where I've been! The Far North!'

'I heard you'd gone a lot further than that! I've had it on good authority that you'd passed on to the next world!'

'What?'

'Dead!'

'I heard you. But what on earth are you talking about?'

He pulled away slightly from her and held her at arm's length, as if he still could not believe it was really her. 'I can't believe you're really here.'

'Well it is me, I'm here and I'm alive and I'd like to know what the hell you are talking about!' She placed her hands on her trouser-clad hips and was grinning despite her demanding tone.

Rory pulled her down to sit next to him on a bale of hay. He held her hand with one of his own and fished in his breast pocket with the other. Out came a piece of newspaper, folded and frail. He opened it carefully and leant over to pull the lantern closer to them. It was the *Register*, dated May 15th, 1851. A month old.

New Evidence: Missing Woman Killed by Blacks In Far North, the headline read. Kate pulled it closer to read the fine text.

Mystery has shrouded the disappearance of domestic servant Miss Kate O'Mara from Wildowie Station in the Far North. The police outpost at Mount Remarkable was alerted five months ago after the woman disappeared in mysterious circumstances from the homestead.

No clue to her whereabouts could be found and she was presumed lost or taken by the blacks.

Fears have been heightened now that Police have found evidence at a deserted blacks' camp near the remote Far North station. A gown and locks of hair were positively identified by Pastoralist Mr James Carmichael as belonging to Miss O'Mara.

Blacks near the area were taken in for questioning by Police, with no result. They have now been released without charges being laid. There is no indication, at this stage, of who the culprits might be but investigations are continuing.

'Oh dear,' was all she said before she read on. She hadn't ever considered that she would be presumed dead. Worse still was that the Yuras were getting the blame for her demise.

The woman disappeared on the same afternoon as the overseer, Mr Angus Campbell, was fatally speared by blacks.

A search was mounted by the station hands from Wildowie and its nearest neighbours after Miss O'Mara failed to appear that evening. It is believed that Miss O'Mara may have gone to Mr Campbell's aid as she did on a previous occasion. It is probable that she was taken by the blacks as a result. The evidence found last week confirms this.

The gunshot wound on Mr Campbell's body still has police mystified. After receiving the fatal spear wounds, Mr Campbell may have turned his gun on himself, although the absence of powder burns around the wound places some doubt on this theory. Police now believe it is more likely that Mr Campbell may have been shot by the blacks with his own gun, presumably taken from him after he had been speared.

'Oh Jesus!' They certainly had that bit wrong! No blame on her, thank God, but she pitied the Yuras now that this theory had taken hold. The next passage confirmed her fears.

This has raised alarm in the Far North since it may signify that the blacks intend to equip themselves with firearms. If so, settlers are at greater risk of attack from these brutal savages. There has been a call from pastoralists for increased police presence in the Far North as a result.

The disappearance and probable death of Miss O'Mara, and the death of Mr Campbell, have prompted further warnings from Police that settlers in the Far North need to be prepared for the possibility of native attack.

Miss O'Mara arrived in the colony, from Ireland, on the Elgin *in September 1849. According to the Superintendent of the Irish Orphans Depot, Mr Moorfield, Miss O'Mara had taken the remote posting against his advice and despite warnings of the dangers of the bush.*

'Jesus and Mary, I never thought for one moment that this would have happened,' she closed her eyes and rubbed one hand over her face. 'The poor Yuras. They save me and then take the blame for my death. And I walked out of there as free as a bird. I should have realised that I would never be blamed. Not in their wildest dreams would the police ever consider that one white would kill another to save the blacks. Never.'

Rory watched her, his thick black brows raised, waiting for her to explain herself. 'Do you think you might let me in on the picture?' he asked.

'Promise me you'll not think badly of me if I tell you? I've not yet told a soul all that happened.'

'D'you think there's anything that you could have done that would cause me to think any less of you? You might have broken every one of the ten blasted commandments and I'd still not hold it against you.'

'I think I have.'

She had committed adultery with James. She had taken God's name in vain. She had failed to remember the Sabbath. Her actions had hardly honoured her father and mother. She had coveted her neighbour's possessions. She had stolen, admittedly only a shirt . . . Her mind struggled to remember the other commandments. There was the one she could never forget: thou shalt not commit murder.

'Tell me, Kathleen.'

Kate sat down on the bale again and bowed her head in her hands. If he was to understand at all then she would have to tell him the whole story, from the beginning to the end.

'Almost two years ago it was that I left you at Bungaree,' she began.

Rory did not interrupt her as she told him about the rest of the journey to Wildowie. She told him about how lonely she had been on the station, how desperate she had been for company, how much she had missed Brigid. He didn't say 'I told you so', even though he had. She didn't tell him how much she had missed him. It was no point saying that when she was about to tell him how she had become James's mistress. She explained how it was that James had played so skilfully on her loneliness, how he had made the most of her yearning for security. How she had gone to his bed. Then she paused, her eyes flicking up to his.

The look in Rory's eyes was hard. His mouth was held in a grim line. Tiny muscles flickered in his jaw as if he was struggling to control himself. And no wonder. He had wanted her himself and now he had to listen to the story of how another man had taken her.

'You were right. I should have listened to you. James used me. I can see it now. But he was so clever about it. I fell for it completely.'

'You always have been pretty naive, as much as you like to think that you're not. How old were you at the time, Kathleen? Eighteen?'

'Just seventeen.'

'Well there you have it. James was a damned scoundrel then.'

'But you can't blame him, Rory. It was my choice. I knew what I was doing. I walked into his arms with my eyes open.'

'He had a duty to protect you. He was in a position of power as your employer and as a man of the world.'

'I was no innocent. I lived in a workhouse, remember.'

'Rubbish! You were still wandering about with your head full of dreams. He took advantage of you.'

'You can't blame him entirely. You know that.'

'Sure I know that. I wanted you myself, remember. Maybe I'm just a bad loser.'

Her hand went to his arm and she said, 'You wouldn't have done what he did, though. You've got a sense of decency. James hasn't. There's more to the story.'

She went on.

'So what did he do? Offer to marry you?' Rory snorted.

'No, of course not.' She told him what James had said and done, and how she had refused to go along with his plans.

Finally she recounted the story of that fateful day when Angus had discovered the blacks.

'*You* shot him!'

She nodded. 'Dead.'

'Not the blacks?'

'No, me. I did it.'

His jaw had dropped down and his eyes were alight with a strange light.

She paused a moment while she tried to read the message in his blazing eyes. 'I had to. It was me, the baby and the Yuras, or it was him. If I didn't do it then, it would have been the end of me. There was no choice, really, there wasn't!'

'Oh, Kathleen!' he shook his head as if he could not believe it, '*You* shot Angus Campbell!' He started to laugh. 'With the pistol that I gave you?'

'Yes, I'm sorry. You didn't mean me to go shooting someone when you gave it to me. I'm sorry, Rory.'

But her apologies went unnoticed. Rory threw his head back and laughed, a throaty laugh full of joy that reverberated around the stables.

'What are you laughing for? It was no joke!'

Rory jumped up and hugged her to him, then he held her at arm's length, admiration written all over his face. 'Oh, Kathleen! I don't hold with killing, but you're a wonderful woman. Never was there a bastard more deserving of being shot and never has there been a better woman to do it. Good on you!'

'Rory! It was a crime! And a sin as well!' The very thought of it made her look over her shoulder to ensure that no one was listening there.

He became serious. 'No, it was not murder and don't be saying that it was. It was self-defence, plain and simple, and no jury would convict you otherwise.'

'I'm hoping it doesn't ever get to a jury.'

'So am I, my darlin', but we'll get to that later. Tell me the rest. What happened then? What did you do? What happened to the baby?' He had not forgotten the baby.

She told him how she had the baby while still living with the Yuras. She explained her reasons for leaving him there while she came south to build some sort of life for him.

There were tears glistening in her eyes as she finished, 'I didn't want to leave him, I wanted him to be with me forever, but I had to. You see that don't you, Rory?'

She hadn't cried when she told him about Dan, the pregnancy, Adnyini or even that scoundrel James and the way he had treated her. She hadn't cried when she told him about her near brush with death. But she cried about leaving the baby. That hurt more than all the rest put together.

'Sure I can see that. There was nothing else you could do at all.' He pulled out a rain-dampened handkerchief from the pocket of his moleskins and dried her tears.

'I miss him so much.'

'I'm sure that you do.'

'You don't think that I'm a bad mother, then?'

'Not at all, Kathleen. You had a hard choice to make and you looked after his needs instead of your own.'

He watched her in silence for a moment before saying the next words: 'So I suppose you'll be looking for a good father for young Patrick, then?'

His tone was easy but his gaze was sharp.

She shook her head. 'No, he has a father, a father who will be made to acknowledge him. I'll find a way somehow. I won't let James get away with this one. He might have ridden roughshod over me, but he won't be allowed to ride roughshod over Patrick. I'll find a way to make him claim his son as his heir if it means that I pursue him to the ends of the earth.'

'I thought by now you'd have learnt that no good will ever come of you pursuing James and his station.'

'You're right. I'll not pursue him. I don't want his blasted station. Not for myself. But one day it will belong to Patrick, I'll make sure of that.'

'Can't you just let the past go? Have you not learnt that lesson? Put it all behind you.'

'I have. I don't give two hoots for the man.'

'If that were true then you'd forget all about him. But you haven't done that. It's like the famine, you once told me that you'd put all of that behind you too, but you hadn't. That drove you into James's arms and it will drive you to your grave if you don't let it go. Let it all go, let the famine go, let James go. Forget him, start again with a clean slate and decide what it is you really want out of life. Don't keep chasing these hopeless dreams!'

'They are not hopeless.'

Memories of Ireland flashed through her

mind. The cold, the hunger. Patrick dying in her arms. They were not just dreams that drove her. They were realities. She shook her head as if to brush the memories away.

Rory picked up a piece of hay and stuck it in his mouth. He watched her for a moment, the piece of hay on his lower lip. 'So what are you going to do?' he asked.

'I'm not sure. I have to get enough money to set myself up, to give Patrick a reasonable home. Then I will go back to get him.'

'You'd best start by going to the police and telling them what really happened up there.'

'What? Go to the police? Are you mad?'

'You have to. They're still looking for you.'

'They wouldn't be looking now. They'd have given up hope.'

'At least clear the blacks. They think the blacks took you.'

This gave her reason to pause. She didn't want the Yuras to take the blame for her disappearance.

'No, if there were going to be reprisals, then they would have been carried out already,' she said, thinking aloud. 'They would have happened in the months when I was with them.'

'What about Brigid? What about Harold? They are grieving your death, just as I was. Even that bastard James must have some feeling. He must have your death on his conscience. Don't you have some responsibility to let people know that you're still alive?'

She placed her finger between her teeth. 'Yes I

do. But how do I do that? If I go to the police and tell them that I have walked out of the bush, alive and well, after six months, they are going to ask me why I disappeared in the first place.'

'Tell them you got lost in the bush.'

'And survived on my own for six months? They won't believe that!'

'Then tell them the blacks helped you. Give the blacks a better reputation.'

'They'll ask why the Yuras didn't just take me to Wildowie or to another station.'

'You've got a point there.'

Rory chewed on his piece of hay and Kate sucked the tip of her index finger.

'You could tell them that the blacks found you a long way from Wildowie and by then the baby was on the way.'

'The last thing I want to do is to tell them about the baby! They will ask me where he is! If I tell them I left him with the Yuras they will be horrified. They'll dash up there to save the white baby from the influence of the savages. I'll never get him back. They will think I'm neglectful. They'll put him into an orphanage and I know how orphans get treated. No way will I do that.'

'Simple. Tell them the baby died in the bush.'

'Then I would have to register his death.'

'So?'

'So then when he reappears he can no longer claim to be the son of James Carmichael.'

'Does it matter that much?'

'Yes it does. You forget that I was an orphan.

I had no father to look after me. I had no advantages in life. Look where it got me. Nowhere! I won't let that happen to Patrick.'

'Listen to me, Kathleen. I lived through the hunger too. I saw people dying every day. I won't forget it for as long as I live, but I've decided not to let it blight my life. I'm determined to enjoy myself. I'm not going to waste my time striving for things that are beyond my grasp. If they come my way, fine. If they don't, so be it.'

'Well, that isn't my way and it doesn't solve my problem here and now. What will I tell the police?'

'If you're not prepared to tell them the truth then it sounds like it is better to say nothing at all.'

'That's what I said in the beginning.'

Rory just shook his head. First light crept through the tiny windows. His face seemed somehow older, the strands of silver sprinkled at his temples more pronounced as the cold grey of first light illuminated his face. She had relieved herself of her burdens by sharing them with him. Now he looked weighed down too.

'You and trouble certainly seem to be attracted to one another.'

'I know,' she said, her voice catching as she spoke.

He drew her into his arms and rested his chin upon her head.

'My darlin' Kathleen,' he said, 'I can't say it

wasn't that bad, for it was all worse than I would ever have imagined it to be.' He put his finger under her chin and tilted her face up to his. 'But it is in the past now and you won't be making the same mistakes again.'

'You don't think I'm bad?'

'No, I don't think you're bad at all. For everything you did wrong you did something right as well. You saved the blacks, you saved Harold's life. You loved that baby enough to leave him behind where he would be safe. You did your best and that is all anyone could ask of you. I'm just sorry that I wasn't there to protect you from all of it. I should have been the one to stop you from going in the first place. I'm the one who told you in the beginning about the bush being the only place to get work. I could kick myself for it now, though. I'm sorry about it all, I really am.'

'You're the last one to be held responsible. You only told me the facts about the colony. I was the one who made the decision to go. I was the one who shot Angus. D'you think I'll go to hell?'

Rory smiled a slow, sad kind of smile. 'I'm not the one to grant you absolution, Kathleen,' he said, and then his mouth spread in a wider grin. 'But there is one thing that we'd best give our thanks to God for.'

'And what is that?'

'That he didn't give us more than ten commandments, for you'd still have some left waiting to be broken!' he said, smiling in a lopsided way.

She laughed through her tears, 'Oh Rory!'

'Come on outside,' he said, taking her arm. 'The grooms will be up and about soon and in to harness the horses.'

They strolled down to the Burra creek to see the aftermath of the flood. Rory talked as they walked, telling Kate how he had been up north to cart goods to another station, leaving Clare soon after the rains had begun. He had arrived at Mount Remarkable some time after the news of her disappearance. After delivering the goods he had continued on to Wildowie to help to look for her.

They had given her up for dead and he had returned south, taking the route from Bungaree to Burra Burra instead of to Clare, with the intention of taking on work carting for the mines. Burra was one place he had not been before and he was keen to see the mine first-hand. He had arrived yesterday afternoon and had taken a room at the boarding house in Creek Street. He, too, had been washed out when the creek flooded.

They sat side by side on a rough rail fence and looked at the mess left in the wake of the flash flood. The dugouts were a scene of utter devastation. Many were mud-filled as the walls and roofs had collapsed under the pressure of the rising water. Everything from crockery to dead chooks lay partially submerged in mud. It was a dismal scene.

'And here I am again with disaster following

close on my heels,' she said wryly. 'Trust my luck for the creek to flood on my first night in the Burra!'

Rory laughed, 'Maybe it was me who brought the bad luck into town, this time. I arrived at the same time, you know.'

Kate looked up into his laughing eyes. Rory always made her feel so good, even when everything was going wrong. His eyes held hers as the seconds ticked by.

His hand slid surreptitiously to hers and he clasped the tiny fingers in his own broad hand. 'Did you not wonder why I went looking for you in the first place, Kathleen?'

She hadn't thought much about it at all. She was thinking more about James. Had he grieved when he found her gone? As much as she had hardened her heart against him when he rejected her, she couldn't stop herself from thinking about him, wondering about him, about what made him tick, about whether there would ever be any hope for Patrick.

Her eyes dropped away for a moment then returned to his. She had forgotten his question.

'What about James? Did he seem upset about my disappearance? Did he say anything about the baby?'

Rory's face fell. 'Jesus, you're a mug! It beats me why you'd be concerned about that man now.'

Kate did not reply. She was thinking. If there was no murder charge, there was no reason not to see James again. She wanted to see him. She would tell him about his son. Maybe she should wait until she had the boy with her again. Maybe the sight of him would stir James's paternal feelings. Surely no one could fail to respond to that beautiful blond boy of hers.

Her thoughts returned to the man beside her. Rory would be a good father and she knew that in his earlier question there had been an unstated offer. She looked up at him. She realised from the hurt in his eyes that she had been neglecting his feelings entirely. She was instantly full of remorse.

'Here I am talking about James when the far better man is right here next to me. Thank you for coming to look for me, Rory, I'm sorry it was nothing but a wild-goose chase. Mother of Mary,' she laughed, 'I now understand why you thought you were seeing a ghost last night!'

He shrugged his great shoulders. 'I'm just glad you're alive and kicking.'

'You're not the only one. Thank God I survived it all,' she said, crossing herself.

'And what d'you think you learnt from the experience? Anything?'

'I guess that I learnt to heed your advice, especially about men, guns, and the Far North!' she grinned at him. Then her look became more serious. 'I learnt that it wasn't going to be as easy to make my fortune as I thought it would be—'

'So you'll give up on that crazy dream, then?' There was a look of hope in his eyes.

'It was not a crazy dream! I'm still aiming to make my fortune. I still want a sheep station. It's not that I want to be the grand lady any more. It's for Patrick now. But this time I'll be more sensible in the way I go about it.'

'So what will you be doing differently this time?'

'I have learnt to think twice before I go dashing off in search of my dreams. I'll not be taking off anywhere to be a domestic servant. That's no way to get ahead. And I'll not be taking up with any rich squatters until the ring is firmly on my finger!'

'You are joking I hope?'

'Well . . . sort of . . .' she said, and her words trailed away lamely.

'You're a worry sometimes! Haven't you worked out yet that the life of a lady would hardly suit you at all? A woman with your spirit could never tolerate the confines of that life for too long—'

'I don't know about that,' she snapped.

'Well I do know and I say you'd be kicking over the traces in no time. A woman who likes working the bullocks and living with the blacks in the bush is not going to be happy sitting quietly in a drawing room.'

'I'll be the best judge of that.'

He shook his head as if disgusted with her, but he smiled nonetheless. 'You've not exhibited a great degree of judgement so far.'

'I don't know,' she smiled. 'I have chosen you as a friend!'

'My point exactly!' Rory gave her a wicked look and twirled his moustache.

Kate laughed at him.

Then he became more serious again. 'So what will you do right now?'

It was a question they were to discuss often over the next few days, but never when Aidan was present, for Kate did not want to let him in on the secret of her identity; not yet. The three of them were working together, reconstructing Aidan's dugout so that they had somewhere to sleep. Accommodation was short since so many homes had been destroyed.

Kate had insisted to Rory that she keep her disguise, at least in the near future. She did not want her identity to be discovered. Not until she had worked out a plausible story for the police. Besides, there were three men for every woman in the Burra and she didn't want the attention that her female status would bring. As well as that, there was plenty of work for bullockies and their offsiders but work for female domestics was scarce. None of the miners' wives could afford to pay for help. And the mine captains needed no more domestic help than they had already. She felt sure that as soon as she donned a gown she would lose any hope of continuing her current work.

It was a good time to be in the Burra. The community feeling was strong. People had banded together to help each other overcome the difficulties caused by the floods. The price of copper was high and the people of the Burra had the satisfaction of knowing that it was their mine and their hard work that had saved the colony from financial collapse. The first elections in South Australia were due to be held and there was much campaigning and excited talk of reform going on in the electorate.

Since Kate, Aidan and Rory were not property owners in the Burra they would not be voting. Even if Kate had owned property, as a woman she would still have been unable to vote, so she took little interest in the relative merits of the rival candidates.

She noticed that Aidan was watching her closely and she wondered if he suspected she was not what she appeared. She said nothing to him, since she didn't want to fuel any doubts that he might have about her or her identity. She was not sure just how the police would react if they found that her death was nothing but a hoax and a waste of their precious time. There were very few police in the colony as they were not at all well paid. Those that were present were very thinly spread indeed.

Within two days they had put the dugout to rights, although it was still fairly damp inside. Aidan had offered Rory a place to stay and he had gladly taken him up on it. In return, Rory offered to shout Aidan and Declan a meal at the Burra Burra Hotel. For both Kate and Aidan it was a real treat. Aidan even lent Kate a clean shirt for the occasion.

The hotel was always a wild spot and even more so on Saturday nights when the miners had been paid. But it was not Saturday and the hotel seemed to be in full swing nonetheless. There was a sense of high excitement in the air. There were people in every condition: sober, drunk, elated, joyous and quarrelsome. Some were singing, others crying, and the din was astounding. It was certainly one of those nights when the publican would be clearing the place at midnight with the swing of his cricket bat.

Before Rory's party had even found themselves a table or chairs they had heard the news shouted across the room.

'Gold!'

It was the word on everybody's lips. Gold had been found in New South Wales. A copy of the Adelaide *Register* from the previous day was shoved in front of them. There it was in big letters. Gold! It had been found at a place called Ophir and the rush was on. It was said that there would be more gold than had caused the rush of 1849 in California.

Kate, Rory and Aidan listened to the excited talk going on around them. People were already making plans to leave. The Cornish miners here were not well paid and gold offered them the chance to make a fortune.

'I'm going too!' Kate announced, her eyes shining bright with the thrilling thought of making a fortune.

'Hold on, Dec!' Rory cautioned her, 'New

South Wales is a hell of a long way from here. How were you thinking of getting there, might I ask?'

'However these others are going to get there, I suppose. It doesn't matter, just as long as I get there before all the gold is taken.'

'It would be a dangerous overland trip of many months. That or you'd have to go 'round by sea! Where would you get the money?'

'I'll get it somehow!' she asserted enthusiastically. She was not going to let a little thing like money get in her way, not when there was a fortune to be made!

Aidan shook his head. 'There's plenty of fools who will join a rush before there's any certainty of enough gold to be found. I'd wait for a while if I were you.'

'He's right, Dec, wait a while, see if it is all it's cracked up to be before you rush off. At least wait until you have enough money to get there safely. If there really is enough gold to make a fortune, then it'll be there waiting for you in a few months' time.'

When Kate had slept on it she had to admit that rushing off might be unwise. She had already rushed off to one remote place to make her fortune and she had come back with nothing in her pockets. And she had learnt a little about heeding Rory's warnings. She would wait and watch what happened at Ophir.

In many ways, her decisions about the immediate future were dictated by two things: the fact that she owned no more than the clothes she stood in and her fears about the repercussions of her disappearance. She wanted to reclaim Patrick and see James but she would have to wait until the smoke had cleared. She wanted to see Brigid and Harold, to tell them that she was not dead, but that would have to wait now too. She would continue working for Aidan until she had saved enough money to move on.

She enjoyed the company of the bullockies and she liked working the bullocks. Most of all, she loved the open air, the bush and the sense of freedom that came from travelling the rough tracks. She certainly knew enough about working the bullocks to be a good helper to Aidan and that in itself was a great source of satisfaction to her. As each day went by Aidan seemed to be getting slower and slower, as if his age had finally begun to catch up with him.

Rory was working his team alongside theirs, so she got to see him during the day too. She loved to watch him as he worked, the play of muscles under his flannel shirt as he tossed logs onto the drays, the sight of those legs and hips firmly encased in moleskins, the view of him from the back, the way his body tapered from his broad shoulders to his slim backside. She loved the way he grinned with his teeth showing white against the healthy tan of his skin, the way he joked and told yarns with the other teamsters. Watching him took her breath away.

If only Rory was the type of man she was

looking for, she thought, and not for the first time. But Rory was Rory. He would never be anything but a rover. It was part of his charm, and without doubt it was a good reason not to treat him as anything more than a friend.

She got to know Aidan a lot better as they worked in the bush. He was a dear old fellow. He, too, had lost his family in the famine. It was something they had in common. Rory had brothers and sisters back in Ireland and he hoped to convince them that they ought to come out to the colony too. It was a close companionship that the three of them had developed. They were all Irish, they all had a sense of fun and they all loved the bullocky's life. Rory claimed that there was nothing in the world that he would trade it for.

As it turned out, Kate was glad that she had not left precipitously for the Ophir goldfields, for within a month even better news came their way.

Gold had been discovered in Victoria.

'The new diggings at Clunes are only three hundred and sixty miles from Adelaide! The journey would not be that much greater than the journey from Adelaide to the Far North!' she enthused as they ate dinner that night.

'Hold on, Dec,' Aidan warned again. They were eating stew and the gravy was trickling down his chin and into his white beard, 'You're too keen on just rushing off without really thinking it through. What are you intending to do, dig for the gold yourself?'

'Why not?'

'Well, for one thing, you're not strong enough, lad.'

Rory added his piece. 'I've talked to men who joined the 'forty-nine rush to California. Most of the Forty-niners came back disappointed. It's a rare few who will make their fortunes by digging for the gold. For every man who makes it rich there are another fifty or a hundred who will come back penniless. The only men who make fortunes out of gold rushes are the gold dealers, the pimps, the shopkeepers and the publicans, anyone who speculates or who can provide things needed by those who are digging for their dinner.'

Aidan agreed with him. 'When you've been around as long as I have you know there's no easy road to riches for most of us.'

Kate was barely listening. She was thinking about Patrick. If she could get rich in the gold rush, she could buy a station to set him up. It was the opportunity she had been looking for. Her attention returned to Rory and Aidan.

'Well then, how are we going to make our fortunes?'

'Are you determined to go then, Dec?' Rory asked her.

'I am.'

'Is there nothing that will stop you?'

She shook her head.

Rory let out a long sigh. 'I must admit it, my feet are getting itchy, too. There are too many restrictions in this company town. I get tired of hearing that I can't do this or that just because "Sammy" has said so. And we'll not be making a good living out of carting timber for the smelters. Sammy's too mean. What about you, Aidan? Feel like roaming again?'

Aidan looked shrewdly from Kate to Rory. 'D'you two young ones want an old feller along?'

'The more the merrier!' It would be a pleasure to have Aidan along, but she was so excited at the prospect of gold that she'd have accompanied anyone to the goldfields.

'I won't be slowing you down too much?'

'Not at all. What do we need, then? Shovels, picks . . .?'

Rory held up his hand, 'Hold your horses, Dec. I'll not be digging for gold, and if you have any sense, neither will you!'

'Oh,' she felt her heart sink. Why bother going?

'We'll have to think of some other way to make money there. Maybe we could take a few others on the drays and charge them for it.'

They all thought for a moment.

'I have a better idea,' Kate said slowly.

The other two looked up at her, their knives and forks poised in mid-air while they waited expectantly.

'What is the thing that everyone needs on the goldfields?'

'Gold, of course,' muttered Aidan.

'It's what they're wanting, not what they're needing. Think about it.'

Rory shrugged, 'Food and water, a place to sleep . . .'

'There will be water in the creeks at this time of the year and they'll sleep in tents if not under the stars,' Aidan added.

'Which leaves food,' Kate said, nodding sagely. 'There will be people rushing over there without packing so much as a picnic lunch—'

'Just like you would have done if we hadn't stopped you,' Rory laughed.

'True enough! There won't be enough food in Victoria to feed all the people coming in from all over Australia, never mind those rushing from the rest of the world.'

'So?' Aidan waited.

'So what does South Australia already produce in great quantities?'

'Wheat,' Rory said, tucking into his dinner.

'Well then, that's what we'll be doing. We'll be carting flour to sell to the hungry hordes! We'll be able to ask any price we want. They'll be swapping their precious new-found gold for some real food in their bellies!'

'Great idea, lad.' Rory rubbed his beard with one hand as he thought about it.

'He's no fool this boy,' the older man added.

'Duffy, O'Leary and O'Connor, Flour Merchants!' she extended her hand to shake with the two men.

They talked far into the night. They would take both the drays: Rory's and Aidan's. And they would take all the flour that could be hauled by the bullocks. Rory had enough money to buy the flour. Aidan had some too. Kate could pay them back from the first round of profits. Anything they needed for their journey could be bought cheaply. People were leaving the Burra in droves and they were selling up everything they owned to get to the goldfields.

If their venture was successful they would make as many trips as they could possibly manage. All going well they might be able to hire other teamsters to help them.

Finally Aidan nodded off in his chair.

Kate woke him. 'You'd be more comfortable in your bed.' She gave him a hand as he stumbled towards the other room.

'There's just one thing we haven't discussed yet,' Rory said, his voice lowered so as not to wake Aidan from his sleep.

'And what is that?' She sat down again and picked up her pannikin of half-cold tea.

'How are you feeling about us two travelling together?'

'What d'you mean?' she asked, putting her tea down again.

'I thought you said that you weren't that naive any more. You know I'm attracted to you. That hasn't changed.'

'. . . I did guess as much,' she admitted reluctantly.

'And you can't deny you have feelings for me too.'

The look in his eyes made her heart flip over

as he said it. She felt the heat rush to her cheeks. No, she couldn't deny the attraction she felt towards Rory. But he was not a part of her long-term plans.

'I am sure that we can place our feelings aside—'

'Can we?' he interrupted.

'Well I can, at any rate.'

His eyes appraised her coolly before he replied. 'And what if I can't?'

'You'll have to. Otherwise it would look pretty damned strange. You're a man and I'm a boy, after all. I don't intend to go to the diggings dressed as a woman, that's for sure. There'd be ten men for every woman. It causes too much unwanted attention. I learnt that the hard way.'

'So you think you can ignore what is between us?'

No, she couldn't ignore it. It would always be there. But nor could she give in to it. Falling in love with Rory O'Connor was something she wasn't going to let herself do.

He was watching her, waiting for her response. She felt hot and uncomfortable. She didn't want to hurt him. She didn't want him to be angry with her. She needed him. She wanted his friendship, she wanted the security of having him there. She wanted him to be around to pull her out of the scrapes that she inevitably got into.

She wasn't mercenary, but she did need the capital he would provide.

She stood up. 'Rory,' she said, 'I do want you, I do need you, but as a friend. Can't we just leave it at that? Isn't that enough?'

Rory stood up and pushed his chair back violently.

'God, Kathleen! You'd try the patience of a saint. You can never see what's in front of your face. Your ambition stands in the way!'

'Keep your voice down!'

'Don't tell me you don't feel it too!' he ground out in a quieter voice.

'Not so much that it can't be put aside—'

Rory covered the distance between them in one long stride. His hands came around on either side of her and were placed firmly against the mud wall, forcing her to move backwards, imprisoning her without touching her, forcing her to look at him.

She could not release herself from the confines of his arms unless she touched him to do so. He leant close, looking down into her eyes. She could not look away without acknowledging the truth of his words.

'Tell me the feelings are not strong for you too, Kathleen!'

She felt his breath against her cheek. She looked into his eyes. They shone with an intensity that owed nothing to the soft light of the slush lamp. The laughter lines had disappeared, and been replaced by a look of utter vulnerability. Her heart bumped against her ribs. She could not deny it. She could not tell him that she felt nothing. She could not lie while she looked into his face so close above hers.

'Oh, Rory,' her voice came out in a sigh.

His lips met hers, gently at first. She did not resist. His hands slid to either side of her face. His eyes searched hers, looking deep into her soul between kisses more sweet and tender than she had ever felt before. She could not have stopped him now, even if she had wanted to.

His lips, firm and warm on hers, sent wave after wave of exquisite pleasure coursing through her. The kisses deepened as the seconds went by. Kate could not check her response to him. Her arms went up about his neck, her fingers toying with the curls on the collar of his flannel shirt and she felt his arms come around her, holding her to him. She felt the heat of those wide hands on her slender back. His arms could have encircled her more than once, she was so small against him.

His lips broke away for no more than a moment and he murmured, 'Tell me you don't feel it now.'

She melted against him, her hands pulling him more closely to her and her only response was a groan, lost in the depths of their kiss. Her hands roamed over his body, his back first, then his chest, broad and muscled, down his flat stomach and to his hips. His hands sought out the contours of her body and their breathing became ragged as each explored the other, their yearnings denied for so long.

'Oh God, Kathleen,' he groaned, raining kisses on her throat.

There was a sound from the other room. They both paused to listen. It was Aidan. The spell was broken. Kate pushed away from him.

'He must be talking in his sleep,' Rory whispered, and pulled her back to him.

She put her hands against his chest to hold him away. 'Rory, no! Not now, not here! I don't want him to know,' she whispered urgently.

He released her and she spun away from him. 'Can't you see? It's no good! We can't allow this to happen again!'

'I can't help myself!'

'Don't be ridiculous! You'll have to, or we cannot go together to the diggings, it's as simple as that!'

'It's not simple at all. I'm a red-blooded man, not a saint.'

'We keep it strictly friendship and business, or not at all, Rory. They're my terms. Otherwise let's call the whole thing off. I'll not have you giving my identity away and I'll not go to Victoria as a woman.'

She didn't say the words that were on the tip of her tongue. She could not tell him the truth: that there could be no future for her and Rory. Patrick must come first.

'Even if it means us not going over there together and you not making your fortune?'

There was a moment of silence. '. . . Yes.'

If it came down to it, she would go on her

own. As much as she wanted Rory to go with her, it was not worth sacrificing her goal. Patrick and the money were the things that she wanted.

'You drive a hard bargain, Kathleen.'

'I have to.'

Rory shook his head and ran his hands through his hair again, 'This is the last thing I wanted. We're quarrelling like a couple of children. What are we going to do?'

'Let's just stay as friends—'

'What if you do make a fortune, what then?'

'I can make no promises. We will have to see.'

Chapter

Twelve

Accommodation in Adelaide was easy to get. Many of the colonists had already made their way over to Victoria and there were plenty of cheap rooms. Adelaide was like the Burra in that most of the able-bodied men had already gone. The rush was on and soon only the old, the sick and the women would be left.

Rory tracked down Brigid Mulcahey. She was still working as a nanny just out of town, at North Adelaide. Rory and Kate walked up there to see her. Rory went in first to let Brigid know that Kate was not only very much alive but was outside the house, and dressed in boys' clothing.

Brigid dashed back inside only long enough to dump the baby into the cook's lap and then came tearing out again, down the central pathway from the front door of the house, through the flower garden and the gate and into Kate's arms.

Rory tactfully left them alone to exchange

their news. Kate told Brigid the bare bones of all that had happened since she had left Adelaide.

'Well I'm pleased you've come to your senses now,' Brigid told her after she had commiserated on Kate's ill fortune. They were strolling up and down the roadside looking at some of the grand houses of North Adelaide as they talked.

'Pardon?'

'You've finally come to your senses—giving up on that high and mighty Mr Carmichael.'

'I haven't—' she murmured.

Brigid didn't stop to listen, she just carried on, '—and taking up with Rory O'Connor, he'd have to be one of the best men this colony has seen.'

'Rory is just a friend, Brigid, that's all.'

'He's more than that, surely!'

'No, indeed he is not. I'm determined to get ahead, for Patrick's sake. I won't be doing that if I hitch up with Rory. Patrick is my first priority. He has to be.'

'Rory won't stop you!'

'I'm not so sure about that. He's not interested in the things that I want. We've discussed it many times. Besides, there's no hope of James ever taking his paternal responsibilities seriously if Rory shoulders them for him. I have to think of that first.'

'You sound like a schemer, Kate, and it is not like you. In the old days you never had a merce-nary bone in your body!' She looked her friend up and down.

'Well I've changed. And no surprise it is after what I've been through. I've learnt a thing or two about the world. I must ensure Patrick never faces a future as bleak as ours has been. And there's no way I'd marry Rory, not until I can ensure that!' She had lowered her voice so that Rory could not hear her from where he was waiting.

'I can just imagine how he feels about that. I've seen him a couple of times since you met on the Great North Road and he adores you!'

'It's not just him that hurts, you know. I have to deny my own needs for Patrick's sake.'

Brigid looked at her. 'I think you have it all back to front nevertheless. A loving family here and now would be better for young Patrick than the hope of a rich but unloving father later in life.'

'We lived in loving families. What good did it do us? We still starved in the famine. Did we not?'

'There is nothing I can reply to that, Kate.'

'Exactly my point.'

Kate changed the subject, hoping Brigid would not come up with a better argument. She didn't want to hear it if she did. She told Brigid that she, Rory and Aidan were off to the diggings to sell flour.

'Will you come with us, Brigid?'

'No, Kate. I'm not that adventurous. You should know that by now. I'll stay here and save steadily. It's more my style.'

Kate shrugged. 'I understand that. You're settled here and you're happy. What else has been happening in your life? We've only been talking about me so far.'

'Nothing so exciting or so dangerous. I was at the depot until February last year, then I came out to this position as nanny to the Jenners' baby. They treat me very well, I'm happy here.'

'What about your young man?'

'I'm waiting for him to come back. He left for the goldfields last month. He says that once he has made enough money he will come back for me and we'll buy a small shop or something,' she smiled shyly.

'Well good on you, you had better snap him up as soon as he gets back! Or hang on, maybe you should set your sights on Rory since you think so much of him!'

'Don't say that, Kate, I may well take you up on the offer and you'll be sorry you ever made it.'

The two friends laughed together. It was the sign that Rory had been looking for. He caught up with them on the roadside.

'Have you two had enough time to catch up on news? We've got to get going out to Harold's, Kate,' he said.

Brigid and Kate hugged again and made plans to see each other when Kate got back from the goldfields. After they left Brigid's they went on out to Enfield, further north of the town, to see Harold. His private comments to Kate were much the same as Brigid's.

That night Kate thought about what her old friends had said to her. Was she wrong in turning Rory down? She really was terribly fond of him. She had to admit at least that much to herself. She couldn't imagine anyone she would prefer to spend time with, not even Brigid herself. But it would seem a shame, such a terrible shame, to forsake everything she had been striving for. After coming so far, after struggling for so long, after getting so close to her dream. To let it all go would be crazy!

And what about Patrick? How would he feel growing up without ever having the chance of knowing his real father or claiming the inheritance that should rightfully be his? Rory would make a good substitute, but that was all he would ever be.

Just thinking about him made her grow warm. A tide of longing swept through her. Thank God Aidan was with them and she had to maintain her disguise or she might have given in to her desires long before now. And she just couldn't afford to. Hell! Imagine if she got pregnant, but to Rory this time! It would be an even worse pickle. No, she had learnt her lesson the hard way. She must not let passion carry her away. She had a duty to her son now. She must keep her sights firmly fixed on their future.

She thought about the journey ahead. Money was what she wanted and needed right now. If they could make good money from the flour then she could return to get Patrick. Maybe she could make enough to buy into a station. She and Patrick would never face starvation. She was determined about that.

Aidan, Rory and Kate left Adelaide three days later, their two drays piled high with sacks of flour. It was mid-September and already there had been further gold discoveries at Buninyong and Ballarat. It seemed as though there would be a fortune for anyone who was prepared to go. They were by no means the only ones on the road. There was a slow but steady stream of people heading east. Many were on foot, some were on horseback and others were taking any kind of conveyance they could get their hands on, from spring-carts to bullock drays like their own. Most people were loaded up with picks, shovels, tents and other gold-digging paraphernalia.

Kate noticed with a growing sense of satisfaction that there were few people taking provisions over there to sell. Most of them had dreams of digging up their own fortune in gold. They did see one or two women, but the overlanders, for the most part, were men.

Kate was now so used to life on the track that she took the minor mishaps in her stride. It was nothing to her now to unload a dray and to help prise it out of a bog. Meetings with the blacks no longer held the same sense of danger and it was commonplace to go searching in unknown scrub for bullocks which had strayed too far in the night. Their journey from the Burra down to Adelaide had seemed quite uneventful in comparison both to her journey to the unknown and remote Far North, and her escape from Wildowie with the Yuras.

This time, of course, she was with two men in whom she had complete trust. She could never come to harm with Rory and Aidan.

There were two routes to the diggings. The first went through Wellington and across to Bordertown through the Hundred Mile Scrub. The Hundred Mile Scrub was very sandy and surface water was almost non-existent in warm weather. Only experienced parties and those not using bullocks could use that track.

The more southerly route would take them from Wellington, through Meningie, along the Coorong, past McGrath Flat, Woods Well, Salt Creek, Tilley's Swamp and the Mosquito Plains. The two routes then joined at Mount Arapiles near the tiny village of Horsham.

Kate, Rory and Aidan chose the southerly track through the Coorong.

The country became more interesting as they crossed the Murray River at Wellington, where the punt operated. The river, the widest she had seen in the colony so far, was beautiful. Its banks were a lush, bright green, like cornfields, stretching as far as the eye could see. The reeds were long and the waterbirds plentiful. Rory shot enough ducks for a feast that night for dinner.

Kate watched him as he roasted the ducks on sticks over the campfire. She sensed a tension within him. There was a frustration there and she had no doubt that she was the cause of it. She could understand it, for the same tension existed in her, too. The only difference was that she was prepared to ignore her attraction to him. Her goal was more important than anything else.

The sun was setting, painting the cloudy skies golden, red and violet. Kate glanced over to Aidan. He was watching them again, as if trying to fathom the roots of the tension.

She had noticed that he seemed to be tiring very easily and was often short of breath after the least bit of exertion. His face had recently taken on a strange purplish hue.

'Are you feeling well, Aidan?'

'I'm well, Dec, don't you worry about me. You won't get rid of me yet!'

'I didn't mean to suggest that you had one foot in the grave!' she laughed.

'No, I'm fine, sonny, really I am . . . It's you two I'm worried about, though. You seem to be a bit twitchy, the both of you. What's up?'

Kate's eyes flew to Rory's. He raised one black brow as if to say that it was her responsibility to make excuses, since it had been her decision to ignore the attraction between them and to maintain her disguise.

She then looked back at Aidan. She didn't know quite what to say. She had been hoping that Aidan hadn't noticed. Despite his relaxed appearance he was astute when it came to people. He must know, she thought, but opening the subject for discussion was another thing.

'Must be the gold fever upon us,' she said lamely.

'That is it, is it now?'

'Must be,' Kate shrugged her shoulders. She looked up at Rory again, hoping that he would say something to back her up, but he said nothing. She was left to squirm uncomfortably on the log she used as a seat.

They served the duck onto their tin plates and sat around the fire eating their meal as the sun set. The landscape took on the deeper tones of the twilight.

Kate sent glares in Rory's direction. He should be helping her to cover their tracks. She didn't want Aidan to know her identity. He would feel as if he had been used. He had been honest about himself with them but she had not given the old man the same respect. It was too late now to admit to him that he had been lied to all along. Besides, if she told Aidan, what would keep her and Rory apart?

Rory returned her glares with bland looks. He was making it difficult for her and he knew he was.

She tucked into the duck's leg on her plate, trying to ignore him. It was juicy and full-flavoured. When she next looked up Rory had finished his meal and was licking his lips.

Something about the way he did it sent shivers of desire down her spine. The movement was so sensual, so suggestive. She dragged her eyes from his face.

Dinner finished, they cleaned up. Aidan wished them a good night. He was tired from the day's activities.

Rory and Kate were left alone, staring at the campfire. Rory said nothing. She felt disinclined to make small talk. What could she say to him? Talk about the weather when there were other more pressing, more consuming issues to be dealt with? The uncomfortable silence stretched between them. Only the night-time insects filled it with their droning and buzzing.

The fire crackled and spat tiny sparks.

Still they said nothing.

He prodded the fire with a stick. More sparks spiralled their way towards the infinite night sky.

Kate cleared her throat. 'I might get an early night.' She stood up and wiped her dusty hands on her moleskins.

Rory watched the gesture, his eyes lingering on her slim hips for just a moment. "Night, Dec.'

She had to walk past him to get her swag off the dray. She knew she wouldn't be able to sleep without clearing the air between them. As she passed him she placed her hand on his shoulder. He was still sitting on the log and he looked up to meet her eyes. It was an unmasked appeal.

'I'm sorry, Rory, sorry about all of this,' she said quietly.

'That's two of us, then.'

She squeezed his shoulder, about to go, but his hand came up to grasp hers. He held it for a moment then pulled it to his mouth and opening her fingers, he kissed her palm in the centre where the flesh was soft and sensitive.

'I'm not mad at you, I couldn't be if I tried. I just regret that it has to be this way,' he said. There was so much sadness in his voice that she felt her heart reach out to him.

He had not let go of her hand and she would not pull it away. She turned her body towards him and he rested his head against her lower abdomen. She could feel his forehead against her pubic bone and his warm breath through the fabric of her trousers. Her fingers toyed with the thick richness of his hair.

'We should never have set out on this trip together. I told you that I could not tolerate seeing you every day like this, without being driven crazy with desire.' His voice was muffled against her.

Those ever so masculine hands slid up the back of her legs to the top of her thighs and he held her there. She felt the tide of warmth spread through her. She could not pull away, nor could she stop herself melting towards him. 'Oh Rory!' it was no more than a sigh.

If only they could stop it here. If only she could have his love, his tenderness, his friendship and his affection, without the inevitable consequences. But the thought was in vain, since neither of them could stop the sensations that overpowered all thought and reason.

His hands dropped down to the back of her knees and her legs buckled, bringing her down into his lap. His arms went around her and her lips found his. It all happened so naturally, so smoothly, without thought or volition, as if in a dream.

She could feel the hardness of him against her and her muscles tightened in response as she wriggled herself closer to him, more deeply into his lap. He smelt of the bush, fresh and a little smoky. His hands moved down over her hips and buttocks, adjusting her to his shape, and then went to the fastening of her trousers.

'God, Rory, this is madness!' the anguished cry broke from her lips. The sound carried clearly in the still night air and it must have been just enough to rouse Aidan slightly.

'You all right, Dec?' he mumbled. He was on the other side of the dray and could not have seen them but Kate still sprang away from Rory guiltily.

Rory placed his fingers to his lips and pulled her back towards him. But it was too late, the moment had passed. Again. She held him at arm's length.

'I'm sorry, I shouldn't have let it happen, I can't let it go on,' her whisper was as anguished as her earlier cry.

'For God's sake give in to it. Why fight it, you can't resist it for ever.'

'I must, for Patrick's sake.' She had disentangled herself from him and was backing away, towards the dray. 'I'm sorry, Rory,' the pathetic words repeated themselves over and over again in her mind, 'I'm sorry, forgive me.'

Chapter
Thirteen

The track hugged Lake Alexandrina for another two days. Beyond the lake lay a long narrow inland sea, about fifty miles in total, separated from the ocean by a narrow peninsula of bright white sand dunes.

The water itself was known as the Coorong, the name given to it by the blacks. The bird life was more prolific than she had seen anywhere else in the colony. Groups of enormous pink-billed pelicans flew overhead. Gulls set their faces into the wind and hovered hopefully over the gentle waves, ready to dive for small fish. Ducks and geese flew overhead in formations, their silhouettes black patterns against the bright blue sky. Swans as black as coal glided graciously across the still waters. Long-necked black cormorants dipped and dived through the water after fish. The pied oyster-catchers picked through the sand for cockles at the water's edge. Emus, startled by the approach of the drays, raced over the sandhills, their long feathers bouncing as they ran.

Kate's eyes drifted away from the scenery to the two Ngarrindjeri women walking down the track towards them. One was wearing an enormous possum-skin cloak. There was a pouch which held her baby warm and snug against her back. Kate could just see the baby's face peering at her in fascination over the mother's shoulder. He looked like a little dark version of her darling Patrick. A savage tide of longing swept through her suddenly. God! She missed him so much. She could have turned around right there and then to return to the Far North to claim him.

The woman held in her hands two thick pieces of bark which sandwiched coals to make a fire. Her companion wore a thick woven seagrass cloak and carried a net bag, a woven rush basket and a digging stick. They were going to collect their share of the food for the day.

She had noticed that the people lived quite differently here along the coast. Unlike the Adnyamathanha, the Ngarrindjeri constructed permanent humpies. They were made of thick seaweed and sand. Those that were built for the winter months were strong and thick enough to shelter them from the bitter cold and misty winds roaring off the Southern Ocean. They were dome-shaped and made of more sturdy materials: logs, branches and bulrushes made waterproof with mud.

They were a healthy people. Their glossy skin

indicated their sources of food were varied and plentiful. They paddled and poled their wooden canoes and reed rafts along the Coorong, taking fish and other sea creatures with nets and spears. Kate had seen them with several different types of fish as well as freshwater crayfish, cockles and mussels. They also hunted the ducks and geese, catching them with nets and nooses. In addition, there were the usual animals—kangaroos, possums, wallabies, snakes and lizards. The women collected the yams, fruits, berries and seeds. The land and the sea were bountiful providers.

Seeing the Ngarrindjeri women brought back memories of the Yuras. Adnyini, Arranyinha and the others. She missed their companionship, their sense of fun and her regular lessons in bush survival. Strangely enough, she even missed the food they had gathered together and eaten.

Kate gazed at the landscape, the white gold of the sands in vivid contrast to the bright blue of the sky and the water, for mile after mile. Its incredibly serene beauty was simply observed, not appreciated, as it might have been at another time. Her mind kept wandering back to Rory. She could not deny her love for him. It was too powerful, too pervasive. If it hadn't been for Patrick, she could toss her future to the wind and wander the world with Rory. However, a mother's love was a powerful thing—not stronger than her feeling towards Rory, but different, more compelling. She must protect

Patrick from the harsh realities that she had faced in her tender years.

Admittedly it was Rory who was getting the bad end of the bargain. What she was doing to him was heartless, but she had no choice right now.

The next day Kate gathered bush food to supplement the ducks that Rory shot. The fruit of the pigface was the size of a gooseberry and tasted rich, juicy and sweet. The bulrushes yielded tender young shoots as well as tubers, which she baked in the coals of the fire.

'Nice tucker, Dec,' Rory said, stretching back against a log after dinner.

'Where did you learn all of this?' Aidan asked her.

Kate's eyes flicked to Rory and away again.

'I worked in the Far North on a station before I came to the Burra,' she replied. 'I was taught about bush foods and medicines by the local women . . . and men,' she added hastily, covering her error.

The women would hardly have taught those things to a young man and Aidan would know it. She hoped he hadn't noticed her slip.

'He's more suited to a life in the bush than most boys, or girls, his age,' Aidan commented to Rory. The way he paused before saying 'girls' was significant. He knew, Kate realised, and he was letting her know that he did.

Rory looked over to her, his eyes burning blue and bright with unspoken messages. He would not break the promise he had made to her. It was up to her to be honest with Aidan. 'More than he realises himself,' he replied eventually.

Kate's glance flicked towards Aidan and away again. She couldn't acknowledge it now. There were many reasons that she could have given: her past, her safety, Patrick's future. But she knew, deep down, that Aidan's supposed ignorance was the barrier she had erected to keep Rory at arm's length. She could not tell him.

The tension between them was eased somewhat the next evening when they camped down with some other folk who were bound for the diggings. Everyone was in high spirits. They had bought fresh fish from the local people and the smell of it frying over the fire whetted their appetites. One of the party of three men was an Irishman named Mick. Inevitably the musical instruments appeared when the dinner had been eaten. Mick brought out an accordion to join in with Rory's fiddle. Once again the old Irish ballads were sung, sometimes with an Australian flavour, like the ballad of *The Wild Colonial Boy*.

Kate had joined in, consciously lowering her voice to sound more like a lad. The songs of home brought a tear to her eye, as they did every time she had heard them. It was Rory who saw the shimmer of that unshed tear.

'You can't deny the blood in your veins,' he said quietly to her in the break between songs, 'nor your love of all things Irish.'

To anyone who was listening the words would

have seemed innocent enough, but coming from Rory, she could not miss their meaning.

'Just the smoke of the fire drifting into my eyes,' she said, her husky voice belying her words.

Was there something special between them because of their common ancestry? Did that explain the fact that she could not harden her heart against him no matter how hard she tried? Was that why her thoughts turned to him over and over again, even when she wanted to banish him from her mind?

They travelled the next day with the other party and at sundown camped with them again. They had reached Salt Creek, which was poorly named since the water in the creek was sweet to drink.

That evening the musical instruments were laid aside as they spun yarns around the fire. Mick and his party had delighted in ribbing Kate, thinking that her strong accent indicated that she was a 'new chum' and that her sweet voice and absence of facial hair were the signs of youth.

Kate did not enlighten them at all. She was glad enough that they thought her a boy. They had not been long in the company of others since they had left the Burra, so this had been a real test.

They were spinning some pretty tall stories which Kate listened to with the wide eyes of innocence. It amused them greatly to think that they had her believing every word that dropped from their mouths. Then it was her turn to spin them a yarn.

'I'm sorry,' she said, shrugging her shoulders, 'I only know one and it's true.'

'All the better,' said Mick. 'It's the kind that we like the best.' The others hastened to agree with him.

'I've only been out in the colony for six months, just me and my old Dad came out. Mum had died some years before,' she began.

The others nodded sympathetically. Rory wiped the smile from his face.

'We went straight up to the Far North to help out on Price Maurice's station at Pekina. I can see it all as if it were only yesterday,' her voice broke a little and the laughter from the others died away. 'The blacks were terrible up there, killing sheep and cattle. At that time it was as far north as a white man could go. We were living in a bark hut on the furthest outstation.'

She looked around the group and then continued. 'Early one morning they attacked the hut when we were still asleep,' she paused and put a hand over her eyes. 'Put a spear through Dad, killed him, they did.'

There was total silence.

'They grabbed me, took me into the bush,' her voice was strange as she continued, 'and they threw me on top of a pile of dead wood. Then they set fire to it. I can see that fire now, rising up around me, and me too weak to get up and run away . . .'

'What happened lad, did the fire burn you?' Mick asked her.

'No,' Kate replied slowly, 'no, it didn't. I was too green to burn.'

Rory let out a shout of laughter. Aidan slapped her on the back, 'Good on you, son!'

The others laughed too, acknowledging a fine tale and a fitting revenge on those who had ribbed her so mercilessly.

It was later on, when they were rolling out their swags, that Rory spoke to her. 'Dec, that was a grand yarn you told tonight.'

'Thank you, I thought it was rather good myself!'

'You make a fine bullocky, there's no doubt of it. You have all the skills. You work the beasts well, you can light a fire and cook a great damper, you sing sweetly and you tell a good yarn. Why you want to coop yourself up in a stuffy drawing room I have no idea!'

She looked at him glumly. What was she supposed to say to that? She looked around to see that no one else would overhear them.

'Maybe I'd be good at embroidery and playing the piano as well,' she whispered.

'And there's painting in water colours too, don't forget!' Rory tried to wipe the grin from his face.

Kate grinned in response. 'You're a devil, Rory. I'll thank you not to tease me. I won't know till I've tried it. Even you may be surprised!'

'I may well be,' and he winked at her before crawling into his swag.

The next morning Aidan looked ill. His face was suffused with purple. Rory ordered him to rest. There was no hurry to move on today. The bullocks, too, could do with a break.

Mick and his party went on their way just after breakfast.

Aidan was still lying in his swag when Kate heard him groaning.

'What's up, mate?'

Aidan shifted, trying to get comfortable. 'Pain in the chest,' he gasped.

Kate went over to where he was lying. 'Whereabouts?' she asked.

'Here,' he said, placing his hand over his heart. 'And here, out towards the shoulder. Must be that duck we ate last night, too rich. I can't digest it.'

Kate didn't know much about medical things but this didn't sound right to her. Besides, it was fish they had last night for dinner, not duck. But she didn't argue with him. He was too ill for that.

'Rory!' she cried, barely stifling the alarm in her voice.

'Yep.' He had his shirt off and was sewing a button back on.

'Come over here, I'm worried about Aidan.'

She absently watched the interplay of muscles on Rory's chest while Aidan explained the pain again.

'Aidan's right, probably indigestion,' he said. 'I doubt that there would be a doctor anywhere near but I might see if there's anyone locally who would know about such things. Dec, help me pack something for lunch, it might take me a while.' He pulled his shirt on again.

Over by the dray he spoke in a whisper to her, 'Doesn't look good, Kathleen.'

'Sounds like his heart to me.'

'Me too, but don't alarm him by saying so. Keep him comfortable. I'll see if there's anyone who can advise us on what to do. Luckily we're at Salt Creek and there are a few settlers hereabouts.'

After Rory had gone Aidan's pain worsened. Kate began to feel quite worried.

She filled a flour bag with salt and heated it in the camp oven. When the bag was warm she placed it around Aidan's chest. It seemed to ease the pain a little for him and he was able to speak.

'Dec,' he said, 'come closer, I must speak to you and I have little breath.'

Kate bent her ear closer to him to catch his words.

'Have the grace to tell me your name, now.'

Kate's heart began to hammer. What could he mean?

'Declan O'Leary it is—'

'Arrah! Don't be wasting what little time I have left t'me, girl! Decla is it?' He did know. He'd been trying to tell her for some time.

'Kate O'Mara it is, and I can explain everything,' she hastened to add, heat rising to her cheeks.

His hand rose feebly to silence her. 'I'm not interested in your explanations—'

'I didn't want to deceive you but I have had no choice. A life on the road as a girl was no easy thing. I'm safer as a boy. I'm sorry that I couldn't tell you, it wasn't that I didn't trust you—'

His hand silenced her again.

'Kate, there's no time for explanations. You no doubt had your reasons and I don't particularly care what they were.'

'Don't talk, Aidan, it's too much of a strain for you now.'

'No, let me go on. There's not much time left—'

'Don't say that!' she interrupted. 'There's plenty of life in you yet!'

She didn't want to admit it, even to herself. He was dying. He knew it just as surely as she did.

'Kate, let me say what I have to say,' he said, gasping for breath. 'I've lived near on seventy years and I know a thing or two . . . I too have lost my family, I too made it through the famine, I too made the long journey to the colony . . .'

Kate waited for him to come around to what he was going to say.

'I've seen the looks exchanged between you and Rory. I've seen how he looks at you and how you look at him . . .'

Kate's fingers itched to still the words on his lips. She didn't want to hear what he was going to say. She didn't want his advice. Not about

Rory. She couldn't have Rory getting in the way of her plans.

'The air has been so thick between you I could have cut it with a knife on any day! He wants you.'

Kate moved.

'No, don't interrupt me! It's as plain as the nose on that pretty face of yours . . . And it's just as obvious that you won't have a bar of him. Well, lassie, if you won't have him and you won't leave him, then it's a cruel wretch you are, just using him to take you to the goldfields—'

'I'm not using him, we're partners—'

'Go on with you! Partners indeed! There's more than partnership between you and you can't deny it! He's a strong man. He knows what he wants and he wants you as more than a business partner. You've just about used up every bit of patience the poor devil has. I'm warning you, Kate, you're on a path to destruction if you don't heed your heart.'

'Nonsense, my heart wants gold! I'm heeding that!'

'It's that damn fool head of yours that's after the gold. If you follow that then you'll deserve all the unhappiness that awaits you,' he winced and then went on, 'and if you ever listened to your heart you'd know it sings a different tune. You love the bush and you love the roving life. You love to sing and laugh and to tell yarns around the campfire. Your spirit is wild and free. You might not have been born here but you're a colonial girl, there's no doubt about that . . .'

Kate pressed her lips tightly together.

'You probably think that I'm old and a fool, but I can see that Rory and this life are in your veins. And if you turn your back on love you'll live to regret it, my girl.'

Any more advice he might have had was cut short by Rory's return.

Kate's heart fell when she saw that he had returned alone. There had been no one who could profess to know anything about medical matters, he told them.

Aidan lapsed into a deep sleep. Rory and Kate sat with him, watching him and looking occasionally at each other over the top of his body. The sound of his laboured breathing was the only thing that broke the silence while they waited for what seemed to be the inevitable.

'He's not got long in this world, Kathleen,' Rory whispered, and then corrected himself, 'sorry, Dec I should say.'

'There's no need to call me Dec,' she whispered, not wanting to wake Aidan from his sleep. 'He knows. He's known all along. He told me so while you were away.'

Aidan stirred a little and moaned.

Kate took his gnarled old hand in her own. The skin on the back was thin, like tissue paper, almost transparent. She could see the veins, blue and purple, tracking across the bones, and the fine muscles and tendons that stretched between them. The skin on his palms and fingers was rough and dry, calloused from hard work, the fingernails chipped and broken. She turned his hand back again. The skin was covered in scars, some old, some recent, many of them scaly from too much exposure to the harsh Australian sun. It was a hand that told a story. A story of hard work in the outdoors, a long life . . . Maybe he did know better than she did . . .

Aidan stirred and grasped Kate's hand more tightly.

'Rory!' Aidan's voice came out rough and thin.

'I'm here, Aidan.'

'It's a shame . . . I won't be seeing all that gold that Kate's been dreaming of,' he smiled and paused for breath. 'Everything I have, the dray, the bullocks . . . it's for Kate now, you understand . . . so she can be equal partners with you.'

'That's fine by me.'

'She's got . . . a fierce hunger to get rich and I know you don't care so much.'

'I understand you, Aidan. I'll make sure it all belongs to Kathleen,' Rory assured him.

Kate pressed Aidan's hand, a feeling of panic beginning to rise in her. 'You'll be right, Aidan, just rest, you'll be right. Hang on,' she urged him, 'there may be a doctor travelling the road to the goldfields.'

She was babbling, she knew it, but she didn't want Aidan just to slip away from her like that. She loved him. She didn't care if he was leaving her the entire goldfields themselves.

'Kathleen!' Rory's whisper was urgent.

She looked up at him and he shook his head at her. 'Shush, let him be. Leave him some dignity. Let him go in peace.'

Kate pressed her lips together and looked down again. Rory talked quietly and calmly to Kate as if there was no dying man between them at all. He talked about everyday things, the condition of the track and the nature of the bullocks, the exquisite beauty of the Coorong with its silver sands stretching starkly for miles, the red glow of the plant called samphire covering the ground and the delicate pink of the salt lakes in the distance.

It struck her that Rory loved this wild land in the same way that she did. Its austere and arid landscapes held a more subtle and powerful kind of beauty than the rich deep greens of Ireland and England. The intricate and minute patterns displayed by sands and shells, bark and leaves, and rocks and grasses were painted in colours of grey, brown, parchment and gold. Their beauty was almost elusive, more delicate and more gentle.

And somehow more profound.

She remembered saying something like that to James once. And he had replied that the English park-like landscapes were more to his taste. But Rory and Aidan loved them like she did.

It dawned on Kate that the hand she held in her own had grown cold as Rory talked. A chill shiver of sadness ran through her. Aidan had died. She looked up at Rory, tears gathering on her lower eyelids.

'He's gone, Kathleen.'

'I know.' She just looked at Rory, her lips parted, saying nothing, contemplating what he had done.

How could a man so strong and so tough be so sensitive? How could a man so rough in his ways be so finely attuned to another's needs, so caring? That seemingly carefree monologue of his had, in reality, been so very well thought out. Rory was refined in his own way, more graceful than James who had been born a gentleman.

Aidan had died on the track, with his friends around him, near his beloved bullocks, as he listened to the description of the landscape that he, too, had loved so much. Rory had made sure that his parting was a happy one and that there had been no indignity.

An exquisite kind of pain rose up in Kate's heart, not so much for Aidan, but for Rory. It was a feeling she could not understand, a feeling too powerful to comprehend, a feeling that she had never had before for anybody.

It was a sadness and a joy somehow mixed together. A delirious kind of elation that hurt, that tormented her and brought fresh tears to her eyes.

It was as if she had seen Rory for the first time and understood who he really was. She didn't want to love him, but knowing him as she now did, how in God's name was she going to stop herself?

Kate knew that Rory was watching her. She knew that her heart was in her eyes, her feelings unmasked, bare and raw for him to see.

Her realisation was surely written all over her face. It wasn't only a physical attraction she felt for him. He wasn't just her best friend in the world. It was more than that. She really did love him. And realising now what she should have known long before was a bittersweet experience, a sweet, tender torment. He must have waited for this moment for a long time.

Kate saw his eyes become shuttered and shift away. She could almost taste the disappointment in her mouth. He would not take her in his arms. She couldn't expect his comfort or his affection. He had told her so, back on the track, near the banks of the great Murray River. He would not take responsibility for what must happen between them. The choice was hers. She must choose him, she must want him and the first move must be hers. If she made that move, she then would accept the consequences.

She would be the one to open the lid of Pandora's box and thereby unleash the fiery passions that lay within. She alone would be responsible for getting burnt.

But Rory did not know the whole of it! It was not that simple. It was not just a matter of choosing to love him or not to love him. What about Patrick? What about the station? What about everything she had hoped for and dreamed of? Was she to throw all that to the wind? For Rory? Or was Aidan right, that she would never be happy if she ignored her heart?

Was the choice really hers or had the divine

hand of God somehow taken control? She didn't want to love Rory but how could she stop herself? And what of the consequences if she continued to shut him out?

Clouds passed over the sun, darkening the landscape momentarily.

'We must bury him, Kathleen,' was all he said. He got to his feet and walked away.

Kate watched him as he collected the spade from the dray.

She was lost in a maze of indecision that had nothing to do with Aidan.

She struggled up, her legs cramped from sitting still on the ground for so long. She looked down at Aidan, his eyes closed and his face peaceful, as if asleep. She thought she should be feeling more sadness at his death but her mind was full of Rory instead. Not that Aidan would be offended that her mind was elsewhere. He had wanted her to examine her heart and that was just what she was doing.

It was his death that had caused her feelings for Rory to surface so suddenly and so powerfully. She had known that she was attracted to him long before this. She had realised that her body responded to his in a way that she could barely control. And she had counted him as a friend, almost since the day they had met two years before. But she had never realised before the depths of his personality, or the way that he might ensnare her heart.

She helped Rory to cover the grave with earth.

They had said very little other than to murmur words of prayer. Just as there had been no doctor, there was now no priest. Other travellers on the road to the goldfields just passed them by, their eyes firmly on the track before them.

Evening fell and a cloak of darkness slowly enveloped the land. There was no one else camping down with them that night, no one to break the tension, no one to lighten the mood. Kate and Rory sat watching the flames creep over the logs, licking them into coals and eventually breaking them down to ash. What could they say? There was too much between them to bother wasting words on everyday pleasantries.

Kate watched the flick of muscles in his jaw, the dance of firelight over the hard planes of his face, the strong chin, the firm lips. She wanted him, so much. Aidan's death and the way Rory had handled it had left her raw, exposed, more in touch with her feelings than she could remember for a very long time. More close to Rory.

God! How she wished she could just throw it all to the wind and live only for the moment. She wanted to leap across the space that divided them. He was only six feet from where she sat but somehow the distance seemed too far for her to cross.

Rory stood up.

''Night, Kathleen,' his shoulders seemed to shrug and he said the words without looking at her.

He was turning his back on her, going to his

swag. The precious moment was about to be lost. She wanted him. Her feelings were too close to the surface to be ignored any longer.

Damn the future, damn the goldfields, damn everything she had ever wanted!

She stumbled to her feet. 'Rory!' It was barely a croak.

He turned slowly back to look at her and his eyes locked with hers. One eyebrow raised itself ever so slowly.

'I . . .' she was lost for words.

She watched as he unhooked his thumb from the belt loop of his moleskins and extended his hand towards her. The message was clear. If you want me, come to me.

Kate closed the distance between them without conscious thought. An involuntary cry was loosened from her lips as she moved past his outstretched hand and into his arms.

For this night, at least, the future could go to hell!

Her lips sought his and the guttural cry in her throat was lost as his mouth came down upon hers. There could be no restraint between them now. All control, all caution was thrown to the wind. Their kiss was hungry, desperate and urgent. Their needs, finally let loose, burst like a volcano and it was as if the searing heat, molten lava and steam enveloped them both from head to toe.

She wound her fingers through his rich black curls as his hands moved up and then down her spine, crushing her against him. Then his hands moved to her moleskin-clad buttocks and he pulled her up hard against his hips. She could feel his arousal, hot and rigid against her pubic bone.

Their kiss deepened and Rory penetrated her soft warm mouth with his tongue, sending waves of liquid heat searing through her breasts, down her belly and between her legs.

'Oh God, Rory!' Her lips left his only long enough for her to groan the words that she could not hold back and then she was kissing him again, their tongues entwining deeply together, their bodies pushing against each other, squirming and writhing to maximise the contact between them. It was if their bodies moved with a will of their own in an endless, urgent yearning to become one.

One broad hand moved to her shirt front and, slipping between the buttons, found her breast. His mouth continued to explore hers, tasting, feeling, while the other hand teased her nipple into a hard, tight peak. Hot tremors ran through her body.

She arched against him, her body wanting to meld with his. She ran her hands over his back to his buttocks, around his slim hips and to the front of his body. His chest was so broad, so masculine, so strong. She opened the buttons of his shirt and then, caressing his chest, she felt his nipples rise at her touch. She drank in the warm male smell of him, the smell of fresh creek water and clean skin made smoky by the campfire.

Could she ever get enough of him now that she had begun?

He unbuttoned her shirt and in response she peeled his shirt down over his shoulders to expose his skin to the warm light of the fire.

He withdrew his lips from hers even though reluctant to break contact for even one moment.

'Get those clothes off while I bring the swag over,' his voice was barely more than a growl and his eyes flashed her a devilish look of pure pleasure.

She sat down with a bump and began to pull off her boots and socks, her blood hammering in her ears. He was back in a few moments and the swag was tossed onto the ground between her and the fire. Taking her by the hands he pulled her up from the ground and against his body again. Then those wide hands came up to either side of her jaw, the thumbs roving over the soft skin of her cheeks, and he paused.

She could have drowned in the liquid blue eyes that looked down into hers. The pupils were wide and open, reflecting the soft light of the fire. They looked at each other for what seemed like a minute or two. It was as if he could hardly believe she was there in his arms and he wanted to drink in the sight of her to make sure. Then he pulled away from her ever so slightly, his expression less devilish and more serious.

'Are you sure, Kathleen?'

'I'm sure.'

'There will be no going back,' his tone was serious, throbbing with emotion.

'I want you,' she said, pulling him back towards her.

There was no doubt in her mind. She wanted to make love with him, more than she could say. Her mouth met his again and he slipped his arm behind her knees, bringing her feet off the ground and her body against his.

He laid her down on the swag and lowered himself on top of her so that she could feel the hard length of him against her. His weight spread her beneath him and she opened her legs and curled her pelvis up against him.

His fingers, surprisingly deft, undid the buttons on her shirt to expose her uptilted breasts to the glow of the fire. Slowly, agonisingly, his lips moved down her throat towards the rose pink of her nipples and he took each one in his warm mouth in turn, tasting, licking, teasing and nipping, until they were twin peaks of pulsating fire sending sparks coursing through her body, the pleasure almost unbearable.

'Rory!' She pulled his face up to her own. 'I can't bear it any more!'

Her hands slipped to his trousers to open the fastening.

'Not so fast, miss, I've been dreaming of this for a long time,' he growled, 'and I'm aiming to extend every moment for as long as I can!' The devilish grin that Kate loved so much spread across his face.

He began a trail of kisses down over her breast and across her belly, making her stomach contract suddenly and tightly, his hands working to remove her clothes and make way for his mouth as he went.

He slipped her trousers down over her feet and followed with his own. Then they were naked, the warm glow of the fire lighting up the glorious contours of their bodies.

'Oh Kathleen, you're more beautiful than I could ever have imagined,' he said as his hands stroked down smoothly over her breasts and hips and between her slender legs.

Her hands mirrored the movement of his as they glided over his muscled torso. The mat of fine hair on his chest tapered to a fine line over the flat plane of his belly and she followed it with her hand until her trembling fingers closed around his manhood, revelling in the sensation of the soft velvet-covered hardness. She heard him groan against her as she moved her hand to feel the throbbing rigid length of him.

And still he continued the onslaught on her body, his fingers slipping in between the petal-like folds to stroke the silken flesh that lay within. His touch was sure and confident, determined that she, too, would take as much pleasure as he. The tension was mounting within her, the centre of her being pulsating and humming with an unbearable, exquisite kind of hunger. Just when she thought she could take it no more he entered her. Plunging into her welcoming body more deeply, she felt her own sweet, agonising tightness reach its pitch around him. All other thoughts were driven from her mind as they rocked together, the whole universe revolving around them, absorbed only in each other as the blazing soul-shattering passion raged between them. Wave after wave of the most incredible pleasure imaginable swept through her and they called out to each other simultaneously. Entwined together their bodies shuddered and quivered in the momentous force of release.

He held her to him, softly kissing the dew from her brow as her body continued to flick with pleasure.

'Oh, Rory!' It was no more than a whimper, her body now too helpless to be brought willingly under control.

'Oh, Kathleen!' he replied, mocking her quivering tone and making her laugh.

He rolled over, bringing her on top of him. She could feel him softening and wet inside her still. He looked up at her, his eyes still smoky from passion, a grin spreading from ear to ear.

'That was worth waiting for,' he murmured.

Kate knew not what to say. She bent forward and kissed him playfully on the mouth and then on the nose. God, how could she not love a man who could make love like that!

'If I keep you waiting just as long for the next one do you promise me such a good time again?' she teased.

'Mother of Mary! You used up every last drop of patience I ever had. I've none left at all now.'

'None at all?'

'Not a single drop,' he grinned wickedly. 'I cannot wait a moment more.'

He held her hips on either side and pushed up against her so that she could feel him, inside her still, hardening again.

Her breath caught in her throat and she felt her tummy suck in with surprise. Surely he could not repeat a performance like that so soon!

But she was to find out that he could and that her own body would respond to his, move for move, sensation for sensation, until they were joined once again in a searing, mindless ecstasy so powerful she thought she would never recover from it.

Utterly spent, they lay side by side on the swag, basking in the warm glow of the fire. Rory traced the line of her jaw with his fingertips and looked into her eyes, as if baring his soul for her to read. Her heart seemed to flip right over in response and she kissed his warm lips once more.

'D'you think we should get some sleep?' she asked him dreamily.

'If you want to get up and cover a few more miles between us and that gold we had better get a couple of hours.' He pulled the swag over them both and Kate rolled over so that she could nestle her back against the warmth of his body.

She could feel his soft sleeping breath on her shoulder but she did not fall into sleep immediately.

She looked up at the stars from time to time,

watching their ever so slow march continuing across the universe. Her sense of satisfaction was deep and profound. Her body was relaxed and spent and her mind was still buzzing and excited.

Something about him made her feel more alive, more fiercely conscious than she had ever felt before.

What on earth was she going to do now and where the hell would this all end? If she was to stop this right here and now it would be like tearing her own heart in two. But what of her plans? What of her dreams? What about Patrick?

At this moment he seemed a million miles away. There was only the here and now, and Rory.

She had thought that James was a wonderful lover . . . Until Rory had made love to her. It was as if she had now discovered true passion for the very first time. He was not only a physical man in his appearance, he was physical in his wants and needs and she felt fiercely alive because of him.

James had been smooth, sophisticated, skilful, gentle. The true gentleman at all times. But his interest in her pleasure, she realised now, had been to heighten his own. He had wanted her willing and pliant.

Rory . . . My God! How could she describe him? Raw, virile, powerful. They were equal partners from beginning to end. The way he made love was breathtaking, glorious, magnificent. The very thought of him had her body stirring and her muscles tightening again.

Rory shifted in his sleep and his hand moved to cover her breast, as if he was responding unconsciously to her thoughts. She wriggled to nestle in closer to him and placed her hand over his, the thrill of his closeness coursing through her body.

Her eyes drifted up to the heavens again and she looked at the thick cloud of stars splashed across the night-time sky from one horizon to the other. God had indeed finally smiled on Kate O'Mara.

The future could go to hell. She was happy, deliriously happy, and she was going to revel in that happiness without thinking of what tomorrow would bring.

Kate was now such an experienced bullocky that she and Rory alone were able to manage both of the teams and drays. The remainder of their days on the track were outwardly uneventful, for the weather was fine and there were no bogs or fast rivers to cross. Nor were there any breakdowns or sick bullocks with which to contend. Bushrangers were scarcely a danger since they left alone those who were on their way to the diggings to concentrate more seriously on those who were leaving the fields with gold in their pockets.

But the nights were something else again.

Most of the time they camped alone, with only the possums and the night owls to witness the glory of their lovemaking under the stars. Occasionally they were encamped with other travellers for the night and at these times Kate insisted on maintaining her disguise. Then it was not the wild freedom of unrestrained passion they enjoyed but the sudden thrill of secret stolen kisses when no one else could see them.

Kate felt alive, earthy and radiant. She refused to think about tomorrow. For the time being, she was happy. Too happy to dwell on dilemmas which could not easily be solved. She loved both Rory and Patrick with equal ferocity, and only Patrick's presence right here and now could have made her more happy.

The countryside changed significantly as they travelled through Victoria. Gone were the sandy plains and salt lakes that had hugged the Coorong. The dense low scrub of mallee gums and paperbarks had given way to taller eucalypts and forests of stringybark. The deep narrow gullies were filled with the luxuriant green growth of lacy ferns.

The mountainsides were thick with an understorey of flowering shrubs. Waist-high thryptomene flowered in delicate shades of pink and white. Wattles drooped under the weight of masses of blooms that were every shade of yellow from lemon through to the deepest gold. Thick yellow banksia flowers thrust up through the bush like huge brushes.

A carpet of wildflowers of all colours and perfumes spread underfoot. Snow-white everlasting daisies with yellow centres were contrasted with the purple flowering sarsaparilla that crept and twined in every direction. Pink boronia clashed violently with the coral-red of the bell-shaped correa flowers and the red-orange of the low-growing grevilleas. Bold yellow guinea flowers stood out against the greens.

And in the midst of it all the modest orchids and delicate ferns quietly provided their own show for those who would take notice.

It seemed that everything on earth conspired to make her happy. Rory was loving, passionate, adoring. The air was heavy with sweet perfumes of every description and the bush vibrated with every colour under the sun. The birds and animals rejoiced in the spring warmth as they built their nests and readied themselves for the birth of their young. Spiny echidnas trundled across the tracks before them, koalas smiled sleepily at them from the forks of trees and sugar gliders soared over the top of them as they made love each night by the warm light of the fire.

It was as if God had created this paradise just for her. She revelled in its heady sensations and gloried in its divinity. The all-consuming soul-soaring communion that she shared with Rory was sacred, much too sacred to be spoilt by words, by plans or decisions. Their joining together was a celebration of what they had and she gave thanks to God for it every day.

The track became busier as they neared the Ballarat diggings. Not that there was one formed track, for there were countless tracks cutting up the fragile soil and disappearing into the bush in all directions. There had been no attempt by the fledgling Victorian government to build roads of any kind to the diggings and they were lucky that the fine spring weather had dried the worst of the gluepots.

Most of the travellers were on their way to the diggings but there were already some diggers on their return journey to Adelaide. Some had tales of good finds, others had barely found enough to make a living and the remainder, dispirited, were returning to warn their families and friends that it would be better to stick to their steady jobs in Adelaide. Regardless of whether they were on their way to or from the diggings they all had one thing in common—they carried the ubiquitous digger's swag and wore the uniform that proclaimed them as diggers.

Their swags were by no means light, since they contained not only blankets and changes of clothes but also firearms, drinking and eating utensils, almost always tin pannikins and plates, candles, calico for tent-making, chamois leather to hold the gold that was dug and food and water as needed. Kate was glad that her own swag was carried on the dray and not on her back. The diggers carried knives and tomahawks in the wide belts at their waists and some shouldered guns or stout sticks, fit to fell the fiercest of bushrangers.

Their uniform was not unlike that which Kate herself was wearing. Blue or sometimes red serge shirts were worn. These were tucked inside trousers or fastened at the waist with a wide leather belt. Sometimes they were worn, as Kate did, simply hanging loose at the waist. The trousers were of moleskin and were wide and loose. Long boots were worn to keep out the mud and water in which they might be working shin-deep. Wide-awake hats of straw or felt graced every head. Kate felt confident that she looked like yet another young digger on his way to the goldfields.

The bullocks hauled their drayloads of flour up yet another steep hill. Kate and Rory shouted out words of encouragement and lashed the whips forward alongside the heads of the leaders to keep them moving. At the top they slowed to a stop ready to rest the bullocks before the long descent.

A strange noise assailed her senses first of all, a noise like a million bees at work, and alerted by Rory's gasp, she looked ahead.

There it was, spread from one side of the valley to the other. Ballarat had burst into view! She felt her mouth drop open as her eyes moved over the scene before them and her mind grappled with the enormity of what she saw.

Never would she forget that scene. Never could she have imagined that it would look like that. Just looking at it more than repaid the long journey they had taken across unknown lands. It was breathtaking, it was ugly and it was the most exciting panorama she had ever seen.

They had been travelling through a landscape of forested hills, ferny creeks and grassy slopes. Wattle groves had been thick with yellow blooms and the entire scene had been peaceful and pleasing to the eye.

Suddenly it had changed.

It was now a scene of unbelievable wreckage. Almost every tree on the diggings had been cut down. Every bit of earth had been dug up and lay in mounds and heaps as far as the eye could see. Acre upon acre was covered in heaps of disgorged gravel and muck. There were pools of green slime and puddles of yellow clay-stained water. There was dirt, refuse and disorder in every direction. There were thousands of human beings engaged in digging, wheeling, carrying and washing. The heads of men bobbed up and down as they worked their holes in the ground. Sandwiched between the mounds of earth were tents, hundreds and hundreds of tents. There were flags flying and washing flapping on lines in the breeze. It was a hive of buzzing activity.

The cacophony of noise that she heard came from a multitude of activities, the rattle of the cradles used to wash the gold from the dirt, the hammering of picks and the scraping of shovels, the calls of diggers to their mates, the barking of dogs, and the clip-clop of horses drawing creaking cartloads of dirt to be washed in the creeks.

There were cries of elation and groans of

despair, the bawdy calls of poor men made suddenly rich and still drunken from the night before.

This was Bailarat.

Chapter

Fourteen

Kate was itching to get down into the throng of humanity and experience the goldfields at first-hand. But she had to hold her enthusiasm in check. It was better to take this safeguard than to risk breaking the legs and necks of every beast in the team. Rory fixed huge logs to the back of the two heavily laden drays with ropes and chains, to slow them down as they went downhill.

When both teams reached the bottom of the slope Kate and Rory unhitched the drags and rolled them to the side of the track. Kate watched the play of muscles on Rory's arms as he handled the logs. He was a strong man and his body moved with easy grace.

'Well here we are,' Rory said, stretching his back and looking around at the mayhem before them.

'What now?'

'Let's find a place to camp for the night. Then

we'll go for a walk and take in the sights.'

It was not easy to find an area that would meet the bullocky's needs for water, grass and wood. The ground was so disturbed that it seemed almost impossible to find all their requirements in one spot. Eventually a site was found on the outskirts of the diggings.

They unyoked the bullocks, camped down, lit a fire and made preparations for dinner. With an hour or so until sunset there was still time to take a good look around.

'Are we going for a walk, then?' Kate asked.

'We'd best not both leave the drays. I saw more than one shrewd glance in our direction as we came through. If we both go we might come back to find the drays have already been unloaded for us!'

'Surely no one would steal from us here?'

Rory gave her a dry look. 'Don't forget that most of the people here are driven by greed. Nothing is safe, Kathleen. One of us will have to stay with our things at all times. You go take a look first and I'll look later when you return.'

'I'll be back in half an hour,' she said and swivelled on the heel of one boot and took off to join in the commotion of the goldfields.

It was the time of day when the diggers were knocking off work and hunting clean water for a much-needed wash at the end of a day's hard labour. Hundreds of small fires had been lit and the afternoon air was rapidly filling with smoke.

Almost everyone lived in a tent of some kind.

Mostly they were made from pieces of calico strung up over the long boughs of trees, which in turn were propped at either end by more boughs or rough-hewn logs. The trees had also been used to make three straddle-legged structures from which to hang cooking pots over fires. No wonder there were so few trees left to grace the landscape!

Furniture consisted of packing cases or pieces of timber set upon rocks. The bedding, often lain straight onto the earth floor, served as seating as well. There was little point in building more permanent homes when the gold might run out tomorrow.

Most of the people on the diggings were men, of course, but there were a few women and Kate could see where their influence was present. Through the open flaps of the tents she saw sheets as well as blankets on the beds and either dry sacks or carpet squares on the floors. Tempting aromas rose from the cooking pots. The women did not look up at her as she passed. They kept to themselves here. Dressed in gowns of plain dark fabric which buttoned up to the neck, they did their best to avoid unwanted interest. Women were a commodity in great demand.

Kate was glad that she passed as a boy.

Some of the tents housed stores and sly-grog shops. Empty bottles lay scattered on the ground and even at this time of the day there were men reeling about, shouting, fighting and swearing.

Prostitutes beckoned the men who had money to burn.

She made her way back to their camp well before sunset, not wanting to get lost in the chaos of the diggings when night fell. In her absence they had been joined by another teamster. Kate gave him a nod and a hello.

'I'll be back soon,' Rory said as he, too, went off for a look.

'Evening, laddie,' called a voice. The woman who greeted her was a sorry creature, thin, with a sallow face and lines of anxiety etched into her gaunt cheeks.

'Evening, ma'am.'

'Been here long?' she asked, her eyes shifting to the drays then back to Kate.

Kate wondered what she was wanting. 'No, not long.'

The woman joined Kate by the campfire and stretched her hands out towards the warmth. Kate could see they were red and rough from hard work.

'You've brought in flour to sell I see,' the woman remarked.

'Indeed we have. We've just arrived. D'you know the going price at all?'

'Almost any price is yours for the asking. Its been scarce here from the beginning, like everything else on the goldfields.'

'Except the gold, I guess.'

'Even that is scarce!'

'I thought there was plenty here. I've heard

that people have just been picking it out of the creeks in lumps.'

'Aye, the lucky ones have. But most of us are yet to find enough to cover the cost of the licence. Thirty shillings for a licence. It is robbery, highway robbery.'

Kate raised her eyebrows and the woman continued.

'It is those blasted squatters who are behind the licence fee. They've been living off the fat of the land and they want to continue that way, with the rest of us bowing and scraping.'

'Do you think so?'

'Too right. They're against us making our fortunes on the goldfields. They even petitioned the government to find some way of preventing the labouring classes from leaving their jobs! So the government came up with the licence. They hope to drive the diggers away from the goldfields with the wretched licence fee. They'd rather us all go back to their stations and mind their sheep for a pittance. But we'll not go back, no matter what. We'd rather starve here than go on with them as our masters.'

Kate listened to the woman's outburst and thought of James. Would he be the type to push for a hefty licence fee in order to drive shepherds back to the stations? It had been hard enough for him to get workers before the gold discoveries. She wondered how he was faring now. Her thoughts returned to the woman's words.

'Is it that bad here, then? Are people really starving?'

'My husband has shot a cockatoo. We'll eat that for our dinner but it will be the first meal of the day for us. There's nothing for breakfast tomorrow. We'll just have to tighten our belts,' she said, looking over to the drays with a wistful expression.

'Have you found no gold at all?'

'Only enough to pay for the licence. Everything we've found has gone to pay for it. My husband can't afford to be found without one or we'd have no chance at all. We'd be hungry and penniless. Now that we are here we have no choice. We have to keep on digging for gold,' she replied, shrugging her shoulders.

Kate could see the weariness in the woman's face. She had lived a rough life, this one. It was a terrible thing to be hungry. She knew that better than anyone. This woman had all the marks of hunger, there was no doubt about that. She wasn't just trying to get something for nothing.

She stood up. 'Come over to the dray, I have plenty of flour. Take enough to last you for a few days.'

'I can't take it, sonny. I've no money to pay you with at all, and don't know when we will have any.'

'I don't want money for it. Never let it be said that I'd turn away a hungry soul. I'll give you as much as you need to tide you over.'

Kate handed the woman a flour bag while she

opened one of the sacks. 'Help yourself,' she said.

The woman half-filled the cloth bag with flour.

'Will that be enough? Take more, go on.'

'Aye, that's enough, thank you, sonny.' The woman closed the bag without taking more. 'God bless you,' she said.

'You're welcome.'

The woman wiped her face with her dusty apron and put her hand on Kate's arm. 'Just one thing though, if you see him, don't tell my husband, will you? He's a proud man and wouldn't take nothing off nobody. I'll tell him that we had it all the time and that I forgot it was there.'

'I won't tell a soul.'

'What is that you won't be telling a soul?' It was Rory, back from his stroll.

Kate glared at him playfully. 'None of your business it is. This lady and I were just having a chat.'

Rory looked at the open sack of flour and the bag in the woman's hands and raised one dark eyebrow in Kate's direction.

'Mrs Wedderburn is my name,' she said, extending her hand to Rory, then she shook hands with Kate. 'Thanks, sonny, and let me know if I can do you a favour any time.'

She hurried away into the fading smoky light of the afternoon, her head held low. The sun was just setting.

Kate turned to Rory, about to explain, when

there was the deafening explosion of a blunderbuss being fired nearby. Before either Rory or Kate could react there was a volley of shots from all directions.

'Jesus!' Rory cried as he pushed Kate to the ground underneath the dray. He rolled in after her and then covered her body with his own to protect her.

'What the hell—?'

The noise was deafening. Gunshots continued in every direction for several minutes.

Kate's heart hammered. She pulled her derringer from her pocket and checked it. She could feel Rory's breath coming fast and ragged against her cheek. They peered out from under the dray into the faded dusty light of dusk. Rory pulled a knife out of his belt. He didn't have his gun on him. They waited ready for an attack of some kind but none came.

Then it was all over. The gunshots had finished. There were only the usual noises of crackling campfires, barking dogs and human voices. And those voices contained not a hint of alarm.

'What in God's name was that about?' Kate asked.

'Beats me,' Rory replied.

They crawled out to the edge of the dray and looked out. People moved about in the twilight as if nothing untoward had happened at all. They could see people stirring pots over their fires, eating their dinners and making preparations for the night as if there had not been a single firearm discharged.

'I think we can get out from here,' he said.

Kate pocketed her derringer and made moves as if to crawl away. Rory's arms pulled her back against him. 'Second thoughts, while we are here though,' he said, his voice almost a growl. Kate couldn't see him well in the fading light but she sensed he was grinning, his teeth showing white and even against the swarthiness of his skin, his eyes twinkling in devilry.

'I've been waiting for this moment all day,' he continued.

His mouth descended on hers and his tongue darted deeply into her mouth.

It happened every time he kissed her, the feeling that her heart was plummeting down through her body and then flying back up again. She didn't pull away, she didn't want to and she could not have done so anyway. There was something magic about Rory, the heat of his lips on hers, the feel of his hands on her skin, the strength of those arms around her.

'Um,' she said as her lips broke free of his.

'Um indeed.'

Their hearts were still hammering but now it was excitement, not the fear of flying gunshot. Rory pulled her towards him again.

'Let me go,' she laughed. 'I've got to check that the dinner is not burning. I'm hungry.'

'I'm hungry too,' he said, his voice low and throaty.

She laughed, 'There's mutton stew and damper for main course, and you're in charge of the dessert!' She gave him a saucy look and broke away from his hold to crawl out from under the dray.

The other teamster camped near them came over to say hello as Kate lifted the lid off the pot to stir the stew.

'Evening, son.'

'Evening to you,' she replied and gestured towards a rock. 'Have a seat by the fire there.'

It was the custom of the bullockies to invite each other to share their campfires, sometimes their meals and always their quartpots of tea. The other bullocky was a middle-aged man with fiery red hair and a thick beard of the same colour that spread over his chest and reached down almost to his waist.

'Ah,' he said, sitting down.

'G'day, mate.' Rory dipped his hat to the newcomer.

'G'day, Blue's the name.' He shook hands with Rory who then introduced himself and Kate in turn.

Blue for his red hair. Typically Australian, Kate thought.

'What were all those gunshots about?' Rory asked.

'Newcomers to the goldfields, are you? If you'd been here before you'd have known that the diggers fire off their weapons at dusk, to check that they're working and as a warning to thieves. I saw the two of you duck for cover and figured you were new to this game.'

Kate was hoping fervently that he hadn't seen anything else, for he would have thought it more than strange to see two bullockies in each other's arms!

'I'm glad that was all it was, then,' she said. 'It sure had us worried for a while!'

'Going to sell a load of flour before you start digging then, are you?'

'No, we'll leave the digging to those who are here already,' Rory replied. 'We'll sell this lot of flour and head home to Adelaide for another load to bring over.'

'Smart move,' Blue said and scratched his beard. 'Carting provisions for the diggers will bring you a reliable income, gold digging won't. I'm bringing stores up from Melbourne myself. This is my second trip. I did well last time and the profits can only get better. There are thousands flooding in from Van Diemen's Land, New South Wales and your own colony. They'll all need provisions.' He broke off to light his clay pipe with a twig from the fire.

'What are you carting, then, Blue?'

Blue drew on the pipe to get the tobacco well lit before answering. 'All the diggers' paraphernalia—all sorts of foods, moleskin trousers and blue serge shirts, wide-awake hats, tin plates, pannikins, cooking pots, knives, axes, picks, shovels, cradles. They reckon you can't make a better living than the blacksmiths and the carpenters in these parts. There are eight thousand people on the fields between here and Buninyong alone. They're selling picks and cradles and the like as fast as they can turn them out, so there's plenty of room for speculation on the gear from Melbourne as well.'

Rory nodded. 'So how is old Melbourne town?'

Blue let out a loud bark of a laugh. 'Old Melbourne town has been turned upside down! You'd have to see it to believe it. There's been a run on the banks, with everyone withdrawing their savings to buy food and equipment for the diggings. Shopkeepers, mechanics, clerks, tradesmen, farmers, policemen—everybody is throwing in their work to get up here. The schools are closed, houses are to let and business is well-nigh at a standstill. Some suburbs are entirely deserted. I've never seen anything like it in all my days. The prisoners have no stone to break because the quarrymen have all left. All public works and surveys have ceased. Buildings have been left only half constructed, painters have downed their paint pots and brushes and disappeared, leaving walls half painted—'

'Will you eat with us?' Kate had to interrupt to get a word in. She had already served food for herself and Rory.

'Thanks, son,' Blue nodded, taking a plate from her, and he continued right on. 'And you ought to see the harbour. It's already clogging up with the ships that have brought the emigrants in.'

'Why's that?' Kate asked.

'The crews are jumping ship to get to the goldfields and there's no one left to man them for the homeward journey—'

'Wait till the news of the rush reaches the rest of the world, then!' Rory broke in.

'God almighty, you're right! This time next year and we'll have hundreds of thousands of newcomers. Imagine the chaos, if you will!'

Kate's eyes were shining. 'How exciting it all is! Aren't we the lucky ones to be getting in on it all at the beginning?'

'We are indeed, you'll be a rich man yet, Dec!' Rory grinned at her and winked.

They went on to discuss with Blue the going price of flour and the best way to sell it. If they had the time to wait, he said, they should sell it in small quantities. Prices varied according to location. The newest rush areas generally had the highest prices. If they wanted to sell it in bulk, Buninyong was the place. It was just seven miles south of where they were and many of the diggers coming up from Geelong stopped there to stock up.

'Up to one shilling and sixpence for a pound you'll get for it,' Blue told them.

'Threepence a pound it was selling for back in Adelaide!'

'Not a bad profit for you, then.'

'Thanks for the advice, mate. We should do well, as long as young Dec here doesn't give most of it away!'

Kate opened her mouth to protest but Rory raised the palm of his hand to her. 'You can give away as much as you like, Dec.'

'She was hungry, I could not deny her enough to eat for a day or two!'

'As long as you don't give away the whole lot—'

She didn't let him finish. 'Rory, I cannot bear to see anyone starving! Don't you remember Ireland? They watched us starving and did nothing. I'll not be doing the same to others!'

Rory's hand came down heavily upon her shoulder. 'Dec, you just do what you think is right, I was only teasing you. I have no doubt at all that you'll have your sights fixed firmly on the profits the rest of the time.'

The thought of making profits while anyone might be hungry was something that continued to worry her. She wanted wealth and the security it would bring. She wanted that more than anything. But not if anyone else went hungry as a result.

She had never had to think about that before.

Blue brought over a jar of jam, taken from the stores on the back of his wagon. It was a welcome addition to their simple dinner and tasted wonderful spread on hunks of warm damper.

'Ah, now Blue has given us this delicious jam you don't have to worry about the dessert, Rory,' Kate said and winked at him, knowing the innuendo would be lost on Blue.

'No, indeed I don't, but I might be needing some exercise to work off this grand dinner.'

'Well I'd not go strolling about at night if I were you,' Blue said, quite ignorant of the undercurrents in the conversation. 'You're more than likely to get shot by some overzealous digger protecting his patch.'

Kate turned away, hiding a laugh. She could see that people had built up their fires to keep their tents and their claims well lit overnight. Occasionally they heard the crack of gunfire echoing across the diggings.

Blue wished them a good night and retired to sleep under his own wagon.

Kate and Rory also retired, their firearms ready to protect themselves and their stores of flour should the need arise. They put both swags under the one dray and when they lay down Rory took her in his arms again.

'Now for your just desserts, young lady,' he whispered. 'This will teach you for teasing me over dinner.'

Even with Rory's warm arms around her and his soft, sleeping breath on her cheek Kate could not drive her new worry from her mind. Was it right to make a profit from the hardships of others? Should they sell off their flour at the highest possible price knowing that someone might go hungry? She had never faced a dilemma like this before. She had never owned more than her neighbour.

. . . The wind blew bitterly cold over her body as she lay in the ditch at the side of the road. She

clutched her young brother closer, pulling her threadbare cloak over them both. But his body was cold, too cold. He had died while she had slept. She began to cry . . .

She could feel someone shaking her. 'Wake up, Kathleen, for God's sake what is it, wake up!'

She was struggling, the mist floating thick around her, as she stared at his dead body. Patrick was gone. She had failed him.

'Kathleen, wake up!' She could feel warm hands on her body. The mists cleared suddenly. And there was Rory, his face above hers.

'Kathleen, wake up, you were dreaming. Wake up, darlin'.'

He gathered her up in his arms. She was in Australia, not Ireland. It was a balmy October night, not the bitter cold of an Irish winter. The hunger was over. She was safe.

'Oh, Rory!' She put her arms up around his neck and clung to him, weeping into his neck. He kissed her face and murmured words of comfort to her, over and over again, until her shaking subsided and her sobs died away.

'What were you dreaming about?' he asked, looking into her troubled face again.

She shook her head. She couldn't speak, it would only make the tears flow again.

'It was Ireland, was it not?'

She nodded her head. It was no use lying. He knew. She tried to stifle another sob but it broke loose despite her efforts. Rory took her in his arms again, rocking her as if she were a baby.

'So you were dreaming about Ireland, about the famine,' he said and she nodded again.

Rory sighed, 'Kathleen, listen to me.' His fingers were splayed either side of her face and he forced her to look up at him. 'You can't just ignore those memories and hope that they will go away. If you bury them deeper and deeper they will eat away at you. A nightmare is nature's way of telling you to get it off your chest and out of your mind. It is the only way to put it behind you. Tell me about it, don't make me drag it out of you bit by bit.'

She began to tell him about the dream, her voice shaky.

Responding to his gentle coaxing, she moved from the dream itself and began to recount the story of her life through the famine. She cried until there were no more tears inside her, Rory holding her, comforting her, as the story came out, until finally she came to the point where she had been selected to come to Australia. The rest he knew.

She was lying back against him now, a feeling of numb exhaustion taking over. His cheek rested against hers and his arms were clasped around her, over her midriff, underneath her breasts.

'And what made you dream of it tonight, do you think?'

Kate told him about her worries. About making money from the misfortune of others.

'How on earth d'you think you'll ever be rich if you're worrying about such things as that? D'you think that the rich lie awake at night with such things as these on their minds?'

'No.'

'Well what are you going to do, then, give up your wish to be rich?'

'No!'

'Well if you're not going to change your mind and you're not going to dig for the gold then you'll have to live with the fact that you're taking money from other people . . . Won't you?' he prompted when she did not reply.

'I suppose so,' she agreed reluctantly.

'Just think of it this way, Kathleen, if we don't bring the flour over then they'll be even more likely to starve, won't they?'

That at least was true. She could stretch the truth and look on it as a mission of mercy.

'And you have my permission to give it away to anyone you think is at death's door.'

'Yes,' she said, but the worries lingered there still.

'D'you think you'll ever get over what happened to you in Ireland, my darlin'?'

She liked it when he called her his darlin' like that.

'I don't know, Rory. I really don't know. It's just when I think that it is all well and truly behind me that it seems to jump up at me again.

Maybe I'll never get over my fear of going hungry.'

'Maybe when you're rich enough you won't worry about it all any more and you can be free of this blind ambition of yours. Maybe then you'll realise that there are more important things in life.'

'It is not a blind ambition,' she said, ignoring what he was saying about there being more important things in life.

'No?'

'No it isn't, Rory.'

He changed tack. 'What if I were to promise you that I would make sure that you and young Paddy would never go hungry again. Would you give up this crazy striving for wealth at all costs?'

'You couldn't promise me that and well you know it.'

He tried another approach. 'D'you often have dreams like this?'

'Occasionally. Less so as time goes on.'

'When was the last time?'

'Not since I met up with you.'

'Doesn't that tell you something then?'

'. . . I don't know.'

The following morning dawned clear and fresh. Before they had time to finish their breakfast they had been approached to sell flour. The news of their load of flour had spread through the gully. The diggers, hoping for a fair price, had come with their flour bags to be filled.

Rory managed the money while Kate helped to fill the bags. That way she didn't have to think about making money from the misfortunes of others. At any rate, she heard no one claim that they were too poor to pay and her conscience ceased to bother her. Judging from the steady flow of people throughout the morning, the price was not too high. But it was high enough for Kate and Rory to feel pleased with their profits.

By the time the rate of customer visits had slowed down there was little point in yoking up the bullocks to move on, so Kate and Rory decided to stay put. Kate could tell that there was something bothering Rory. It was not something he was ready to talk about. She often looked up to find his eyes on her and a look of speculation on his face. At other times he was far away.

'A penny for your thoughts,' she said to him that evening as they both stared into the flames.

'I'm thinking about us.'

'And what are you thinking?'

'I'm wondering where all of this will end,' he said, a hint of sadness in his voice, as if he had guessed what was on her mind.

'Can't we ignore the future, just for a little while?'

'After last night I don't know that we can . . .' his voice trailed away.

'What do you mean?'

'You're obsessed by the famine. It drives you. Money and security will always come first with you.'

'I can't help being driven by it.'

'So I've seen. It rules your life. I thought you loved me enough to not always worry about going hungry, but now I'm not so sure.'

'Rory, I can't make any promises to you, not now. I can't tell what the future will bring or how I will feel.'

'And you expect me to wait patiently for you while you take you time deciding. Is that it?'

'Well . . . I don't know what else we can do.'

'My patience is running thin,' he said, and tossed a lump of wood into the fire. Fragments of burning coals spat in all directions and sparks shot skyward.

Kate swallowed. She did not know what to say. She wanted it all. She wanted Rory to love her, to make love to her, to look after her, to make her laugh and sing and dance. She wanted wealth, she wanted security. She wanted the life of the station mistress, the security of land and a home from which she and Patrick could never be evicted. She wanted a place in society, a place that would guarantee security forever. She wanted the polish and sophistication of the English gentry.

She knew, a sense of dread weighing down her heart, that she could not have it all. She would be forced to make a choice. The day of reckoning could not be postponed forever. And she could see already who was going to lose out. And when she lost him she would lose a part of herself. But there was no other way.

Rory was watching the play of emotions over her face.

'You lived through it all too, Rory. How is it that you are not fearful of another famine?'

'It was an awful time for us too but I did not lose my family. We owned our own land and could not be evicted. There was many a night when there was no food upon our table, though.'

'So how did you all survive?'

'On our wits. We were near enough to the coast to take up fishing. After the first potato crop was hit with the blight we began to plant other crops. We turned our hands to anything and everything that could bring in a few pennies. I went up to a big farm owned by an Englishman and worked in the stables there. We sold off everything that wasn't going to put food in our bellies. We survived by being flexible, by grasping at every new opportunity that presented itself and by making opportunities for ourselves when there were none in sight. We were prepared to change, we didn't just plant another crop of praeties and pray for the best.'

'You learnt to live off your wits.'

'Mm. It's like I said, Kathleen. We saw plenty starving on the roads and in the ditches. We saw that there was nothing that you could take with you when you go. There was no point amassing wealth or possessions just for the sake of it if you didn't know how to make use of the opportunities that stared you in the face. We were prepared to take risks.'

Kate was thoughtful. Would her family have survived if they had taken more risks, staked their lives on new ventures and grasped hold of the future with both hands?

'I don't think it was within our natures to do what your family did. We didn't even think about new ways to earn our bread. When we were evicted it seemed as though my parents just lost the will to survive. Your nature is different, I can see that. You love adventure, you love to gamble, you're happy to drop one job and move to another without so much as another thought.'

'Arrah! Adventure is in your nature too!'

'It's not, I'm sorry to say.'

Rory snorted, 'Jesus, woman, you hardly know yourself at all. You love adventure. Hell, you went up to the most remote and dangerous part of the colony. You've dressed yourself as a boy and carted wood for the smelters, you've dashed across to the goldfields without so much as a second thought. You can handle a firearm, swear and tell yarns like the best of them. Aidan said it too, didn't he? He called you the wild colonial girl. Good God, you can't tell me that you don't have an adventurous bone in your body!'

'I don't feel adventurous! I don't feel like I'm a risk taker! In the depths of my soul I'm not!'

Rory shook his head and smiled at her. 'At the risk of sounding arrogant, I reckon one day your eyes will be opened and you'll find that you're a different person than ever you've imagined yourself to be.'

'Do you really think so?'

'If you spent more time in female company you'd realise that you're different from most women. But that reminds me, it does, talking about women, there's been something I've been meaning to talk to you about. Another baby would really throw a spanner in the works for you.'

'I won't get pregnant.'

'How can you be sure?'

'The Adnyamathanha women told me how to do it, by making a medicine from the she-oak.'

Rory's eyebrow raised in question.

'Yes, I know what I'm doing. It has worked so far.'

'You're sure?'

'Yes, and I've been carrying some of Widow Walsh's Female Pills on me just in case. I'll not get caught out twice.'

He looked . . . disappointed somehow. The diggers had already retired, so she walked across to where he sat, squatted down before him and took his face in her hands.

'Don't look like that,' she said and tilted her face up to kiss him. She touched her lips to his.

His kiss was fleeting and he turned his head away to stare into the fire.

'Come to bed, Rory,' she said.

Whenever they made love the dilemmas were banished from her mind. When she lay in his arms the rest of the world and her worries simply failed to exist. She wanted to bury herself in that sweet, wild oblivion and forget the inevitable choices she would have to make.

She ran her hands up his thighs to his hips. 'Come to bed now, we can worry about all of that later.'

But he pushed her hands away, ignoring her invitation. 'No I can't sleep now, you go, I'll join you in a little while.'

But he did not join her after a little while. She waited until, despite her best efforts, she fell asleep. When he did crawl into the swag beside her she stirred but he rolled the other way and went to sleep. She could not remember him ever turning down her invitation before.

When she awoke the next morning he was up already. He was distant. She could feel it. As she poured a pannikin of tea from the pot he told her he was going off in search of the bullocks.

A cold kind of aloneness seeped through her soul. A premonition of what was to come. She could not have it all. This was the first lesson.

'I think we should move on,' he said when he had rounded up all the bullocks. 'We'll be here for ages if we sell the flour pound by pound. We should go to Buninyong and sell it to the stores there and then get back to Adelaide.'

'Oh . . .?'

'I've been thinking. The way to make the best profit is by bringing over as many loads as quickly as we can. Bring it in bulk, sell it in bulk. We may even be able to hire some other teamsters to help us do it.'

'So what are you suggesting?'

He poured himself a cup of long-stewed tea and sat on the bare ground beside her.

'Kathleen, I don't know how to say this so you won't be hurt. I'm not saying it to pressure you or anything like that. I had hoped that you would care for me enough to throw all of your worries to the four winds, enough to give up on these ambitions of yours. Sure, we're in this money-making thing together and it would be just grand if we got rich because of it. But it won't break my heart if we don't make our fortunes. It would break yours though. I realised how important it was to you last night.'

He put down his tea and took her slender fingers in his own. Her nails were chipped and short. They were working hands like his. But her own small hands looked so slender and white against his. Even in the Australian sun her hands would never tan as much as his had.

'I'll do everything in my power to help you make your fortune and I'll be making one for myself at the same time. But I think you need some time alone, away from me. I think as long as we are on the road together I'll be frustrated with your ambitions and you'll be unable to decide what it is you really do want from life.'

A bitter taste rose to her throat as her heart began to sink.

'So I propose we handle things this way. We should get back to Adelaide as quickly as possible and buy another two loads of flour. I know someone who will help me to bring it over.'

'And what about me?'

'You say you don't care for the roving life and you want your security, so you have the chance to test that out. Stay in Adelaide and buy the flour at the best price that you can get it. At the same time keep your eye out for any drays or teams for sale, so that we can build up our business. Find some more teamsters who we can contract to bring it over for a reasonable price. You look after the Adelaide end and I'll look after the journeys to and fro. You might even want to look into the cost of shipping it across.'

Kate stared at the ashes of the dying fire. A wisp of thin smoke spiralled towards the perfect powder-blue sky.

She should be feeling quite happy with the plan, she reasoned, but she wasn't. She couldn't say why. He was right, it would be the quickest way for them to make money. So why was there this sinking feeling in the pit of her stomach?

Rory tossed the last sack from the back of the dray. Blue had been right. The storekeepers in Buninyong were anxious to get their hands on the flour. And the price was very good indeed.

Rory leapt down in one fluid movement. Beads of moisture clung to his forehead and there was a damp patch on the front of his shirt.

Kate had counted the money and was placing it carefully into a chamois leather bag.

'Well, Dec, I'd say that it was a successful venture, wouldn't you?' He shook her hand and winked at her.

'We have done well, my friend.'

'With nothing left to steal from the drays I think we can afford an hour or two to celebrate, don't you?'

'What do you have in mind?'

'How does a long bath, a hot meal and a pint of beer sound to you?'

'Sounds like heaven!'

'Mother Jamieson's Inn is just down there on the next corner, we'll see if she can squeeze two more guests in anywhere. John Veitch, the storekeeper here, said his son will look after the bullocks and the drays for the night if we like.'

'I didn't realise there was an inn here.'

'No, you've been too busy counting flour sacks and pennies since we got here!'

'Well they got an inn up fast then. The gold was only discovered here in August!'

'Buninyong was born long before gold was discovered. It's the third-largest Victorian town after Melbourne and Geelong. The timber cutters have been here for ten years supplying split and sawn timber to the stations. The store and post office, the school, the brewery, the log kirk and the manse—they all predate the gold. Only the police camp is new. But take a good look because I'll guarantee you this town won't be the same in ten years' time!'

'Rory, about dinner and the inn—we don't want to spend all of the profits we've just made, maybe we should just camp out as usual.'

'We deserve a treat now and then, we've been working damned hard. Don't worry about the money!'

'I can't help but worry about it. I've never seen so much before in my entire life!'

He placed his hand on her arm. 'You're a funny one. I thought it was a chance for you to sit at a table piled high with food, just as you've always wanted!'

'I do want it, but when we've got more money.'

'All right, we'll not touch your precious profits then. It will be my shout.'

'You can't afford it either.'

'I can afford any dinner and comfortable bed that your heart desires. Just enjoy yourself. You deserve it.' He laughed and said, 'There's not too many women who would choose a wash in a creek and a sleep on a swag over a hip bath and a feather mattress!'

The inn was clean and comfortable, a far cry from some of the inns that Kate had stayed in on the way to the Far North. The paintwork was fresh and the walls were papered with a pretty pattern. It was obvious that it was frequented by the squatters on their way between the western districts' stations and Geelong.

Cleaner than she had felt for a long time, she had put on her only spare change of clothes. They weren't really flash enough to wear to dinner in the dining room but at least they were clean and without obvious patches and darns. Her hair was growing longer and the wash in warm soft water had sent it curling in a sooty halo around her head.

'You're looking less like a boy with every passing day,' Rory had whispered with a glint in his eye as they made their way to the dining room.

Rory smelt fresh, the scent of the soap lingered on his skin and his hair shone clean in the candlelight. It still looked unruly but that was Rory's style.

They started with a beer to quench their thirsts. Kate relented a little and insisted that they were her shout since he was paying for dinner and the night.

'May the road rise up before you!' she said, raising her glass.

'And the wind be always at your back!'

They took long gulps of the cold beer.

Rory looked at her. 'I have another toast, too. To silk dresses and sumptuous dinners!'

'I'll drink to that!'

They both laughed.

First they had soup. It was lobster bisque. Kate had never heard of such a thing before, never mind tasted it. The flavour was subtle and the consistency smooth and creamy. The waiter, a young member of the Jamieson family, told them that the lobster had come up fresh from Geelong that day.

Rory ordered a bottle of wine to go with dinner. Kate repressed a shudder at the thought of how much it would cost but by now she was getting into the mood. It was exciting having a dinner like this. It was more than a treat, it was a dinner better than Kate had ever had in her life before. She knew that her eyes were shining and her cheeks were tinged a delicate rose pink.

Main course was a succulent pork roast with all the trimmings—golden brown potatoes and the freshest green vegetables she had seen in a long while. The gravy was smooth and rich and there was a slightly tart apple sauce as well. Fresh oven-baked bread and a golden yellow butter came with the main course.

Kate noticed that Rory's eyes had not strayed from her face all evening. Her eyes had not left his face either and she had the sensation of almost drowning in his gaze.

A buttery baked caramel pudding was brought to them for dessert. Rory swathed the pudding in thick, rich cream from the jug on their table.

Kate looked across at him. He was devilishly handsome, deliciously masculine. She could feel the wine they had shared was going slowly but surely to her head. If only she was dressed as a woman they could have held hands across the table that divided them. She could not wait until dinner was over and they could retire to their room and the thick feather beds that awaited them.

It was as if Rory could read her thoughts. The smile he sent her across the table was as intimate as a kiss.

He leant forward. 'Kathleen,' he said softly, 'I've made a decision . . .'

Another voice drifted across to them, '. . . I could hardly believe my ears last week in Melbourne . . .'

The cultured voice intruded into Kate's consciousness. It was a voice like James Carmichael's, the same accent. Her attention became riveted to the speaker at the next table as if it were James himself. It was the first time she had taken her eyes off Rory's ruggedly handsome face all evening.

Rory stopped mid-sentence as her attention swung away.

The speaker was relating a story.

'*"Eighteen pence!"* I said to the shopkeeper, *"My good man, it is hardly worth eighteen pence!"* And do you know what he replied? *"You can keep your lousy eighteen pence. I don't make my living off the patronage of bloody squatters!"* '

There was a chorus of tutting from around the speaker's table.

'Imagine it, if you will,' he went on, shaking his head. 'There is no doubt that the lower orders are getting above themselves. And it is all the fault of the gold.'

'Yes, it's true. I tried to get workers to my station this week for the shearing and was met with absolute rudeness.' A middle-aged Scot now held the floor. 'They showed great interest at first, asking about the wages and the number of sheep to be shorn. Then one of them got quite cocky. He suggested that I sell the run to him and that I stay on as the manager!'

'Good heavens!' exclaimed the gentleman wearing a clerical collar.

'I just walked away in disgust, of course. The fellow called out after me, *"You wouldn't like to come and cook for us, would you?"* I was never so shocked before in my life.'

Rory had listened too but he was sitting where they could not see him. An unholy grin split his face in two.

It was all that Kate could do not to burst into giggles. The wine had indeed gone to her head and she could barely hold herself in check. Her eyes danced with glee.

'Isn't it shocking!' he said in a low voice to Kate.

She inhaled, about to laugh, and nearly choked on a mouthful of the luscious pudding.

'. . . But they'll learn, all of them. The gold will soon run out. Wool will be king in the end. By the time these ruffians work that out, all the land will be bought up,' the clergyman was saying with an air of self-satisfaction.

That wiped the smile from her face. The gold would run out! How would they make their fortunes? This might even be the last profitable trip they could make!

Rory watched the changing emotions flit across her face. 'Don't panic yet, my darlin',' he said, leaning forward suddenly.

'Sh!' She was listening to what else the squatters had to say.

'. . . The farmers with small holdings will be selling up and rushing to the goldfields and we can buy everything that they dump at a low price . . .'

Kate felt her lips part in alarm.

'We should be investing in wool, Rory!' she whispered urgently across the table.

'There'll be plenty left for you to invest in when you've made enough money. Australia can support a hell of a lot more sheep yet,' he said dryly. 'Just remember that if the farmers are dumping everything at a low price then they'll be dumping their wheat harvest as well. We can buy it up cheap and make twice the profit.'

But it was no good. His words did not placate her. Their lovely dinner of celebration had turned sour. Her downfall was staring her in the face. The money was in wool, not gold!

That night should have been the most glorious night they had spent together. They had privacy. They had comfort. Soft candles lit their room. They were full of wine and rich food. It should have been wonderful. But it wasn't. It had been spoilt by the squatters. Kate knew her attention was elsewhere and for the first time, all of Rory's competence as a lover was entirely lost on her. He knew it too.

Wool will be king! The words echoed through her mind again and again as she tried to sleep. *Wool will be king!*

If wool was to be king, then she wanted to be part of it. Patrick must be part of it. It was the only path to a secure future.

Chapter

Fifteen

Kate walked alongside the polers, her whip dangling carelessly over her shoulder, the fall trailing along in the dust. The dray creaked ceaselessly, providing a rhythm to her thoughts. *Wool will be king, wool will be king*.

It was November and the scorching summer heat had begun. Rory was some distance behind her. He had fallen back so that he and his team would not have to walk head down, eyes closed against the dust that she and her team had stirred up. Without the potent presence of Rory sauntering along in front of her she could turn her mind to the question of her future.

He had been right. She did need to spend some time alone, away from him and the domination of his personality. She would stay in Adelaide and think this whole thing through. Yes, she did love him and there was no way that she could deny that, especially to him. But her parents had married for love and that hadn't stopped them dying in the famine.

She would have to stop this relationship with Rory and concentrate on more important things. As he suggested, they should keep their business partnership going, with her in Adelaide and him in Victoria. It was the only way. She wanted Patrick, she wanted a station—Wildowie if she could get it—and she wanted everything that it symbolised. She would not make the same mistake that her mother had made. And with Rory away from her she would gain the strength she needed to turn her heart away from him.

He must know what was going through her mind. She did not have to tell him. There was no need for words. They had fallen into a pattern of thinking and feeling like one. He was cheerful on the surface, but beneath that there was a thoughtful, almost melancholy mood. It had persisted ever since they had left Buninyong.

No matter how hard she tried it seemed as though her head, her heart and her body moved in opposite directions. Knowing that soon it would all be over, she didn't want to make love with him. But she was still drawn to him irresistibly as if her mind was no longer in control of the rest of her.

Their lovemaking had taken on a new quality. It was no less passionate, no less exalting, but it was different. It was born of desperation, as if each time they came together it might be their last. There was nothing gentle about it, nothing soft or sensitive. It was raw, destructive, as powerful as dynamite. On the nights they were camped alone, they could barely wait for the cover of darkness to descend before they tore off each other's clothes, their bodies hot and aching for the satisfaction that their hearts, in future, would be denied. Sometimes it seemed as if they made love in despair, as if it would stave off the hurt and pain that was sure to come. As if the wilder their lovemaking was, the more the memory of it could compensate for all that they would lose.

They would come together in a swirling maelstrom of passion, a hopeless denial of the inevitable tearing apart. It was a searing, blissful torment that raged within them and between them, leaving them breathless, their bodies spent but their hearts no less vulnerable to the pain than when they had begun.

Finally their journey had reached its end. They were at the Tiers and they could see down to Adelaide, spread out between the hills and the coast. They were sitting on a boulder, looking down at the plain together. The air was still and the twilight was that dark inky blue that hovers for a moment just before the darkness takes over. It was as if time was standing still, waiting for the acknowledgment that the end of their togetherness had come.

'What are you thinking?' she asked.

'It's the end for us two together now, is it not?' his voice was ever so soft and low.

She looked up at him, her heart in her mouth. She hadn't wanted to say it out loud herself in case her words shattered the thread of control that held her together.

'Don't say it, Rory!'

'It's the truth and I'm one for facing the truth head on. I thought you were too.'

'I don't want to . . . to . . . leave you,' she stumbled over the words, 'but I have to, Rory, I have to. You understand, don't you?' her voice was small at the end of the sentence. Tears gathered on her lower eyelids, not yet ready to spill over.

'In some ways I do, I can see what is driving you,' he stood up in a gesture of impatience and kicked the ends of the logs into the fire. 'God almighty, I wish it didn't drive you. I wish that you could put all of Ireland and the famine behind you. But I can almost see into your mind and this thing has a hold of you, so strong that sometimes even I doubt that you'll overcome it. At other times I dream that you'll just wake up one morning and it will all be over. You'll find that the security is inside yourself and that you don't need silk gowns to be sure of it. I had hoped that I would be there when it happened, but maybe I won't.'

Night had now fallen and Kate turned around to stare into the flames of the campfire. There was a physical sensation deep inside her, a sensation that her heart was bleeding, a trickle of blood squeezing out with every heartbeat.

Rory squatted by the fire and looked up at her. 'It's the only reason I'm prepared to continue on with this flour thing with you. Because I hope against hope that when you're wealthy in your own right that your fears will simply evaporate and you can go along with the choice your heart has made.'

She did not respond.

Rory came to stand in front of her. 'My darlin' Kathleen,' he said, taking her slender hands in his broad ones and pulling her up towards him. The moment of silence seemed to stretch forever, then his words came slowly, 'Make love with me one last time.'

His hands slid up her arms and she allowed herself to fall against him. Parting her lips, she raised her face to meet his kiss. His hands, warm and strong, stroked the contours of her spine, her hips and her bottom, sending her belly into a wild swirl. Her hands moved over his body, returning the sensations, stroke for stroke, caress for caress.

It was different this time, more sweet, more romantic, more poignant, as if Rory wanted to leave her with a memory of a love that could never be forgotten. He lowered her to the ground, his eyes never leaving hers for a moment, his lips seeking hers again and again as if to imprint the taste of him forever on her brain. He removed her clothing piece by piece, kissing each new expanse of flesh as it was exposed. Love flowed in her veins like warm honey and a golden tide of loving bliss ebbed through them and between them.

Just at the moment it reached its peak, Rory took her face in his hands and looked deeply into her eyes. His mouth took hers in a kiss of warm velvet and she shattered into a million stars like the Milky Way stretching across the ink-black sky above them. It was a bittersweet ecstasy, unspeakably divine and more tender than words could express.

She lay against him, listening to the beat of his heart. After a few moments he pulled her upright to sit in his lap. She dropped her head down to avoid his gaze but he placed his fingers under her chin to tip her face up to his.

For the first time ever, in the aftermath of passion, the tears gathered in her eyes. And by the light of the stars she saw in his eyes the drops of moisture that came in response.

'Oh Rory, I'm breaking both our hearts I am, but I can no more help it than I could stop the sun rising in the morning.'

'I know that, my darlin'.'

He didn't ask her why she was doing it. He didn't beg her to reconsider. He didn't even blame her. It was ground that they had covered so many times before.

Mrs Applebee's Family Boarding House was exactly the sort of accommodation she had been looking for. It was the kind of place that was entirely unexciting. Nothing untoward would happen there. There would be no midnight drunks roistering in the hallways or ladies of questionable virtue giggling in bedrooms in the early hours.

Mrs Applebee was a respectable widow. The quiet and genteel boarding house that she presided over, Kate realised, lent a certain respectability to the boarders themselves. Kate could feel safe from the unwanted attentions of men, since she had shed her disguise, but at the same time there were one or two rooms where she could entertain friends or people with whom she was to do business. While it was respectable, it was not so strict as to prevent her coming and going as she pleased.

It was situated on the corner of Rundle and Pulteney Streets right in the heart of the town. Five minutes' walk would take Kate to the sale-yards on North Terrace, to the auction markets in Hindley Street or the shops close by in Rundle Street.

The boarding house was a charming building of two storeys, surrounded by a pretty waist-high picket fence. The upper storey had a fine wide balcony. Kate's window looked over that balcony and across the town to the eastern hills. Her room was furnished with a bed, covered with a patchwork quilt in shades of blue and pink, a washstand and a wardrobe made of rose-wood and a small writing table. The walls were papered with a tiny print of pink and cream roses and blue floral-printed curtains swayed in the breeze that blew through the window. It was the prettiest room that she had ever lived in.

Kate sat at her writing table from where she could see through the window and watch the street life unfolding.

Rory had left yesterday. Already today seemed empty without him. The other boarders were nice enough but their company paled in comparison to Rory's vitality and easy charm. They were not the kind of people who would enjoy a hearty joke or a tall story. She pushed the thought of Rory out of her mind. She had other things to do right now. There would be time enough to worry about him later. And if last night were any indication, she would be spending many a long hour thinking of him, missing him and wishing that his strong arms were around her once again. He had told her not to come to a final decision until he had returned. And she wouldn't. She simply wasn't capable of saying a final goodbye to her relationship with Rory. Not now when her feelings were yet to be brought under control.

It was December 1851 and here she was back in Adelaide where she had started. She had been in the colony for just over two years. And what a time it had been! She had travelled to the Far North, to the Burra, to the Victorian goldfields and back again. She had learnt to use firearms and to drive a bullock team. She could cook a damper in the campfire as well as the next man. She could survive alone in the bush. She had saved a man's life. She had lived through two long hot summers in the bush, a flood and an attack by Aborigines.

Thinking she had loved one man, she had become his mistress and had his baby, only to find that it was a hollow love built on loneliness and hopeless dreams. She now loved another, more than she wanted to, more than she planned for. Her dream had grown into a driving force, fuelled by the needs of her child, sharpened by her fears, forcing her to sacrifice all else as it propelled her away from the man she loved.

It had been a time like no other. She had grown up enormously. She had turned from a skinny innocent girl into a passionate woman. She had learnt to stop rushing in where angels would fear to tread. And she had learnt about better and worse ways to make money.

Would she have come to the colony if she had known what awaited her? If she had known that no rich husband or benevolent employer had been awaiting her on the docks? Yes, she would—anything rather than struggle through each day in a cold, dirty workhouse waiting in fear for the next famine to strike.

Could she fulfil the dreams that had driven her since she had stepped onto the boat at Cork? And if she did, would she ever be able to erase the imprint that Rory had left on her heart?

She had three months, maybe a little more, to think it through before he returned to Adelaide. He had been patient with her. More patient than she would have been had their positions been reversed. Three months to think through her future, to buy the next loads of flour, and to find more bullock teams, teamsters and drays. She was going to be busy.

Kate had caught up with her old friend Harold Simpson again. He had been delighted to see her and equally delighted to take on the contract to cart a load of flour to the diggings for her and Rory. He was keen to do Kate a favour since she had been the one who had saved his life. He would have no intention of staying on at the goldfields as he was an old man now and the spear injury to his chest meant that the hard physical labour of digging was beyond him. Many sources of the work that he did previously had dried up now that so many people had left Adelaide.

Harold's oldest boy, Simon, a tall lanky lad with a mop of chestnut hair and a personality not unlike his Dad's, was now old enough and experienced enough to drive a team on his own. He would go with Harold and Rory, taking Kate's team and dray, also loaded with flour.

Rory had looked up an old friend of his by the name of Roger Serle and Roger had readily agreed to take his dray and yet another drayload of flour financed by Rory and Kate. He wanted to check out the goldfields for himself. If he liked what he saw and wanted to try his own hand at digging he could stay over there. By all accounts Roger was a steady sort of fellow who seldom made spontaneous decisions. He was unlikely to stay there and dig for gold himself. There was a good chance he would keep contracting for Kate and Rory.

Of course, their profits would not be quite as high if they had to pay other contractors but the volume sold would be increased dramatically now that they had four teams on the road to the goldfields. They would also establish ongoing markets, in as far as it was possible, given the fluctuating state of the goldfields. Already there was a new rush on, this time to Mount Alexander, where further large deposits had been found. It seemed as if all they had to do to find new gold deposits in Victoria was to turn over a shovelful of earth. South Australians were prospecting for gold too but there was yet to be a find anywhere near as big as the smallest find in Victoria.

In South Australia the wheat harvest was under way. In the next few weeks farmers would be bringing their grain into the markets and Kate would be in a position to haggle for the best price. She had heard already that many of the farmers were just waiting to sell their crops before they left for the goldfields. Then, if they did not do well as diggers, they could be back again in time to sow the next year's crop.

Her mind drifted to Patrick. He would be almost a year old now. God, how she missed him! How she longed to hold him in her arms. But she would have to wait, at least until Rory returned. Then she would know exactly where she stood financially. Maybe then she could return, finally, to get him.

The ceaseless churning thoughts were interrupted by a tap at the door.

'I'm coming!'

She opened the door. 'Brigid! You're earlier than I thought you would be!' She gave her friend a hug.

'I couldn't wait to see you again! I'm sorry I couldn't talk the other day when you called in to see me but the baby was fractious and I'm not supposed to be entertaining visitors when I'm working.' Brigid returned Kate's embrace and then took off the bonnet that had almost completely hidden her face from view and placed it down on Kate's bed along with a large cloth bag she had brought.

'So you're all settled in, I see,' Brigid said, looking around.

'Not that there was a lot to put away!' Kate laughed.

'We'll soon fix that! What are we shopping for this morning?'

'Since this is the only gown I own I think I had better get some more!' She smoothed the fabric of the plain blue gown she wore. The gown and a cheap bonnet to cover her shortened hair were the first things she had purchased with her money from the flour. She and Rory had enlisted Mrs Applebee's help. As soon as Mrs Applebee was let in on the secret, she had quietly taken Kate up by the back stairs to her new room, so that she wouldn't be seen by the other boarders.

Then Mrs Applebee herself had dashed out to get Kate a suitable dress to wear.

'And when we've bought me a couple of spares we can start on the underwear, the night-gowns, bonnets, shawls and everything else that I need besides!'

'Have you gotten rid of those dreadful boys' clothes yet?'

Her friend grinned. 'Indeed not, you'll never know when I might be needing those again. They've been washed and folded and stored away for my next adventure!'

'I thought you would have had enough of those by now!'

'You never know . . .'

'Well I hope you are staying in Adelaide for a while now for I missed you, Kathleen. I certainly don't want to read of your death in the *Register* like I did last year.' Brigid's eyes went a little misty at the thought of it.

'I missed you too, Brigid,' she replied, and then on a lighter note she continued, 'and I don't want to read of my death in the newspaper again either!'

They laughed together. No matter how long they had been apart the bond sprang up instantly between them again. Kate had not been conscious of missing female company on the trip to the goldfields but she was very glad to have Brigid close by her again. Their friendship had passed the test of time and the long months of separation.

'Well, I've brought my scissors over, so let's get started on that hair first of all!'

Kate drew the chair over to the centre of the room and sat on it. Brigid fished out the scissors, a hairbrush and a small mirror from her bag.

'Thank heavens it has grown a bit,' Brigid said, brushing out the sooty black curls that now lay on the collar of Kate's gown. 'I'll only cut enough off the back to even it up a bit. But I don't know what we should do about the front. It's not quite long enough to part it in the middle and pull it around to the back. That would have been the more fashionable way to do it.'

She pulled the hair round the sides towards the back but even with the curls stretched out they were not long enough to be held in place there.

Brigid brushed Kate's hair this way and that, trying to decide how best to turn her boy's locks into a woman's hairstyle.

'Why not just leave the sides loose,' Brigid suggested. 'Your hair is curly enough to be brushed into ringlets; even if they are a bit old-fashioned they will have to do. We can still part it in the middle . . .' she fished in her bag again and this time pulled out a narrow black velvet ribbon. 'For the time being you can hold it in place with this.'

She threaded the ribbon underneath the ringlets at the back, bringing it up behind Kate's ears to tie it on the top of her head, so that the hair at the front of her face was smoothly drawn to the sides where the ringlets then fell naturally over the ribbon.

'Yes, that will do nicely. What do you think?'

'Sure, Brigid, that looks good.'

Brigid removed the ribbon then snipped the hair where it needed to be made more even.

While Kate removed the hair from the floor Brigid emptied the rest of the things from the cloth bag onto the bed.

'Now, Mrs Jenner throws out her clothes just as soon as they have a tiny tear or a scorch mark on them. She has given lots of them to me, for we're a similar size, but they should fit you too, so I thought you might like some of them,' Brigid said, 'that way you won't have to spend all of your hard-earned profits on a new set of clothes. I've brought you over a couple of nightgowns, some stockings, some chemises and drawers that have hardly been worn and a few petticoats, since skirts are getting wider all the time. There's also a few handkerchiefs here for you.'

'Brigid, are you sure that you don't want them yourself?'

'No, I've plenty, honestly, I have. She throws things away even if she thinks they no longer suit her, so I have more than enough.'

'Thank you indeed. They are lovely!' Her fingers travelled over the soft cool cottons, the edgings of lace and the tiny embroideries that decorated the underwear.

'These are just the things that she passes onto

the likes of us! Her silk things she considers unsuitable to give to servants.'

'Well we'll both be wearing silk one day if this flour carting continues to go as planned.'

'You really think so?'

'Sure, and you should join with us, Brigid.'

'I'm not the type to make a good teamster,' Brigid laughed. 'But if you need some help with the books I am good at that sort of thing and I can do it when the baby is sleeping.'

'Good idea. I've never been confident with figures like you have. The Jenners obviously don't work you too hard at this job of yours.'

'No, my only duties are as nanny to the babies. There are other servants to look after the house and the garden, the laundry and the kitchen. It's not a bad life at all. There are no risks. I'm well looked after. I think you should be doing something similar, Kate, instead of chasing wealth at all cost, trying to get ahead fast. You'll likely come another cropper.'

'No, it's not for me, but I'm glad you found something that suited you. And what about that gardener who was keen on you?'

'Goldfever! I'll see him again, he said, when he makes his fortune. That or he'll give up when he finds that there's not enough gold there. Either way, he'll be back and we can set a date for our wedding then.'

'I'm pleased for you, Brigid,' Kate said, suspecting that Brigid might have done much better for herself elsewhere and with someone else.

Brigid shrugged. 'But what about you, Kate? I sensed the tension between you and Rory when I saw you the other day. What is happening?'

She told her friend what had happened between them.

'Be honest with yourself!' Brigid broke in. 'It's that James Carmichael that you're after!'

Kate sat down on the bed with a sigh. 'No, not any more. Not for myself. If it had not been for Patrick I'd still have been dreaming of him. As much as I don't like to admit it, he used me, then just discarded me when he had finished. I don't want him for me, but I want him for Patrick. I'm determined to find a way to make him take responsibility for his son if it's the last thing I do! That is the most important thing right now—to set Patrick up for life. If I can make James pay it will be all the better.'

'So Rory is irrelevant to all of that?'

'I want Rory in a way that I have no control over, as if the attraction that pulls us together takes over and I am powerless to fight against it. We think alike, we feel the same way about everything, we love the same things. He makes me laugh and sing. He plays the old Irish tunes on the fiddle and the blood quickens in my veins . . .'

Kate was gazing into space as if remembering the nights spent with Rory, a rapt look on her face.

'But you'd marry James if he asked you, wouldn't you? You don't want to admit it, even to yourself, but you would. And there's more to it than Patrick, is there not?'

'I want James to say sorry. I want him to make it up to me. I could forgive him for what he did. I would take him back for Patrick's sake, if there was a chance. And there's something deep inside of me, I can't put my finger on it exactly, but it's something that compels me to seek him out again despite what happened up there. He seems to be tangled up with everything that I came here for.'

She looked up at her friend, her eyes stormy. 'What am I going to do?'

'Is there actually a choice? Do you have any power over James? Would he offer marriage?'

'Probably not.'

'I don't think so either. I think you're all mixed up about him. You want him. You also want him to be sorry for what he did. You want to see him crawling on his knees to you. If he won't apologise then you want to make him pay. It's revenge and jealousy all bound up together with desire.'

'You're reading things into it!'

'Am I?'

Kate didn't answer.

Brigid just looked up at her friend with one eyebrow raised.

'I want James to be a proper father to Patrick. I want a station. It's just that Rory is standing in the way and I can't stop myself from loving him.'

'You've always been one for just rushing towards your goal as if nothing else mattered. Slow down! There's no hurry. Take it one step at a time and think it through.'

Kate rested her jaw on her hand. 'I've got to do something soon. I want it all set up for when I go to get Patrick.'

'Then why don't you buy yourself some land and forget all about James?'

Kate looked thoughtful and it was a moment before she replied. 'It's not just the land, it's the security of knowing that you're part of the establishment. They're the ones who will never suffer starvation if another famine comes.'

'So it's Rory, love and the fear of the famine, or it's the station and lifelong security for you and the boy. Is that it?'

How could she put it so bluntly? It made her feel so mercenary. It was more complex than that.

Her gown was particularly well tailored and she always felt smart in it. It was a lovely lustrous tan colour with a contrasting black plastron in a triangular shape that extended from the top of the bodice down to a point below her waist. The bodice was heavily boned and quite tight, making her waist appear even smaller than it was. The tan sleeves were fitted to the wrist, with an oversleeve of the contrasting black fabric that reached halfway down her upper arm. The skirt was wide and she was wearing no fewer than nine petticoats underneath it, including one of horse hair. She had a matching bonnet made of the same fabric, in the modern style, smaller, set lower on her head and not so closed-in around her face.

It was the outfit she wore when she went to do business at the saleyards and the auction mart, or if she was negotiating directly with the farmers themselves. It was a good colour that did not show the dust that inevitably blew around Adelaide streets in the summer. Her kid boots were of the latest style and she had kid gloves of the finest quality to match. She held a delightful hand-painted and deeply fringed parasol over her head to shelter herself from the hot February sun.

'My driver and the dray are just over here,' she said to the flour miller, pointing to her new dray and team.

'Come on, lads, be smart about it. All of this flour here has to be packed onto the lady's dray.'

The two young men began to toss the sacks on unceremoniously.

'Pack it on neatly,' Kate directed them, 'I want to get it all on this one dray and it won't fit if you just throw it on like that!'

She stood with one hand on her hip and the other holding the parasol.

The lads did not even blink at the commands coming from a woman. With most of Adelaide's men away at the goldfields many of the remaining farms and businesses were run by wives and daughters.

Kate could see that across the yard a well-dressed man had stopped and was staring at her but she did not spare him more than a glance, for she was counting each sack of flour as it was packed onto the dray.

'Right, that's it,' she said to the flour miller, 'thank you very much indeed.' She shook hands with him.

'Good day to you, Miss O'Leary.'

She turned around, about to leave. Intuition told her that the gentleman who had been watching her earlier was watching her still. He was on his way across the yard towards her. There was something about the way he walked, it was a walk that was full of confidence, the slim hips and long legs moving gracefully. Before her conscious mind could respond to those clues, her heart had begun to hammer and a sensation like butterflies fluttered deep inside her.

'James Carmichael!' the name rose to her lips without volition.

And indeed it was.

'Kate O'Mara! Good heavens!'

'James!'

He closed his mouth, which had dropped open in a most ungentlemanly fashion. 'Kate . . . I can't believe my eyes. What on earth are you doing here? I . . . I thought you were dead.'

Kate looked around, conscious that someone might overhear them. He advanced to meet her and took her hands in his own, looking at her intently. She knew not what to say.

'Kate! It's like a dream come true. Seeing you again. Where on earth have you been? What has happened to you? We gave you up for dead! I just can't believe my eyes. Tell me I'm not dreaming!'

'You're not dreaming.'

He was absolutely shaken. No wonder. 'And aren't you looking fine!' his eyes raked her from head to toe as if taking in the new Kate, fashionable gown, bonnet, parasol and all.

'Things have changed, James. How are you?'

'All the better for seeing you, my dear. I had thought never to see you again!'

'Kate O'Leary is the name that I use now, James,' she said quietly.

'Mr Carmichael, your flour is ready to be delivered! Where do you want it taken?' they heard someone calling.

'I'll be with you in a minute!' he called back.

'Kate, we have so much to catch up on. This is no place to talk. What say I meet you at Johnson's Coffee Shop in half an hour? Do you have further business in town? Can you wait for me?'

'Indeed I can, I'll see you there.'

He raised her hand to his lips. 'Johnson's in half an hour, then.'

Kate turned on her heel and left him to his business. God! He was as smooth as ever. She had forgotten just how urbane he was. Those cool grey eyes and that butter-coloured blond

hair were an unusual combination. The sight of
him had brought back so many memories!

Kate chose a table away from the window,
towards the back of the room where they could
sit without being disturbed or seen.

'You look absolutely wonderful, my dear,' he
said as he took off his grey tophat and gave that
and his cane to the waitress.

'You're looking pretty swell yourself!' she
replied. 'Last time I saw you, you were every
inch the squatter!'

'I've been to see the bank manager today so I
was dressed for the part,' he replied, 'otherwise
it would be the squatter's togs as usual. But
enough of that, how are you? What happened?
Where have you been? I thought that I would
never again see you alive!'

The waitress brought their coffee.

'It is a long story.'

'I've got the time, tell me.'

Kate made up the story as she went, telling
him how she had heard gunshots and had taken
off, on foot and with her pistol, to investigate.
She had not found the source of the commotion
and somehow she had got lost, strange as it may
sound. She wandered around in the bush, dis-
oriented and obviously going in the wrong direction. As night fell she had become frightened
and had started to run in what she thought must
be the direction of the homestead. She fell

heavily, breaking her ankle. At that stage of her pregnancy it was too hard to crawl, so she lay where she was, knowing that Angus would have set up a search party and hoping that she would be found.

She was found, but not by Angus. It was the blacks.

'You could not have known that Angus was dead by then,' he interrupted her.

'Dead?' she feigned surprise.

'Yes, the shots you heard would have been the blacks. They must have ambushed him, taken his gun and shot him. He was found dead on the evening you went missing.'

'Good God! Angus dead? I can scarce believe it! And by his own gun!' She was pleased with herself. She did sound surprised. 'He did get what was coming to him, I suppose,' she added as an afterthought. 'He'd attacked them twice to my knowledge. They had a right to defend themselves.'

She didn't like to let the blame rest with the Yuras, but her own part in the story could never be revealed, especially to James.

'Maybe, but to kill him in cold blood!'

'True,' she said, not looking at him.

'But he was no friend of yours, was he?'

'No, he treated me shamefully, more so after you left to go south.'

'So the others told me. They thought that maybe you had run away.'

'I was tempted to,' she replied, looking him

straight in the eye. The more she told the truth, the more plausible her story would be.

'So what then? The blacks had you?'

She nodded. 'I was frightened at first, but they were very kind to me, they were.'

'I'm surprised they did not kill you outright!'

'I was too,' she lied. 'Maybe it was the baby. They love children so much; I found that out.' She continued her story, saying how the blacks looked after her till the baby came.

'It must have been awful living with them. So primitive and savage as they are. Why did you not contact us? We'd have fetched you.'

'I didn't know how to. I thought about sending someone with a message but I felt sure that Angus would shoot any black that walked up to the homestead. Even if the message had gotten through, I had my doubts that Angus would do anything to help me in your absence.'

'But you knew I would be back up there sooner or later. Why did you not let me know what had happened? Why did you not return? We were looking for you.'

Kate met his gaze as squarely as she could and spoke quietly. 'I thought you'd be well pleased that I was gone. You'd have been rid of me before that if you'd been able to.'

He looked at her as if her accusation was unfounded. 'My dear girl,' he protested, 'we had our differences, but I would never have left you with the blacks if I had known of your fate.'

She let his comments pass. Now was not the

time to tell him what she thought of him. She was playing a deeper game; a game in which she hoped that Patrick would be the winner. She went on to tell him that the blacks had eventually taken her down to Burra Burra.

She stopped her story then and looked up at him searchingly. 'Are you not going to ask me anything about your baby, then?'

James shifted in his chair before answering her. 'The baby was your concern, my dear.'

'You don't want to know about him at all?'

'Tell me about him. It was a boy, I take it.'

She told him about little Patrick, the fact that he took after James with his blond hair and grey eyes. She realised as she was talking that Patrick would have changed a lot since she last saw him. He would have teeth, and maybe less baby fat. He could even be walking.

'Where is he now?'

'With friends,' was all that she replied.

'So, what since? What have you been doing since then? You look like you have struck gold!' He was looking at her dress and he had closed the subject of the baby.

She told him about the flour carting and he whistled before commenting, 'Smart girl, aren't you?' He looked thoughtful.

She nodded.

'You are doing well, then, by the sounds of things,' he said.

'I'll be a wealthy woman in no time at all. That is if the gold lasts, as I said.'

'That will be two of us then, but I'm still living off the sheep's back. There's even more money to be made from wool than I had originally thought. The Far North is for sale—well the fourteen-year leases are—that's why I've been to see the bank today. The more money I can lay my hands on now the more runs I can buy to add to Wildowie.'

She sat up. 'The Far North is for sale, you said?'

He must have literally been squatting on it before. Now the leases were for sale. Her beloved Flinders Ranges! The land she had come to love.

'Yes, all of that land has been released this year. I had first option on Wildowie, of course, since I had the possession of it, and I now own that lock, stock and barrel. But the more land you have the more profitable it is. You need big tracts of that kind of land if you want to keep sheep on it. Plenty of land and good sources of water. I have been searching out the best runs since I established Wildowie, waiting for the release of the land. If I can get the money I'll be the lucky one to snap it all up.'

They had finished their coffee as they talked and Kate could tell that he was ready to leave.

'Listen, Kate, I have another appointment and I will have to go. I'm going to stay with friends out of town for a few days. I must see you again. Where can I find you when I get back?'

What could he want with her now?

'Mrs Applebee's, on the corner of Rundle and Pulteney. You can find me there or she will take a message if I'm not in.'

He placed a gloved finger on her arm. 'Can I escort you home or anywhere else?'

He was always the gentleman. His manners really were impeccable. But she could tell that he was in a hurry now.

'No, I'm about to do a little business, I will wait to hear from you. You won't forget now, will you?'

She didn't want to appear too anxious to see him but she couldn't help herself. Rory would be back soon. She had to find out if there was any chance at all with James, for Patrick's sake.

He drew her chair out and gave her his hand to rise. 'I could never forget you, Kate,' he said, his voice lowered so that she was left in no doubt of his meaning.

Kate felt her heart flutter in response to the throb in his voice. James still wanted her. There was no doubt about that. Maybe there was a chance that Patrick could have his father.

'I'll call to see you in a few days' time,' he promised as they parted.

Kate gazed through the leaded shop windows as she made her way home. But she was taking no notice of the goods displayed. Faulding's Chemist could have had wild lions for sale and she would not have noticed. The thoughts tumbled around inside her head.

James Carmichael! How she had wanted to

see him. Now they had finally made contact again! He was everything she had remembered him to be. Boyishly handsome and so very polished, everything about him bespeaking the gentleman, from his shiny leather shoes to his dove-grey tophat. She could almost forget how selfish he had been. He must be made to accept Patrick as his son. He must.

And if he didn't . . . she would think of something that would make him sorry.

He wanted her, there was no doubt about that. He had been unable to take his eyes off her. But she was no longer the naive young girl who had stepped off the ship and onto the wagon destined for his station. She was a woman, a woman rapidly coming up in the world and she was going to call the tune this time!

But there would be time to think about all of that later. In the meantime there was something else pressing on her mind. The land! The leases were for sale. That wonderful land that she had come to love. She should be buying it as quickly as she was able. Land would last forever but the gold wouldn't. She remembered the squatters at Mother Jamieson's Inn at Buninyong. *Wool will be king*, they had said. They, too, were buying it up as fast as they could. Land! Land! Land! The word ricocheted around in her head.

Only the foolish would be left chasing after dreams of becoming rich from gold when there was land for sale. If only the flour business had been going longer and she had saved more money. She didn't have enough on her own to buy the lease for a large tract of land. Not enough to run a successful sheep station. But with James? If they were to team up on it? Then they would have enough between them.

Land! It was land that would give her the security she needed.

She could never settle down happily with Rory while she lacked the security that only land could bring. She would put everything into making enough money to buy land for herself and Patrick and she would worry about her heart later.

And if she kept land as her goal the rest would surely fall into place.

Chapter
Sixteen

When Kate got back to Mrs Applebee's that afternoon, she was amazed to find a number of large boxes had been delivered and had been left at her door. Wondering what could be in them she quickly unlocked her door and pulled them inside.

She pulled the lid off the largest box. Whatever was inside was wrapped in sheets of fine tissue paper. There was a note on top and she unfolded that first.

It was Rory's bold handwriting in thick black ink.

> *My darling Kathleen,*
> *I will pick you up for dinner at seven o'clock. The trip went even better than expected. I will tell you the news tonight when I see you.*
> *Rory*

The note fluttered from Kate's hand to the floor as she pulled aside the tissue paper, impatient to see what the box contained.

At the first sight of the fabric she took a sharp inward breath. It was silk, beautiful silk of the finest quality. The colour was exquisite, a lustrous blue, almost a violet. French blue it would be called, or maybe periwinkle. It was almost opalescent, reflecting the dual colours of violet and blue.

'Glory be to God!'

She pulled the gown from its box with one hand and pulled the leaves of tissue away from it with the other.

It was an evening gown. A divinely beautiful evening gown of the finest silk. Rory had bought it for her. Tears sprang to her eyes. Trust Rory. A beautiful silk evening gown and Rory had bought it for her to wear to dinner tonight!

Through the shimmer of tears she could see the delicate light reflected from the fabric, refracted through the moisture on her eyes, making the gown magically illuminated. She moved closer to the window and looked closely at the fabric.

Her first silk gown!

She had been so overawed by the gown that she had forgotten the other boxes. She lay the gown over her bed and pulled the lids from the smaller ones. The next box contained thin-soled black satin evening slippers and the following one evening gloves, embroidered and beaded.

The last box held silk underwear, soft and almost transparent, in the softest peach colour, and a pair of the finest silk stockings.

Kate sat down on the edge of the bed, careful to avoid crushing the gown. Trust Rory to have catered to her wildest fantasy! Only a man like him would do something like this. Only Rory would spend his hard-earned profits on such a wickedly expensive outfit. He cared only for the present. The present and her happiness.

Well she had better begin to get ready!

She tried on the dress first, just in case it needed any alteration. The fit was perfect. She checked the shoes and gloves next. Rory had guessed her sizes correctly. The man had talents that she was still finding out about! She smiled to herself. He knew her body intimately from head to toe so it was probably no surprise that he could guess her size with reasonable accuracy!

She pulled on one of her more simple gowns and flew downstairs.

'Mrs Applebee! I won't be in for dinner tonight. I am going out. Could you arrange for a hot bath to be drawn for me?'

'An important engagement, my dear?' the older woman asked her.

'Very,' she grinned.

'Do you want a hand to dress? I could come up to help you myself.'

Kate had never had anybody help her to dress before but she did not refuse the offer. 'That would be lovely, thank you.'

Mrs Applebee would know exactly what to do with her hair and how to arrange the gown to best advantage. Kate sent up a silent prayer of thanks that she had chosen Mrs Applebee's as her home. She and the older woman had hit it off immediately.

'What time is your dinner?'

'I will be collected at seven o'clock.'

'I'll come up at six, then, dear.'

Kate ran back up the stairs, not so much because there was any great hurry but more because she was so excited. God! She had missed Rory so much! She was aching to see him again, regardless of the strain between them when they had parted. On top of that, to be going out to dinner, and in a gown like that! It was what every poor orphan must have dreamt of at one time or another! And not least of all herself. It was a special dream, a fairy tale come true.

Mrs Applebee's maid knocked on her door a short time later. The hip bath was brought in, followed by bucket after bucket full of steaming water. This was a special treat since normally the boarders took their baths in the bathroom at the end of the corridor.

Kate soaked for a good half hour and then washed her hair, using the last bucket of water to rinse it thoroughly. She had already put on her peach-coloured silk drawers and chemise and her petticoats when Mrs Applebee knocked on her door.

'Come in!' she called.

Mrs Applebee entered the room and was drawn immediately to the gown laid out on the bed.

'My dear girl, it is absolutely gorgeous. Where did you get a gown like this?' The question was probably superfluous since Mrs Applebee had most likely been at home when Rory delivered the boxes.

'Beautiful, is it not? It is a gift from a very good friend.'

'I wonder where he bought it. It must have come from England, if not originally from France. The garments produced in the colony are seldom made of such beautiful fabric.'

'I would not know. It's the finest gown that I've ever seen, never mind owned.'

'Now you sit down here,' Mrs Applebee said, drawing a chair in front of the washstand so that Kate would be able to see in the mirror above it. 'How are we going to do this hair of yours?'

'That I don't know. It's not easy to do much at all with it at this length.' She pulled a lock down. It had grown to just past her shoulders.

'It's a shame that you ever cut it.'

'Necessity.'

'So you told me, dear.'

Mrs Applebee began to brush her hair. Kate was very much aware that it was a real condescension on the part of the older woman. Indeed it would have been more fitting if she had sent her maid along to help. Mrs Applebee must have taken quite a liking to her to offer her personal help. Maybe it was because they had something in common. They had shared confidences not long after Kate arrived and Kate had learnt that Mrs Applebee had struggled too. She had been an only child. Her mother had died in childbirth. Her father had been a successful merchant and the family had come up in the world. Before he had died he had refused his permission for her to marry Mr Applebee, a man whom he believed was a no-hoper and little better than a fortune hunter. The so-called fortune hunter left for Australia but continued to keep in touch through letters which she had kept secret from her father.

After her father died she arranged to follow her beloved to Australia and to marry him. Sadly, her father's judgement had proved correct. Her husband was charming when sober, but when he drank he abused her mercilessly and gambled her money away. Since all her money and possessions transferred to him on her marriage, she had no control over his spending and she could not divorce him without losing all that she had. Fortunately, before all the money was gone, he was killed in a knife fight. She scrimped and saved, living on little else but bread and dripping, while she built up her boarding-house business. She, too, had learnt that it was a harsh world for a woman without friends or family. She, too, had been taken in by the slick promises of a selfish man. They had a lot in common.

'What will you be wearing in the way of jewellery, dear?'

She hadn't even thought about jewellery. 'Oh, I don't own a single piece of jewellery, ma'am, I'll have to go without.'

'Wait one moment then,' Mrs Applebee said, and shuffled out of the room.

While she was gone Kate drew on her stockings and her soft new satin shoes. Mrs Applebee returned a few minutes later with her jewellery box in her hand. 'Now I won't lend you anything too expensive and then you need not worry about thieves or loose catches. Ah, this is what I thought might suit!'

She pulled out a necklace made of finely worked silver and black shining stones. 'The jet necklace will highlight this lovely black hair of yours,' she said, 'and there are some matching beads that we can thread right into your hair. They are very simple but that is the best, I think. Too much fussy jewellery would only detract from your beauty and your youth.'

She proceeded to part Kate's hair in the middle and to draw the strands smoothly from the front across her ears and then upwards to be fixed at the crown of her head. Fortunately the hair was just long enough to reach around without being pulled too tightly. Then all the hair at the back of her head was caught up, braided and wound into a circle at her crown.

Kate turned her head to the side to see the effect since she had never worn her hair that high before. It made her neck look longer and more slender. The individual strands that were shorter than the others had already begun to loosen from the rest and they hung down raven black against the white of her neck. The effect was soft and feminine.

'Keep still!'

Kate stopped moving her head to look. She would have to wait until Mrs Applebee had finished her creation.

Eventually the jet beads were pinned into place. They were woven in with the braiding and some had been left draped loosely to hang down below the mass of hair at her crown. The effect was to make her head glitter with mysterious lights when she moved.

'It looks beautiful,' Kate sighed when the older woman had finished her hair and she was able to turn her head to look in the mirror.

'Now for the gown,' Mrs Applebee said briskly.

Kate stood up while her lacings were drawn tight.

'Stand still now.'

The gown was dropped over her head without it touching so much as a single hair of her new hairstyle. Mrs Applebee twitched it into place and began to do up the fine buttons that stretched all the way down her back.

'You are lucky that you have such a lovely small waist, my dear. Now, turn around and let me have a look at you.'

She turned towards the older woman and tilted her head up, conscious of the weight of the hair and beads high on her head.

'You look beautiful. The dress is absolutely perfect for you. It matches exactly the colour of your eyes. The blue with the hint of violet. If only the pansies were in season we could have woven them into your hair as well. They, too, would match your eyes perfectly. Never mind though. What I find hard to believe is that any man could have guessed your size so well.'

Kate's eyes twinkled in response and the corners of her mouth lifted.

Mrs Applebee did not press for an answer to her question, but there was an answering twinkle in her eyes too. 'Now, the jet necklace to finish it off.'

She picked up the necklace and clasped it around Kate's neck and then she adjusted the gown on her shoulders. 'Now, don't look in that small mirror, come and have a look in the full-length mirror in my rooms.'

She led Kate to the other end of the corridor and to the mirror in her dressing room. Kate looked herself up and down in utter disbelief. Never before had she worn a gown so beautiful. She looked at the expanse of ivory skin that was exposed. The gown was both décolleté and off the shoulder. The curves of her breasts were just visible above the *de coeur* neckline. The necklace was made of silver that had been skilfully worked to look like fine lace and the jet beads hung from it, black like a silhouette against the white of her skin.

Kate wasn't so sure that she was comfortable with so much skin exposed and she pulled the shoulders upwards a little.

'No, evening gowns are supposed to be worn well off the shoulder. It looks charming,' Mrs Applebee assured her, and twitched the gown down over her shoulders again.

Kate stared at herself in the mirror unable to believe the transformation. Her eyes glittered like the jet beads. Wait until Rory saw her in this!

She turned around to Mrs Applebee and hugged her. 'Thank you for helping me to dress and thank you, too, for the loan of the jewellery.'

'My pleasure, dear girl. Don't crush that gown! Now one more thing, if you don't have a suitable shawl I'll lend you one. The evening might get cool.'

She pulled a lacy black evening shawl from her wardrobe and draped it around Kate's shoulders. 'Perfect!'

'Miss O'Leary!' it was the voice of the maid, 'Miss O'Leary!' She knocked on the door of the room. 'A gentleman here to see you! He's down below.'

A hush fell on the room as Kate descended the stairs to the entrance hall. Two of her fellow lodgers who had been conversing in earnest about the goldfields stopped abruptly as she came into view. Rory went forward to take her hand.

'Kathleen!'

'Oh, Rory!'

Each looked at the other as if mesmerised. Rory was dressed in evening clothes too. His cutaway jacket was black to match the trousers that were buttoned down at the foot. He was wearing the latest style of elastic-sided black shoes, highly polished, and he wore an elaborate silk waistcoat that combined the colours of black, grey and blue in a shimmering pattern. His snowy cravat was tied in a large bow. His hair and beard had been trimmed and his skin shone as if he had scrubbed it with soap. He held a black tophat in his hand and looked quite unlike the dusty bullocky whom she had last seen waving her farewell.

They might have stared at each other for longer if they hadn't been interrupted by one of the other lodgers. 'Miss O'Leary, you do look lovely this evening!'

'She does indeed,' Rory added, drawing her hand into the crook of his arm.

'You look pretty swell yourself, Mr O'Connor!' She looked up at him and from where she stood in her thin-soled shoes he looked taller than usual. And so damned handsome!

'And where are you off to this evening, Miss O'Leary?' the other lodger asked, his eyes still as round as saucers at the sight of Kate in such a stunning gown.

Kate looked up at Rory, one eyebrow lifted.

'Only the best for Miss O'Leary tonight. We are going to the Blenheim for dinner.'

'Ah well, you will have a lovely time then. You won't get a finer dinner than at the Blenheim. Enjoy yourselves!'

Kate picked up her skirts and they swept through the front door and out onto the street. She was determined that her gown was not going to collect the dust off the unsealed streets of Adelaide. She let go of Rory's arm so that she could hold the skirt well clear of the ground.

'Oh, Rory, I've missed you so much!'

'I've missed you too, darlin'. I reckon I made the fastest trip any bullocky has made to the goldfields and back.'

'I wasn't expecting you back so early. It's lucky that I already have the next load ready for you. And I've managed to get another three teams and drays as well.'

'Well done. What price did you give for the grain?'

She told him and he whistled in response. 'You did well!'

'I managed to get in touch with a couple of farmers who were headed for the diggings. They were willing to sell at almost any price so that they could get going. I negotiated a good price on the milling too. How did you go with selling the four drayloads?'

'Very well, but I'll tell you all about that later. There was something that I wanted to tell you before we got to Blenheim's.'

'Oh?'

'Yes, something that I know you'll be interested in. We were camped by a party of Irish diggers when we got there. The old fellow had died and they were holding a proper Irish wake for him. The type that we've not seen the likes of since we left Ireland.'

Here he goes again, she thought. 'I can just imagine.'

'There were plenty of spirits provided and most of his family, never mind the guests, were roaring drunk by the time I was invited to join them.

'I said to the widow, *"Well, Mrs Kennedy, what was it that your husband died of, then?"*

'*"Gonorrhoea,"* she said to me.

'*"Gonorrhoea?"* said I, *"I heard it was diarrhoea, the fault of the water, it being so scarce and so dirty."*

'And the widow lowered her voice, she did, and she whispered in my ear, *"'Tis better that he be known for the lover that he was not than for the shit that he was!"*'

'Oh, Rory!' Kate laughed. 'For all the fine clothes you've not changed one bit! I'm glad you didn't save that one for the dining room of the Blenheim, I'd not have been able to raise my head for the shame of it all!'

'That would be the day!'

'Well I've become quite respectable since you saw me last. What with staying at Mrs Applebee's and doing business with the nobs and snobs! You'd never believe that I was once a rough bullocky.'

'Well you can't be too respectable otherwise you'd not have laughed at poor old Kennedy's sad demise,' he grinned.

Kate schooled her features into a more serious expression as they entered the Blenheim. Rory had made a booking and they were shown to a table in a quiet corner away from the entrance and the door to the kitchens. The room was decorated in a sumptuous deep red wallpaper. A chandelier holding hundreds of candles hung in the centre of the room and made the silver cutlery and gold-rimmed plates sparkle with reflected light. It was without doubt the place for the well-to-do to dine in Adelaide.

Rory had ordered a bottle of champagne and the waiter poured them each a glassful, placed the bottle on ice and left them to study the menu.

'Kathleen,' he said her name quite softly and she looked up from the menu and into his face.

'To you,' he said, raising his glass to her. 'You look so beautiful tonight.'

The fine glass in her hand tinkled as it made contact with his and she took a sip, the first sip of champagne she had ever tasted, and the bubbles fizzed in her mouth. 'I feel beautiful too, Rory. This gown is wonderful. It's the kind of gown I've dreamt of all my life. You knew that I've always wanted a silk gown and you bought it for me. How can I say thank you?'

'I could think of a suitable way,' and he wiggled both brows up and down.

'I'm sure that you could.'

'No, seriously, the pleasure is all mine.'

He paused, looking at her through narrowed eyes, his head tilted to one side. 'It reminds me of something . . . something you only get to appreciate when you're on the track every evening. You would know what I mean, for I think you've commented on it to me before now. That blue-violet, the colour of the sky when the sun has set and the light has nearly faded away, the colour that is there for those few moments just as Venus comes twinkling into life above the horizon.'

'I know it.'

'Well, you're like that evening sky, the colour of your eyes and your gown are the shimmer of that violet-blue, and your hair is like the velvet black of the night sky that follows on just a few moments later. Those beads and the sparkle of your eyes are the galaxy of stars that are coming to life.'

Kate felt her lips part in wonder. This Rory was such a rough diamond! The more she knew him, the more complexities his nature revealed. Only he could be so poetic and graceful one moment, all sweat and muscle the next, hilariously funny a minute later. How much more of him would be revealed to her?

'You chose a gown that could not have suited me better.'

'I did indeed.'

She lowered her voice, 'And the underwear and everything. It's beautiful. And all of it fitting me so well. How did you know what size to buy?'

Rory set his glass on the table. 'I just figured you were about this size,' he said, one dark eyebrow raised and his hands making gestures indicating the shape of her body.

She nearly choked on the mouthful of champagne she had just taken. She laughed and coughed again. 'Rory! You could charm the skin off a snake, you could!'

'Ah, the snakes can have their skins. I'd rather charm the trousers off an Irish girl!'

She felt the colour rise to her cheeks and she looked around her. No one had been close enough to overhear him and, besides, the comment would have made no sense to anyone who might have overheard.

'Well, this is a celebration,' he said, changing the subject. 'Kathleen O'Mara, I have great pleasure in telling you, you are now a rich woman!'

'Tell me more!' she leant forward, clapping her hands together.

At that moment the waiter came to take their order. Rory did the ordering for her and she could not believe it when he ordered every course and several side dishes as well.

'I want everything of the best,' he told the waiter. 'Never mind the cost. Give us the best wines in the house, I don't know which ones they would be but I'm sure that you would.'

'Certainly, sir!'

'We'll never eat that much,' she said when the waiter disappeared. 'I'm so tightly laced I'll be lucky to fit in the first course!'

'We don't have to,' he replied, 'but I've got to make absolutely sure that all your dreams have come true. You wanted silk gowns and tables piled high with the best food that money could buy and that is exactly what you're going to get!'

'Oh.'

'Exactly. You'll either decide that you've had enough or that you can't stand the waste and you don't want it any more. Either way, you'll eventually get to the point where you don't dream of Ireland any longer. That's my plan. I figured it out on my way back from the diggings.'

'And what if I decide that I can never get enough of it?'

'Then I'll have to turn to bushranging as well as the flour-carting business! Bullocky by day, bushranger by night.'

'You'd make a good bushranger. You've got that romantic look about you!'

'I'd need more than romantic looks. I'd have to get a lot tougher for starters,' his eyes narrowed as he demonstrated the mean look of a bushranger, 'that way I could keep you under the thumb like a bushranger's woman should be.'

'Ha! That'll be the day! But I can just imagine you sweet-talking the weary diggers into handing over their gold! It has not come to that just yet, though. Now what were you saying before we were interrupted?'

'I can't remember.'

'You can too!'

'What was it about?'

'About me being rich!'

'Ah that!' he teased her, his eyes glittering.

'Tell me!'

'I'm deadly serious now, Kathleen,' he paused for effect. 'We made six hundred per cent on the flour.'

'What?'

'Six hundred per cent.' He watched as his words sank in and Kate did the necessary arithmetic.

'Glory be to God! We are rich!'

'Getting there. We headed straight for the new diggings at Forrest Creek and Mount Alexander. Ballarat is finished, only a few hundred left there by all accounts. But at the new fields you should have seen it. It made the Ballarat rush look like a Sunday picnic. With all the new arrivals from South Australia and Van Diemen's Land, the number has swelled to twenty thousand all told! Twenty thousand people working up huge appetites. The flour was all sold within a day. There are storekeepers there who will pay in advance for us to bring them the flour.'

'How can they be sure you'll return?'

'They can't, but they're willing to take the risk to get the stores there. Apparently the roads between the diggings and Melbourne are atrocious. They say that once the rains come they will be impassable. The Victorian Government is doing nothing at all to improve the roads or to provide any services despite the licence money they're collecting off the diggers. There'll be trouble over all of that before long, for sure.'

'But in the meantime they're looking to South Australia for flour.'

'Exactly. We can make this business as big as we want to, my darlin'!'

The waiter appeared with their appetiser of fresh duck liver pâté served with tiny, thin pieces of buttered toast.

'Mm,' Kate said as she bit into a piece. It was absolutely delicious. She washed each mouthful down with a sip of champagne.

'So did you take orders in advance?'

'Some, but not all. The price of flour may go higher yet. If it does, we can make a bigger profit on the rest; if it doesn't we still have certain buyers waiting for our flour.'

Rory entertained her with all the stories of the wild goings-on at the goldfields until their next course came.

It was a wonderful rich cream of chicken soup, with a subtle flavour that reminded her of the one that they had at Buninyong, full of cream, with finely chopped chives on the top.

Entrée was some tiny puffy pastries filled with a seafood mousse. With it came another bottle of wine, this time a German riesling. Kate had already slowed down, realising that if she washed down each and every mouthful of food with a mouthful of wine that Rory may well have to carry her home.

God, it was fun to be with him again! She almost regretted her decision to stay in Adelaide. It would have been great to have made the last trip with him.

With their main course of veal escalope finished, Rory pushed back his chair a little. 'Well, my dear, what do you think we should be doing with this business of ours? Should we take as many advance orders as we can? Or do you think we should just take our chances on every load?'

'It probably depends on how much we want to reinvest in each run, I suppose. We might want to invest some of the profits in other things—'

Rory was about to give his opinion when he was interrupted by another gentleman who had strolled over to greet him. 'Rory O'Connor!'

'George Hawker! How do you do?' Rory stood up to shake hands with the man who looked familiar to Kate.

'George Hawker, this is Miss Kathleen O'Leary. Kathleen, this is George Hawker from Bungaree,' he said, remembering to use her assumed name.

No wonder he had looked familiar. She had seen him from a distance when they had passed through Bungaree Station on the way to the Far North. The way that George looked at her suggested that he remembered her face from somewhere too.

'How do you do, Mr Hawker,' she said.

'What are you up to these days, Rory?'

'Kathleen and I are in business together carting flour to the diggings.'

'That would be a good business to be in at this stage, I would imagine.'

'Indeed it is.'

'How much longer do you think the gold will last?'

'A good while yet, I'd say.'

'You're not thinking of buying up land instead? The Far North is for sale now, you know. I could see you up there, Rory, you're the rugged Far North type.'

Rory shook his head. 'No, that life is not for me. I'll stick with the flour carting for a while. The lifestyle suits me down to the ground.'

'I imagine it does! Well, if I need any wheat taken off my hands where can I contact you?'

'Contact Kathleen. She's managing the Adelaide end of the business. You can find her at Mrs Applebee's.'

George nodded. 'Good, I might do that. Must get back to Bessie now or she'll be wondering where I've gotten to. Evening, Rory. Nice to meet you, Miss O'Leary.'

Kate stared at his back as he made his way across to the other side of the room. George Hawker was probably the wealthiest squatter in the whole of South Australia. He had made a great success of wheat and wool. He was a man who knew what he was talking about. Even he was talking about land!

George Hawker's words were forgotten for

the moment as the waiter had brought their dessert of apple and pear tarts served with rich crème anglaise. The pastry was light, flaky and sweet and the fruit was fresh from local orchards. The thick sweet muscat complemented the food. It was absolutely delicious and the flavours lingered long in her mouth after each taste she took.

The richness of the food and the luscious flavours of the wines were combining, affecting Kate in such a way that she felt deliriously sensual, happy and excited. If there had been no one else in the room she might have leant towards Rory and taken his face in her hands to kiss him on those wine-sweetened lips. Conscious that they were not alone, she slipped one satin shoe from her slender foot and felt for his foot with her own. It was a bold thing to do but she wanted to touch him, to feel his body against hers. This was as close as she could get.

Rory's lips parted when she made contact with him. His mouth curved with tenderness. 'I'm glad to be back with you, my darlin'.'

'I'm glad you're back here, too. I missed you when you were away. Being here with you, dressed like this, drinking sweet wine, it could not be more perfect. I wish that this night would never end.'

He leant forward to clasp her hand. 'Let's forget the proprieties. I don't give a damn if we are in the snootiest restaurant in town. We're rich in our own right so the dictates of the upper classes can go to hell! Kate, I love you, more than any woman I've loved before. This night never has to end. It can go on for ever. It can go on for the rest of our lives. Marry me.'

Marry me. The words seemed to hit her hard in the gut. Rory waited for her response but she floundered. His proposal had for some reason come as a surprise. It was not that she hadn't guessed that he would ask her one day. She had thought that he probably would, even though he had once told her that he was not the marrying type.

Kate felt her own lips part and her heartbeat hammering away in her head. What was she to say? Her heart said yes, overwhelmingly yes! But her head seemed to have taken control and was silencing her tongue.

'Say something, Kathleen. Don't just sit there looking at me as if you were struck by lightning. You know that I'm more in love with you than any man could be.'

Yes. She knew that. So what was it that was stopping her from saying yes? Why could she not throw all caution to the wind? She loved Rory, in a way that was almost beyond description. He was like, like . . . like fire in her veins, inflaming her, exciting her with everything that he did and every word that he said. Hadn't this dinner proven that?

'I've never seen you lost for words before. Surely you knew this grand dinner was for some good reason.'

She felt a tear form slowly in each eye and then spill suddenly over the lids to trickle down her face.

'What is it, my darlin'?' he took her hand in a firmer clasp.

'I don't think that I can!' the words tumbled out suddenly, 'I don't think that I can!'

'You love me, don't you? It's in your eyes. It's in your lips each time that you kiss me. It's in that adorable body of yours each time you wrap it around mine.'

'I'm too scared.'

'Scared? You scared? I thought that Kathleen O'Mara didn't have a scared bone in her body. Scared to say yes? Or to marry me?'

'Both. I love you more than anything, more than anybody. I love you to distraction. But I cannot marry you, Rory!'

'Jesus! What is it, not still this famine thing is it?'

She nodded her head.

'But you've got your silk dresses. You've got your table piled high with the best bloody food that money can buy. Why the hell did you think I did all of this if not to convince you that you need never go without? We're onto the best money-making racket I can think of. Isn't that enough security for you?' His voice was getting louder as his frustration increased.

'Sh!' she lowered her own voice, noticing the stares of the other diners. 'You can't tell me that the gold will last forever!'

'I can tell you that it will last one hell of a long time. You can't kick the dirt with the toe of your boot over there without unearthing a nugget by mistake. The Forty-niners say the country all through Victoria has the look about it that guarantees there is gold. There will be enough to keep the diggers going for years.'

'How can you be sure?'

'No one can be one hundred per cent sure of anything. But I'm willing to stake my life on it. Anyway, if I am wrong, so what? There will be other ways to make money. I'm confident that I can live on my wits anywhere, any time.'

'Well I am not!'

Rory shook his head. 'After all that we've been through together you don't trust me, do you?'

'It isn't that I don't trust you, Rory. It's not that!'

'It is. My God! You don't trust me to look after you, to provide for you,' he was getting upset, she could tell by the way his eyes were flashing. He was the sort of man who seldom lost his temper but this was one of those times. She had pushed him too far.

'Rory, I trust you to do everything in your power to make me happy. But there are some things that just aren't in your power. You're not the type to settle down. No, don't interrupt me. You'll try, I've no doubt of that, but at heart you're a rover. You'll want to move on some time to try your hand at other things, to see new parts of the world. You can't deny it! And I don't want to do that!'

'What the hell do you want then?'

'I want land! It's the only thing that will last! I want a station. I want to be sitting pretty on something that will always hold its value. I want to be up there with the landed gentry. For they and they alone will never starve!'

'God, Kathleen! It is a new country. The rules that applied in Ireland do not apply here! There is no guarantee that the land will give you that security here. You've seen almost as much of it as I have. And I reckon you can get seven good years and seven bad years. If we have a long drought, which I suspect will happen one day, then your station will be worth nothing. The blacks have told us again and again that there will be a drought, as surely as night follows day. If you don't believe me then at least believe them. They aren't only saying it to scare off the white man. You'll sit on that wide verandah of yours and watch your precious sheep die of thirst and starvation!'

'I don't believe you! George Hawker, James Carmichael, those squatters from Buninyong. They said it! The land will last. Wool will be king! And here we are, building our future on fool's gold!'

'Oh, Jesus!'

Tears continued to gather, of their own accord, on her lower lids and spilled silently down her face, causing the thick black lashes to bunch together and her eyes to look like stars. 'My family lost their land, Rory. Look what happened to them. They died, the most awful deaths, and I had to watch them! I don't want that to happen to Patrick and I never want to go through it again myself. I'm sorry, Rory. I really am. I didn't want to hurt you, because it hurts me too. But I can't marry you. I can't do that.'

Rory sighed, a look of bitterness twisting his mouth. 'Not even if we invested our profits in land?'

'Your heart would not be in it. It would never work, you said yourself that you don't want to settle down on a station.'

'I would if it meant that much to you.'

'You don't really want to, though. You'll never put your heart and soul into it like I would. You'd never give your all to something you don't believe in. You'll want to sell up one day. You'd want to go off and do something else. Patrick and I will be forced to sell out too and where would that leave us? No, I couldn't do it to you even if you offered. It would never work!'

'You're not prepared to give it a try.'

'I can't afford the risk.'

'Jesus, Kathleen! Do I mean nothing to you at all? We are relatively wealthy now. We don't have to worry about where our next meal is coming from! You're driven by all of the wrong things. You, I and Patrick can be happy together, it is all that counts in the end. Are you going to let sheep stations stand in the way of that? Can you not see that it is the love of a lifetime?'

They stared silently at each other as the minutes slipped away.

Finally Rory sighed, 'All right then, what are we going to do now? I'm not interested in sticking around here watching you chase rich squatters. I've never been one for suffering. I'm no martyr. It has to be all or nothing. It's the end of the road for O'Leary and O'Connor the Flour Merchants. I say we drop it all right now and I shall find my comfort in someone else's arms.'

Someone else's arms! The end of their business! No! She didn't want that.

'But I've got everything ready for taking the next load!'

'Oh, Kathleen!' Rory looked at her in disgust.

She could read his thoughts. It looked as though she was more upset about the loss of her profits than she was about losing him. It wasn't true, for parting from Rory would tear her heart in two.

The seconds ticked by.

'Well then, I'll take the next load since you have it ready and we planned it together. But then that will be that. When we've split the profits it will be the end of our partnership for good. As I said, Kate, I'll not stick around to watch you do what you're going to do. It won't just make me unhappy, I reckon it will make you unhappy too. But if you want to ruin your own chances of happiness it will be entirely upon your own head. I don't want to watch it.'

'Rory, you've got the wrong idea. I've never said that this is the end of the road for us. I don't want it to be. I love you. You are still a friend, no matter what. You know that I have other things that I must do. I must get some land and I must return to claim my son. When I have done those things then I can consider myself and my own needs and—'

'Me?'

'Yes, you. But I can't make any promises. I know I've kept you waiting for a final answer from me for too long. I won't make you wait any longer. I don't want you to find someone else, but I'm not going to prevent you either. We've both got to be free to do what we want to do. Right now, there is no hope for us to marry. We have to call it quits in that way, but there's no reason for us not to see each other as friends.'

Rory said nothing in response.

'And let's not throw the business in. It is too good a money spinner. Right now I need it to finance my land. You can do what you like with it.'

'I don't like the idea of it. As long as it brings me into contact with you then I am going to want you. It won't work.'

'Well, you've always said to let the future look after itself, so let it. Let's take it one load at a time and see how it goes. If we can handle it, fine. If we can't, we'll split the business. You said so, Rory, you said that the future looks after itself, so let it.'

He had his head lowered and he looked up at her from under his heavy black brows as if he knew that she was twisting the things that he said to her own advantage.

'Sometimes I don't understand you,' she said, ramming home her advantage. 'You say that you want a life of footloose freedom. You say "Easy come, easy go", you say you just want to roam around and enjoy yourself. Why don't you then? Why don't you forget about marrying me, shrug your shoulders and carry on with life?'

'People change, Kate.'

'Do they?' She didn't want to listen to what he was about to say. 'I don't think so. I will always be Kate O'Mara, the ambitious and grasping famine survivor and you will always be the devil-may-care, roaming Rory O'Connor, is it not true?'

'Is it?'

Chapter

Seventeen

The day after Rory left, James sent a note to Kate, asking her to join him for a picnic lunch at Waterfall Gully. It was such good timing that she almost wondered if he had known that Rory had been back and had now gone again.

And what could he want of her? Part of her wanted to throw the invitation back in his face. She still seethed with resentment about what he had done to her. But she could not afford to put him off-side, not when Patrick's future was at stake. He arrived in the late morning driving a smart little buggy. Kate went out onto the street to greet him and sprang lightly up to sit beside him on the seat.

This was the first time she had been on an outing since the disastrous dinner with Rory a week ago. She pushed those memories aside. The March day was fine and, fortunately, not too hot. The conversation was kept to generalities as they made their way to the foothills below the Tiers.

Kate was wearing another of her new gowns, this time a pretty printed muslin with narrow sleeves and a lace collar. The flimsy fabric swayed about her as she walked up towards the waterfall. She thought how different she must appear to James now that she was no longer wearing the practical dark fabrics and narrower skirts of the gowns she had bought when she had first arrived in Adelaide. They had been suitable for a servant. This gown was suitable for a sophisticated woman of means and that was exactly how she wanted to feel.

The waterfall was still flowing and they found a grassy spot by the water's edge. They had the place all to themselves. James spread out a rug for them to sit on and unpacked the picnic lunch from the basket. There were fresh bread rolls, still warm from the oven, scotch eggs, finely sliced ham and fresh, furry peaches neither blemished nor bruised. There were fine white linen napkins and china plates with delicate patterns painted on the edges. James had also brought a bottle of wine. He poured a glass each for them.

'To the future!' James said and Kate clinked her glass with his.

'Indeed,' she said, taking a sip.

'Have some of this,' he said, passing her some of the scotch egg on a plate.

'Thank you,' she said and took it from him. 'Don't tell me you've been cooking, James.'

He smiled that condescending smile of his. 'Not I! The hotel kindly packed it for me.'

'Where are you staying this time?'

He swallowed a mouthful of food before replying, 'The Southern Cross. I always stay there. The service is good.'

She remembered meeting him there, for the first time, two years ago. As they ate their picnic lunch she told him about her trip to the gold-fields. He seemed very interested.

'And this Rory?'

'He was the one that I met on the way up. You must remember him. He went with us as far as Bungaree.'

'Ah yes, I do remember him now that you say that . . . Do you mind me asking, what exactly is your relationship with him? Is there some kind of understanding between the two of you?'

She swallowed the sweetish mouthful of bread roll before answering. 'No, there is no under-standing between us. Rory is not the type to set-tle down. He is my business partner and my friend and a wonderful friend at that, but there's nothing more than that between us.'

'I'm glad.'

The way he said those two words made her heart bump and the blood surge in her veins. What did he mean? She looked at him, waiting for him to say more.

'Would you like some peach?' he asked, pick-ing up a knife.

'Thank you.'

She watched as he peeled away the furry skin and cut the white peach flesh into slices. The juice ran down over his fingers and dripped onto the plate.

Kate watched those long slender hands at work, remembering the feel of them on her skin and the cool, smooth way he had made love to her at Wildowie. There was a certain delicacy about those hands. He slid some of the slices onto a plate for her.

She took the plate and looked at him. If it had been Rory he would have tossed her the peach whole. Or if he had been feeling romantic he may even have fed her luscious mouthfuls of it with his fingers. They would have exulted in the sticky juice dribbling down their throats. But James would never do that. The two men could not have been more different.

'And tell me more about this business of yours. How well are you doing? Do you think it will continue?'

He really had no right to ask her but she was proud of what she and Rory had done and it pleased her to tell James about it.

He whistled through his teeth when she told him the expected profit from this trip alone. 'I'm impressed,' he said.

James wet the napkins in the creek and they both wiped their hands clean of the juice. He took off his hat and lay down face-upwards on the rug. Kate did likewise, gazing up through the tracery of leaves to the powder-blue sky. They lay there for a few moments, saying nothing. She closed her eyes. The wine and food, combined with the hazy warmth of the afternoon sun, had made her feel relaxed. There was only the soft buzz of bees and the cascading sound of water over rocks.

Then James rolled towards her, one hand propping up his head. 'I really missed you, Kate. I wished like hell that things had not worked out the way they had.'

Her eyes flew open at his words and she looked up into his face. Was this for real? Was he really sorry? Was he trying to make amends?

'I count it as one of the greatest mistakes of my life,' he said ruefully. His hat lay on the grass and the dappled sunlight played on the gold of his hair.

'Do you?' Her heart began to thump again. She had hated him for what he had done to her. He had used her, then tried to kick her out. So why did her heartbeat quicken when he looked at her like that?

'I do. And I know we can never have that time over again . . . But we can start afresh.' He moved towards her and his lips brushed softly across hers. 'Tell me that it's not too late, that I've not made you hate me forever.'

'I could never hate you forever, James,' she said honestly. Not if he claimed Patrick as his son. Then she would not hate him.

She thought about the way he had just brushed her lips with his. Rory had done the same thing yesterday. And yet the same physical sensation had aroused quite different emotions.

Yesterday the sensation had been a bittersweet anguish. It had reminded her of what she had let go. She had longed for more.

Today, James's kiss had sparked off another kind of need. She longed only to be comforted. She longed to be told that she had made the right decision, that it would all be worthwhile, that putting Patrick's interests before her own needs was the right thing to do. If things kept moving in the right direction then James might do something for her precious Patrick. She would even put up with the ever-so-smooth James if it meant that her son would have his father.

His hand came up to her face and he traced a line across her jaw and down over her throat. She swallowed self-consciously, wondering what was coming next. She wanted to knock his hand away, but she restrained herself. There might be some small chance that he would make it up to her and Patrick. His lips brushed hers again and she felt his hand trail past the pulse at the base of her throat, over her collarbone to her breast. He cupped it gently in his hand and she clenched her hand in an effort to forestall her reaction to him. Their kiss deepened, acting like a drug upon her senses, numbing the pain that throbbed deep inside her, giving her hope.

She had forgotten how polished he was. There was none of the raw power that exuded from Rory but his lovemaking was pleasant nonetheless. His hands roved over her body as she returned his kiss. The fabric of her bodice was so sheer it felt like his hand stroked her skin directly. She could feel her nipples hardening to his touch. He moved closer and his leg came to rest between her thighs, from where she could feel the tide of warmth spreading through her body. She knew then that if he did take her back, she would be able to learn to live with him again in an intimate way.

'I've missed you so much. I've ached for your beautiful body more than you could ever know.' His hand slipped down the outside of her leg to her ankle from where it made the journey up again, this time underneath her voluminous petticoats against the soft, stockinged skin of her inner leg.

Her hands roved over him, first his slim hips, then up his spine as she remembered the familiar territory of his slender, golden-skinned torso. More refined than Rory, less muscled . . . And then she remembered what she had told Rory as they sat looking at the aftermath of the Burra Creek flood. He had asked her what she had learnt from her Far North adventures.

I have learnt to think twice before I go dashing off in search of my dreams. And I'll not be taking up with any rich squatters until the ring is firmly on my finger!

The words rang in her ears as James slipped her skirts and petticoats out of his way. She was a fool if she let this go any further! He was a selfish scoundrel, she had found that out already. A sophisticated, charming scoundrel. She had no idea what his motives might be this time. Not yet. He had made no promises about Patrick's future. They had not even discussed it.

'Uh uh!' She pushed his hands away from her and sat up.

She wanted to tell the arrogant James where to get off, right now, but she couldn't. She was playing a deeper game. She was here for Patrick, not for herself.

'What is it?' he said, and reached for her again.

'No, James, don't,' she said breathlessly, 'I don't intend to get caught that way again.'

She did not raise her eyes to meet his. It was not exactly true, since she now knew the Yuras' secret of preventing pregnancies, but it would suffice as an excuse to hold James off. She wanted the control over what happened between them this time.

'I want you,' he said, and his mouth lowered towards hers again. He kissed her deeply and then broke off, 'And you want me too, my delicious Kate.'

She did want him, long ago, but not now. Now she wanted something different. His name for her son. Eventually his property for Patrick, too. She restrained herself from landing her knee right where he deserved it.

'I do want you, James,' she lied, 'but I'm no

longer the naive young girl that stepped ashore two years ago. If we come to an understanding it will have to be two-way.'

He was resting back on one elbow now and his eyes were hooded. 'What do you mean?' he asked.

'I mean this. I am now a woman of means and I can make some choices. I'm not going to choose a man who is not prepared to offer me the security that I want. I don't ever want to be pregnant and unmarried again.'

'It is my fault that you feel like this,' he said, changing tack suddenly. 'I blame myself entirely. No wonder you can no longer trust me. Hell, I've handled this badly too. There was so much that I wanted to say to you today. So many things I have wanted to tell you. I spent last night rehearsing them in my mind.'

She looked at him expectantly.

'Of course, as soon as I look at you the words just leave my head. You do something to me . . . I don't know how to describe it. I want you so much. After what happened between us at Wildowie, when I realise how badly I handled it all, I start to think that there can be no hope for me.'

'Pardon?'

He rolled over to her so that his face was close to hers. 'Kate, do you forgive me for all of that?'

She looked at him but did not reply.

'Would you take me back?'

Kate felt her lips part and her eyelids open

wide in surprise. Could this be for real? Could it be this easy? Did it mean that she was not going to have to fight tooth and nail for Patrick's rights? Could it be that he was actually proposing marriage to her?

'Are you talking marriage?'

He looked at her straight in the eye, sincerity dripping from his voice. 'To be perfectly honest, I don't know myself. I just know that when I saw you, the feelings that I thought I had buried came back even more powerfully than before. I've never felt for anyone what I feel for you. Let's spend some time together, see what comes of it. Let's not try to cross our bridges before we come to them.'

He took her in his arms and rolled her over on top of him so that she could look down directly into his eyes. 'I mean every word that I say.'

She looked down at him, his grey eyes smoky with lust. He wanted her, there was no doubt about that. But what did it mean?

She let herself be drawn down towards him, till her lips met his. She could feel his tongue opening her lips and entering her mouth. It was too good to be true. She could never love James like she loved Rory, never. A love like that only came once in a lifetime. But Rory was not the father of her child. James was. He was a devil, a smooth, charming devil, but she was going into this with her eyes open this time. Yes, he would probably use her. She was not sure how. But he surely would.

And she would use him as much as he would use her.

She felt his hands at her skirts again, pulling them up so that she could sit with her bare skin against him. The kind of drawers she wore had no centre seam. The two legs were simply sewn separately to the waist elastic and were left open in the centre for convenience. She could feel the hardness of him, through his trousers, against her.

He pulled her down to kiss him again as his hands worked at the buttons on his trousers. She moved back just a little so that he could free himself from his clothing. Then she thought better of it and lifted her hips away from him completely.

'No, James, not like this.'

'How else do you want it? Like this?' He rolled her over onto her back and pressed himself against her.

She wriggled away from him again. 'No. Not now, James. Let's start again. Let's start afresh. This is too much like last time. Let's take it slowly, as it comes, like you said.'

She pulled her legs up and drew them together, presenting her knees as a barrier.

'Kate, don't be coy,' he said, and reached for her hands to pull her closer to him again.

'No.'

'Don't you trust me? What sort of a beginning will it be if it starts out like this? You said you had forgiven me.'

'I have forgiven you. I'm no longer the naive young girl that you first met. I'm calling the shots this time and I say that I won't be making love to you until we know where this thing is going.' Until the ring is on my finger or Patrick's name is on your will, she finished silently.

Her heart was beating fast. She could feel the pulse at the base of her throat. It was a risk. A big risk. She could lose him. If she did, then that was the way it was meant to be. If he wanted marriage then he could wait.

He looked at her shrewdly, the grey eyes cold and almost calculating. Then his mind was made up. 'Of course, my dear, how crass of me! I got carried away, and why not, with such a beautiful woman in my arms. Our reunion will be all the sweeter for having waited. You are absolutely right.' He rolled away from her and lay on his back, looking up at the sky once more.

'It is how it has to be right now.'

'For you, anything.' He smiled at her and drew her over for a gentle kiss.

They made their way back to town.

'Have you thought of where you will invest your money? You should invest it in something secure, you know.'

'Yes, I have been thinking of that.'

'You won't find an investment more secure than land.'

'My thoughts entirely.'

'Trouble is, you need a big piece of land to

make a good profit from it in South Australia. You would be better off buying land in partnership with someone else.'

Is this what he wanted from her? Had the whole afternoon been about charming her into this? She knew what his next words would be before he spoke them.

'I'm looking for someone to partner me in the expansion of Wildowie.'

They were travelling into the late afternoon sun, her eyes blinded, and she could not read his expression, but she guessed it would be as innocent as a new-born babe's.

'Wildowie? I thought the station was the Carmichael empire! You'd hardly want someone else involved, would you?'

He ignored the underlying tone of her comment. 'As I said the other day, Kate, I want to expand. I'd be willing to let you have a share because I am fond of you, very fond of you. I know how much you've always wanted a station like Wildowie.'

His eyes slid to her as she sat contemplating his offer.

'And I want to do something for the boy.'

Could she believe that this was really happening? How should she respond? Thoughts tumbled through her head. On the surface it was the opportunity she had been looking for. But she was no naive new chum now. She knew James well. Well enough to know that the share he was offering her was in his best interests and not hers.

'Tell me more about it. What are you thinking of doing, exactly?'

'I've scouted out the areas around Wildowie. There are no big parcels of land left to the south. I don't think the land to the east has enough water, but to the north, there is one big creek, the Barcowie, where water is plentiful. It is that parcel of land that I want.'

What about Elatina? Had he discovered that yet? 'And to the west? Is there no decent land there?'

'No, as you will remember, it is all mountains to the west, as far as anyone can see. The land is worthless. It would not be good sheep country. They would all get lost and it would be hard work to find them again.'

Kate breathed a sigh of relief. He wasn't talking about Secret Gully where the Yuras would hide Patrick if he were in danger. He wasn't talking about Elatina Valley. He didn't even know that they existed. She would find Patrick and the Yuras safe there when she returned.

'So, how much money would you want me to invest?'

'Let's talk about all that later. Think about it. If you're interested, we'll sit down and consider it properly . . .' He paused. '. . . I've always thought you'd make a wonderful station mistress, Kate. You handle the bush as well as any woman I've ever met.' He squinted slightly in the afternoon sun, the fine wrinkle lines fanning out from his eyes. 'You would look wonderful, dressed as you are today, in a beautiful gown, looking out from the verandah of a gracious homestead over your land. I can picture you there.'

Cunning beggar! He had always known how to pull the very strings that would make her dance. Had she actually said that to him at Wildowie? Had she shared her fantasy with him? Or had he simply just guessed it? By God, he was clever.

But she was getting more clever. She could pick it now when that smooth tongue of his was at work. She knew now when he was playing on her emotions to suit himself.

'Why me? Why are you asking me to join Carmichael Enterprises? Why hasn't someone else snapped up this offer already?'

He turned his head to look at her. 'Oh, Kate, I am sorry. It is my fault that you don't trust me. I can't blame you for that. I am trying . . . to make amends to you, you know. And to the boy. If you made a sound investment in a profitable station there would be something there for him as he grew up, maybe a home to call his own, a future for him. If you wanted to, you could sell off your share, either to me or to someone else, at a huge profit later on. Then he could buy a station of his own . . . But it is up to you. You might have other plans for your growing bank balance . . .'

He let his last comment hang in the air.

No she didn't have plans. Not yet. James was

right. It would be a good investment for Patrick's future. It was exactly the kind of thing that she wanted for him. She knew Wildowie. She knew that it was profitable. Rory had voiced his doubts about the land in the Far North, but she hadn't agreed with him at all.

On its own, it was an offer worth thinking about. James did seem to be sorry about what he had done. He was fond of her, as he phrased it. He wanted her in his bed, she knew that. She would never trust him wholeheartedly like she did before, but maybe there was a chance to build their relationship again, this time on wiser foundations. You never know, she thought, maybe she and James could get back together again and jointly build the station into the place that they both dreamed of. It would be a dream come true for Patrick. Both of his parents and the station . . .

His voice interrupted her thoughts. 'I forgot to tell you. After Angus was killed by the blacks I got a new overseer. You know him.'

'Who is it?'

'Sid, one of the teamsters who came up on the same trip that you did, remember him?'

'Sid! Of course! I'd never forget him. He was the one who helped me get the spear tip from Harold's chest. How is he?'

'Well. And he makes a good overseer. He's tough and he's shrewd, but he's good with the men, always fair to them. Which is good, for I can't afford to have the shepherds leave now.

There are few enough who'll stay when the glitter of gold promises higher returns for their labours.'

'You've had trouble with the shepherds leaving, too?'

'Sure have. Everyone has.'

'Ever thought of using the Yu—' she paused mid-word '—the blacks to help you?'

'You know what they're like. They cannot be relied upon, they roam around too much and they'd be stealing all the sheep to feed their tribe. No, I wouldn't trust them myself.'

Kate shrugged but did not pursue the matter. In her view the Yuras were no longer able to wander as they willed and they would happily swap some work to get a regular bellyful of good mutton and some respite from the constant harassment and hounding.

'Here we are,' he said, pulling up in front of Mrs Applebee's.

'Thank you for the lovely day, James', she said, giving him her hand. 'And I'll think about your offer. I am interested.'

'Good, I thought it would be in your best interests. Maybe we can talk about it some more . . . I tell you what, I've been invited to Government House for a reception on Tuesday evening next, would you like to come? We could talk about it more then.'

'A reception at Government House?'

'Nothing too flash, I assure you, but I'm sure you would enjoy it. It would be the sort of crowd that you'll enjoy more often if you become a station owner.'

Clever James, pulling the right strings yet again! 'I'd love to come!'

'I'll pick you up at eight. Formal dress. Have you got something suitable?'

'I have a silk evening gown. Will that do?'

'I'm sure it would be perfect.' Then his eyes flicked over her, and he remarked, 'You have come up in the world, haven't you?'

'Yes and it is only the beginning.'

'We'll make a good pair, you and I.'

'I hope so, James. I hope so.'

'Mr James Carmichael and Miss O'Leary,' the head footman announced as they entered Government House.

Kate's eyes were glittering with excitement. She knew that she was looking her best in the fine gown that Rory had given her. Not that he would be too pleased to hear that she was wearing it for James Carmichael. But she pushed those thoughts aside.

Her eyes flicked quickly around the room. Her gown rivalled any of the others worn here tonight. She had finally made it. She was at Government House and was part of Adelaide society. She might soon own part of Wildowie.

The room was already full of people. The noise of the voices raised above the music made quite a commotion. There were twenty couples dancing and the rest of the guests were helping themselves to the sumptuous refreshments piled high onto tables around the sides of the room. A waiter approached them and Kate took a glass of champagne from the tray that he held.

James began introducing her to his friends and acquaintances.

'George Reynolds, may I introduce to you my friend Miss Kate O'Leary—Kate, this is George Reynolds and Mrs Reynolds from Kulpana Station in the south-east.'

'Pleased to meet you,' Kate said as George Reynolds took her hand. Of course, with her Irish accent it sounded more like 'Playsed to meet ye'. She saw their eyebrows rise in response.

'You're a new arrival, dear?' Mrs Reynolds asked.

'No, I've been here for nearly two and a half years. I came on the *Elgin* in '49.'

She saw their eyes widen a little further and she felt the pressure of James's fingers on her own, warning her to say no more.

'Kate has done a bit of travelling since she arrived,' he said, steering her away from the dangerous subject of her background.

'Well, if you like travelling you'll have to come down to have a look at the South East. We think it is the finest country in the colony.'

'It is fine country indeed. I have been down there, ma'am. I took my team right past your property I think.'

'Beg your pardon, your team did you say?' Mrs Reynolds's double chin wobbled as she spoke.

'My bullock team. I drove a bullock team over to the goldfields.'

Mrs Reynolds's mouth dropped right open as if she could not believe her ears. It turned her double chin into a triple and Kate had to suppress a desire to laugh at her expression of shock.

'Miss O'Leary owns a very successful flour-carting business,' James interposed, trying to smooth the way for Kate more successfully.

'And you've actually driven them yourself? Good God! I've never heard of that before! A woman driving a bullock team!' the older gentleman pursued.

'With most of the men having left for the diggings we'll see women doing a lot more than they used to,' James said quietly.

The conversation was steered successfully away from Kate and onto the gold rushes.

'Yes, life has certainly changed,' George commented. 'Gold seems to be turning society upside down. You only have to look at the *nouveaux riches*. Their antics are comical right now, but if it goes on too much longer it might well be as they threaten.'

'What exactly are they threatening, Mr Reynolds?'

'They are saying, Miss O'Leary, that they are the masters now and that we shall be their servants—'

'And it's partially true already,' Mrs Reynolds broke in, 'I hear that women from good families are now forced to do their own housework. The shortage of servants in Adelaide has become serious since so many have joined the exodus to Victoria.'

'Well I must introduce Kate to John and Mary Challoner,' James said eventually, trying to move Kate away from the Reynoldses.

Kate's glance flicked back to them as they walked away. Both the Reynoldses were looking at her still, consternation on their podgy faces. Kate tilted up her chin. Damned snobs! They were not going to ruin her night!

James leant closer as they strolled through the throng. 'Might be best if you didn't let on too much about your past, Kate,' he said quietly. 'They are a conservative lot. Once they know you and see how delightful you are they will welcome you with open arms, I'm sure. But in the meantime, all that about your background and being a bullocky will only shock them.'

'I'm not ashamed of my past, I don't see why I should hide it!' she whispered back fiercely.

Anything else he might have been going to say was cut off as a young gentleman approached them. 'Ah, James! You're back in town I see! How are you, my dear friend?'

'Well thanks, Edmond,' and he proceeded to introduce Kate.

She looked Edmond up and down. He was one of those sallow young men whom one would expect had lived in the tropics for too long.

He kissed Kate's hand in a very dandified way. 'Where did you find such a pretty girl,' he simpered. She thought it unlikely that his interest was in women.

'It's a secret,' James told him.

'I heard that your overseer was killed by the blacks, James. Shocking thing!'

'Yes, most unfortunate.'

'And your maid is still missing?'

'Lost or taken by the blacks is the opinion of the police.'

'Tut! Tut! Tut! Did they catch any of the culprits?'

'Not yet. Unlikely to, either. Who knows who did it, except the blacks themselves, of course, and they're not saying.'

'Mm, they've got plenty of guile even if they're not that bright—'

'Oh, if you knew the blacks well you'd know that they're an intelligent race. Look at the way they survive in the bush. Not many white men could do as well,' Kate broke in.

Edmond looked at her in surprise. 'Come now, Miss O'Leary, give a black a tail and you'd have a monkey complete.'

Kate felt James press her hand meaningfully and she bit back the hot words on her tongue.

'Ah, Lucy Hobhouse!' James drew another acquaintance into the conversation and introduced both Kate and Edmond.

He continued on his round of introductions until, it seemed to Kate, he was exhausted by his efforts to keep her hair-raising conversation topics within bounds. 'Would you like to dance, my dear?'

Fortunately dancing was something that she did well and she knew that she would not embarrass James on the dance floor. The love of music was part of her Irish heritage. While she would have preferred a fast Irish reel she was happy to be swept about the room in a waltz.

'You are looking absolutely ravishing.'

'Thank you, James.' She looked up into his eyes and the rest of the room disappeared into a blur of chandeliers and wallpaper. 'You look very handsome yourself.'

She felt so proud to be here with him, in Government House. God! It was little more than two years since she had stepped off the *Elgin* a penniless orphan, and here she was now at a Government House reception, dancing with a successful squatter and one of the Adelaide upper crust. It was exactly what she had wanted for herself and now it was what she wanted for Patrick, too.

She should be totally happy, but her feelings were mixed.

What was it exactly that James wanted? He always put his own needs first, so what was in all of this for him? And what about these people, what would they expect of her if she joined their set?

'Am I doing all right?' she asked him.

'You are doing beautifully, my dear. If you looked around this room right now you would find that everyone's eyes are on you. They are wondering who the beautiful woman is and why she is in my arms.'

It was a kind thing to say, typically well mannered of James, but it did not really answer her question.

'I've never had to curb my tongue like this before.'

'Kate, you can discuss the blacks and the bullocks any time you like with the right people, and any time with me, but these are not the right people and this is probably not the best place. If you want their respect, which I'm sure you will do, then keep the conversation on lighter and less controversial subjects.'

'Talk about the weather, you mean, or other women's gowns, babies, growing roses, that sort of thing?' She couldn't help but smile. The thought of discussing those things all evening would bore even her to death.

James smiled back. 'You're a minx, Kate. Life will never be dull with you around the place.'

'James, why do I have to worry about their respect? They don't seem to be too worried about mine. The things that they were saying about the antics of the *nouveaux riches*—don't they realise that I am one of the new rich? If I was the type to be easily offended that would have seemed very rude!'

'They weren't conscious of that. Take it all with a pinch of salt. If you don't knowingly offend anyone here then at least you are doing the right thing, that is all that matters. Just keep it light and you'll be fine.'

Kate tried that a little while later.

'What brought you out to Australia, Miss O'Leary?' another of James's friends asked her.

'Want,' she replied honestly without thinking, and then she laughed, trying to keep it light, 'though why I came here for that I don't know, for there was plenty of want in Ireland!'

The response was dead silence.

'I was joking.'

'Oh! Of course, yes,' the man replied, giving a pathetic little laugh.

Kate spun around, about to put her glass on the table. At that moment a waiter walked by. He bumped into her. Several glasses of champagne slid from the tray and crashed to the ground. Champagne splashed onto her gown and fizzed a darker blue on the fine silk.

'Oh! I am so sorry, madam!' the waiter cried out, torn between picking up the broken glass and dabbing at her gown with the white cloth that had hung over his arm a moment before.

'Don't worry, it was an accident,' she said. 'Here,' she took the cloth from him and began to mop at the stains on the silk herself.

'Find a maid to help the lady sponge her gown, please,' James said to the waiter.

He went off immediately, returning a moment

later followed by a maid in a crisp black and white uniform.

'Yes, madam, follow me,' the young maid said.

Kate was taken through the reception room and along a corridor to a private room that adjoined the ladies' room. The maid pushed the door so that it was almost closed. Kate sat down on the only chair. The maid got down onto her knees and lifted Kate's skirt a little so that she could sponge the champagne stains.

She heard a couple of women enter the room next door. She could just see them through the crack in the doorway. It was Mrs Reynolds and Miss Lucy Hobhouse and they were both fixing their hair in front of the large gilt-edged mirror.

'So, what do you think James Carmichael is up to, bringing that young woman with him? I wouldn't have thought that she was his type. He's been on the lookout for a rich wife with the right connections for so long, I'd be highly surprised if he fell for a pretty Irish face,' Lucy Hobhouse said.

Kate cocked her head and listened more carefully. She put her finger to her lips and winked to signify silence to the maid.

'Money,' the older woman replied. 'He's been trying to raise some cash to finance the expansion of his station. The banks have turned him down. He can't find anyone else to finance it on his terms because he won't let anyone else gain any control over the station. Money here is tight with so many leaving the colony. She has a business of her own, she told us. So there is no doubt in my mind that money is his motivation.'

'Waste of a good man, I'd say.'

'Yes it is a shame, he could have done much better for himself than that. Not that he will marry her, of course, he's too shrewd for that. He'll charm her into his bed and out of her money, I should think.'

'Mm, still a waste of a good man.'

The older woman twitched at her grey hair. 'Shame that you're not well endowed yourself. But still, with Captain Tolmer escorting the gold back from Victoria, South Australia should be much better off again soon and there will be gentlemen with money once more.'

The maid stood up. 'There, madam,' she said quietly, 'that should fix it. Hopefully there will be no permanent stain.'

'Thank you,' Kate replied.

She sat there for a moment, pondering. The two women were probably right in what they said. James did want her money, but she hadn't realised that it was only because no one else was forthcoming. She knew that there had to be a reason. So much for him taking an interest in her and Patrick! So much for him being sorry that he had treated her so callously! She should have known better.

He was so charming and so downright selfish. She would work out how to deal with him later.

She wondered if she should leave the room

while the two women were gossiping outside. She decided she would. Why should she feel embarrassed when it was they who had been caught out behaving in a very unladylike manner?

She stood up and opened the door. She walked to the mirror nonchalantly and began to tidy her hair.

The expressions on the faces of Mrs Reynolds and Miss Hobhouse were reflected in the mirror. Mrs Reynolds's mouth had dropped open and Lucy Hobhouse turned a bright red.

Kate couldn't help but grin. She hoped that they were feeling as embarrassed as they looked!

She turned around to face them. 'I can assure you that he won't be wasted on me,' she said with a very saucy and provocative look. 'I'll make very good use of him.' She then strolled from the room with a swish of her silk skirts and without a backward glance.

She returned to the reception room with glittering eyes and a smile plastered firmly onto her face. James, not noticing anything amiss, introduced her to the Governor, Sir Henry Fox Young. The excitement of meeting such an important person almost made up for the fact that she had found out that James was up to his old tricks again.

Looking around the room, she had to admit it, the company was generally pretty dull and most of the conversation boring. If all James's friends were as insipid as the ones she had met tonight had been, then she would rather be on the track swapping yarns with the bullockies and watching the Milky Way on its journey across the glorious black sky.

Kate kept James at a distance as she said goodnight.

'I'll call around to see you tomorrow and we can finalise the details of your investment,' he said, rubbing his hands together, presumably to keep them warm.

'Is there any hurry?'

'Of course not,' he said, but his gestures belied his words.

'Good, then leave it for a couple of days,' Kate replied. 'I'll have to see exactly what state my finances are in and have a chat to my bank manager first.'

'Certainly, my dear, do that, but don't take too long about it, since someone else might snap up my offer first. I did want you to have first bite.'

Someone else? If those two women had been right then there was no one else and he was trying to hurry her into the deal.

'I'll let you know when I'm ready to talk details with you,' she said, as he saw her to the door.

As she got ready for bed she thought about the conversation she had overheard and she went over every detail of their conversation at the picnic the other day. James had questioned her at length about her business, the profits and the longer term future of flour carting. It was only after that conversation that he had told her how much he regretted his treatment of her and how much he still wanted her.

Then he had talked about land and wool and how much money there was to be made. He would have known how impressed she would have been by all that.

I've always thought you'd make a wonderful station mistress, Kate. You handle the bush as well as any woman I've ever met. You would look wonderful, dressed as you are today, in a beautiful gown, looking out from the verandah of a gracious homestead over your land. I can picture you there.

They were the words he had said. She had twigged at the time that he was playing on her dreams, just as he had before, up at Wildowie when he had lured her into his bed. She had guessed at the picnic that he wanted something from her and she had hardly been surprised when he had offered her a share of Wildowie on the drive back.

I am trying . . . to make amends to you, you know. I thought it was something that I could do for the boy.

Yes, he had said he was trying to do something for the boy, but he had actually offered nothing for the boy at all. He hadn't said that Wildowie would one day be Patrick's. He hadn't said that he would help Kate, in any way, to make a future for their son.

He'll charm her into his bed and out of her money, I should think. That's what those women had said, and they were probably right. That was exactly what James had set out to do.

No, by financing the expansion of Wildowie, Kate would be helping James, not the other way around.

She was going to enjoy this meeting immensely. He had long deserved what she had in store for him. He had tried to fool her once too often. The man had the impudence to try to use her again while apologising for treating her badly the time before. But she had changed. God, how she had changed.

'Hello, James,' she said coolly, rising as he entered.

The maid ushered him in and left, closing the door behind her. Mrs Applebee had made sure that no one would interrupt them during this important meeting.

'Hello, my dear,' he replied, pressing his lips to her hand. 'You are looking absolutely gorgeous again.' His hand still held hers as he stepped back a little to admire her gown. It was some moments before he dropped it again and not before he had caressed the soft inner flesh of her palm with his thumb.

'Have a seat, James,' she said, sitting down again herself. 'Let's get straight down to business. So now, I've had time to put my affairs into order. What exactly is your proposal?'

'Very businesslike, my dear. I haven't seen you in this mode before.'

My dear. How those words grated on her ear now that she knew what he was up to. Rory always called her 'my darlin'' and it was like a caress in comparison.

'We have never done business together before, have we?' she replied crisply, then added, 'well . . .?' and waited, pen poised, for James to describe his proposal.

'Well, it is like this. I figured that since you have the boy to look after, you'd want to keep things as flexible as you could. After all, you might want the money one day to pay for his education or something.'

'Yes.'

'So I thought you might like to put in as much money as you can now, and after that, as much or as little as you like, when you want to.'

'And what sort of legal agreement would we have? How would we document all of this?'

'I thought there would be no real need for all that. Those sorts of agreements never work. I trust you, and I'm sure that you can trust me, so I thought we'd keep it simple and flexible.'

'Nothing on paper, you mean?'

'No, nothing on paper. That way you are free to invest however you like.'

'Very kind of you,' she murmured. 'But we would need to put some things in writing, surely? What if one of us were to die?'

'Of course, if that is what you want. We could keep a record between ourselves.'

'Good. Now what about the leases? Would they be in my name or in both names?'

'I thought it would be best if they were in my name. That way whatever taxes had to be paid would be paid by me.'

'I see. And what about the profits? I assume we'll make plenty of those. How will we split them?' she smiled.

James started to shift in his chair. 'Of course, plenty of profits. We can come to some agreement on those as need be. You may want to plough then back into the station or invest elsewhere. You can make that choice when we see how things go. I want you to have the power to do with your share of the profits whatever you like. That way we can both do what is best for the boy.'

'I'm glad you raised the whole issue of your son, James,' she said, emphasising the words *your son*. 'Let's put Wildowie aside for a moment while we talk about him. If I'm coming up to Wildowie, what are we going to do about Patrick?'

'Well, he can come too. The boy won't want to be parted from you, I shouldn't imagine.'

'No, but that is not what I'm asking. I don't intend to hide his paternity from anyone. The station hands will remember that he is your son. I'd honestly have to tell anyone who asked me that you are his father. Will you be openly claiming him as your son when we come up?'

'I hadn't thought of that exactly.'

'What had you thought of?'

'Well, I'm not a dishonest man. If anyone charged me with it, I would not deny that he is my son.'

'No, of course not. You couldn't do that. But what will you be doing about him?'

'What do you mean?'

'Well, I take it that if I invested enough, that we would be equal partners in building the expanded Wildowie?'

'Yes.'

'And that, if we were to have any relationship together again, er . . . do you know what I mean?'

'Yes.'

'Then we would do something to make it all above board—'

'Let us cross that bridge when we come to it, my dear. Let us see how it works this time. I don't want to tie you down in any way.'

'Kind of you to think of me, I'm sure. But no, let us not worry about me at this point in time. It is Patrick I'm worrying about.'

'That is fair enough.'

'What do you mean, "fair enough"?' She knew her eyes must be glittering dangerously.

James faltered as he searched for the right words, 'Well, I . . . I . . .'

'Are you, or are you not prepared to take on your rightful share of responsibility for Patrick?'

'You've got to understand one thing, Kate,' he interrupted. 'Having the child was your choice. I told you then that I would have nothing to do with him. It is up to you what you do about him. It is not up to me. What could I do for him now anyway?'

'There's a lot you could do. You could, at the very least, ensure that I get fair dividends from my investment so that I can provide for him. But you don't seem to be prepared to make any guarantees of the safety of my investment by documenting anything. God knows, you could even contribute some of your own money—'

'Maybe—'

'Don't interrupt me. You asked me a question, let me finish answering it. That would be the least you could do. A real gentleman would be falling over himself to do more. He'd be offering to take the boy on, train him to step into his father's shoes, even naming him as heir—'

'Kate!'

'But if you were really the gentleman you claim to be, if you really cared about Patrick's future, as you say you do, and if you genuinely felt any love for me, then you'd marry me so that Patrick didn't grow up as a bastard!' She sat back in her armchair to watch his reaction.

He was lost for words and made several false starts before beginning. 'Oh, Kate! How could you doubt my intentions,' he ran his fingers through that smooth butter-coloured hair. 'I do care for you, more than you realise. I do care about the boy's future—'

'Can't you call him by his name?'

'Patrick's future,' he corrected himself, saying his name for the first time ever. 'That's why I offered you this opportunity. I was concerned that you didn't use your new-found wealth unwisely. I thought that this would be the best way to help the b . . . Patrick. You have misconstrued the situation entirely. I just wanted to keep it as flexible as possible—'

'I'd hardly accuse you of trying to hoodwink me,' she broke in sweetly, her tongue in her cheek.

'I thought that was exactly what you were accusing me of!'

'We can argue about that point later. What about what I have said?'

'Er . . . what was that again?'

'Marriage, James.'

James stood up and took a deep breath before turning to her. 'Kate, I love you. You must know that. I regret the bad blood that has passed between us, but I thought it was all forgiven. I would marry you if I could, but I can't. I'm being honest with you, I really am. I just can't marry you, as much as I would like to. I have my family to think of. Not knowing you as I do, they would be horrified to learn that I was to marry someone who had been a p . . . poor orphan from Ireland . . .'

He had been going to say 'peasant', she knew it.

'. . . It simply can't be done. Not now. Maybe when they get to know you and when they know just how much work you've put into Wildowie it will be different. They would be concerned right now—my place in society—not wishing to be rude—the way they would see it, I would be cast down several rungs of the ladder. People would gossip. I could not marry you now. I'm sorry, my dear. I just could not do it.'

'But you didn't mind taking me to meet the Governor!'

'That was different!'

'Yes, so I understand, you wanted my money pretty badly, didn't you?'

'No, I didn't. I have other options!'

'Do you? I think you had better take one of those then.'

'What do you mean?'

'I mean that our deal is off.'

'Kate, you are overreacting!'

'Am I?'

'Yes. These are but small hurdles to jump.'

'Small hurdles? You say that the presence of a bastard son is a small hurdle? Not to me it isn't. It is all right if he lives on the station, if he has to and you have no other choice, but you won't recognise him and you won't contribute to his well-being or his future.' She laughed bitterly, 'James, I'm not the naive fool that you think I am. On top of all of that you think you can sweet talk me into handing all of my hard-earned money over to you, with no written agreement, no contract, for you to buy a lease that won't have my name appearing on it anywhere.'

'Kate!'

'No, don't interrupt me,' she held up her hand, 'I haven't finished yet. To crown it off, you want to lure me into your bed with your slippery promises of me being the station mistress. Don't you remember you tried that one on me last time? I can only fall for it once, for God's sake!'

James's mouth dropped open slightly and he raised his shoulders as if falsely accused on every count.

'Jesus! Don't play innocent! Say something honest to redeem your character just a little!'

'Kate, my dear—'

'Don't call me that unless you are prepared to treat me like it too!'

The smooth charm was wiped off his face as he realised his usual tactics were not going to work.

He took a deep breath and straightened his back. 'Are you saying that unless I meet the conditions you want to set, that our deal is off?'

'That is exactly what I'm saying. Make Patrick your heir. Put my name on the land leases and get a legal agreement drawn up between us to cover all of my concerns. Or you don't get a penny from me!'

'Is that all?'

'No, it is not all. I thought once that we could

make a reasonable family, despite the bad start. I thought we could forget what happened, for Patrick's sake—'

'We can—'

'Don't be ridiculous. We can't. I cannot trust you at all. What basis is that for a relationship? I had been going to say, that if you want my body, even one more time, then there'll have to be a ring on my finger. But now nothing would induce me to make love with you again. There is no way that I would marry you. I'll not let you charm me into your bed and out of my money, despite what your friends say!'

'Who said that?'

'Find out yourself, James.'

'Well,' he said, standing up and reaching for his dove-grey tophat, 'I think you are making a bad mistake. You've been listening to some kind of despicable gossip. You will miss the opportunity to invest in a very profitable station.'

'Nothing you have ever done would cause me to doubt the gossip, James. What else am I to think?'

He ignored her question. 'You are not the only string in my bow. I do have other options. There are people falling over themselves to invest in Wildowie. There is one option that you would love to know about.'

What could he mean? Who else had he approached? 'Is there? I have it on good authority that the banks aren't interested. Everything they had has been taken to the goldfields.'

'Well, your information is incomplete, my dear. I pity you. You have missed out on the chance of a lifetime.'

'Oh no, James. I've got news for you. I have not missed out at all. It's you who have missed out.'

'What do you mean?'

She let the silence hang for a moment.

'Look at this,' she replied. 'My first piece of land. I have purchased the lease.'

She pushed it across the table for him to have a look at.

'I am not interested,' he said, picking up his cane. 'You are welcome to your measly patch of soil, wherever it is.' He strolled towards the door, not waiting for her to rise.

'I'm not sure whether I'll call it O'Leary's or Barcowie, what do you think?'

He whirled around at the word Barcowie. 'Pardon?'

'O'Leary's Station,' she said the words slowly, 'or Barcowie Station? Which sounds better?'

He pulled the papers from her hands and his eyes scanned the top sheet. He tossed the lease for Barcowie, the piece of land that he had wanted himself, down on to the table. 'You rotten bitch!'

'It was there to be taken. Free enterprise and all of that.'

His top lip curled as he regarded her. 'It is. But it is a tough world too. You poor fool. There isn't enough land there to ever build a profitable station. You'll live to regret it.'

'No, it's not the only land I'm leasing.'

'Well, there's no other grazing land adjoining that.'

'Is there not?'

'No, impenetrable mountains to the west, arid lands north and east and my property is right on your southern boundary.'

'Is that right?'

He looked at her, suspicion written all over his features. Did she know something that he didn't?

'Unless your friends have bigger secrets than the ones I've heard about so far.' He was obviously referring to the Yuras.

Kate shrugged her shoulders.

'Well, I'm sorry it all turned out this way. Sorry for you. You'll never make a success of it. And don't expect a single penny from me for you or for your son. Nor will you get any help from Wildowie, you can be certain of that,' he grasped the door handle.

'James!'

'Yes?' he said coldly, the muscles clenching in his jaw.

'All you had to do was to show one bit of consideration, for me or for Patrick, and it would all have been different. I'd have handed that lease right over to you. I tested you and you failed the test. Had you not been so damned selfish Barcowie would have been yours. I pity you.'

'No one pities James Carmichael, my dear.

You will be pitying yourself before too long, I can assure you of that.'

The door closed firmly behind him.

'I'll show myself out!' she heard him say in the corridor.

Mrs Applebee popped her head around the door a moment later. 'Everything all right in here?'

'Yes,' she said, her shoulders sagging. 'It was as you said it would be. He really is a self-centred, avaricious scoundrel.'

'He failed the test.'

'He did.'

'So you'll go ahead with the second part of your plan?' Mrs Applebee entered the room and sat down.

'Yes, I'll make sure that he'll live to regret what he's done to me and Patrick. I've got the letters to Sid, Craig and Robert ready to send. If I can get his overseer and two of his shepherds for Elatina then he'll really be sorry he ever used me.'

'With most of the shepherds rushing off to the goldfields he'll have trouble getting replacements.'

'That's right. And he's too damned arrogant to even think of employing the Yuras as shepherds. They're beneath his notice.'

'Maybe he's right about the Yuras.'

'No, I know them as well as anybody does. They're good with animals. They know the bush like the back of their hand. They're sick of the reprisals and the harassment and they need a reliable source of food. I reckon they'll make damned good shepherds. My station won't be suffering from lack of labour. Wildowie will, especially if Sid, Craig and Robert decide to join me. My revenge on James Carmichael will be sweet.'

'You don't look all that happy about the outcome, though.'

'I'm not sure that he's feeling the least bit sorry, either for what he did or what he was about to do. The man has no conscience at all.'

'He'll be sorry when you have finished with him.'

'Maybe I'll be sorry too.'

'Why should that be?'

'He says that I don't have enough land to make a profit. I knew that already and I was preparing to buy more later. I'm scared that he'll discover Elatina before I get it.'

'Well, lease it now.'

'I can't. I haven't got the money right now— at least not enough for a piece of land that big.'

'Why do you need such a huge piece of land? Surely with Barcowie as well you'd have enough for a profitable station?'

Kate put her fingernail between her teeth, and thought about her reply. 'The land at Elatina is not just for me,' she said finally.

'Who is it for?'

'The Yuras. The black people up there. I owe them my life. They have exacted a promise from me, a promise that cannot be forgotten.'

'Which is?'

'To save some of their precious land for them.

I have tried every avenue I can think of—the Surveyor's Office and the Governor included—but there is no way the Crown will reserve it for them. I would buy it for them outright, but that cannot be done either. A fifteen-year renewable lease is the best I can do for them.'

'Do they need such a big tract of land?'

'No, they could do with less, but then there would be a hitch. If they don't improve the land, or at least build upon it, within the term of the lease, the government is entitled to consider them as land speculators.'

'Pardon?'

'Speculators, people who buy up land leases in the hope that they can sell them later for a profit. The lease could never be renewed.'

'But no one in their right mind would consider the blacks as speculators!'

Kate shrugged. 'They would not improve the land as we see it.'

'So what will you do?'

Kate sighed. 'The only way that I can see to get around it is to lease a huge tract of land, in my own name. I will set aside part of it for their exclusive use, and I will use the remainder myself. I will build my homestead on that lease and run sheep both there and at Barcowie. That way no one can claim that the land has not been improved.'

'And you don't have the money for the lease?'

'No, not until Rory gets back. And in the meantime someone else might get Elatina. James might lease it just to stop me expanding Barcowie.'

'There's a simple answer to that. Let me lend the money to you. If you can pay me back when Rory arrives, well and good. If not, I'll just charge you the going rate of interest until you do pay me back.'

'What is in it for you? You hardly know me.'

'I know you well enough. I've seen how hard you work. I've seen how shrewd you are. Besides, I like the thought of giving a helping hand to another woman. I know how hard it is to get into business on your own. I've struggled too, you know.'

'Money is so scarce, though. You could invest your money anywhere you wanted.'

'I think that you're a very good investment,' her eyes twinkled as she regarded Kate.

'Thank you, then, I'll gladly take up your offer.'

'But there are two conditions.'

'What are they?'

'The first is that your name, not the Yuras' names, must be on the lease. I know you and trust you. I don't know the Yuras and I'm not prepared to lend them the money. They would have no way of repaying me if anything happened to you.'

'Fair enough. My name goes on the lease. The second condition?'

'That you promise me you'll make that slimy gentleman pay!'

Kate laughed, a hollow kind of a laugh. 'Oh, he'll be made to pay all right. I haven't finished with him yet.'

Part

Two

Chapter
Eighteen

MAY 1866

*A*t seven o'clock the autumn morning was already warm. The air was perfectly still and the blue smoke of a Yura campfire spiralled lazily up to the wide, open, cloudless sky. The spiders had been at work overnight, spinning webs of golden threads between the trees. The dewdrops, suspended on the threads, sparkled like diamonds in the bright morning light. Kangaroos grazed on the grassy slopes of the valley floor and stood to attention as the station hands began their morning's work. Sensing no danger, unconcerned at the movement, they continued their leisurely feed.

Kate watched from the breakfast table on the verandah with a sense of deep satisfaction. Elatina Station was her dream come true. She had founded a grand station, built a gracious homestead and made it a financial success.

'You're looking very satisfied this morning, Miss Kate,' her overseer commented as he took a sip of tea. He still called her Miss Kate, the title of respect she had earned years ago when Harold had been speared.

'I am that, Sid. Is Elatina not the most beautiful station you've ever seen?'

Sid's face broke into that twisted smile that she had learnt to trust. 'It is. You have a right to be pleased with yourself.'

The homestead overlooked the conjunction of two creeks lined with stately gums. Beyond the gums grew the graceful she-oaks with their weeping grey foliage. Further up the slopes were the native pines. The effect was one of layers of colour: gum green, she-oak grey and pine emerald.

There was a magnificent rock wall along the other side of the creek, where the ancient layers of red and brown sedimentary rock had bent, buckled and split vertically, giving the rock face a sense of movement, as if it flowed along in concert with the water.

'We should all be pleased with ourselves. I couldn't have done it without you.'

'We all pitched in. Craig, Robert, myself and not forgetting the boy here,' he leant over and ruffled Patrick's dark blond hair in a rough but affectionate gesture.

'Hey!' Patrick's hand shot out to tilt Sid's wide-brimmed hat down over his eyes.

'Cheeky galah that he is!' Sid exclaimed, placing his hat down on the verandah where Patrick couldn't reach it.

'No, not forgetting Patrick,' Kate said, putting down her teacup and grinning at her son. 'We couldn't forget him, now, could we? But it has all been for you, son. A couple more years and I'll hand over the reins. Elatina will all be yours. I could not be placing it into more responsible hands.'

Patrick's wide mouth curved into a slow smile, but the light of mischief was in his eyes as he replied, 'There are plenty of years in you yet, Mother. I can't imagine you not running Elatina.'

She was proud of her son, he was mature for his years and very responsible in his outlook. But he was not grasping, nor was he ambitious. He was a curious mixture of traits. There was a good sense of humour there and a quiet assurance. He tackled things in a competent, confident way. But he had no plans for an empire. Without her guidance he might well carve the whole place up and give out the pieces to the shepherds and the Yuras.

'It's hard to believe that he's fifteen already,' Sid commented. 'Almost the same age as you were, ma'am, when you first came up to the Far North.'

'I probably just looked that young. I was seventeen, you know, when I took on the Far North.' She was only eighteen when she had given birth to Patrick, just south of the station near Elatina Creek where the Yuras now made their permanent camp. And she was nearly twenty when she had returned, with Sid, to claim him in the spring of 1852.

After nearly two years, he had been, to all intents and purposes, a Yura baby. Healthy, happy, tottering around on his sturdy little legs . . . It seemed as though it was just yesterday. He had accepted her as his mother without a hitch. Maybe it was because they had camped near the Yuras for a few months, easing into his life, rather than taking him away from theirs. Sid hadn't liked it, of course, but she called the shots and he had no choice.

The Yuras had helped in the process too. They had spent those first two years talking about her to him, weaving their magical stories around him, his birth and her eventual return. Soon he had been talking both Adnyamathanha and English with equal fluency and moving frequently between the old hut and the camp. He seemed to love his mother and his Yura family with the same intensity and he had grown up with the advantages of both.

Fortunately the two cultures had never clashed. He had never been caught between them, as he might have been had they not lived on the station. A shiver trailed down her spine at the thought of what could have happened, and what might have gone wrong, but relations between the Udnyus and the Yuras, at least on Elatina, had always been good.

'The years have gone quickly,' she said. 'The Far North is no longer the remote place it once was. There are plenty of stations further north than us now. Mining towns, too. It has certainly changed.'

'Speaking of mining towns, do you still want me to go up to the Blinman store today?'

'Yes, if you would, Sid. I want to get in some nice things for when our guest arrives. From what Rory said in his letter, he's due soon. See what they've got. There might be some nice fresh fruit and vegetables or some specialty foods brought up from Clare Village. See what is there, I'll leave it up to you.'

'Are we needing any of the regular stores?'

'You can check with cook to see if we're running short on anything.'

'What about the Barcowie run? I intended to go up there today to take the rations to the outstations and to check on the water.'

'I'll go up instead,' Patrick said. 'I'm looking forward to a decent gallop through the bush.'

'I'll be off, then,' Sid said, rising from the table and picking up his hat.

'Oh, I nearly forgot,' Kate said, folding her napkin. 'Pick up the mail and er . . . keep your ears out for news, of course.'

'What sort of news were you wanting?'

'How things are in the neighbourhood. How the drought is affecting people. That sort of thing.'

'You want to know how James Carmichael is faring, is that it?'

Kate shot a warning glance in her son's

direction. 'I'm interested in how all of our neighbours are getting on, not just James.'

'I thought you knew already that James, like most of them in the Far North, is struggling to get enough feed and water for his sheep. His clip was down last year too.'

'Divine justice, I'd say,' she muttered.

Patrick watched them silently.

'Well, I wouldn't wish this wretched drought upon anybody. Neither should you, Miss Kate. The Far North has not seen decent rain since November 1864. It's now May '66,' he said, and began counting on his fingers.

'Eighteen months,' Patrick broke in.

'Eighteen months,' Sid nodded. 'Elatina may not get through it unscathed if we don't get rain soon. I wouldn't be gloating if I were you.'

'Elatina Valley has a flush of green from that shower we got a week or two back. All our major creeks—Elatina, Barcowie and Middle Creek—are still flowing. Deep waterholes remain in Secret Gully. If any rain falls, Elatina will be the first to get it. It's these mountains, they attract the clouds.'

Their eyes travelled around the rugged blue peaks that formed the perimeter of Elatina Valley. They were shrouded already in the haze of the hot morning sun.

'Well, the water and the feed won't last forever with the number of sheep we run here. Another month or two and we could be facing trouble ourselves.'

'The Yuras say Elatina water has never completely dried up,' Patrick broke in.

'Well they only ever had themselves to water. One hundred blacks don't drink as much as fifteen thousand sheep,' Sid's lip curled.

Sid never called the Yuras by their proper name. He always called them the blacks, no matter how often Kate corrected him. An undercurrent of dislike always ran through his comments. He had never liked the fact that Kate had used them as shepherds and he had never trusted them. If it hadn't been for Sid, Kate would have paid them for their services. 'I'm not staying on at a station where the blacks get paid. I have my pride!' was what he had said. She couldn't afford to lose him. He was a hard worker and was well liked by the men. He had a reputation for fairness.

The Yuras received rations for themselves and their families, which was better than nothing, Kate told herself. But she knew that Elatina Station would not have survived without them in the early gold rush years. It was their help that allowed her to get ahead when the other stations had been hampered by the shortage of shepherds. She respected their knowledge of the land.

'You might be right, Sid. I might check with Arranyinha, see what she thinks our chances are.'

'You do that,' he replied. He stepped down from the wide cool verandah and strode off towards the stables.

Patrick watched until Sid was out of sight.

'Mother?'

'Yes?'

'Will you answer one question for me?'

'Depends what it is.'

'What have you got against Mr Carmichael?'

Kate felt the tension ripple through her. She looked at her son. Had he heard something? All the people she had poached from Wildowie had been sworn to secrecy. Even Arranyinha and the other Yuras had promised not to say anything to him. He had asked her about his father several times before, but she had always told him that she would tell him the story when he was older. Lately he had not asked her. Maybe he had learnt that she didn't want to talk about it.

'Why do you ask?'

He shrugged his shoulders. 'You always want to get one up on him. You speak of him with loathing. He's never done us any harm, has he? He keeps to himself over there at Wildowie.'

It appeared that he knew nothing. No one had told him.

'It's a long story and an old one. One day I will tell you all about it. All you need to know now is that James and I fell out. He swore that he would never extend a helping hand to me or to anyone at Elatina. And he never has. He's not been a good neighbour to us.'

Patrick looked at her speculatively, as if he knew that there was more to the story. She knew she should tell him about James but she didn't want to. She didn't want him to know how foolish she had been. Nor did she want to open the lid on those feelings.

'Udnyuartu and Virdianha! Nunga?' It was Arranyinha, greeting them as she came through the garden.

Kate was glad that they had been interrupted. She would explain everything to him one day, she promised herself but not now.

'Warndu,' Patrick replied, responding to his Yura name.

'Nunga?' Kate asked her old friend in return, as she gave her a hug and a peck on the cheek.

'Warndu,' Arranyinha nodded, patting Kate's arm in return.

'Join us,' Kate said, offering Arranyinha a chair.

She shook her head and sat on the edge of the verandah.

'I'd best get organised to be off before it gets too hot,' said Patrick. He gave Arranyinha a pat on her shoulder as he passed.

'Don't forget to check on the water at Barcowie!' Kate reminded him.

'Will do. I'll be back by dinner,' he said to his mother.

Kate tossed her napkin onto her plate and left the table to join Arranyinha on the step.

'How's life?' she asked her friend in Adnyamathanha.

'Good,' nodded Arranyinha.

'Have you been down to the camp lately?'

'I have just come back. I went down to see my daughter for a few days.'

'I wondered why I hadn't seen you for a day or two. How is everyone there?'

'They're all good, Udnyuartu. My daughter will be having another baby soon. When her time comes I will go and stay with her.'

'Another grandchild!'

'Five now,' grinned Arranyinha.

'So how are things down at the camp? Is everyone well?'

'Yes, very well.'

'Is the water in Elatina Creek going to hold out, do you think? Will there be plenty there for the Yuras if the drought goes on?'

'Plenty now.'

'Sid thinks that we may run short of water if it doesn't rain soon.'

'Elatina and Barcowie have always had water, ever since the Dreamtime.'

Kate laughed, 'But there weren't any sheep in the Dreamtime!'

'True. No sheep in the Dreamtime, just the two great Akurras. They drank up all the water.' She shrugged her shoulders. The loose, wrinkled skin that hung flap-like under her arms quivered as she did so. Arranyinha had grown older, too.

'So, barring the return of the Akurras, do you think we'll have enough?'

'I cannot say, Udnyuartu. Enough for the Yuras and the Udnyus, yes. But for the sheep, I do not know. They are not important creatures.'

Not to the Yuras, Kate thought. They would not care if all the sheep dropped dead tomorrow. As long as the people survived, that was their chief concern.

'Do you think it might rain soon?'

Arranyinha's eyes roamed slowly over the landscape, then over the ground closer to them. It appeared that she examined even the ants before giving her verdict. Her eyes, crinkled against the sun, twinkled bright amongst the folds of dark tissue. 'Not soon,' she said.

Kate looked up into the wide, cloudless sky, her eyes partially closed against the bright light. No rain in sight. Rory had warned her that this might happen. He had talked about seven good years and seven bad years. She remembered it clearly.

She hoped that the dry conditions would not deter him from his trip up north to see her. It was almost a year since she had seen him, six months since he had written to say that their carting business had been sold for a very healthy sum. She had hoped, now that their business no longer gave them the cause to meet, that they would find other reasons to stay in touch.

He had continued as manager, occasionally making the trips with the teamsters himself. She had mostly left it up to him, using her share of the profits to establish Elatina. They had continued to meet once or twice a year, sometimes in Adelaide, and at other times at Elatina. They had been business meetings, but it was obvious that the friendship, and the spark, were still there.

He had never again mentioned marriage, but she knew the offer always stood open. And she had always told herself to wait—for Elatina to become established, for Patrick to grow up a little . . . The time had simply slipped away from them. Rory. Her heartbeat quickened as she thought of him. Her feelings had not changed one bit in all those years.

He was coming to see her. What could it mean? It had been fifteen years since she had turned down his offer of marriage and then tried, albeit unsuccessfully, to turn her heart away from him. A decade and a half since she had told him that she must set up a successful station and in that way provide a secure future for Patrick, before she could attend to her own desires.

And now she had done it. She had built the secure future that she wanted for her son. Mrs Applebee's loan had been repaid in the first two years. All of Kate's money from the flour carting had been invested in building Elatina since then. Sure, it had taken much longer than she had thought it would. The years filled with hard work had flowed past much faster than she had reckoned on. Was it too late for her and Rory? What if she told him that she was ready to hand over the reins of Elatina to young Patrick? Would he still want her?

There had been no one else in his life when

she had last spoken to him. Sure, he had seen a number of women over the years. He was a red-blooded man, as he said. And she couldn't begrudge him that. She would have done the same if she were a man and it hadn't been for Patrick. As far as she knew, none of his women had worked out right. He had once told her rue-fully that not one had measured up to his mem-ory of her. She crossed her fingers and hoped that no one had since.

The anticipation of seeing him ran swift in her veins.

It was later in the day, when she was prepar-ing the guest room, that she looked out through the window to see dust arising from the track into Elatina. Her heart skipped a beat. She slipped out of the house. Somebody was on that track. There was a vehicle stirring up the fine red dust. It might be Sid, returning from Blinman, she told herself, willing her heart to slow down. She stood waiting, her eyes straining into the distance. It was two horses, not one. It was not Sid. The station buggy was drawn by only one horse. She stepped off the verandah, barely con-trolling her impulse to run down the track to greet her visitor.

It was him! Her eyes never left his face as he pulled up the horses. 'Rory, you made it!' she shouted out.

The horses had barely skidded to a halt before he had jumped down and she was in his arms, the cloud of dust enveloping them completely as he took her in that bear-like hug.

'Oh Kathleen! It is grand to see you!' He held her at arm's length, looking her up and down.

'Are either of you going to help me down or shall I jump?' came a female voice from the vehicle.

Kate's heart plunged abruptly. Who had he brought with him? She lifted her eyes to see Brigid grinning from ear to ear.

'Brigid! What in God's name are you doing here?' She ran to the side of the wagon to offer her old friend a hand to get down.

'Oh, Kate!' said Brigid, when she had disentangled the hoop of her crinoline from the wagon.

'What a lovely surprise!' Kate hugged her. 'Rory never told me that you were coming too! Jesus, you gave me a fright for a moment. I wondered just who he had brought with him.'

Swift looks were exchanged between the visitors. The innuendo was not lost on either of them. Kate felt her heart drop as the realisation hit her that her first assumption might not be as far from the truth as she had thought.

She drew her head up proudly, determined not to let the thought bring her down until the reason for Brigid's presence became clear. There was no point jumping to conclusions.

'Welcome to Elatina, both of you. You're a sight for sore eyes, that's for sure. Come in, come in. You must be hot and parched.'

One of the station hands came out to take

care of the horses. Rory turned to get the baggage.

'No, leave that, one of the boys can bring it in later. Come inside out of the heat. So, Brigid, tell me, what brought you up here? You once swore you'd never venture into the bush!' she asked as they moved inside.

'Ah well,' Brigid replied, shaking the dust from her skirts, 'that was before Rory talked me into it. You know what a smooth tongue this man has!'

Secretive smiles flashed between the two travellers again.

Rory removed his hat and wiped the sweat and dust from his brow with the back of his forearm. 'I told her that you had civilised the place, Kathleen, and I convinced her that she'd be safe with me.'

'And you believed this rogue, did you?' Kate asked, looking from one to the other as they sat down. What was going on here?

'No, to be perfectly honest, I was dying to see you. And I was sick to death of the Jenners' place. You were right when you said that I'd not get anywhere fast by working there as a nanny. The children are almost grown up now and I was relegated to the life of a domestic once more. I was getting so sick of it. When Rory said that I should toss it in and come up to see you, I figured there was nothing to lose.'

'Well, I'm glad that you came. I've not seen enough of you, either of you,' she said, looking up at Rory, 'for a long time.'

Mary, Kate's cook, brought in cool drinks.

'So, how was the trip? Hot?' Kate asked.

'Dusty!' Rory said, taking a great gulp of the drink.

'You would be used to that. But what about you, Brigid? How did you find it?'

'Exciting. Much more fun than I thought it would be. I don't know why I've not travelled outside Adelaide in all of these years. And camping out was great fun too, nowhere near as scary as I had imagined.'

'Don't tell me you camped out!' She looked from one to the other.

Rory looked at Brigid, back to Kate, then grinned. 'Yep, I had to give her a real taste of bush life!'

'I can't believe it. There are inns all the way now. You didn't have to camp out! None of us are as poor as we used to be!'

'It's in my veins, Kathleen, as well you know. Brigid here took a bit of convincing, but she soon got used to it. You'd never know now that she had slept most of her life in a bed!'

'Should I make up a swag for you out in the garden, then, Brigid?'

'No, I might frighten the sheep out there!'

They all laughed.

'Well, you two will be wanting to wash off that dust and get changed for dinner. Come through, I'll show Brigid her room and we'll set up another one for you, Rory.'

'Where's that lovely boy of yours, Kathleen?'

'Visiting the outstations. He'll be back in time for dinner,' she said as she took them down the wide hallway. 'Just relax for a while now while I check how dinner is going, have a wash and get changed myself.'

'You'll not be wearing those trousers to dinner, then?' Brigid asked.

'No, we're not quite that rough out here!'

'I thought you'd have thrown them out years ago!'

'No, I don't want hoops and skirts tangling me up in the bush. Trousers by day, a dress for dinner. We have to keep up the standards out here in the colony!' she said with a plum in her mouth and a twinkle in her eye.

Kate chose her gown more carefully than she would have done if she was dining as usual with Sid and Patrick.

Silk was still her favourite fabric. The dark blue gown that she had bought when she was last in Adelaide would be the very thing. It was simple, with little ornamentation, but the cut was particularly elegant. The neckline was low and wide and the skirt floated out around her in an enormous circle, highly fashionable and now made possible by the use of hoops rather than multiple petticoats. She chose small pearl earrings and a matching necklet with a single pearl around her neck. Yes, it was just the effect she wanted. Simple, classy, graceful. Not too formal for a dinner with friends at the homestead, but elegant and indicative of her success.

She looked at herself in the mirror. The gown was not the exquisite blue-violet of the one that Rory once gave her, the one that matched her eyes so perfectly, but the depth of the blue made her skin appear a translucent ivory and set off her eyes, making them seem more brilliant against the depth and richness of the colour.

She looked closer, assessing her face. She was thirty-three. Did she look it? When her face was relaxed and her eyes lit up with excitement and pleasure, she looked little more than the seventeen-year-old she had been when she had first met Rory.

But she knew that when she was tired or worried the mirror told a different story. Fine horizontal lines of anxiety surfaced on her brow. When she gazed at the wide bright sky looking for rain, the delicate laughter lines fanning out from the corners of her eyes changed subtly to marks of anxiety. She smoothed her hair back and fixed another comb to hold the heavy coils of hair at the back of her neck.

Rory was the only one in the dining room when she arrived. He turned from his contemplation of the dusk view from the window. His eyes travelled down her body and back to her face.

'You're the one who's a sight for sore eyes, Kathleen.'

'Thank you.'

'If you look like this at dinner every night then I'm one guest you'll not be getting rid of too easily!'

Kate smiled and looked at him. He was still a devilishly handsome man. The years had not added appreciable weight to his strong frame, as it did with so many men, and he must have been forty at least. His face was now clean-shaven. He no longer wore the closely trimmed beard that he had sported when he was a bullocky. The sprinkling of silver hairs at his temple extended back along the sides of his head. His eyes, true blue, still twinkled with the same humour and zest for life.

'Don't worry about that. I've been waiting a long time to see you again, I'll not be tossing you out too soon.'

'Good.' His face became more serious. He rested his hands on the back of one of the tall, carved dining chairs. 'I've come with a particular purpose in mind. We need to talk, Kathleen. Soon. I want to let you know what I've got in mind.'

They heard Brigid's voice in the hallway. 'It's a long time since I've seen you, Patrick.'

'A year it must be, Aunt Brigid, though it's not a day older that you're looking,' Patrick replied as they both entered the dining room. The rhythm of his speech was Irish, if not the accent itself.

'You'd charm the birds right out of the trees, you would, you dear boy.'

'Tomorrow, then,' Kate replied as Rory strode forward to greet Patrick.

Their first evening passed quickly as they

shared news of the previous year. Kate was desperate for Adelaide news. Rory was interested to hear all about the drought and how it was affecting the stations in the Far North.

'Elatina will survive it. Probably the only place that will. Some of the runs have already been abandoned,' Kate told him.

'What about Wildowie?'

'I don't give a damn about Wildowie, you should know that!' she said, dismissing the subject.

Rory persisted, coming at it from another angle. 'So you made the better choice of land, then?'

'Of course I did. I was the only one who had the Yuras' knowledge of the area. James bought the leases for the land to the north and west of Barcowie to try to stop me expanding, not realising the best land was to the east over the mountains, here at Elatina. He did it to spite me and it has backfired. My land is still green, his land has turned to dust and it damn well serves him right.'

She always felt cross when she thought of James. She looked up.

Rory looked thoughtful. Patrick was watching her, alert again.

'Did he ever marry?' Brigid asked.

Kate laughed. 'Very rich upper-class women who want to live in the remote bush are rare. And besides, there are always some innocent female domestics desperate for a job.'

Rory, Brigid and Patrick all looked at her, as if dismayed by the bitterness in her voice.

'Anyway, let's talk about happier subjects. What has happened to the other girls from the *Elgin*, have you seen any of them lately, Brigid?'

Kate, Rory, Brigid, Patrick and Sid were sitting on the verandah at breakfast the following morning when the sound of a horse's hooves brought them a visitor.

'James Carmichael!' Kate said, rising from her seat. Her napkin, forgotten, fell from her lap to the ground. What in God's name was he doing here?

'Good morning, Kate,' James said, slipping from his horse and raising his hat. He tethered his horse to the hitching rail.

Kate was speechless. James had never once visited Elatina.

'Morning all,' James said, taking in the rest of the party in one glance.

Sid and Rory both stood and stepped forward.

'How are you, Mr Carmichael?'

'Well thanks, Sid. Yourself?' he said, shaking hands.

'Well, sir.'

'Rory, I didn't know you were coming up this way!' James shook his hand too.

Kate looked from Rory to James. She hadn't

realised that they would remember each other from all those years ago.

'Came up to see how the drought was treating you all,' Rory replied.

Brigid and Patrick were the only ones left sitting at the table.

Rory looked at Kate, expecting her to make the introductions.

She was still baffled. What could James possibly be wanting? He wasn't making a friendly neighbourly gesture after all these years, surely?

'James, do you know Kate's friend Brigid Mulcahey?' Rory asked, making up for Kate's omission.

'Yes, of course, I do remember you,' he said. 'It has been many years, hasn't it?'

'It has indeed,' Brigid said and inclined her head graciously. Her confidence had developed as she matured.

James then looked at Patrick. Kate knew that there could be no mistaking the relationship. That butter-coloured hair, the grey eyes . . .

James raised one brow. Still Kate said nothing.

'And have you met Patrick, Kate's son?' Rory asked.

'No,' James replied, stepping forward to shake hands as the young man rose from his seat. 'We've never met. I've seen you around but we've never been formally introduced. I've heard a lot about you, of course. They say that you do a great job helping your mother run the station.'

'Thank you, sir,' Patrick replied.

There was a moment of uncomfortable silence.

Finally Kate spoke. 'What brings you to Elatina?' she asked.

'I hoped to have a word with you, Kate,' he said.

'Go right ahead.'

'You're not going to leave the poor man standing there, are you? Aren't you going to invite him to have a seat and a cup of tea, Kathleen?' Rory prompted quietly.

'No, thanks anyway,' James responded quickly. 'I've had breakfast.'

'Go ahead, Kate, take Mr Carmichael into the parlour. We can look after ourselves out here,' Brigid suggested.

Kate had no choice but to show him inside, as much as she would rather not.

'Have a seat. What can I do for you?'

'Kate, don't be too hard on me, can't we put aside the old enmity and treat each other with the respect of neighbours?'

Kate looked at him silently for a moment. What could he possibly want? He couldn't be extending the olive branch after all these years.

'These are hard times. We all must support each other or we go under.'

'You've come to offer me some kind of support, have you? It's not before time.'

'Kate, I'm sorry. We should never have let things go for so many years.'

'I'm glad that you are sorry, if you are. It's been no easy life here building a future for your son. But if you've finally come to offer help then I'll not be turning it down.'

James shifted in his seat. 'Maybe we could consider some mutual help, then. Let's start with what I could do for you.'

'What you could do for me, for a start at least, is to come clean. Don't try those old tricks on me yet again. You've come for something. Be honest, tell me what you want.'

James dropped his head and rubbed his hand over his forehead in an unaccustomed gesture of defeat.

'It's hard times up here. Rain must be coming soon. It's the longest drought we've had since I came up here nearly twenty years ago . . .' He paused.

In the harsh early-morning light Kate could see the silver sprinkled through the darkened blond of his hair. Lines of new worries were etched into his cheeks.

'The drought must break soon. We've always had good rains by June at the latest. There's very little feed left at Wildowie and precious little water. The sheep are losing condition fast—'

'You only have yourself to blame. You bought bad land to prevent me getting a big enough station to be profitable. You can't deny that.'

'I don't deny it. You made me so angry at the time. You refused to trust me. I meant to do the right thing by you, I did.'

'We won't argue that now.'

'I agree. Nothing I can say will change your mind. But if we had joined forces then, we would have built the biggest and best station in the north.'

'I gave you that chance and you wasted it. There's no point talking of what might have been.'

She could see what he was going to ask, and she wasn't going to make it easy for him.

He ran his fingers through his hair. 'Kate, you might be bitter, and maybe I can't blame you for that, but the time for bitterness is over. I'm no longer out for your blood. I am sorry that I ever hurt you. Very sorry. I want to put it all behind me. I have had to overcome considerable pride to come here to see you today.'

He held up his hand as she made moves to interrupt him. 'Hear me out. Listen to what I have to ask. Consider that it might be the best way for us to start over again as neighbours. You have been clever, you've worked damned hard. You are the victor in the battle that has raged between us over the last fifteen years. But there is more glory for you—you can be gracious in your victory. It will make it all the sweeter in everybody's eyes. What about some of that famous compassion of yours? You have always championed the underdog. Do it now, for I'm coming crawling to you on my belly. There is no one else in the Far North who can give me what I want. You are the only one who has enough feed and water to get through the drought. You chose your land very wisely indeed. Let bygones by bygones. Let me bring my sheep over to Elatina until the drought breaks.'

Her moment of triumph had finally arrived! And it had come at the most unexpected time. Her heartbeat quickened.

'Please, I'm begging you.'

He was on his knees to her. Apologetic. Humbled. Bested. As sorry as she had ever wanted him to be. The grandfather clock ticked as the moments went by. She looked at him, wondering how to make the best use of this, wanting to finish his chances for good, but conscious that she now had her opportunity to get what she had always wanted.

He looked up at her, waiting.

The clock chimed the hour, eight chimes. She said not a word as her mind raced for a strategy that could give her the best possible advantage. She would give him what he wanted, if he gave her what she had wanted for so very long. James would have to pay a price.

It was as if he read her thoughts. 'I'm not asking anything for free. I'm happy to pay you, more than generously if you want it.'

'I'm sure any payment would not cost you as dearly as losing all your stock.'

'True. Name your price. You have the upper hand.'

'Money alone is not what I want. I'm a wealthy woman in my own right. But there are some things that I do not have. No, let me correct that, there are some things my son does not have . . .'

She let the words sink in.

'Yes, some things *your* son does not have.' She paused again. 'He does not have the rights that he should have. He has no inheritance other than from me. He does not have his father's name. He has no legitimacy. Being illegitimate is quite a disadvantage in this world, you know.'

James swallowed.

Yes, she would go the whole way. She would take him for everything he had.

'James, you can bring your flocks over, for as long as you like . . . on one condition,' she looked directly into his eyes. 'That you marry me. I do not want you for myself, it would be a marriage in name only. But I want you for Patrick. You will make him your legitimate child and he will be the rightful heir to both properties. He will own the grandest sheep empire in the colony. It is his right. For that, I will save your station.'

James was white around the mouth, his whole body tense, the muscles flicking in his jaw. 'You always were a prime bitch, Kate O'Mara, always out to get from me what you could. Nothing has changed. I offer willingly a pound of flesh but you want my blood as well—'

She interrupted him, saying, 'Take it or leave it. It is up to you. You can finally do the right thing by Patrick or you can take your sheep elsewhere.'

'There is nowhere else.'

'*That is your problem.* Weren't they the words you said to me when I told you that I was carrying your child?'

Kate had never seen him so angry. His grey eyes were as hard as granite, his jaw was clenched. She revelled in the power she was exerting.

'There is no way I will submit to your ultimatums. You might have the upper hand but you will not walk roughshod over a Carmichael.' He stood up and placed his hat on his head.

He strode to the door. 'The drought will break soon. I'd rather take the chance.'

'The Yuras doubt it. I'd trust their judgement, if I were you.'

'Well, if you want to trust the ignorant blacks, fine,' he said as he kicked open the door onto the verandah in front of him and walked out.

'I'd trust them before you any day,' she called after him. 'And it's not my flocks that will perish, it is yours.'

He turned. The words came out slowly, clearly, maliciously. 'Well I'd rather the sheep died, every last one of them, than lower myself to marry a money-grubbing Irish peasant!'

'Irish peasant is it?' Kate grabbed her shotgun from the hallstand as she made her way through the door behind him.

James unhitched his horse and mounted as she lifted the gun to her shoulder.

'Get off Elatina. I will shoot you as an intruder if I ever see you here again!'

Wordless, he wheeled his horse around and galloped out the way he had come. The puffs of dust kicked up by the horse's hooves were picked up by the northerly breeze and blown along the track as if ushering him away from Elatina.

'Kate!' It was Brigid, aghast.

She turned at the sound of her name. They were all at the table still, Rory, Brigid, Patrick and Sid, mouths open, rooted to the spot.

Tears of anger welled up in her eyes as she looked at them. 'That bastard!' she said as she lowered her gun.

Rory came to take the gun from her hands. 'Let's put that away. Go and sit down.'

'What on earth happened, Kate?' Brigid asked.

'He makes me sick, the selfish, self-seeking . . .' She struggled for the words to describe how bad he was. She could feel her cheeks flushed and her eyes bright with anger.

Brigid leant forward and poured her friend a cup of tea. 'Here, don't say anything until you have calmed down. Sit.'

Kate took a mouthful from the cup and banged it down onto the saucer again. 'Did you hear him? Not lower himself to marry an Irish peasant! Who does he think he is, calling me a peasant? I'm as good as he is! Better! We're no longer in old England. We're in the colony where everyone is equal! And I have proved it!'

'What on earth was he talking about?' Brigid asked.

'Begin at the beginning, Kathleen. Why did he come?' Rory interjected.

Patrick's young face was creased with worry and concern. She must watch what she said.

'He came here begging feed and water for his sheep. After all these years of not giving me one bit of help, of taking no responsibility for what happened and then, on top of it, trying to do me a bad turn.'

'Water, eh?' Sid asked laconically.

'Yes, he wanted to bring his sheep over to Elatina, until the drought breaks. After what he did to me, he expected me to grant it to him like that!' She snapped her fingers.

'Must be desperate,' Sid interjected.

'He is. Another few days and his sheep will be dropping like flies.'

'So what did you say?' Rory was leaning forward, alert, suddenly more interested in the outcome.

Kate glanced at her son. 'I said yes, on certain conditions.'

Rory's eyes were bright. 'And what were they?'

Kate looked at Patrick again. 'Patrick, would you do me a favour?'

'Er . . . yes.'

'Go give the men their orders for the day. I'm in no mood to attend to them. They must be waiting. You can come back when you've finished, if you like.'

Patrick rose, albeit reluctantly.

'I'll be all right, I'm starting to calm down already. Please, go and do that for me.'

She waited until Patrick had disappeared around the side of the house before she continued.

'You all know the history between James and I. You know how he treated me when I was pregnant. I have the upper hand now, so I used it, but not unreasonably, I don't think, in view of the circumstances.'

Brigid rolled her eyes. 'Kate, what have you done?'

'I told him that he could have all the water he wanted, on my conditions.'

'Which were?' Rory said nonchalantly. His hands were in his pockets and he was slouching, but the tension in his shoulders betrayed his interest.

'That he marry me, that he make Patrick legitimate, that the properties be brought together so that Patrick one day receives his rightful inheritance.'

She saw Rory's face fall. He had never understood her obsession with James. He had never understood that, despite how much she loved him, Patrick had to come first.

'I thought you didn't want him!' Brigid said.

'I don't. But I would have put up with him for Patrick's sake, so that he could have a father, a name, all of that.'

'What did he say?' asked Rory, the muscles rippling in his jaw.

'You all heard him, you heard him humiliate me, calling me a money-grubbing Irish peasant! Saying he would never lower himself!'

'Dear me!' Brigid said.

'Bad to worse then, Miss Kate.'

'Yes, and he can forget ever getting a drop of water or a blade of grass from me!'

The rest of the party were silent.

'Well don't all of you look at me like that, your eyes accusing me! He was the one who did me wrong. You can't deny it!'

'There is more than one way to skin a cat. There are other ways you could have gone around it. You could have been more gracious and hoped that later, when old wounds had begun to heal over, that he would have come round to doing the right thing by his son.'

'That is your way, Brigid, but it is not mine. I'm not that patient. I can't wait another fifteen years hoping that will happen!'

'Patience does not come into it. You'll still be waiting fifteen years for what you want, if not fifty! You'll not get what you want by going about it that way.'

Kate looked away from Brigid towards Rory. His expressive black brows had descended over his eyes.

'Why are you looking at me like that?'

'You rush your hurdles, Kathleen. You don't think of what outcome you really want. You don't kick a man when he's already down. We men have our pride. You should know that by now.'

'Well he's the one who'll be sorry, not me.'

'Is that right?' Rory's thick eyebrows flew up again.

'Yes!'

'You might eventually have gotten what you'd wanted and been able to do the right thing at the same time.'

'Rubbish!' She took another gulp of half-cold tea.

Rory shrugged his shoulders.

She looked at their faces. 'You all look as if you think I've done the wrong thing.'

They said nothing.

'Be honest. You do, don't you?'

'If you can face it, I will be honest, Kathleen. It's an unwritten law in the outback. Water is scarce at the best of times. You never refuse a mate or a neighbour when he asks for water, not unless you'll die of thirst yourself. Have you forgotten your life as a bullocky? We relied on the generosity of every property owner we passed. They gave their water and feed freely to us. It's the done thing.'

'No. He's no mate and he is no good neighbour.'

'Then neither are you.'

'Not to him, I'm not.'

Rory shrugged again, as if he had more to say but wouldn't say it.

'Brigid, you support me, don't you?'

'No, I'm sorry, Kate. For once I don't. How can you have forgotten the famine? How can you forget that the English landlords ate from tables piled high with food, that they passed us in their carriages and never stopped to help as we struggled hungry and weak along the road? There was plenty in Ireland, for all of us, but they wouldn't share it. They exported it for profit while we starved! How is this any different?'

'It is different! It isn't the same!'

Brigid said nothing.

'She's got a point, Miss Kate,' Sid said quietly.

'So you are against me too, are you, Sid?'

'No, not against you. I know how you've struggled. But we help each other out in bad times. To deliberately withhold food and water from thirsty men and beasts, why, it's as bad as the cruelty meted out to me at Port Arthur. There's no good reason for what you're doing; it's cruelty.'

It was the first time that Sid had ever mentioned his convict background. Kate had guessed the truth, but never before had he so much as hinted at the hard life he had led.

Anyway, he can't talk, she thought. She had never forgotten how he had treated those Aboriginal women on her first trip north. That was cruel too.

She looked at the disapproving faces surrounding her. Immoral, cruel and heartless. That's what they were thinking. But they had not been through what she had!

'I'm going for a ride!' she said, pushing her

chair back. She added 'Excuse me,' as an afterthought.

Sid stood up to go too.

Kate heard his voice behind her: 'I'll leave you to it, I'm off to check on the water supplies in question.'

Chapter

Nineteen

*R*ory and Brigid were left looking at each other across the table. 'Mother of Mary!' sighed Brigid.

'She's really done it this time,' Rory said, shaking his head.

'What can we do?'

'Nothing.'

'You always had a way with her, Rory. She's listened to you more than she's ever listened to anyone else. Why don't you talk to her again later when she's calmed down a bit?'

'No, I don't think so.'

'Why not? She won't listen to me, never has. Give it a try, at least!'

Rory shifted on his seat.

'Rory? Why won't you?'

'I can't. There's something you don't know. My hands are tied.'

'What is it?'

Rory looked her in the eye. 'You'll promise

not to breathe a word of it to her?'

'God's honour,' she crossed herself.

'I have a stake in Wildowie. If she ever found out, she'd shoot me instead of James!'

'No!'

'Yes, I tell you. When Kate refused to lend James the money for Wildowie he came to me.'

'Oh,' her voice fell away.

'Yes, "oh". At first I refused him, of course. Then, the more I thought about it, the more I figured it would fit well into my plans. As you know, Kathleen always wanted land. If she was ever to marry she swore it would be to someone whom she perceived as secure, like a squatter. Someone who could provide a rock-solid foundation for Patrick's future.'

'She has always had a bee in her bonnet about that. It was the famine. It has warped her thinking.'

'Yes. I figured that if I could prove to Kathleen that I could maintain a steady interest in land, while continuing to make good money in the carting business, that she might eventually have me, especially if she had become more secure in herself. I finally agreed to fund the expansion of Wildowie, not realising that James planned to thwart Kathleen's plans if he could. I hoped that I could eventually gain the controlling share, buy James out. That way, I could ask Kathleen to marry me, demonstrate my respect for her need for security, and as a final inducement, surprise her with the deeds for Wildowie, for Patrick.'

'I see. Nice plan. One or two drawbacks, as it has turned out.'

'Yes. I thought, of course, that my chance was near. I knew that she had made a success of Elatina, that it was finally giving her the sense of security she wanted. I hoped, selfishly of course, that James would go under in the drought, so that I could complete my takeover and reveal all to Kathleen. I sold the business in preparation to buy Wildowie outright. That's the real reason why I came up, other than to see her, of course.'

'So you'd not given up on her all these years?'

'I tried to,' his eyes dropped to his hands as he spoke, 'many times, but my feelings for her have never changed. There is only one love like that in a lifetime. With her, I had that.'

Brigid's eyes misted with tears of sympathy. A moment passed. 'I believe she feels the same way. Won't admit it, of course.'

'No. Too stubborn for that.'

'So?'

'So, what can I do? If I try to convince her to share the water with James, I'll be out of the fat and into the frying pan. If she ever found out that I own more than half of Wildowie she'd rightfully feel deceived.'

'More than that, betrayed.'

'Exactly.'

'Can you not speak to James, secretly of course, get him to meet some of her demands?'

'I don't want him to change his mind and marry her.'

'No, I hadn't thought of that. You are in a pickle.'

'I am that.'

'What are we going to do?'

Rory looked dismayed. 'Nothing. We'll just have to watch her do it, watch her deny him the help, even though we know it's wrong.'

Rory put his head in his hands.

Brigid rose and went to stand by him. 'Don't give up, we'll think of something.' She patted him on the shoulder and he looked up at her, appeal in his eyes.

It was at that moment that Kate rounded the corner, riding hat and whip in hand. She stopped in her tracks.

Rory flinched. Brigid took her hand off Rory's shoulder as if she had touched something hot. They both looked guilty, as if they were up to something.

The silence stretched out like a long, dusty track between them.

Kate could feel her face falling. Her suspicions had been confirmed. Rory had given up on her. Brigid had him instead. Her best friend and her never-forgotten lover, together.

She remembered Brigid's words many years ago: *Rory O'Connor, he'd have to be one of the best men this colony has seen . . . and he adores you!*

Her reply to Brigid flashed through her mind: *Maybe you should set your sights on Rory since you think so much of him!*

Don't say that, Kate, she had replied, *I may well take you up on the offer and you'll be sorry you ever made it.*

And they had laughed.

Kate wasn't laughing now. The silence continued.

'Sorry for my rude behaviour,' she said at last. 'I've asked Patrick to show you over the station this morning. I'll be back after lunch some time. Make yourselves at home.'

Dry leaves and bark cracked and crunched, hard and brittle, under the horse's hooves. It was a stinking hot day, with a strong northerly propelling dust and debris through the air and into her eyes. Not much of a day for enjoying the ride, but that didn't matter, as long as she could be alone with her thoughts.

That wretched James! Not lower himself to marry an Irish peasant! It was the ultimate insult, a comment he knew would offend her deeply. It was like rubbing salt into the wound, reminding her of her stupidity in ever thinking that she might have had a future with him. It was a long time since he had destroyed that dream, but it still rankled.

Well, she had shown him a thing or two. She was better than him. He would suffer and she would derive great pleasure from watching it happen. It was no loss to her that he wouldn't marry her. She would have forced herself to tolerate him for Patrick's sake. She had wanted to marry Rory anyway.

Rory! Now it was too late for Rory! Tears started to her eyes and she bit her lower lip to stop them from flowing. That's what hurt the most! After all these years, finally to be in a position to attend to her own needs in life and it was too late!

She had spent her childhood looking after her younger brothers and sisters, helping her mother. Her adolescence sped by as she warded off starvation. Then she had struggled through the days at the workhouse and had come to South Australia. Life had only just begun and a long hard grind it had been. Before she knew it there was another mouth to feed, another child to provide for. It had taken her so long to build a future for him. And there had been the Yuras to look after as well. She had nursed them personally throughout the years that the white man's diseases, previously unknown to them, ravaged their people. There was the measles epidemic, the influenza and countless other contagious illnesses that they, and their medicine experts, were helpless to deal with.

Finally, she had thought to herself, this is it. Time to look after me. But she had miscalculated badly. She had never believed that Rory would ever find real happiness in anyone else's arms. Evidently he had. And they were her best friend's arms.

She couldn't blame Brigid. Or Rory. She had

been one hell of a fool. The only thing that she had ever made a success of was Elatina. She wasn't going to jeopardise that for James Carmichael, of all people! Sure, she had enough feed and water now. But what if the drought didn't break? What if there were no rains through the winter? Then Elatina would turn brown and dry too. Her sheep would perish.

No, she wouldn't do it. James could go to hell.

She slipped off her horse and led him up the hot shale-covered mountain slopes. The tall shafts of the yaccas stood sentinel on the ridge above her, silhouetted against the quivering brightness of the sky.

If it hadn't been for James, she would not have had Patrick. Then she could have married Rory. Now it was too late. The whole damned thing was James's fault!

She left the horse tethered under the shade of a tree and made her way to the peak on foot. She looked out over the harsh ancient landscape. Elatina Valley, that great, wide expanse of superb grazing country, was faintly tinged with green. She could see her homestead, the out-buildings, the shearing shed and the woolshed, built with her own blood and sweat.

Then she turned and looked to the east. There was Wildowie, the rolling hills and plains. In a good year it was a magnificent and memorable place. This year it was brown and parched, unforgiving and forlorn in the time of drought. The eagles no longer soared overhead; maybe it was too dry, even for them. The wind raised eddies of dust and twirled them across the landscape. James had made his own bed. He could lie on it.

He had caused her to lose Rory.

When Kate returned to the homestead she found that Rory had gone out riding with Patrick. Brigid was on the verandah, reading.

'Good ride?' Brigid asked. Her voice was anxious. No wonder.

'Fine, thanks.'

Kate sat down on the step, picked up a twig and trailed it through the dirt. She had to clear the air. She had to let Brigid know that she was not cross with her. It was her own fault, not Brigid's, and it would be no good to alienate both her old friends in one go.

'So things have changed, Brigid?'

'What do you mean?'

'Is that why you and Rory came up, to tell me to my face?'

'Tell you what?'

'About you two.'

'What about us?' Brigid looked genuinely puzzled. Kate had never realised what a good actress she was.

'You can come clean. I won't be angry with you. I suppose I should have expected it, that you two would hitch up together.'

'No, oh no, you've got the wrong idea entirely! It is as I explained it. I saw Rory. He said that he was coming up to see you, asked me if I would like to go too. I had finally run out of patience, so I agreed. I only came up to see you. I swear it.'

'Well why did you both look so damned guilty when I walked in on that tender little scene this morning?'

'No, Kate, you're jumping to the wrong conclusions. It wasn't what you think it was.'

'Well, what was it then?'

Brigid looked flustered. A slow blush made her cheeks rosier than ever.

'Brigid, I've never seen you blush before!'

'I . . . I—'

'Don't lie for my sake! All I can say is congratulations. He is a good man.'

'No,' Brigid said, shaking her head furiously.

'Not ready to make a commitment yet, is that what it is?'

'Kate, you've got the wrong idea, honestly!'

'Don't worry, I won't say a thing until it's announced.'

Brigid rolled her eyes.

'Tell me, what ever happened to your sweetheart, the one who went after gold?'

Brigid sighed. 'My patience ran thin with him, too, I must admit it. He was always writing to me, telling me he had found gold, but not enough for us to get married. Then he would want to keep digging just long enough to get a bit more. I heard the same story over and over again. I think it was like gambling, it got into his veins. He wanted to marry me, but he couldn't give up the digging, just in case a fortune was under that next lump of clay. I waited and waited. The letters became more infrequent. I would have looked elsewhere, but there was no social life for me, working for the Jenners. I was at their beck and call twenty-four hours a day. In the end I sort of gave up on him.'

'That was when you turned to Rory?'

Brigid shook her head. 'You have it all wrong, I tell you!'

She didn't want to argue with Brigid. She had seen which way the wind was blowing. She didn't want her disappointment, her bitterness, to show.

'I've got to check on dinner now. See you then,' Kate said, leaving Brigid staring after her, open-mouthed.

The conversation that night was strained. No one dared speak about the real issues and the small talk was satisfying to no one. The northerly wind had gained velocity during the day and was now whining around the home-stead, flinging sand and dust against the windows. The air seemed to crackle with electricity, making everyone edgy and uncomfortable.

Kate retired early, glad to remove herself from the atmosphere of disapproval. But she could not sleep, her mind churned over the events of the day. James and the drought, Brigid and Rory.

Tired of tossing and turning on the hot and gritty sheets, she wandered onto the verandah in the hope of finding some cooler air. Brigid was already there. They both sat staring out into the moonlit night, listening to the ceaseless click and whirr of the crickets and the sound of twigs and leaves hitting the house.

It was no cooler outside than it was in.

'Kate, I know I shouldn't interfere, but I can't help thinking about James. He is your nearest neighbour. It can do you no good to ruin him just to spite him. It will cost you nothing to give him feed and water, will it? I can't believe that you could refuse him a lifeline after your experiences in the famine. I thought that those memories drove you. I thought that you could never get them out of your head. Why can't you see the parallels now?'

'Don't remind me of the famine. I feel as though I've finally put all of that behind me.'

'Yes, behind you, but not forgotten. None of us will ever forget it. I just remember the look of the wealthy—fat and sleek—while we starved. It is the same. You will prosper while James's livelihood falls to dust around him.'

'Stop it, Brigid!'

Brigid fell silent. An owl hooted in the distance. Kate tried to ignore Brigid's words.

'I'm off to bed,' Brigid said.

'Goodnight then, sweet dreams.'

Kate's sleep, when it came, was disturbed by the old dream. It was the first time in many years that it had returned to haunt her.

The cold damp mist had settled thickly around

them. She stumbled up, her legs weak, her brother lifeless in her arms. The rumbling sound of carriage wheels penetrated the mist. She stopped, hopeful. Would they take her up? Would they have food?

'Help me!' she called out feebly. 'Help me!'

The curtain was flicked aside as the carriage drew abreast of her. A moment's view was all she had—a cold, hard face. 'Drive on!' he had called.

She stared as the carriage was swallowed up by the mist again. She was alone. A strangled cry escaped her lips.

Kate sat up, her nightdress wet with sweat. She reached for the candle with fumbling hands. It illuminated her room, her pretty room with the oak furniture and the soft cream printed wallpaper. She was here, Elatina. Safe. No longer hungry.

But she was denying her help, just like the stranger with the cold, hard face had done to her.

The wind had dropped overnight, but the air was still oppressive and hot. Kate was wearing her hair up, but she could feel the fine hair that had escaped the pins sticking to her neck and temples, dragging on her skin when she moved her head.

'All right,' she said, looking at the faces around the breakfast table. 'I give in. You lot

win and so will James. He can have the damned
feed and water.'

'You've changed your mind, then, Mother?'

'I have.'

'Well done, Kate,' Brigid said.

Rory and Sid both smiled.

'Thank heavens for that,' said Patrick. 'I was
worried. I talked it over with Arranyinha yesterday. We were both worried. It is not the Yura way.
You told me to always heed the Yuras, Mother,
and they always say that we must share the land,
share the water. Survival depends upon it.'

Kate smiled at her son. He was half-Irish,
half-Yura, but his Yura inheritance was not
obvious on the surface.

'Well, I hope we do all survive. If the drought
continues for too long we may live to regret our
generosity.'

'What made you change your mind,
Kathleen?'

The dream had. The dream that haunted her
at every point of crisis. Once, many years ago,
Rory had held her in his arms when she had that
dream. He wouldn't now. His arms were for
someone else.

She shrugged her shoulders. 'I thought about
it, that's all. Sadly, my ethics won out over my
desire for revenge!' she said with a hollow laugh.

'One question, Miss Kate.'

'Yes, Sid?'

'Which area exactly were you thinking James
could use?'

'I hadn't thought about that yet.'

'Well, I went to check supplies yesterday, and while I'm in favour of it, I don't know how we will manage it.'

'Why?'

'Well, I'm not convinced that we will have enough if the drought continues. I went to Barcowie yesterday. It is the logical place for James to take his sheep, since it is close to him and there is a reasonable supply of water. But there's not that much feed up there. Barcowie didn't get those last showers we had here on Elatina. Would you agree, Patrick?'

'I reckon so. We may even need to move our Barcowie flocks down to Middle Creek eventually.'

'Well then, he'll have to bring his sheep over to Middle Creek, even though it is further. I imagine some of them are in pretty poor condition and he'll probably lose a few on the way, but beggars can't be choosers.'

'We could have trouble with that too, Miss Kate. Our sheep and theirs will be in pretty close together. If they bring any disease with them then they'll infect our flocks. And that land would end up being heavily overstocked.'

'Well, let's have a talk about that after breakfast. We'll sit down and consider the thing right through. Our visitors have probably heard enough station talk for one breakfast!'

'My faith has been restored, Kathleen,' Rory said quietly.

'You thought I had lost all decency, didn't you?'

'It certainly looked that way.' His eyes were warm, very warm. Her heart turned over. Memories of her time with him flooded through her mind. She couldn't remember when she had been happier than those days with Rory.

He dropped his eyes. Then he and Brigid looked at one another. Presumably not aware that Kate was still watching him, he winked at Brigid.

Kate looked away quickly. Pain shot through the centre of her being. There was obviously something going on there despite Brigid's denials.

Kate and Sid met in the office to consider the best thing to do. Barcowie was not an option. Middle Creek presented problems.

'I wish you'd told me all this before I announced my decision at breakfast this morning. I can't go back on my word now. You were the one pressuring me to provide the water yesterday. Why didn't you say it then?'

'Hadn't worked it out then. Hadn't checked out the supplies with that possibility in mind.'

'Well, what are we going to do?'

'There is one other option.'

'What is that?'

'Elatina Creek.'

'No.'

'Why not?'

'I gave that to the Yuras.'

'Not on paper.'

'It doesn't matter. I can't do it. Not after what they have done for me.'

'You don't have a choice. They'll understand. They are the ones who promote sharing. Patrick said it this morning.'

'No, I made a vow.'

'Well, then you have two choices. Put the Barcowie flocks at risk or surround the homestead with fifteen to twenty thousand sheep.'

'What would you do?'

'Send him to Elatina Creek.'

'You would, you've never respected the Yuras.'

'The blacks are unlikely to run out of water. Elatina Creek always runs well. There's never been grazing there so the feed is still plentiful. The blacks don't use it. If there is a shortage of water, they'll move on somewhere else in the short term.'

'They will mind. Anyway, there is no water anywhere else. We are using the rest. It's where the Yuras always came in the dry seasons.'

'Well, it's your livelihood. If you want to run yourself short it is up to you. The blacks won't go without.'

'I promised them that land would be theirs as long as I owned Elatina, and hopefully after that too.'

'No reason why that should change.'

'I don't know . . .'

'Up to you, Miss Kate.'

'All right, I'll think about it,' she said as she dropped her head into her hands.

When Sid had left the office she stood up and walked outside. She had thought that she had already made the hard decision.

Her eyes scanned the sky. It was still hot, oppressive. Cloud cover was descending but it did not look as if rain was in sight. The Far North had seen this weather pattern so many times over the last year, but it had never produced more than a drop or two. Sometimes a little on the high rugged mountain tops, but never enough on the plains.

If only it would rain, then the decisions would be superfluous.

They took dinner on the verandah. The high, thick blanket of cloud was holding in the heat and even the usual cool of the house had dissipated. Spectacular streaks of lightning rent the air on the northern horizon.

'Quite a show. Looks like you will all get your rain at last,' Brigid commented.

'Not likely. When we do get rain it's usually brought by the south-westerly wind. This weather is from the north. Plenty of lightning and thunder, but no rain will come of it.'

'If there was rain close by, we'd be able to smell it and feel it,' Patrick added, 'but you can feel how dry the air is. That cloud will simply slip over the top of us during the night and it will be as hot and dry as ever tomorrow.'

'James must be feeling desperate by now,' Rory commented.

'Yes, he had better get his sheep over here fast.

If he was being honest when he said that he only had a couple of days' feed and water left for them,' Kate said. Then she sighed.

'What have you decided, Miss Kate?'

She had made her decision. It hadn't been an easy one. The only viable option seemed to be Elatina Creek. She would ride down there in the morning and tell the Yuras of her decision. It would only be until the drought broke, then they could have their land and their creek to themselves again. There was plenty of water there, and feed going to waste. They would just have to cope as best they could in the short term. She didn't like to do it, but she had no choice. She wasn't going to let her livelihood turn to dust only to benefit James Carmichael.

And she would underscore her generosity to James by sending Patrick over to him with the news. Maybe Rory and Brigid were right: it might even set the foundation for a relationship between Patrick and his father.

'Patrick, I would like you to ride over to Wildowie in the morning, if you would. Tell James that he can bring his sheep over. He might appreciate it if you bring him back over to Elatina and show him exactly where to put the sheep.'

'Sure. And where exactly were you thinking of letting his sheep water on Elatina?'

Kate swallowed. 'Elatina Creek. You know the area well. Show him where to take them. Make sure that he won't disturb the Yuras.'

A look of dismay replaced the eagerness on

Patrick's face. His mouth opened and closed twice before he answered. 'Won't disturb the Yuras! What are you taking about? Does Arranyinha know about this? Mawaanha? The other elders?'

'No, but—'

'You'll have to talk to them first.'

'You know how long those decisions take them. By the time they get back to us, half of James's sheep will have perished. They are likely to agree anyway.'

'That's not the point. You must ask their permission first.'

'Please just do as I ask.'

'I won't do it, I'm sorry.' He spoke the words quietly, without the impulsiveness or passion of his mother. It was the cool assurance inherited from his father.

Rory, Sid and Brigid sat silent, tense, evidently not wishing to interfere.

'Well I'm telling you to, Patrick. You wanted me to share the water with James Carmichael. You are the one who said that it was the Yura way. I am sharing!' She could see the pain in his eyes as she threw that in his face.

'You can't share Elatina Creek!'

'We can't be risking our own necks to look after James Carmichael. It's the only option.'

'But Elatina Creek belongs to the Yuras!'

'It belongs to me, actually,' Kate said, 'I hold the leases.'

'You gave it to them. You saved it for them. How could you have forgotten that?'

'I haven't. There is plenty of water for them and for James's sheep. There is plenty of feed there. It is only until the drought breaks. The Yuras will come to no harm.'

Patrick was white around the mouth. It reminded Kate of something . . . the look on James's face two days ago. That implacable, cold anger. Their resemblance had never struck her so forcibly before.

'You're a traitor!'

'Patrick!' Sid intervened, 'don't speak to your mother like that!'

Patrick whirled on Sid. 'She has betrayed the Yuras! And I can see who would have put her up to it. You have always hated them!'

'Now, lad,' Rory said quietly, placing his hand on Patrick's arm, 'it's no way to speak no matter what they have done. And no way to put your view forward either. Keep calm, tell us what you've got against it.'

Brigid added her piece. 'Your mother has worked hard for you all these years, she's doing it for the best.'

Rory silenced her with a frown.

Patrick's sweeping glance took in the whole group. 'You are all on her side now, aren't you? Two days ago you were all in agreement with me, that she should give some of our resources to James. Now you are all against me. She's found a way to wriggle out of it. She's going to give away someone else's water instead!'

'We aren't against you, son. Never lose your

temper, remember, or you lose the battle too. Tell us, why would it be so wrong?' It was Rory, pouring oil on troubled waters again.

'It is not just the water that is at issue here. It is the principle! That land was given to them. No, let me rephrase that. It has been theirs for all time, it is the only piece of land that they have retained—'

'Not by law—' Brigid interjected

'No, it is not on paper, but it doesn't have to be. A promise is a promise. The honour of our family is staked upon it.' His gaze flicked to his mother's face. Beneath the passion in his words lay the hard cold steel of his anger. 'Her honour, and mine too! That land was for the Yuras, so that they would have one piece of their own land to call their own. The rest of it has been taken up by settlers. You know, Mother, you know what land meant to the Irish, you told me what happened when your family lost their land. You know what it means to the Yuras. It was to be one small patch of land where they didn't have to fight for their rights to what the earth has provided for them!'

'Well it is still theirs. Nothing will change that,' Kate assured him.

'Then you should be asking their permission before you give their water away!'

'I meant to go down there tomorrow morning and talk to them about it.'

'To deliver the *fait accompli*, you mean!'

Kate sighed, 'If that is the way you see it, yes.'

'Mother, have you forgotten?' His voice broke a little on the words, revealing both his youth and the strength of his convictions. 'Have you forgotten what the land means to them?'

'It is only a bit of water and grass!'

He dashed a tear from his eye with the back of his hand. 'No. It is not just water. It will be desecration of the land. You know how much it means to them. It is precious. The tie will be broken! The link between them and the land will be violated. Those sheep will trample all over it. It will be changed forever.'

'The land will recover, won't it?' asked Brigid.

'No it will not, not in the minds and hearts of the Yuras! It is sacred, like a mighty cathedral is to us. We don't let sheep wander into our cathedrals!'

'But they have done nothing remarkable with it. They have built no beautiful cathedrals. They don't use it for anything,' Brigid said.

Patrick looked at her and shook his head in dismay. 'They don't need to do anything with it. It is a superb cathedral in itself. Every gully, every tree, every animal is integrated in its glorious structure.'

Brigid looked bewildered.

He turned to Kate. 'Please, Mother, remember the vow, remember what we owe them. Don't turn on them now that the going is rough. If you do, your gesture will have meant nothing at all. You will be in the same class as the rest of the Udnyus who have hounded them off the land, shot them, poisoned them, driven them to starvation and death.'

'There is no need for you to be so dramatic!' Kate said. 'I understand what you are saying and it does you great credit to be thinking of the Yuras. But I will not change my mind. I will not give away all that I have strived for. I will not put our livelihood at risk. I don't like doing it, but that is that. The decision is made.'

'Mother, you have forgotten. I was born there near Elatina Creek. My name is Virdianha, I have the name of the firstborn. It is my sacred birthplace. Desecrate my birthplace and you will have violated my spiritual link with the land.'

What had she done? This boy of hers was more Yura than Udnyu. She should have realised before now that conflict would inevitably arise. He would have to choose one way or another, Yura or Udnyu. He could not stand between the two forever. And in reality, both he and the Yuras would have to live in the white man's world. It was her duty to make clear to him where he really stood.

'Patrick, you are not a Yura by birth, so it cannot have that meaning for you. Take James there, I am instructing you to.'

'I will not do it. I will have no hand in your dirty work. You may have lost all sense of what is right, but I have not. Excuse me,' he said and stood up. 'I am sorry, Mother, I cannot do what you have asked.'

He placed his napkin on the table, turned and walked off the verandah into the night.

Kate dabbed the film of perspiration from her neck with her napkin. 'He'll come around,' she said to the others.

Rory raised one thick black brow. 'Do you really think so, Kathleen?'

'He is my son. He had better do as he is told.'

'He is no longer a boy,' he said. He passed his hand over his mouth and both black brows flew up. 'He reminds me very much of someone else at much the same age. Someone else who championed the underdog, someone else who was determined and stubborn about certain principles.'

Kate grinned, despite herself. 'Tell us. Who was that, Rory?'

'A young scamp of a lad, an Irish billy-boy named Declan who I knew in my early days.'

'You're a rogue, Rory O'Connor! Do you think he's right, then? Do you think I should leave Elatina Creek alone?'

'It is your land. You know what promise you made the Yuras. That is up to you.'

The question of the Yuras' water did not leave her mind all night. She went over the options, time and time again. Was Patrick right? Was she forsaking her promise to them? Certainly, Patrick's strength of opposition had unnerved her.

Or was it that Patrick was growing up, and that his view was simply the spark for the many conflicts that must ensue now that he had reached that critical point where boyhood must give way to manhood.

All children go through this stage of development, she told herself. It was only by disagreement with their parents that they made the transition to independence and adulthood. Udnyus did not have the rites of passage like the Yuras had. There was no initiation, no ceremony to help boys to make that final step, nothing to mark their passage. It was only by distancing themselves from their parents' views and values that they could become independent. That was what Patrick was doing. It must be, she told herself. That was why he was so vehemently opposed to her plan. She rolled over and nestled her head into the pillow.

Or was it something else? Was this, she wondered, the inevitable cultural clash? She opened her eyes and stared up at the ceiling. Was this the natural consequence of the way she had raised him? He had spent his infancy with the Yuras. He had lived between the two cultures right through his formative years. He had been educated at home, mostly by her, sometimes with the help of a tutor, and frequently by the Yuras, especially the men. They had been like fathers to him. He had never really mixed a lot in Udnyu society. He had not been sent off to boarding school and Kate had spent too much time working to do a lot of socialising with the local Udnyu community. She tossed off the sheet that had covered her.

Maybe it was no surprise that he viewed the world almost exclusively from a Yura perspective. Had she allowed him to be initiated, as the Yuras had wanted, it may have been worse. The more he identified with them, the more difficulties he would have encountered at some time or another. But who would have denied him the love of the Yuras?

The next morning the air was hot, close and oppressive. Clouds still hugged the sky and Kate could hear the distant rumble of thunder to the north. The weather seemed to press down upon her, heavy and insistent, like the burden of decisions on her mind. She was hot, damp, irritable, pressured. Caught between what others wanted from her, and what she wanted herself.

'Patrick, let me explain what I will do. I will go to the Yuras this morning and ask their permission to bring James's sheep over. If they do not agree, I will accept their decision and the sheep can come to our end of Elatina Valley. Would you ride over to see James some time this morning? You can let him know that I have agreed, that he can have feed and water for his sheep, and that there is no price and no conditions on that. He can get ready to start bringing them over tomorrow.'

'Thank you, Mother,' Patrick said, a slow smile lighting his face.

When Kate walked her horse through the

trees and into the Yura camp, it was obvious that the news of the dissension had preceded her. The children hung back against the legs of the adults, instead of rushing forward to greet her with laughter and cheering, as they usually did. The adults were silent and sombre, and the tension palpable. The atmosphere was like the weather—oppressive, insistent and threatening.

It had always amazed her that the Yuras knew so much about what was going on at the homestead and how quickly they found out about it. There was a constant movement of station hands and their families between the two sites. Kate and Arranyinha exchanged visits throughout the week. Patrick also moved between the two settlements, visiting his Yura family every other day. He may even have come down early this morning to tell the elders about the threat to their land. Sometimes Kate had wondered if the Yuras had special communication powers that she did not know about.

She tied her horse to a nearby tree.

'We've been expecting you,' the old man, Mawaanha, said. But there was no word of welcome.

'I've brought some fruit for the children,' Kate said, holding up a big brown paper bag. 'Apples! Isn't anyone hungry this morning?' She always brought some fruit with her. The Yuras, particularly the children, loved it. But there was no stampede for it today. The children looked afraid of her.

Arranyinha came forward. 'I'll give it to them.

They are shy of you today. Sit down, I've just made a billy of tea.'

Arranyinha handed round the apples and then poured some tea into a number of dented tin pannikins. She handed them out to Kate and the men. Kate walked over to join the group and squatted in the dust, one booted moleskin-clad leg stretched in front of her, ready to talk to Arranyinha and the men for as long as it needed. They were obviously ready for discussion.

Kate told them all that had transpired so far with James Carmichael.

Mawaanha, a very old man now, talked about what had gone before. 'Without the Yuras there would be no Elatina Station. We saved you when you were perishing of thirst. We showed you the land. We raised Virdianha as one of ours. We have minded your sheep and worked on your station for rations of tea, sugar, flour and mutton.'

'I have not forgotten. I will never forget your kindness and your generosity to me.'

'Yes, and you showed your appreciation by granting us this land to be our own. You promised it to me, personally.'

'I did. And I did that in the knowledge that we would all work together for the future of the Yuras and the future of Elatina Station.'

'And we would always do that. But James Carmichael is not one of us. There has not been good blood between Wildowie Station and the Yuras, ever. Now Wildowie hovers over our heads, like the wedge-tailed eagle after which it was named. Like the wedge-tailed eagle, it is ready to strike to take what belongs to us.'

It was a good analogy, Kate thought. The wildu was a huge bird, black-brown, with a wing span of nine feet. When resting it sat in dead gum trees, surveying the land through hard, cruel eyes. When hunting, it was a truly breathtaking creature, king of the sky, soaring upwards in majestic circles, wings upswept, until it spied its victim, then the swoop was fast and smooth, its aim determined with deadly accuracy. The beak and talons were sharp and cruel. At carrion, it was an ugly and loathsome creature.

But the wildu's prey would be killed and eaten. James only wanted to borrow the land for a short time.

'It may only be for a week or two, until the drought breaks,' she said and she took a sip of the bitter black tea.

'Have you come to ask our permission to do this thing, Udnyuartu, or is your decision really made?'

Kate took a long breath and said, 'For your permission.'

There was silence for a moment.

'We cannot give it,' Mawaanha said. 'If we give in once, we will have to give in again. It would only be the beginning. Are not the Yuras more important than the sheep?'

The question sent a shiver down her spine.

Are not the Yuras more important than the sheep? How could she say no? Mawaanha had a point that must be conceded, however much a part of her rebelled against it.

'It is your land. While I am alive, it always will be. I'll not break my promise to you and I'll not use it without permission. James can bring his flocks to Middle Creek.'

Arranyinha spoke: 'Thank you . . . sister,' she said.

Chapter

Twenty

Not long after Kate had returned to the homestead and Patrick had left for Wildowie, Craig McInerney came tearing down the track to the homestead.

She had seen him coming and, alerted by the speed of his riding, had left the verandah to meet him on the track.

The fair skin of his face was reddened with exertion and streaked grey with sweat and ash. His horse was lathered.

'Ma'am,' he blurted out, barely pausing for breath, 'fire up at Barcowie, started by lightning, we think. It has already taken a good hold on the plain. Robert, Ned and the others are battling it, but we fear it's out of control. The northerly has sprung up again and the fire is heading this way!'

'Oh Jesus, this was all we needed, the undergrowth is as dry as tinder!'

'That's right, ma'am, that's why I left to ride

'down to warn you.'

'You did right. How much time have we got, do you think?'

Craig shrugged his shoulders. 'Half a day before it gets here, if the wind doesn't change.'

'Leave the horse with me, go inside, get a drink and something to eat from Mary. Then come back out to the verandah to help Sid and me work out what to do.'

Kate grabbed the reins and called for one of the lads to take the horse and to find Sid. She looked out to the north. The smoke was barely discernible from the cloud, but it was there, dirty and brown, billowing into the northern sky.

She dashed back to the house crying, 'Rory! Brigid!'

They were still chatting over cups of tea. 'What is it?'

'Fire up at Barcowie! We'll be needing your help. Have you seen Sid?'

'I'm here, Miss Kate,' he said as he stepped up onto the verandah.

'Thank God! Sid, there's a fire out of control at Barcowie, heading this way.'

'Yes, I know. I've got the lads collecting supplies already.'

'Good. Sit down, everyone. How are we going to tackle this, do you think?'

'What about Patrick?' Rory asked.

'Too late, he left some time before Craig arrived.'

'Should we send word to Wildowie, d'you think?' Rory pursued.

'Most likely they would have known about it before we did, I would have thought. They would see the smoke clearly from Wildowie.'

'No time to lose, and we have to help ourselves first. The fire is on our property,' Sid added.

'Exactly,' said Kate. 'There are a few things which need to be done. Ah! Here's Craig. Sit down, Craig. Thanks for racing down to warn us. Are you up to another ride, do you think?'

'Sure, Miss Kate.'

He had always sprung into any activity that he thought might please her. He had overcome his boyish infatuation for her many years ago but he still had a tender spot for her, and she knew it.

'Good. All right, there are a few things we need to keep in mind. The sheep are the most important thing. If we lose them then we lose our income. We've got to get them to a place of shelter. Secret Gully could be the best place. It is deep enough to shelter them from the flames themselves and narrow enough that when they panic there will be nowhere to run, stupid creatures that they are. What do you think?'

They all nodded.

'My suggestion is this: Craig, if you would ride up to Middle Creek, instruct the shepherds to take their flocks to Secret Gully, and help them do it. Sid, I want you to take all available hands up to Barcowie to help get the fire under control if you can. Take extra supplies with you: food, drinks, blankets, wet sacks, anything you think you might need.'

'How can I best help?' Rory asked.

'Come with me, I'm going to head up to Secret Gully with the home flocks.'

'I'm not exactly a dab hand with sheep.'

'That's fine, I can tell you what to do and we will have the dogs and the shepherds to help as well.'

'Is it worth trying to get them up there?'

'Yes, sheep have no sense. They will certainly perish if the fire overtakes them here.'

'What about me?' Brigid asked.

'I want you to stay here, Brigid, if you would. Try to save the homestead if the fire comes this way. You'll have Mary, the cook, and I'll leave you a couple of lads to help, too. You can start by dousing down the thatch on the roof. Get lots of buckets and pans of water ready. Fill the bath with water too. Have some wet blankets ready to beat out the flames. Close all the doors and windows of the house and the outhouses. Stuff the cracks with rags if need be. If the fire overtakes the place get down into the cellar and stay there, keep yourself safe.'

'Watch for any sparks that might come down the chimneys,' Rory added.

'The wind is picking up, Miss Kate!' Sid urged.

'Any questions?' she looked around at the group. 'Good, let's go, then.'

Heading the sheep into the smoke-laden wind was no easy task, since their natural instinct was to turn and run in the other direction, or to huddle together, heads lowered. As the wind gained speed, it carried more debris with it: cinders, leaves, dust. It stung Kate's eyes and filled her mouth with grit. The shepherds had covered their noses and mouths with their scarves, and she did the same.

The frightened sheep bleated piteously. The dogs yapped and snapped at their heels. Rory and Kate, on horseback, cracked their whips. The shepherds shouted and swore to keep the hapless animals moving in one group.

As the wind rose further Kate knew that it was a race against time, a race to get to Secret Gully before the fire cut their path.

And time was running out. The enormous churning cloud of smoke ahead of them was indication that the fire was not far away. Pieces of burnt and burning debris flew through the smoky air, making their eyes smart and their chests heave.

Suddenly Rory was up close. 'How much further?' he shouted.

'Not far! Five minutes!' Her nervous horse was wheeling and snorting, difficult to control.

'You think we'll make it?'

'Better to make it than to be caught out here in the scrub!'

'All right!' He disappeared again to her left and they continued to heckle the sheep, pushing them towards the fire.

Dozens of small animals ran towards them and birds screeched overhead, heading south in the lee of the smoke. They were almost there. Kate could see where the gully dropped away suddenly ahead of them.

She galloped towards the left, calling to the shepherds as she went: 'Drive them east! To the edge of the plain! We'll take them into the gully at the shallow end! Drive them east!'

She could just make out Rory to her right, galloping around and up the side of the flock, forcing them to turn and to head east, parallel to the gully.

They worked together, turning them, heading them round while the shepherds prevented them from bolting south, back the way they had come, away from the smoke.

The smoke was thickening, reducing visibility to no more than a couple of hundred yards.

'Move 'em faster!' Kate shouted out. 'The fire is almost here!' Her voice was whipped away in the wind and lost in the roar of the fire. The sounds of sheep bleating, birds screeching and men shouting added to the atmosphere of chaos and panic.

'Faster! Move 'em!' she screamed. The sheep were running now, panicking, but at least moving in the right direction.

It was then that she caught sight of a red shirt through the smoke. Craig's red flannel shirt.

'Mother of God!' The awful realisation hit her.

He was driving the other flocks towards them, also parallel to the gully on this side! He must have had trouble turning them into the gully itself. He, too, was moving along the south side of his flock, stopping them from bolting away from the smoke. The flocks of frightened sheep were moving headlong towards each other, parallel to the chasm which lay across on their northern side. If they panicked they could turn to the north, disappear over the edge of that chasm and fall to their deaths! The shepherds, on foot in the blinding dust and smoke, were ignorant of the presence of the other flock and were preventing them from breaking away to the south.

'Head 'em round south,' she screamed. No one could hear her!

She spurred on her horse; racing alongside the chasm and taking off her hat she waved it in the air to both drive back the sheep and to attract the attention of the men.

'South! South! Head 'em south!'

Rory must have seen it too. He, too, was galloping, trying to place himself between the sheep and the chasm.

They were both yelling, galloping, cracking their whips, trying desperately to turn the sheep.

She saw the disaster unfolding before her eyes, the two flocks racing headlong towards each other, the hapless shepherds and dogs still ignorant of the danger, preventing the sheep from breaking out to the south.

The smoke cleared briefly. There was a moment's visibility and the shepherds saw the danger. But they were in no position to turn the sheep. Both flocks were panicking, running towards each other. Craig was trying to turn them from his end.

'You stupid bloody sheep! The other way!' Kate screamed at them, but they ran head-on into the others.

They turned to the north. Those behind followed their leaders.

'Kathleen! Out of their way!' Rory called to her.

She pulled her horse back just in time. They watched in horror as the sheep plunged over the edge of the chasm.

'Oh Jesus! You stupid damned sheep! Stop!' Kate screamed at them.

But she was helpless to stop the destruction. The rest followed those in front, blindly, unthinking, on and on until all sheep save a few had disappeared over the edge.

Kate and Rory slid to the ground and led their horses to the edge of the chasm. The sheep lay in a miserable pile. Those underneath had been suffocated by those on the top. Some of them were still twitching and moving. Some were bleating piteously, a mass of broken bones.

The shepherds came up to the edge too.

'God, Miss Kate,' Craig panted, his voice hoarse and breaking with strain, 'I'm so sorry. I should have known you would be bringing them this way.'

'No, Craig, it's not your fault. It's mine. I'm the one who should have thought ahead.'

'We should finish them off,' one of the others said.

Kate just stood there, staring down at the catastrophe, her eyes streaming from the smoke.

'No time for that!' Rory shouted above the increasing roar of the flames. The fire was on the other side of the gully and sparks had jumped across, lighting the grass around them. 'Get into the gully! Save yourselves!'

The shepherds ran ahead of them.

Rory grabbed the reins of both horses. 'Come on, Kathleen! It's too late for those poor beasts. Which way into the gully?'

Kate led the way, running, as Rory pulled the horses behind him. They were stubborn, frightened of the smoke and the heat. He stopped to place the wet sacks, which they had carried with them, over the horses' heads.

The fire was now well across the gully at the eastern end and Kate could see it racing across the plain ahead of them, ripping across grasses left dry by the scorching summer sun. The air was thick with debris and smoke. Their lungs heaved and their eyes streamed.

They would not get to the end of the gully where the shallow entrance allowed easier access.

'We'll have to get down here!' she called to Rory.

He handed over the reins of her horse, rubbed his eyes with the back of his hand and started down the steep slope. Kate followed behind him, not too close, in case she started an avalanche, but nor did she tarry. The fire was close at hand, the scorching wind buffeting them from all directions, the air almost too hot to breathe.

They got the horses down.

'This way!' Kate screamed.

She ran along the gully floor, stumbling over rocks and dead branches, splashing through shallow pools.

'There's a cavern up ahead.'

Each ragged breath sent a searing pain through her chest. She looked behind, Rory was still following her. The others must have taken cover under the shallower rock ledges. But there was no room there for the horses.

They were gasping now, breathless, desperate for the oxygen sucked by the savage flames on the plain above them.

Finally, there was the cavern, the one she had come to that day when Arranyinha had shown her this place. They led the horses over the rocky ledge that formed the entrance. The welcome cool of the cavern hit them as they entered.

Rory fixed the sacks more securely over the horses' heads and led them further into the cavern, their backs to the entrance. There was an old log, probably used as a seat by some previous occupant. They tethered the reins to the log. Rory pulled the wet blanket from the back of Kate's horse.

By now the roar of the fire outside was thunderous. Charred leaves and twigs were swirling into the cavern, the heat of the air was ferocious. Kate's eyes were streaming, her cheeks and lips hot and burning.

Rory took her arm. 'Lie down, Kathleen!'

She lay face down on the rock floor, away from the horses, and breathed the cooler, fresher air from close to the floor. Rory lay down beside her and put his arm over her back.

'No matter what happens, keep still,' he rasped. 'Stay here.'

They lifted their heads to see what was happening. The gully itself was filled with fire, a wall of flames leapt and danced at the mouth of the cavern.

The fire seemed to reach out to scorch their hands and faces. Rory brought the wet blanket over their heads. They held the blanket close around them to keep out the searing heat of the air they had to breathe.

They panted for air, sharing what little there was under the blanket, breathing each other's dampened breath.

The noise was deafening. Close by, the horses neighed and shifted uneasily, frightened.

To Kate it seemed as though the breath was sucked right out of her lungs. They battled to expand and inhale. She and Rory clung to each other, panting, breathless, for what seemed like an eternity.

Then the roar was over. The fire had destroyed all in its wake and it had passed on, down across the plain towards the homestead.

'The homestead! Brigid!' Kate started to move.

Rory strengthened his hold on her. 'Stay still, you fool. There's nothing we can do for anyone else now. You can't overtake the fire without being caught yourself. Every inch of soil will be glowing hot like coals, the trees will be on fire, crashing to the ground with no warning. Anyone out there now is on their own.'

Kate gave in. She lay still, worrying about the others, but savouring the security of his arms around her.

'Just thank God that we are safe ourselves, my Kathleen,' he murmured in her ear.

'Thank God indeed,' she murmured, and rolled closer to him.

His arm came right around her. It was then that she noticed how her heart was hammering. Had it been beating like this all along?

She could feel his heartbeat racing too. Her breath came in curious, anguished gasps that bore no relation to the fire passing overhead and down across the plain.

His hands began to travel over her, igniting the fire in her veins, inflaming the passion that lay there, a spark to tinder. And then there was no turning back. The feelings, denied for fifteen years, long smouldering, flared to sudden life.

His lips came down onto hers, claiming her, rekindling the needs she had suppressed for so long. His tongue nudged her mouth where her lips came together and she opened up to him as he probed deeper. Her tongue entwined with his and she explored the once well-known territory of the hot depths of his mouth.

Their bodies came together as if an invisible magnet pulled them inexorably closer. Kate felt her heart beating hard and painfully against his chest. Her heart yearned for more of him. Her body yearned for more of him. She rubbed her breasts against his chest, feeling the sparks course through her. She loved him and it was as if the rest of the world ceased to exist for her. They were caught in a searing maelstrom of desperate, devastating need; urgent and compelling, a need that must be expressed.

Her arms came up around his neck and their bodies pushed against each other, yearning for the closeness they had once known, yearning once more to be one.

Rory twitched the blanket from their heads and they breathed the hot, smoky air. He rolled on top of her, covering her body with his own, claiming her, devouring her with his lips.

'Oh, Rory! Oh, God! How I've wanted you for so long,' Kate gasped, between kisses, running her hands down over his muscled back.

He rolled her over on top of him. His hands came up to the buttons on her shirt. Her hands were at the fastening of his trousers. There was no finesse in their movements, no patience.

Fire raged between them, sucking the breath from their bodies, searing over their skin, flaring through the core of their bodies. They were both slick with sweat, salty and smoky. She guided him to her, easing herself down upon him.

And she was transported back to their earlier days, the smoke of the campfire in their nostrils, the blackness of the wide night sky. Her body responded to his as if they had never been parted, as if it had held the memory of his body, waiting again for the bliss of that all-destroying fire to consume her once more.

They rocked together, the firestorm between them raging more powerfully than the one outside that rushed headlong and forgotten towards the homestead.

The passion reached its explosive, shattering peak and the fire consumed them totally.

Kate let herself down onto his body, her head on his chest, and he rolled to the side, cradling her in his arms.

Neither of them spoke. Each savoured the heat of the afterglow, and revelled in the devastating completeness of their release.

For a few moments they were silent.

'Why did we do it?' Kate asked.

Rory let out a short laugh. 'It was beyond our control, my darlin'. You can't keep something like that damped down for ever.'

'No, I meant, why did we ever stop loving?'

'It was your decision, as I recall,' he said, his tone dry.

'Yes, I know. You should never have respected my wishes!'

'You would have put up a pretty strong defence.'

'Oh, God, Rory! What are we going to do? What about Brigid?' She had betrayed her best friend!

'Listen, Kate. There's nothing we can do about anyone else right now. Let us just ignore the rest of the world. We are stuck here for the time being. Let us just enjoy this time together. Soon we will be back out there, trying to clean up the mess. And you will never have seen such a mess in your life before, I can guarantee you. It will be months of hard work.'

'It isn't exactly what I meant.'

'I don't care what you meant. Just leave those decisions, whatever they are, until then.'

He disentangled himself from her arms. 'I'm hungry and thirsty, I don't know about you. Let's hope some of our supplies are still tied on to the horses.'

'Should we get water for the horses? They must be thirsty too.'

'I don't think we should take them outside. It will be like a furnace out there for some time.'

The supplies were still there. Rory poured some of the water into his hat to give to the horses. The rest he brought with him and, sitting with his back to the entrance of the cavern as if to shut out the outside world, he and Kate shared their supplies of bread, meat and water.

Replete, they lay on the cooling floor of the cave.

At the touch of his hand Kate felt her body quicken to life once more . . .

It was dark when she woke. She felt around her and found Rory.

'It's too late to go anywhere now,' he said, and he pulled her into his arms again.

Patrick laid the saddle on a patch of cool sand in the creek bed. The fire had been fickle. This small area of scrub had not been burnt.

'Lie down here, Mr Carmichael,' he said, his hand guiding the older man, helping him lay his head on the saddle.

'Now, stay here. Don't touch your face or your eyes. You'll only make it worse. There's a pool of water within sight. I'll wet my handkerchief, ready to place on the burns for you.'

He came back with the handkerchief dripping wet. 'Here, I'm placing it on now,' he said.

James winced as the boy touched his face, but the cool of the wet cloth brought immediate relief.

Patrick filled his hat with water. He took the handkerchief off and soaked it again before replacing it.

'What happened, lad? We were riding together one moment, the next thing I knew I was over my horse and you were leading me through the burnt scrub.' His voice was ragged as he struggled to endure the pain.

'We were on our way from Wildowie to Elatina. I was to show you where to bring the sheep, remember that?'

'Yes, I do remember that. Go on.'

'We didn't see the fire coming at first, but when we did, we decided to race for Elatina to give what help we could—'

'Yes, yes.'

'The fire was patchy. Some of the scrub had been left untouched, other areas were only just singed. We heard an almighty crack and you looked up. It was a burning branch falling from a tree. I called out to warn you but it was too late, the branch caught you in the face and knocked you off your horse.'

'Is that what happened? Is that why my face is so painful?'

'It's burnt badly.'

'I can feel it. What then?'

'My horse bolted as soon as I went to your aid. You were knocked out, but I couldn't leave you there in case the fire came back on itself. I put you over your horse and led us to this creek. I think we'll be safe here, even if the fire returns. We're surrounded by great flat boulders, there's nothing to burn and there seems to be enough water for our needs.'

'Good lad.'

Patrick soaked the cloth again.

'I can't seem to open my eyes,' said James, trying to struggle up.

'Just lie there,' Patrick told him, pushing him down again.

'But I can't open them,' he said. 'Can't see a damned thing!'

'Your eyelids and the flesh around your eyes is swollen,' Patrick told him. 'Don't even try.'

Patrick knew more than he was prepared to say. There was a good chance that James would never see again.

'It's dreadfully painful, lad.'

'It must be. You're bearing up well, though.'

'What will we do now?'

'There's not much we can do,' Patrick replied. 'It is no use trying to get through to Elatina homestead now. Not with only one horse. There's no telling which direction the fire is heading. We are better off staying put. Wait for the danger to pass. They may come looking for us.'

'I'm in your hands, lad.'

'I'll look after you, Mr Carmichael, don't worry.'

Patrick took James's hand. 'Now here is the water; feel it?'

'Yes.'

'Good. When the cloth gets too warm, dip it in again and put it back on your face.'

'What are you doing?' There was an edge of fear in his voice.

'I'm going off to look for some special plants.

They can be used to soothe and heal the burns.'

James's arm shot out, his hand found and grasped the fabric of Patrick's shirt.

'What is it?' Patrick asked.

James released him and lay back. 'Nothing . . . Don't go too far, will you?'

'No, I won't go out of earshot. If I don't find what I'm looking for I'll come back.'

Patrick found the right type of eucalypt tree. The precious gum that he wanted oozed copiously from the trunk. The herb that would help the healing process was harder to find. From time to time he circled back to James to re-soak the cloth and to give him water.

He found the herb at sunset.

He did not light a fire. The night was hot and smoky enough without it. Besides, any extra heat on James's face would have been unbearably painful.

He set about his work while the light faded around him. He chose a smooth, flat rock which he used as a table. With another rock, he ground the gum and mixed it with water. The herb was mashed and mixed with water too.

Before he applied them, he would give James some food. He wanted him to lie still once the ointments had been applied.

'Mr Carmichael, I have something for you to eat. I've crushed it up so that you needn't chew too much. It would make your face too sore.'

'Thanks, lad.'

'Here, I'm putting some in your mouth.'

James accepted the food, chewing it just a little and swallowing before opening his mouth for the next mouthful.

'What is it?'

'Lerp,' Patrick replied.

James spat and tried to sit up, 'What?'

'Lerp, Mr Carmichael.'

'Haven't you got anything else?'

'Sure. Some minga nguri, some grass seeds . . .'

'What are you trying to do, boy? Poison me?'

'No, feed you.'

'Well I don't want any. You wouldn't know what that stuff might do to you.'

'It is all food. There is no other. I was not carrying any food supplies with me when I came to Wildowie this morning.'

'Well, you can eat it if you want. I'd rather go hungry.'

Patrick shrugged and said, 'Up to you, sir.' He began to eat the food he had collected.

'How do you know about all that?'

'The Yuras taught me.'

'The who?'

'The Yuras. The blacks.'

'Your mother has always been pretty friendly with them, I hear.'

'I was raised by them,' Patrick replied.

'Pardon?'

'Raised by them. First two years of my life. Always been close to them since.'

'Well, well,' said James. 'I heard rumours but I have never believed them.'

'There you have it,' Patrick replied. 'They taught me bushcraft. They taught me bush medicine too. I've made up two preparations for your burns. One for soothing, the other for healing.'

'I'd rather you didn't use them.'

Patrick sighed. He waited for a moment before continuing. 'Mr Carmichael. There's something I have to tell you about your burns. I think it is very likely that your sight will be affected. It is not just the swelling that is preventing you from seeing. The eyes themselves are burnt, I think. And your face is quite badly burnt too. The sooner the burn is soothed, the sooner the healing process starts and the less scarring there will be.'

There was a moment of silence while James digested the unpalatable news.

'Why did you not say so before?'

'I didn't want to make you more worried. If you don't trust these remedies, fine, that is the way it is. I won't put them on, but you are taking a risk. You may well be partially blinded and the scarring may disfigure you. It is up to you to decide.'

James lifted the handkerchief and felt gingerly with his fingers, wincing with pain as he traced the contours of the burnt flesh.

He then lay still, silent.

'Are you all right, sir?'

'Yes, boy, I am. Do your worst. Put your heathen potions on me. I have no choice.'

'Will you eat any more first?'

'No, thanks anyway, sonny.' His voice throbbed with an emotion that baffled Patrick. There was something there, something unspoken, something about the way he emphasised the word 'sonny'.

Patrick washed his hands. He used the gum infusion first, washing the burnt skin with it.

'That is very cooling,' James murmured.

'Yes, it soothes well.'

Patrick continued to dribble the infusion over the burnt skin until there was none left.

Then he scraped the herb paste off the rock with his pocket knife. He scooped it up with his finger and smeared it as gently as he could onto James's face.

'There, that's done. Don't move now. Let it sit there for as long as you can. I can make up some more in the morning.'

The treatments seemed to have soothed his pain. Patrick could see the tension easing.

'Patrick?'

'Yes?'

'Do you know who I am?'

'Of course I do,' said Patrick, somewhat baffled, 'You're James Carmichael, of Wildowie Station.'

'Has your mother never told you more than that?'

'No. I've always had my suspicions that there was something she wasn't telling me.'

'Haven't you ever wondered who your father was?'

'Yes, often. But every time I broach the subject, Mother shies away from it, so I've learnt not to ask. She'll tell me one day, I know.'

'No one else has even hinted? The Yuras, Sid, any of the others?'

'No.'

'She must have sworn them all to secrecy then.'

'Your guess is as good as mine, I would think.'

'So . . .' he paused, considering his words. 'You don't know that I am your father?'

Patrick jumped as if a gun had fired close by. 'What?'

'I am your father.'

'How can it be? Why have I never been told?' The questions tumbled through his mind one after another.

He now had the last piece of the jigsaw in his hand, the piece that made sense of the rest of the picture. The rivalry between the stations, his mother's bitterness, the veiled references to James Carmichael . . . could this explain it all?

'Well, you will have to ask your mother her side of the story, but this is how I saw it,' James began.

Chapter
Twenty-One

When Kate awoke at first light she heard the sound that they had waited for for so long—the patter of heavy raindrops on the hot, parched earth.

She lifted Rory's arm off herself, rolled away from him, dressed and made her way out of the cavern.

The smell was one that she would never forget. Everything was burnt and much of it was smouldering still. The rain was falling on the hot, dry ash. Its sickening stench was an assault on her senses.

She made her way along the gully to a place where she could climb up the walls without difficulty.

It was a bleak and desolate spectacle that greeted her. The entire landscape was black, with grey circles of ash where bushes had once grown. The trees, or what was left of them, were like charred skeletons: twisted, distorted, deformed, their limbs bare and smoking. Several sheep and a number of bush animals lay amongst the devastation, their bodies charred and bloated. It was the ugliest sight she had ever seen.

Raindrops continued to fall, intermittently, heavily, splashing against her warm skin and sizzling on the hot rock and earth. The rain had come just a day too late. She sat down on an ash-covered rock, still warm, and dropped her head into her hands. God almighty, what had she done?

It was here that Rory found her some time later.

'Kathleen, what are you doing out here?'

She looked up at him through a film of tears.

He drew her up into his arms and she clung to him as if he were the only great river gum left in a desert of shifting sands. Tears seeped through her closed eyelids.

'Kathleen,' he said. 'It looks worse than it is. The fire may have left some parts of Elatina untouched. Some of the other flocks may have survived and those that didn't can be replaced.'

'No,' Kate said, her voice muffled against his chest.

'Yes, I say. It's not over. Not yet. You'll build it up again. This rain will bring the bush back to life in no time. It will spring new green growth within weeks. It will heal itself, just wait and see.'

'No, Rory—'

He interrupted her, stroking her back with his great strong hands, 'Yes. Sure you feel dispirited now. But wait for tomorrow, you'll bounce back. You always have. You can build it again.'

'It isn't that. I'm finished with Elatina—'

'Elatina is nowhere near finished and there is Wildowie too.'

She stopped, raised her head, and looked up through her tears to his eyes, 'Pardon?'

'Elatina might be burnt, but Wildowie probably survived the fire!' His eyes were glittering, exultant, as if he was about to deliver the master stroke.

'So what?'

'Kathleen,' he said, sitting down on the rock and pulling her down next to him. His arm around her shoulders, he drew her to his side.

'I wanted to tell you soon,' he said, 'but I never thought it would be under circumstances like these.'

'Tell me what?' she dashed the tears from her face with the back of her hand.

'I own more than half of Wildowie. I'll make a deal with James to give half of it now, with stock, to you and Patrick, to help you get on your feet again.'

'What are you talking about?'

He told her the story of how he had come to acquire a half share in Wildowie.

'James approached me when you had turned him down.'

'You knew that I had been seeing him?'

'Yes, but I didn't say anything to you. He'd always been a sore point between us, hadn't he? And I wanted you to forget all about him. Anyway, James was desperate by then. If he didn't lay his hands on the money soon he would be out of the land grab. He had to agree to my conditions.'

'And what were they?'

'That my interest would never be disclosed to anyone, especially you, and that we would have joint control over Wildowie and any future developments that might affect it.'

'But he didn't agree to those conditions when I laid them out before him!'

'Yes, but you were out for his blood, and he knew it. Whereas he assumed I was much more naive and had no ulterior motive.'

'And did you have an ulterior motive? You always said you would not put your money into wool, that the Far North was risky—seven years drought and all of that. It's not like you ever really wanted to settle down or become a squatter yourself.'

'I did it for only one reason. Your good self, Kathleen.'

She waited expectantly while he chose the words carefully. 'I knew you would not rest until you had what you believed was true security. I knew that you'd never get James out of your head until Patrick had his inheritance assured. So I decided to get it for you.'

The rest was left unsaid, but she could work that out for herself. 'Oh, Rory!'

'Yes, I'm a soft-hearted fool, I know. And of course it was one of the reasons I came up here. I had been waiting for the chance to buy James out. I felt sure he would find himself in financial strife sooner or later. But he's been a better manager than I counted on. When the drought came, I figured it might break him. So I came up, hoping to see him and to make the ultimate offer. But as it is, other events overtook us.'

'Did you know he'd tried to break me, using your money to buy up the land around Barcowie?'

'No, on that count I was ignorant. But I suspect that you have been as bad as each other.'

She nodded ruefully. 'You're right. But then, why did you not support me when he came for help?'

'I was caught in a bind. Ethically I couldn't approve of your response, even though his loss would have ultimately been my gain. In some ways I would have been happy to lose the sheep in order to get full control over Wildowie. But I couldn't support his view either and if I put pressure on him to accept your conditions, then there would have been no chance for us two to get together again.'

'What a pickle I've landed us all in.'

'You've led us all a merry dance for sixteen years, my darlin'. But there it is, half of Wildowie, if not the lot. It's there for you and

Patrick. You can start again, and Elatina will be as grand as you might ever have hoped.'

Kate tried to digest the news for a moment. 'I don't know what to say. I suppose I should thank you for doing that for me. Had all of this not happened,' she said, indicating the annihilated landscape surrounding them, 'then I would have been thrilled. It would have been just one more feather in my cap. One more triumph over James Carmichael. But, to be honest, I don't think I care any more. It's too late for all that.'

'Too late? What do you mean?'

'Oh, Rory, I realised it this morning, lying in your arms, looking at your sleeping face. I've been a fool.'

'No—'

'Yes! Poor Brigid! And the others, if they are still alive. And Patrick. And poor selfish James, for that matter.'

She searched his face, her eyes troubled.

Rory turned, tilting her chin so that he could look down into her eyes.

'Tell me. What is it? I thought my news would make you the happiest woman on earth. I've waited fifteen years to break it to you.'

'Oh, Rory, what a fool I have been! I realised it this morning. None of this really matters in the end! And it has taken me so long to work it out. Lying there, next to you, this station was the last thing on my mind. I wondered why on earth I had not woken up in your arms every morning for the last sixteen years. Why had I wasted all those years when I could have been as happy as I have been in the last twelve hours. I love you so much. And I cast you aside for this, for this . . . this stupid obsession. This worthless, stupid obsession.'

His arms surrounded her, tightening around her. 'It's not too late!'

'No, maybe this is the one thing that can be salvaged from the fire. But I've lost so much else!'

'What have you lost?'

'All sorts of chances. To think that even yesterday I was telling everyone that the sheep were the most important thing to be saved from the fire. I did not even chase after my own son! I did not ensure that he was protected first! I did not look after the men, or you or Brigid! I did not spare a thought for the Yuras. Do you realise that any of them may have perished while I was busy protecting those stupid, worthless, damned sheep!'

'The others know how to look after themselves. With a bit of luck they may all be safe, too!'

'I pray to God in his mercy that they are safe. If only I had not been hell-bent on revenge against James, my son may have come to know his father. James may have helped out. We could have supported each other. Sure, James is a selfish man, but maybe I'm just as selfish and that is at the root of all our disagreements!'

'It's easy to be wise when you look back.'

'You saw it then, though, didn't you? You tried to tell me. But the stubborn woman that I am, I didn't listen. And now I've done one of the worst things I could ever have done. What a turn to serve my oldest, most loyal friend!'

'Eh?'

'Brigid!'

'What about her?'

'Betraying her with you!'

'Explain yourself, will you?'

'Lying in your arms when I knew you were almost promised to her!'

Rory tipped his head back and laughed, a deep guttural laugh that carried loudly through the damp, smoky stillness.

'What are you laughing at?'

'Oh, Kathleen, where did you get that idea from?'

'I saw the two of you, together on the verandah, Brigid's arm on your shoulder. The way you both started when you saw me made me feel sure of it. Besides, why else did you come up together to see me? You said you had some news to tell me, I thought that was it!'

Rory laughed again.

'Rory! Stop laughing! I thought you'd given up on me. And there was Brigid always telling me what a good man I'd let go!'

'Oh, Kathleen, it couldn't have worked better if I'd planned it that way.' He jumped up and pulled her with him. 'Oh you're a wonderful woman. And you've given the game away now completely. I won't be letting go of you, regardless of the fight you'll be putting up.' He took her in a fierce bear hug, almost squeezing the breath from her body.

Kate laughed with the breath she had left and gasped, 'I give in now!'

'The day that you give up on anything will be the day we lay you out, my darlin'!' Rory hugged her again. 'Well now, we'd better get back before they do come searching for our corpses.'

'Just one thing?'

'Yes?'

'What were you and Brigid talking about that morning, then?'

'James, you, me, Elatina, Wildowie—the whole bloody tumbleweed we've blown around in for the last sixteen years.'

Chapter

Twenty-Two

'Kate! Kate! It's Patrick! Where are you? Patrick is back!' Brigid's voice rang out through the high-ceilinged rooms of the homestead.

Kate ran from her room, still doing up her buttons, her feet bare and her wet hair dripping down her back.

There was Patrick—dusty, dirty, damp, his clothes crumpled, his hair thick with ash, leading a horse. She had no time to take in the presence of the tall, slim figure sitting passively on the back of the horse, his head wrapped in strips of shirt fabric.

She launched herself at her son and flung her arms about his chest. 'Oh, Patrick, my darling boy, I was so worried for you!'

'I'm fine, Mother,' Patrick replied. 'It was just that it was slow getting back on foot. What about you? You're all right?'

'Fine, fine.'

'Everyone else?'

'We all survived it, praise be to God!'

'The Yuras?'

'Fine. They've been through bushfires before. They knew what to do.'

'Good. Then help me get Father inside.'

Kate jerked. Father! She turned to the figure on the horse. She would have recognised that long, slim torso anywhere. But she had never seen the shoulders slumped before, the whole body sagging, resigned. The all-too-familiar arrogance entirely absent.

'James!'

'Yes, Kate, it's James. Help me down, someone, would you?'

Kate stood immobilised. What had happened to him? And what had gone on between them that her son now called him Father?

Brigid had been standing back, evidently not wishing to intrude. She stepped forward. 'Mr Carmichael. It's Brigid. Take my hand,' she reached up to grasp the long, slender hand in her own.

Kate shook herself mentally and stepped forward to help him. She would have to think about that later. Patrick was there before her, grasping James's arm, supporting him as he dismounted.

'What has happened?' Kate asked Patrick.

'He's been burnt on the face, badly.'

'Mother of Mary! Bring him inside, my bedroom will do.'

She led the way, opening the doors, as James limped inside, Brigid holding one hand, his other arm linked with his son's.

Brigid turned him with his back to the bed. 'Here, sit down,' she said.

'We're covered in ash and dirt. Mother, do you want to put an old sheet or something down first?'

'What does the bed matter?'

'It's that beautiful spread you've always protected!'

'Rubbish, it's not important. Lie down, James. Patrick, you too, sit down. You look exhausted.'

Patrick eased his father back towards the bed. Kate laid him back gently against the pillows.

'Brigid, could you ask Mary to find my medical kit and bring some bowls of clean water and bandages? Then she can get some drinks and a plate of sandwiches.'

'Sure,' Brigid said and moved quickly but quietly from the room.

'James, I'll do what I can for your burns. As you know, we are several days' ride from the doctor at Clare. I see no point in sending for him at this stage, unless you want me to. I'll do my best for you.'

'Thank you. I trust you.'

'I don't know why you should,' she said, with irony in her voice.

'I've seen you in action before,' he said, his tone terse. He was in pain.

Yes, she had acted nurse many times before,

Harold's spear wound being the most memorable.

She and Patrick began to make James more comfortable, first by removing his boots. She turned to Patrick. 'What happened? Where have you been? Rory and some of the Yuras are out looking for you. I've been so worried!'

James was silent. Only Patrick answered her questions.

'We got caught in the fire on the way back from Wildowie yesterday. A great thick burning branch fell on James. Knocked him unconscious and burnt his face. My horse bolted when I went to help him. I found a small waterhole in an unburnt patch of scrub and we stayed there overnight. It has been a slow trip home with only one horse, and me on foot leading the way.'

'Your horse arrived back here last night. By the time I arrived back from Secret Gully this morning Brigid had begun to think the worst. When you hadn't arrived by lunchtime we sent out a search party with the Yuras as trackers.'

'You should know that I can look after myself in the bush, Mother.'

'Of course, if you were alive and well. But we were worried.'

'So, looks like Elatina got through unscathed,' he said, brushing aside her concern for him.

'Everyone's alive. That's the main thing. And we're lucky enough to have the homestead intact, thanks to Brigid.'

'The Yuras? You're sure they're all right?'

'All fine, they knew what to do.'

'The rest of the property? The stock?'

'That's another story. Ah, here's Brigid.'

'Here, Kate. Towels, clean sheets and your kit. Mary will bring the water in a moment. She's cooling the water from the kettle.'

'Thanks. Let me go and wash my hands.'

When she returned to the bedroom Brigid and Patrick had covered the bed with an old sheet.

Kate used one of the sheets to cover James's chest and neck.

'Tell me if I am hurting you too much,' Kate said as she began to unwind the makeshift bandage.

'I will.'

Brigid held his head as Kate unwound the bandage. James winced a little as the fabric came away, bit by bit, from the burnt skin.

God Almighty! Kate bit back the words that rose to her tongue as the burnt flesh appeared. What an awful mess. What she had uncovered was red and raw, like fresh meat, swollen and charred. Her stomach turned as she looked at it. She looked up at Brigid.

There was no need for words. The silent message passed between them. It was a ghastly burn. And it had been only partly revealed. It was already evident that his handsome features had been destroyed.

Kate dropped her head to continue her task of gently removing the fabric where it had stuck to the weeping skin. Her fingers were slender and nimble.

Brigid took James's hand in her own. 'You're doing well, Mr Carmichael. Grip my hand if it helps you to bear it.'

He murmured in response and his hand tightened. Brigid placed her other hand on his brow where the blond hair flowed back from his forehead.

Finally the cloth was removed. Kate looked in dismay at the damage. Patrick did not have to tell her. She knew that James would probably never see again.

She mixed some salt in one of the bowls of water and began to dab his face gently, cleaning away the ooze and the ointments applied by Patrick. Loose pieces of charred skin came away as she washed. She knew that if it wasn't clean enough that infection, the greatest risk, might set in.

It was as clean as she dared make it without causing him too much pain. She stopped, looking at that once-handsome, smooth face, and her eyes filled slowly with tears. No one, no matter what they had done, deserved this.

She remembered what it had been like to touch that face all those years ago when she had made love with him. The sophistication, the arrogance, the desire in his eyes when he had bedded her. She remembered the warmth that his passion had brought to the grey irises, like ash still warm and glowing in the campfire, the hardness of grey shale when he was angry, the cold steel of his disdain. She would rather see any of those than to be confronted by this distorted, raw, oozing mess in front of her eyes.

The tears formed into drops and spilt over her lower lids to roll noiselessly down her face. Compassion washed away the bitterness that had once waited, like a malicious seed of vengeance, for the moment to burst open and grow.

No one said a word. Brigid and Patrick waited for her to continue with her task. She looked up. Brigid's eyes had filled with tears, too.

'Well,' James's voice came out croaky, 'what is the prognosis?'

Kate held Brigid's eyes with her own, willing her to say something. She knew that if she spoke James would hear the pity in her voice.

'Well, Kate? What do you say?' he asked again.

She could not respond.

'Too busy gloating?'

His words cut her to the quick.

His dirty hand came up to touch his face.

'No,' Kate knocked it away. 'Don't touch it. You don't want to . . .' she paused as her voice broke. 'You don't want to get the burn infected.' She had given herself away. He had heard the sounds of distress and her thickened voice.

The same hand that had tried to touch the wound came up to find her face and his fingers felt the wetness there. 'I never thought you would cry for me, my dear.'

'I'm not inhuman, James.'

She took his hand in her own. Brigid had the other. The silence stretched away. The tick of the bedside clock seemed suddenly louder.

'It is bad, then.'

'It is, James. I'm sorry. You will be fortunate if you regain your sight. Your face will be scarred. I'm sorry. Very sorry.'

There was a moment of silence.

'We'll look after you, though, Mr Carmichael, for as long as you need us.' Brigid's soft brogue broke the tension. 'Don't be worrying about a thing. We'll get the doctor up from Clare. There may be something he can do.'

Kate continued her task until the loose skin had been removed and the remainder was clean. She covered his face with a light, clean bandage once more and then sat down while Brigid took over.

James said nothing, but they all knew, from his tight silence, that the fire burnt on in the blistered flesh. Brigid fanned his hot face. When he began to fidget and twitch she read to him, drawing his attention away from the pain.

'Patrick, come with me, you look exhausted,' Kate said, rising from where she sat. She was conscious that she and Patrick had things to discuss.

She led him through to the cool, dark dining room. 'Sit here, I'll get you some lunch, and you can tell me what happened after you've eaten.' He slumped down onto a dining chair and rubbed his hands across his eyes.

She returned moments later with some fresh

sandwiches and cake. 'Start eating while I get you some tea.'

She let him take a few gulps of the tea to wash down the food before she began to tell him the story of what had happened at Elatina Station during the fire. When he finished his lunch it was his turn to tell her what had happened to him and James Carmichael.

He eventually arrived at the inevitable question, the one Kate had been preparing herself for ever since she had heard Patrick call James 'Father'.

'Why have you never told me, Mother?'

Kate paused. It was long enough for Patrick to think that he must press her.

'Don't you think I had a right to know? Didn't you think you had a responsibility to tell me?' His eyes were like granite, hardened by a maturity that had come too quickly for him.

'Don't judge me too hastily, Patrick. Hear me out. You've heard James's side of the story, evidently. Now listen to mine.'

Patrick eased his chair out from the table and leaned back, waiting.

Kate started haltingly, for it was a story that had been a long time coming . . .

She had tried not to paint too black a picture of James. He had behaved like a thorough scoundrel towards her, but as she had come to realise in the immediate aftermath of the fire, she must also take responsibility for some of the bad feeling between them.

'It's not a matter of who did right, and who did wrong, Mother,' he interrupted her. 'You both played a role in what happened, as you say yourselves. The question is why no one told me.'

Kate sighed before she spoke. 'There were lots of reasons.'

'Yes?'

'I didn't want you to know that you were illegitimate.'

'Why not? As it was, I began to wonder if the problem was that you did not know who fathered me, or that maybe he was some utter derelict of a man.'

'Patrick!'

'Well, my imagination had to fill the gaps you left!'

'I hoped you wouldn't think about it too much.'

'I'm not stupid,' he muttered.

'No, I know that.' She thought for a moment about the most honest answer she could give. 'I suppose I didn't want to tell you because I didn't want to face the questions you would almost certainly ask. I didn't want to face my own feelings or own up to my share of the blame. I just kept putting it off.'

'You knew that it couldn't be avoided forever, surely.'

'Yes, I knew that. But part of me hoped that I could win James over and that, by the time you heard he was your father, he would be prepared to act like a father towards you.'

'It was more than that, too.'

'Sure it was. As much as I nurtured hope, I plotted revenge. I would have broken James if I had the chance. But then I wouldn't have wanted you to know who it really was who I'd wreaked my revenge upon.'

'But to leave it so long!'

'When you have children of your own, you will know just how quickly those years fly by.'

They sat looking at each other, not saying a word, for what seemed like minutes.

'I'm sorry, Patrick. I failed in my duty to you. There is no acceptable excuse for not telling you before now.'

Patrick sighed and rubbed his eyes. 'I accept your apology, Mother. I suppose I've learnt a valuable lesson in the last few days.'

'Yes?'

'One's parents are never perfect.' He shrugged and gave half a laugh.

Kate smiled grimly. 'None of us are perfect. None of us are right all of the time. We all have to learn that about ourselves.'

Rory and the Yuras were back by dinnertime, having tracked Patrick and James all the way back to Elatina. Sid had ridden back from Barcowie.

They took dinner in the dining room, since the sickening smell of wet ash and smouldering logs was still carried on the breeze outside. It was only James who did not join them for dinner.

Brigid, with her usual tact, had taken a tray to him so that he could eat dinner alone. His struggle to bring the food to his mouth would be unobserved by others.

The conversation revolved around the fire and its impact.

Half of the land that formed the Barcowie runs had been destroyed but most of the flocks had survived, thanks to the hard work of Sid, Craig, Robert and the other shepherds. There was enough feed to keep the Barcowie flocks going until the flush of new green followed the rain.

The fire had sped through Elatina from one end almost to the other. The growth had been higher in the valley than anywhere else and had fuelled a hot fire. Ironically, what had been their advantage two days ago had been their downfall on the day of the fire. Most of the scrub was burnt and the flocks destroyed. Fanned by the wind, the fire had changed direction when it had reached the southern part of the property, sparing the Yuras and their parcel of land. It had turned towards the west, cutting the track which led from Elatina to Wildowie and the main road. It had raced up the steep mountainsides which formed the boundary between the two properties and had died out there. Wildowie had been left untouched.

Kate spent much of the weeks that followed on the verandah, staring out across the ancient bent and buckled landscape, lost in contemplation, caught in her own Dreamtime. Part of her had perished during the fire—the restless, striving, ambitious part. In its place, the fire had forged a new strength in her, a new assurance, not built on the foundations of sheer determination, but on her acceptance of herself and others as they were, and the knowledge of what was important in life.

She talked a lot with Rory, about the missed years, and the years before they had met, the years of the famine. She talked about her family, the things she had done and the things she would do if she had her life over. And with the telling came a sense of peace, a reconciliation with all that had gone before.

She talked with James, too, about where they had gone wrong and what they would do if they had the time over. As for the future, they made no firm plans. There was a commitment to co-operation between the two stations. That was enough. Besides, James was in no position to take up the reins where he had left off.

Doctor McEvoy was unable to do any more for him. His sight could not be restored, but the doctor commended both Brigid and Kate on their nursing and took a great deal of interest in the Yura treatments. But that was all.

Patrick took it upon himself to ride over to Wildowie twice a week and to report back to James on the progress of the station. It, too, had received soaking rains, the creeks were flowing again and lush growth had sprung up across the land.

But James, like Kate, was not particularly concerned about Wildowie. With an overseer and Patrick to keep an eye on it, Wildowie would manage itself. He had other things on his mind. At Kate's invitation, he stayed on at Elatina. Brigid stayed at his side. She not only nursed him, she also helped him to learn the skills he needed to manage without his sight. She helped him to dress, to eat and a thousand other things. Her soft voice, endless patience and desire to help made her his preferred companion. She had a way of helping that did not cut across his sense of pride or his need for independence. She anticipated his every need.

Kate watched as the relationship between James and Brigid grew stronger and closer. She was struck by how much James had changed. He would once have spurned the company of a woman like Brigid, preferring his women beautiful and feisty, like Kate had been. But James was a different man. He had not only come close to dying, but he had also suffered a cruel and permanent injury. She was not sure whether it was one or both of those things that had caused him to re-evaluate himself, his life and his values. The arrogance was gone and in its place was a new warmth and humility. He was no longer concerned so much with his status but with his humanity. There was still a long way to go—a lot of grieving for what he had lost—and further recovery waiting to be made, but Brigid was there, supporting him at each step of the way.

'Mother?'

'Yes?' Kate looked up at her son from where she sat on the edge of the verandah, watching the afternoon sun stretching its dappled shadows to meet them across the new green of the grass.

'We need to make some plans. It is two months now since the fire.'

'What plans?'

'Elatina. We need to work out what we're going to do with the place now.'

Kate said nothing.

'I should leave you two to talk,' Rory said, uncoupling his hand from Kate's and standing up.

'No,' Patrick replied quickly, 'stay, you're part of this thing too. Well, Mother? What are you thinking?'

'I'm not really thinking anything, apart from how beautiful the afternoon sun looks, golden upon the land.' She laughed, 'I'm not much good to anyone these days, am I?'

Patrick sat down on the edge of the verandah. 'I can understand that,' he said, shrugging his slender shoulders. 'It's just that the men are coming to me for orders now. I don't know what you want me to tell them.'

'Tell them what you like,' Kate said, almost disinterestedly.

'What I like might not be what you like or what you want.'

'Maybe that is as it should be,' Rory said.

'He's right, Patrick. I had intended to hand it over to you soon anyway. I've controlled the place for long enough. Is it too soon for you? Am I expecting too much? You're only fifteen, I know. Maybe we should be asking Sid to take up the reins.'

'No, it's not too soon. I know what needs to be done to get the station back on its feet. Sid and I can work happily together on that. I've watched you for long enough to know how to run the place. It's just that I didn't want you to feel that I was taking over.'

Kate ruffled his hair. 'Well, you are taking over. That is how it should be. I don't seem to have the energy for it any more. I suppose I'm finally going to kick over the traces.'

'You'll be right in a couple more months, Mother. It's the shock of the fire still.'

'It's more than that. I've been doing a lot of thinking, a lot of reflecting. There's so much more to life than I've ever considered. Rory and I have been talking of going away. We've missed out on a lot by choosing the paths that we did. As you know, we go back a long time, before you were born. We want to make up for that. I want to live life free and easy while I can. Not strive. Not work. Just enjoy life. Taste the freedom that Rory has always talked about. The only way I can be sure of doing that is to leave here where the work and the demands will keep staring me in the face. So we're going to travel. Maybe go to the west, we're not sure where, and it really doesn't matter. I don't want to make too many plans right now. I've spent too much of my life making plans.'

Rory's mobile black eyebrow shot up, and he winked at Patrick. 'I've got plans, especially for your mother, but I won't be letting her in on those until we're on our very long-awaited honeymoon!'

Kate laughed.

'I'm sure you have, Uncle Rory,' Patrick laughed too. 'Or should I not call you "Uncle" any more?'

'You'll make me feel old if you call me Uncle now that you're a young man yourself, and I've never wanted you to call me "any more" either!'

Kate winced, 'Oh, Rory! Your jokes have not improved over the years!' She turned to her son, saying, 'Seriously, Patrick, I want you to come with us. It seems sometimes that I've spent so much time working and striving that I've never spent enough time with you, just enjoying your company. And we should all three of us spend time together now we're to be one family. Leave Elatina for Sid to look after for a while. Come with us. I want you to. We both want you to.'

Patrick picked a piece of dry grass and placed it on his lower lip.

It was a few moments before he replied. 'Well, Mother, I'd love to come. But I don't think I can.'

'Why not?'

'There's Elatina—'

'Elatina can look after itself, Sid will still be here.'

'I know that Sid is a good overseer. But that's not it. There's the Yuras as well. Someone has to remain here to ensure their claim to the land is upheld. You cannot seriously expect Sid to do that. He has no respect for them,' he held his hand up as Kate moved to interject, 'and it is more than that. I have a connection with this place and the people. My heart is here. The connection to land cannot be easily broken. Mawaanha can't have too many more months in him. Arranyinha is getting old too. She can't last forever. I want to keep an eye on them. My heart is here, Mother.'

'It doesn't mean that you can't ever leave.'

'No. But I can't leave now, while everything is so uncertain. And there is my father as well. I have a duty to him. To help him with Wildowie now that he's lost his sight.'

Kate was disconcerted. 'That is very commendable of you, I'm sure, and I won't stop you doing that if it's what you want to do. But be warned, I know him, he's a selfish man, underneath his new-found humility. I told you the story of what happened between us. I've forgiven him now. But you're better off to concentrate on Elatina. I doubt that Wildowie will ever be yours.'

Patrick looked her in the eye, his own eyes clear and grey like water in a still rockpool. 'It matters not if Wildowie comes to me. We have plenty . . .'

We have plenty. The words sent a strange shiver down her spine. They did have plenty, and it was her own Patrick who was saying it. Things had changed so much. She listened as he continued.

'But you should know that James has promised that I shall now be his son in every way, not only in terms of the inheritance. We have been close, ever since the fire.'

'I still find it hard to believe!'

'Well he has.'

'Well I wouldn't entirely trust that promise, if I were you.'

'I can only judge people on how I find them. I do trust him. People change, you know.'

Kate looked at him, the hot words of denial on the tip of her tongue, but she hesitated. *People change*. She had said those words herself. James had changed, so had she. It was just that her distrust of him was so ingrained.

There was a moment of silence.

'I still want you to come with us.'

Rory placed his broad brown hand on her slender one. 'The lad has grown up, my darlin'. He has changed too. He knows his own mind. You, too, have changed, no one would deny that. But there's one thing you still haven't learnt.'

'And what is that?'

'You can't be having it all.'

They had two visits to make before they left. The first was to the Yura camp.

The late afternoon sun slanted shafts of light through the trees. Smoke drifted from cooking fires. Dogs yapped and children screamed with delight as Kate and Rory entered the clearing.

Women were preparing the evening meal and some of the men, back from the hunt, were cleaning the firearms that Kate had given them. Many of them rose from their tasks to welcome them as they dismounted.

'Udnyuartu!' Arranyinha called, and Kate went to her old friend for a hug.

They sat around the campfire talking to the Yuras as the pale winter sun slipped down behind the hills. Kate told them that she and Rory were going away and that Patrick would be looking after the place while she was gone.

She apologised again that her ambition and her desire for revenge had jeopardised their control of the land, and they accepted her apology.

'I am about to ask you to make another decision about your land,' she said and she saw the wariness in their eyes.

'What decision?' Arranyinha asked.

'If you are in agreement, there is something that I want to do.'

'Yes?'

'I promised you fifteen years ago that I would try to save your land for you. I put some of my own aside, but that is not the same and it is not enough. I have more influence now than I used to. When I go to Adelaide, I'm going to see if I can have the title divided, and get your names put on the lease for Elatina Valley. It is not much land compared to what you once had, but there must be some way to do it. I'll do whatever it takes; start with the Surveyor-General's Office I suppose, put lawyers onto it, see the Governor if I have to. But I want to ensure it is yours legally. What do you think?'

Rory broke in before they had a chance to reply, 'We will try, but there can be no guarantee of success.'

'We understand that you will try,' said Mawaanha, 'and yes, you have our permission.' A spark of amusement, or maybe it was triumph, lit his eyes.

When Kate and Rory arrived at Wildowie neither Brigid nor James came out to greet them. It was no surprise, since the house was now sheltered by trees and could not be viewed from the road. James had returned to Wildowie a month ago. Brigid had gone with him, ostensibly to help him settle back into Wildowie again, but she had shown no sign of wanting to return to Elatina.

A young girl of mixed ancestry came to the door.

'They bin gone for a walk, Missus,' she told them. 'Come in, I'll fix you a drink.'

'No, we'll track them down. They can't have gone too far,' Kate replied.

Kate turned to Rory. 'It's a good opportunity to look over the place. It's hard to believe that it has been sixteen years since I was last here.' They stepped onto the path that led through the garden. 'We'll go up this way, there's a fantastic view from the hill, looking over towards the red gorge wall on the other side.'

Kate led him up through the orchards towards the place where she had sat her first day, and many times thereafter, looking over Wildowie. She remembered that she had suggested to James at the time that he place a garden seat there.

And there was a garden seat there. But someone was there before them. It was James and Brigid.

Kate and Rory stopped abruptly as they took in the scene before them. Kate felt her jaw drop. The father of her child and her best friend were locked in a close embrace. James was talking to Brigid, his hand trailing over her face. Brigid was leaning back against his chest, her head on his shoulder. She was looking up at him, absorbed, adoration written all over her face. They were oblivious of the rest of the world and evidently had no idea that visitors had arrived and were watching them now.

Kate and Rory looked at each other. Rory shrugged his shoulders. He took Kate's hand and they turned slowly and went back the way they had come.

'We wouldn't want to embarrass them, now, would we?' he said in a whisper. 'Let's try it again.'

'James! Brigid! Where are you?' he called as they made their way through the trees again.

Brigid had disentangled herself and had looked around. 'Kate! Rory!' She jumped up, pleased to see them, not a trace of self-consciousness in her manner.

In fact there was something new there, a new confidence in her bearing, a new spring in her step as she came to greet them. 'What a lovely surprise!' she exclaimed and kissed them both.

'How are you, James?' Rory said, extending his arm to clasp the shoulder of the man who was beginning to rise. 'Don't get up,' he said, shaking the hand that James had extended towards him.

James stood anyway and Kate kissed him lightly on the cheek. 'How are you, James?'

Times had changed. She could afford to be gracious now. They all sat down. Kate sat on the seat next to James, and Brigid sat on his other side. Rory lowered himself onto one of the boulders that had originally marked the place.

'What brings you over?' Brigid asked. 'We

weren't expecting you. If we had known you were visiting we would have had some cakes baked up.'

The use of 'we' was not lost on Kate. Brigid spoke for both of them.

'It's just a quick call and there's no need to go to any fuss on our behalf. We came to see how both of you were getting on and we wanted to let you know of our plans, since they might affect you, Brigid.'

'Oh?'

'Yes, Rory and I have decided to have a break. We'll be leaving in a couple of days and may not be back for some time.'

'Where are you going?' James asked.

'On a honeymoon. A good long one,' Rory replied. 'Wherever the fancy takes us.' He paused for a moment. 'Assuming we locate a priest in the meantime!' He laughed.

Kate laughed too. Travelling priests were still a rare commodity in the Far North. 'Adelaide first,' she added. 'We'll call on Harold Simpson, Mrs Applebee and a few others.'

'That will be nice for you, you need a break,' Brigid replied, smiling at Kate.

'Yes, we can leave Elatina in Patrick and Sid's hands,' Rory said.

'We thought we'd better find out whether you wanted to return with us, Brigid. Or whether James still needs you here to look after him. I trust she's been doing a good job?' Kate asked.

Smiles flashed between James and Brigid and their hands touched briefly, as if in assurance to each that the other was there. Kate was intrigued about how much further the relationship between them had developed.

'I don't know how I could have managed without her,' James replied. 'It was no easy thing to come back here and try to take up the reins again since the accident. She's taken over the books and paper work entirely, never mind all the day-to-day things . . .' his words trailed away.

'So, had we better whisk you away now or were you intending to stay on longer, Brigid?'

'I don't know that I could do without her right now,' James replied.

There was a moment of silence.

'Well, it seems then that you won't be going with us when we leave, so you're welcome to go back to Elatina and stay on there if you want to. Or Patrick will arrange for you to get back to Adelaide whenever you want to go,' Kate said. She didn't want her friend to feel that she was stuck here at Wildowie after they left.

'Thanks, Kate, but I think I'll be here for a while.' She paused and touched James's arm. 'Shall we tell them?'

James's hand moved to cover hers. 'Why not? Now is as good a time as any.'

Brigid raised her shining brown eyes to Kate's. 'We are getting married,' she said simply.

'No!'

'Oh yes, we are,' James said, his voice as cool and assured as ever.

'James, I can't believe it!' the words burst out before Kate could stop them. 'You said you'd never marry an Irish peasant!'

Rory burst into laughter.

'Don't be laughing! He did say that! You heard it with your own ears.'

James smiled and pulled Brigid's arm into the crook of his own. 'I suppose I hadn't met the right kind of Irish peasant then. I was a different man then than I am now, in more ways than one.' His hand went up to touch the patch on his face in an unconscious gesture.

'Anyway, I'm not an Irish peasant any more, Kate, and neither are you. And I'm no longer afraid of the bush. I love it. I love being here, having an important job to do. I want to do it for the rest of my life.'

'Don't get me wrong, I think it is wonderful, but you've only really known each other for a few months.' She didn't want Brigid to make any of the same mistakes that she had. She hoped that Brigid wasn't just beguiled by station life, as she had been.

'When you spend almost every hour of your waking day with someone, and you're as close as I have been, nursing James, touching him, caring for him, then the barriers just fall away. They do.'

'So I see,' Kate laughed. 'Oh Brigid, is it not ironic? Do you not remember what we said all those years ago on the *Elgin*? I told you that I wanted to become the mistress of a grand station, live off the fat of the land for the rest of my life—'

'Dine from tables piled high with food and dress in silk,' Rory interjected.

'Yes, all of that. And it took me, the impatient, striving, determined Kate O'Mara, sixteen years to achieve it. And here you are, the loyal, steadfast, patient, careful Brigid Mulcahey, and it has all fallen into your lap, without you even trying.'

'I said that I'd get there the slow way.'

'You're a damned fast worker, my friend.' Kate leant across James to hug her. 'I'm happy for you. I'm happy for you, too, James. Congratulations, and look after my best friend, won't you?' She kissed him lightly on the cheek.

'Absolutely. I know what you'll be like to contend with if I don't. Your best friend and our son, I'll look after both of them.'

'Thank you, James.'

The frost settled onto them where they lay on the ground. She shivered, pulling the blanket more closely over them both . . .

The thin light of the misty dawn wakened her. She heard the crunch of wheels over frosty ground. Another traveller on the road already.

His body, next to hers, was still. Her arms reached out to him, pulling him closer. He stirred in his sleep and his warm arms came around her once more. She was here, on the track, with Rory. And she need never fear cold or hunger again.

Di Morrissey
Tears of the Moon

Two inspiring journeys
Two unforgettable women
One amazing story

Broome, Australia 1893

It's the wild and passionate heyday of the pearling industry, and when young English bride Olivia Hennessy meets the dashing pearling master, Captain Tyndall, their lives are destined to be linked by the mysterious power of pearls.

Sydney 1995

Lily Barton embarks on a search for her family roots which leads her to Broome. But her quest for identity reveals more than she could have ever imagined . . .

TEARS OF THE MOON IS THE STUNNING NEW BESTSELLER FROM AUSTRALIA'S MOST POPULAR FEMALE NOVELIST

'. . . a sprawling saga . . . skilfully atmospheric'
THE BULLETIN

John Lewis
Savage Exile

Two lives . . .

England. 1803. Will and Jessica were destined to be together. Forever.

Two victims . . .

But change is in the air, and Will is forced to leave the woman he loves.

Two journeys . . .

From the bloody waters off Cape Trafalgar to the treacherous coastline of colonial New South Wales, *Savage Exile* swings like a pendulum between personal lives and history. A novel of fabulous scope and almost unimaginable hardship, of life and love and tremendous spirit, *Savage Exile* combines all the tyranny of Robert Hughes' *The Fatal Shore* with the passion of Vivian Stuart's *The Australians*.